Praise for *The Gai*
Johnny Worthen

'A riveting story of personal obsession and epic-scale
horror. Pray you never hear the Gaia Chime!'
Tim Waggoner, four-time Bram Stoker Award-
winning author of *Lord of the Feast*

'*The Gaia Chime* is a mind-bender of a cultural
and global horror-thriller that will take you
down twists and turns you will never see coming!
Highly recommended!!'
Jonathan Maberry, *New York Times* bestselling
author of the *Joe Ledger* thrillers and *NecroTek*,
on *The Gaia Chime*

'A chilling discourse on class, culture, and capitalism,
underpinned with ancient myth, Johnny Worthen's
The Gaia Chime is a provocative and visionary near-
future narrative, and an unsettling call to action. If you
haven't already put Worthen on your must-read list,
you should rectify that now.'
Lee Murray, five-time Bram Stoker Award-winning
author of *Grotesque: Monster Stories*

'*The Gaia Chime* is a fascinating story with shocking
twists. The vivid characters and dialogue that just sings
makes reading the latest tale from Johnny Worthen
an absolute pleasure. You're going to be delighted or
terrified – possibly both.'
Kate Jonez, Chief Editor at Omnium Gatherum

'*The Gaia Chime* is ringing and calling out to a receptive generation. We know of many of the changes that have happened to our world, but now there is something more, something deeper, driving people to take up the fight. Johnny Worthen addresses the issues of the day by casting a dark reflection of what could be when the chime strikes.'
Daniel Yocom, Guild Master Gaming

'Johnny Worthen is a bold and imaginative writer; his *Coronam* work is a fascinating look at our troubling history through the lens of tomorrow.'
Bryan Young, author of *BattleTech: Honor's Gauntlet*

'Worthen shows himself a master of style and substance.'
Michael R. Collings, 2016 World Horror Convention Grand Master

JOHNNY WORTHEN

THE GAIA CHIME

FLAME TREE PRESS
6 Melbray Mews, London, SW6 3NS, UK
flametreepress.com

US sales, distribution and warehouse:
Simon & Schuster
simonandschuster.biz

UK distribution and warehouse:
Hachette UK Distribution
hukdcustomerservice@hachette.co.uk

Thanks to the Flame Tree Press team.

The cover is created by Flame Tree Studio with elements courtesy of Shutterstock.com and: PeopleImages.com – Yuri A and Cassandra Madsen. The font families used are Avenir and Bembo.

Flame Tree Press is an imprint of Flame Tree Publishing Ltd
flametreepublishing.com

A copy of the CIP data for this book is available from the British Library and the Library of Congress.

1 3 5 7 9 8 6 4 2

PB ISBN: 978-1-78758-893-6
HB ISBN: 978-1-78758-894-3
ebook ISBN: 978-1-78758-895-0

Printed and bound in Great Britain by Clays Ltd, Elcograf S.p.A.

JOHNNY WORTHEN

THE GAIA CHIME

FLAME TREE PRESS
London & New York

Don't trust anyone over thirty.

– Jack Weinberg

Jayden

In the unrealized imagination of the child, it was an inexplicable idea. Sourceless, it was like a sound that came from the inside out, a distant murmur or a hum. Not of his own – unless an antenna could claim genesis of invisible signals by forming them into perceptibility. In that sound, that gurgle, grunt, or chime, a seed of intent and correlated action took root in the back of Jayden's mind as a directive for which he had not the words to explain nor could himself understand if he had those words.

It rose to his consciousness in a sliding moment of daydream, just as he rocketed his toy truck over the coloring book, made it do a loop-de-loop in the air, and land among the building blocks in a slow-motion crash, end over end. In the short space of the aerial trick, in his seven-year-old mind, surrounded by up-churned memories and pretended violence, it formed.

Across the house, the child's mother, Susan, fried four chops on a new electric stove and swallowed back her worry. She'd dressed up for the meal – put on makeup, the red lipstick Tom liked, the tight gingham skirt and loose blue blouse. Her hair was up. Her lilac perfume would only be hints beneath the sizzling pork, but both scents should work on Tom if things had gone to plan.

The plan was for things to get better, and they had been. Finally, things were getting better. Tom, after waiting so long, after struggling with his mid-management position for three years, was now on the brink of upper management. Today was the interview, and tonight they would celebrate with his favorite meal – pork chops and beer.

The house had been cleaned, the laundry done. She'd vacuumed and dusted the big suburban house, noticing pleasantly when the HOA mowed their front lawn. That morning she'd waved to brown-skinned workers who'd waved back.

All was well and their lives were finally living up to their three-car garage.

It had turned around the moment Tom was asked to apply for the position. She remembered that day well, for it was such a stark contrast to the day before it. It had been a Friday and he came home happy and playful. They made love that night. He'd been tender, though she was hard put to relax, her enthusiasm marred by Thursday's coupling.

"Fucking illegals get promoted over me," Tom had railed Thursday night, three whiskeys deep before dinner. "And that dyke is now a comptroller. She doesn't even know what that does."

Susan had made the mistake of asking Tom what a comptroller was, not knowing herself and wanting to sympathize. He'd looked at her for a moment, confused, bleary, and then smacked her. "Duh," he'd said.

It hadn't been a bad smack. Hadn't even bloodied her nose. A mild moment, a reaction to his disappointment. The whiskey talking. They both knew he was too good for the job he had. He was executive material at least. He could go into politics. He had the looks and the breeding. It irked him. She understood that, and before the night was over, he'd apologized and took her for make-up sex in the bedroom. She showed the proper enthusiasm at the appropriate times, tried not to flinch at the violence, and didn't say a word when he'd been unable to finish, grateful when he gave up and took his side of the king-size bed.

Then the Friday. That was two weeks ago when things had turned. He'd been brighter and energized thereafter. He came home most nights directly from work and stayed with beer only. They talked again like they had at the beginning, before the job, before the house, the cars, the time-share, and Jayden.

Jayden.

A strange little boy, she thought. He was quiet. His teachers all said so. Which was strange because when he was a baby, he was reckless and adventurous and loved the sound of his own voice. He'd not stay in his room after bedtime. How often she'd wake in the middle of the night to find him playing in the front room or crunching cereal on the kitchen floor.

Or walking in on Tom beating her up.

As Thursday to Friday two weeks ago had been a turn, so too had that bad day.

Jayden had doubtlessly heard them fighting before. Heard the crying, heard the police, saw the patrol cars outside when the neighbors called them in their last apartment, but it was that one night, when Tom was particularly in his cups – not his fault, the booze acting on him – that Jayden changed.

She'd seen him in the doorway and turned to him, intending to rush him back to his bedroom, when Tom had struck her from behind. It was her fault. If she'd been watching, she'd have been able to duck the blow or at least lessen it. As it was, she was knocked senseless, and when she woke up sometime later, Tom was passed out in the bathroom and Jayden was nowhere to be found.

She'd always intended to talk to him about it, had planned to, practiced even, but the moment never came up.

He stayed in his room all nights after that.

★   ★   ★

Two weeks of new spring, Tom in a good mood, and she slowly coming out of her nightly fear of seeing him. She still had the butterflies thinking of her husband walking in the door every day, but lately they'd been undeserved. He'd been the perfect gentleman.

Tonight, she knew, he'd be in the best mood possible, or the worst. She shuddered to think the latter.

The door opened.

Susan's breath caught in her throat and she waited, the chops sizzling at her side.

"Honey, I'm home," Tom called from the hallway.

"Great!" came her enthusiastic response. She hadn't heard rage in his voice. "You got it?"

"Let me tell it," he said, coming into the kitchen, his voice a little sharp.

She felt her pulse in her ears.

"I got it!" he said and swept her up in his arms.

She shrieked and laughed but cut it short, remembering the same scene playing out when he'd gotten the mid-management job three years before. It struck her then, sadly for the briefest moment, that all joy was temporary.

Jayden heard his father come in, heard his parents talking, heard them laughing, heard his mother's voice cut off and felt the idea bloom in his mind like a silver cloud of calm acceptance.

He walked down the hall to his parents' bedroom and tried to remember how different this big room was from their last house. He couldn't remember. He dropped his truck on the floor and went to the nightstand.

"It's about time, you know," said Tom, cracking a beer. "When my father was my age, he was already a district manager over half the state."

"He didn't have to struggle the way you did," she said, and then when she caught his gaze, added hastily, "Affirmative-action stuff."

"Yep. Then a man was measured by his worth, not his tan," he said. It was an old joke and she smiled at it.

"Dinner will be ready in ten minutes," she said, giving him time to drink before feeding him.

He patted her rump and kissed her on the neck and she hardly jumped at all.

Jayden stood in the doorway watching his parents' affection. He could appreciate it. He liked seeing it. Liked seeing his parents getting along – no, more than getting along; actually enjoying each other. This is how he thought of his parents. This was a scene right out of his imagination, the 'truth' as he knew it. Already at seven, he'd compartmentalized and suppressed the other things. The present moment, especially this one, was his definition. At seven what else was there? And things were getting better. If he had any grasp of the past, it was short, and the weeks preceding this day were all good. Days deeper than that, days past, history and eons and ancient times untold, were buried rightly deep in his developing mind, hidden by him intentionally or slumbering and waiting to sprout. And from an ancient seed it bloomed then, the sound pulsed in him and like instinct, like a drowning man gasping for air, or throwing your arms out to catch yourself if you fall. Thus, the sound acted.

In the kitchen, on that Friday, amid the smell of peppery pork and love-me liars, with Tom's own pistol, Jayden shot his father six times while his mother watched.

By the second shot, the man was dead on the floor. The last four were delivered point blank. Susan remembered to turn the burner off before reacting.

The scene was unnoticed by the public, a common occurrence. A barely reported accident, with a moral calling for responsible gun ownership and pistol locks.

When asked if he'd had a reason to shoot his father, had intended to kill him, the child had shrugged and said he didn't know. It was just an idea that had come to him.

Part One

Incidents

Chapter One

Seth and Charlotte stood outside looking in as the eager hordes entered past them. They had been waiting at the side gate for twenty minutes for someone to acknowledge their credentials and let them in.

"We're going to miss the match," said Charlotte.

"No, we've got at least an hour," Seth said, looking up from his phone. "It's a set all on the court Bobby's scheduled for next. They'll be playing for a while."

"So now would be a perfect time to be with him in the locker room, catching all the pre-match jitters."

"We'll make it."

Charlotte wasn't so sure, but she deferred to Seth and his experience. He'd been doing this for years, whereas this was her first outing. She was the face of the documentary, the reporter, onscreen interviewer. The 'eye candy', as it was called. Seth would stay behind the camera. They'd share producer credit and together try to make the most of the grant that had led them here.

The Olympus Bank Open was newly named for their newest sponsor, but the venue, the famed Indian Wells Tennis Garden, was venerable and venerated as a true tennis temple. The largest two-week event outside of the four Grand Slams, it was required play for all serious contenders, and for this fortnight, with the aid of a new broadcasting agreement, it would be the epicenter of the global sporting world. Such was mid-March in southern California.

Seth shifted the camera to his other sweaty hand, remembering not too long ago when the presence of such an expensive piece of equipment was as good as a pass into any venue. Concerts were usually the only problem, where rabid groupies and fans would try anything. Getting backstage at a

Mutter show required a bogus press pass and he'd had to bribe some idiot to get into the World Relief Fund-A-Palooza – the dumbest name for any concert ever. Those were tricky, but now the VIP gate at Indian Wells took the mantle for the highest security venue he'd ever filmed at.

He thought to take more footage of the rich and famous passing them with their curious disdain, but he had plenty of that already. This was to be a positive documentary, not a social dissection. He was basically ignored as a functionary, standing around cases of equipment, camera in hand, and dressed in his work clothes – short-sleeve buttoned shirt, jeans and comfortable shoes. At forty-six he could pass for upper thirties with his ruddy Dutch features and black Bohemian beard. He looked the part of the filmmaker and when he wasn't pointing the camera directly at them, these elite fans had little use for him. Charlotte, on the other hand, was young and bright, twenty-four years old and dressed up in pearl earrings, clean white dress, modest heels. Professional tennis casual if such a thing existed. Youthful and thin, she could fit in with the train of young aristocrats flowing past them into their reserved catered boxes, if it weren't for her skin. In a sea of rich white tennis fans, her Indian features and natural tan made her conspicuous and drew not a few sidelong, accusatory – dare Seth say it – racist stares, particularly from the older onlookers. He hoped she hadn't noticed and wished he had a cigarette.

The looks that worried Seth were ignored by Charlotte who had had a lifetime to develop a resistance to them. She was not so jaded as to think that their delay in passing this gate had nothing to do with her heritage. Nevertheless, she put on a smile and approached the guard again.

"We're working for Robert Weller," she said.

"Who's he?"

"He's the CEO of the bank this event is named after," she said.

"Olympus Bank? Wow. That's interesting."

"His son is playing on center court."

"Big day for him, huh?" The guard was not moving.

Charlotte turned to Seth for backup. He shook his head and pulled a pack of cigarettes from his shirt pocket. He tapped one out, looked around and then put it all back.

She returned to the fence where they and their equipment had waited for an hour, sighed through a forced smile. Then Charlotte's phone beeped.

"Finally," she said.

"What?" said Seth.

"Kinsley is on her way."

Seth looked through the viewfinder and framed the gate, imagining Bobby's girlfriend appearing and getting them inside. "I've never seen anything like this, you know," he said.

"The crowd?"

"That, but also the security. It's tighter than that congressional debate I did back during COVID."

"Don't take it personally," Charlotte said. "It's me."

"You?"

She gestured to her face.

"No. You're perfect for the part. Just the kind of PR these types need. They don't want to look stodgy and exclusive. They are stodgy and exclusive, but they don't want to look that way."

She shrugged, thinking that there was probably something to what Seth was saying, on the grander level anyway. Her Hindu heritage had surely played a part in getting the grant from Olympus Bank to make the documentary. Robert Weller himself had interviewed her before ponying up the money.

"We'll make Bobby look good," she'd said.

"No," was his response. "Be honest. Show the trials of the tour. Show that it's not who you are, but what you do, that wins success."

Her plan was to follow a single up-and-coming tennis player for a year through the Grand Slams. It wasn't that she loved tennis, but she'd seen Bobby Weller, Robert Weller's son, getting some recognition. Searching for ideas to finish her journalism degree, she lit upon the idea and figured the school, with Weller money behind it, would foot the bill and start her on her career. She'd put together the proposal, pretended that she was approaching several avenues for funding, and then presented it to the board of regents of Commondale University, where Robert Weller Sr. was a sitting board member.

He was a regal man who beamed aristocracy and old money, though Charlotte didn't know how old it was. His silver-gray hair was precisely combed and his skin the healthy tan that spoke of tropical junkets and tanning beds. His suit was tailored, gray and crisp, like his eyes; a silk white tie was pinned with a diamond stud that refracted the seeping daylight off his breast. His face was gentle and nobly lined for his age, but any softness was belied by his eyes which Charlotte found piercing and subtly accusatory.

"I don't want it to look nepotistic," he said. "Raw is good. Show some warts."

This was during the interview and the way he spoke had thrilled her, and she knew she had it. Everything had happened so quickly that when he asked who she intended for her crew, she stammered and remembering Professor Lian in the film department, offered up his name. She hadn't spoken with the man in years, not since he was demoted to part-time.

"He's good," said Weller, "though maybe a bit past his prime."

"He'll work cheap," she said, and then changing the subject, "We'll aim to have the film ready for the indie circuit next year."

She looked around at the other regents. None of them said a thing. The room was impressive, a boardroom table from another time. Rich brown oak smelling faintly of furniture polish. It seemed too ancient for the school, which was only half a century old. The table, the chairs, crown molding and oak paneling all looked antique, something she'd expect to see at Oxford. None of the other buildings had such décor. All the rooms in the Robert Weller Administrative Office Building were opulent, but this one, the only place where Robert Weller was likely to be seen on campus, was a different animal entirely. To her right, windows, floor to twelve-foot-high ceiling, showed an idyllic snowy courtyard with benches and evergreens she'd never imagined existed on the campus. To her left, paintings too big to be anywhere else.

The president spoke into the silence. "You're aware of Seth's drinking?"

"I understand that he had a problem," Charlotte admitted, wishing then that she'd chosen someone else. Had she even imagined things would move so quickly, she would have, but of course, she'd barely had time to put together a tentative timetable. Luckily, she could just copy and paste the professional tennis schedule and have it done the night before. "He is teaching again," she offered.

"Yes," said the president, who glanced at Weller, who looked on.

Two of the regents were women, one of those was Black. They, like the other five, were all past sixty, though the women hid it better. There was an air of weighty decision, grim faces pondering how to use the largess Weller had bestowed on the school.

"We'll let you know," said Weller.

Dismissed, she collected her portfolio, smiled her practiced anchorwoman smile, and left through the heavy wooden door, noting the lack of squeak in the hinges.

Three hours later that afternoon she was awarded the grant and had to find Seth Lian to tell him about his new job.

From his cracked window, Seth had seen her skipping up the sidewalk to his office in the Arts Building and somehow knew she was there for him. He remembered her from an undergraduate class he'd taught when he was still teaching full-time. A journalism student with ambition, not afraid to put in the work, but looking for the quick turnaround on her plans.

As an adjunct professor, tenure now forever out of reach, he'd listened attentively to the proposal and readily agreed to Charlotte's plan. "It'll be good to get in the field again," he said. "Thanks for thinking of me."

"We'll start right away."

He filled out the leave request that afternoon.

★   ★   ★

Kinsley took a while to arrive. Seth, feeling the need for a cigarette more acutely than the slipping schedule, deliberately never looked at his watch, hoping that would somehow calm Charlotte. He hadn't changed his earlier opinion of her much. She was eager but impatient, and not for the first time, he wondered if she would be up to the challenge of actually making a live documentary.

"I told you that some things are going to go wrong," he said to her. "This isn't even one of those. Stop pacing. You're sweating."

"I don't sweat," she said. "I'm Indian."

"Oh, Ganesh removed those glands from the subcontinent? How lucky for you."

She glared.

His cool was partly staged, partly a product of his fatigue. He'd never made an actual documentary like this before. He'd been second unit on a couple of projects that turned into documentary-like things, but this was different. Charlotte was right, if this thing took off, it could put him in the big league, or maybe, at least, get him back in the game. He thought of Travis and wished he could have a cigarette. Or a drink.

Kinsley finally showed up at the gate and waved them to the turnstile. Seth picked up the bags while Charlotte trotted forward to meet the dilettante. They exchanged perfect smiles. Charlotte's real, Kinsley's uncertain.

"Sorry it took so long, Bobby's in a mood."

"Not a problem," said Seth, taking the offered lanyard and hanging the pass around his neck with one hand.

"Was there some confusion that we were coming?"

"I don't know," said Kinsley. "Come on."

Charlotte had tried to hide her impatience but knew she hadn't. She was, therefore, a little taken aback by Kinsley's disinterest. They'd been waiting at the door for a good long time. The text that had finally brought Bobby's girlfriend to the gate was sent over an hour ago. Indian Wells was not that large.

With her VIP pass around her neck, Charlotte fell in behind Kinsley, trying to remember why they were there. Seth took up the rear with the bags.

Seth had no illusions about Kinsley and her reaction. It had actually been better than he'd expected. She'd brought the passes herself rather than finding someone in the servant class to do it. That scored her points in his book. He'd been around the classes that separated themselves from little people enough to predict them, if not understand them. He'd not spent a lot of time there, but some – mostly at posh parties where he was taking glorified wedding pictures with a thirty-thousand-dollar camera. That was decades ago, before Commondale, some while he was still married. After he'd been tasked by a guest to fetch them hors d'oeuvres for the third time while he was filming, camera to eye and everything, he was pretty sure where he fit in on their totem pole.

He felt much the same vibe crossing the grounds of the tennis venue to wherever Kinsley was taking them. The people were all worshippers of tennis, which, as he understood, was one of the last exclusive sports. Right up there with polo and yachting, tennis kept the riffraff out. Mostly. There were some fans, regular fans, with enthusiasm and blue-collar ways, probably supporting the newest middle-class upstart to challenge the circuit, but the majority were there for the society – their society, not his. For a lark he counted non-white people and after Charlotte, and disregarding staff, he got to two. The others were of a kind, little changed in the decades since he filmed bar mitzvahs and Sweet Sixteens in the Hamptons. Here also their uniforms were consistent, clean white – very white – attire in keeping with tennis tradition and ideology. Young and old mixed at the bars, where a martini could be had for a day's salary. They swarmed like the WASPs they were, perfect hair, airy disregard for prices and people like him who moved invisibly, like a blood cell, among them.

He noticed a group of long-haired 'rebels' with a continental look about them. The posh from across the sea. Fabian would envy that hair, Seth thought, and realized how old he was to think of that comparison.

"What?" said Charlotte. "What's with that noise?"

"Sour grapes, maybe," he said. "Envy."

"For what?"

He didn't answer. Charlotte, he knew, still had the belief that she could enter this world, that success in front of the camera would open these doors. Doors did open for fame, but celebrity was never enough to join these blue-blooded circles in earnest. They were the ultimate clique, a segregated private club where two generations of obscene wealth was entry level. If there was an Illuminati, they were it. In a way, he envied Charlotte's innocence and realized it would help in the documentary. Hell, her education into these realities might even play into it. Or not. It was to be an 'upbeat' documentary, after all, even though they were free to 'show warts'.

Charlotte caught up with Kinsley, who had put a step between them. Since Kinsley had been so nice before, Charlotte read it as she was in a hurry, maybe worried. Seth read it differently, but Charlotte took the lead.

"Can you tell me more about Bobby's pre-match routines?" Charlotte asked. "Is he nervous?"

"I think he might be this time," she said. "Something...eh... I don't know."

Kinsley Carreau would play a big part in the documentary. She and Bobby had been a thing for years. Nothing official, but the Wellers and Carreaus shared business interests and, like royalty of old, the prospect of uniting their kingdoms played a part in their pairing. Kinsley and Bobby had joked about that in Miami. Her family lived in Marseilles, Bobby's currently in Boston, though they had houses all over. They'd visited him in three different states already, Massachusetts, Florida, and now California. Jet-setters. Kinsley had flown in from Bern to attend this match. It was unclear if she'd remain for the next, particularly if Bobby lost.

Charlotte sensed Kinsley was distracted. It was not something she usually felt from her. Usually, she'd been amiable and open. Her affability was something that Charlotte had wanted to emulate. She'd never be able to get the Gallic nose or perfect cheekbones and svelte figure – not in her DNA – but she could maybe master Kinsley's makeup and attitude, both of which added to her natural gifts to make her a standout even among these peers. The slight accent was also adorable. Charlotte thought they were friends, or could be.

"I don't suppose you know if we've been granted access inside the locker room?" asked Seth. It was usually against the rules, but rules didn't always apply to people like Robert Weller, and hope against hope, he'd hoped.

"Did you know that Olympus Bank funded that fracking debacle in Oklahoma?" said Kinsley.

"What?" said Charlotte, glancing at Seth, who shrugged. "No, I didn't. Why?"

"Oh, never mind," said Kinsley turning with a smile to regard the two filmmakers. "Yes, you can get into the locker room. I'm taking you there now."

Seth was surprised at this and made a metaphorical leap. Looking at the clean white-clad people milling around under the sponsor sign, it probably wasn't a reach to imagine them as gods walking the gardens of Olympus. Indian Wells was called one of the temples to tennis, so the coliseum would be the *cella*, or inner sanctum, the court the altar. The locker room, secret and off-limits, a holy of holies. A strange heretical thought that unnerved him even as he formed it. Feeling his own place in the pantheon, or lack of it, his outsider status slid to 'interloper', and as the door to the interior was opened, 'thief' and 'burglar' also crossed his mind as ideas if not words. As they entered the hallway, their path planing downward beneath the structure, Seth rounded out the simile, and, to no one in particular, said, "I feel like Orpheus."

Chapter Two

Through the windowless hall, event functionaries fluttered by like cherubs with iPads and radios, slowing only long enough to glance at their passes and then move on.

Kinsley navigated swiftly through the labyrinthine halls, walking with purpose which Charlotte could appreciate. Moving like that was always a powerful thing; it kept disruptions to a minimum, kept guys from hitting on her in the halls of Commondale and got her into trendy nightclubs where she'd hit on the guys. The pace was a nice counter to the earlier long inertia. No one spoke and the background sounds of murmured commands and low conversation were all beneath the threshold of understanding, and together with the strange air-conditioned, artificially lit space, cast the mood from festive above to surreal here below.

The weird otherworldly nature of this behind-the-scenes glimpse into elite sporting did nothing to banish Seth's classical delusion of ancient gods and little people. Naturally his thoughts traveled to Barney Faro, his longtime friend in the Commondale teachers' lounge. A kindred spirit who by virtue of his discipline – history, humanities and philosophy – hadn't had the oversight Seth had had. He'd also never worked outside academia. And he wasn't an alcoholic. But of course, when they talked and joked, it was all because Barney had cushy, pedestaled Sophists to protect him, while Seth lived film noir, tragedy through a whiskey glass.

Hardly watching where he was going, flighting in daydreams, Seth didn't notice Ivano Madic coming down the hall until he was past. The upcoming Croatian tennis star was Bobby's opponent. It was only when Charlotte called after him that he realized the opportunity he'd missed.

Charlotte had caught it too. "Why don't you film the walk?" she asked him a little peevishly.

"Is that okay?" said Seth to dodge his error. He'd talked about asking forgiveness before permission several times when planning their techniques for the shoot, outlining the techniques of guerrilla filmmaking. It was an obvious deflection and as such he considered it an apology.

Kinsley answered the question over her shoulder. "Walking? Sure. Why not?"

Seth took up the camera, toggled image stabilization, and followed behind.

The door to the men's locker room was as nondescript as a utility room. A pair of steel double doors opened, with a simple laminated sign declaring its contents and promoting its restricted access. A single white-clad club official stood in the way.

Kinsley flashed him her smile; Charlotte and Seth their passes. The man opened the door for them, and Kinsley marched in, ignoring the signs and gender restrictions.

Charlotte had imagined the room would be opulent in keeping with the superstar athletes who used it and had braced herself for the shock after the utilitarian corridors, but it was not like that. It was different than the hallway, with warm full-spectrum lighting and softer carpet, but there were no divans, no catered high-protein smoothie bars like she'd imagined. The room was wide and warm, a space of rich dark chestnut cubbies – classy, unadorned, except the rich dark browns of the wood. The design was understated, functional, a place for clothes and locking cabinets. Towel stations were frequent; shelves for clean ones, bins for used. Water and cups. Sunscreen. A faint smell of soap wafted in on a cool air-conditioned breeze and the only sound Charlotte heard, as she ached to hear fading noises, was her own party shuffling forward.

They came upon Bobby Weller lacing his shoes. He was alone; his locker door hung open and his racket case was on the bench beside him.

He looked up when he heard them approach. His gaze passed over the two filmmakers with barely a note of recognition, then held on Kinsley. He watched them come but no one said a word until they were right in front of him. Seth held back to get a wider angle.

"Sorry we're late," said Charlotte, digging into her bag for a microphone. "There was some confusion at the gate."

"Confusion," he said.

"Yes. But Kinsley sorted it out."

"Confusion," he repeated.

Seth zoomed in on the man, sensing something off about him. In their past interviews he'd been open and ebullient, friendly even. Strikingly honest about his position in the tour and background. Now, he was distracted. The camera showed a glassy stare that never wavered from Kinsley. A pan to her face showed the same kind of thing.

Charlotte found the mic and turned it on. "What's going through your mind right now?" she asked him.

At that Bobby turned and regarded her. He looked at the microphone like it was some alien artifact, then returned to Kinsley.

"Is my father out there?" he asked her.

"He's in the VIP box with the club president and some other people."

"My mother?"

"Yes. How're your ears?" asked Kinsley.

"Yeah, yeah," he said and rearranged rackets in his bag.

"You've played in front of television audiences before," began Charlotte. "Do you feel added pressure knowing your parents will be there or do they give you strength?"

The expected answer was 'strength' of course, maybe a bit of making-daddy-proud stuff. This would be followed up with an after-match interview with Robert Weller, and apparently Vanessa Weller too, his mother, to get their reactions seeing their son's triumph or failure.

The question brought Bobby's gaze to Charlotte. Seth zoomed in. The vacant eyes blinked and focused. He noticed the camera then, looked into the lens – something he'd been warned against doing. Turning back to Charlotte, he squeezed his eyes shut and brought his hands to his ears as if shutting out a crippling din.

Charlotte stole a glance at Seth, who was lucky enough to capture it in the camera. He didn't know what was going on either, but her questioning eyes made for good film. When Charlotte squeezed her eyes too, it was surreal. He zoomed in. He didn't see what Kinsley was doing. She was out of frame.

A soft chime preceded a warm, melodic female voice announcing, "Men's match 4-A players to the court. Men's match 4-A to court. Good luck, gentlemen."

Bobby Weller stood up and hefted his bag over his shoulder.

"Good luck," said Charlotte.

He smiled at her and said thanks, looking like he had before. Like he was supposed to, Seth thought. He left through a door at the back.

"I'm going to get a seat," Kinsley said.

"Will you be sitting with Robert and Vanessa?" asked Charlotte.

"No, but not far away. Your passes should grant you press access to the upper levels. I've heard it's better to film up there since you can move around more without getting in trouble." Having dismissed them, she turned to go.

Charlotte said quickly before she left, "He looked distracted. Is that normal?"

"His tendon has been bothering him. Nothing big."

"Thanks."

Kinsley left the locker room the way they'd come. Seth moved to find good angles for some establishing shots, filming the empty spaces, the showers, the bins. Online he'd been unable to find as much as a camera still of the locker room since its newest remodel. Plus, it'd make good filler under Bobby talking about tennis being a lonely sport. Good stuff from a previous interview, the one in Florida yet to be edited.

"You have enough?" asked Charlotte. "I'm not sure they'd like you filming all this."

"Yeah, I got plenty." Seth lowered the camera and switched it off. "Turn off your mic to save battery."

Charlotte nodded and put it away.

"Do you think we could leave some of these bags here? I'm sick of carrying them."

"I doubt it."

"Me too."

He hefted the bags over his shoulder with a grunt and followed Charlotte back out into the hall. She asked an usher how to get to the upper press locations and his advice was to leave the clubhouse and try from the outside with the fans.

The blast of heat stunned them. Seth felt sweat bead on his forehead before they found the stairs. By the time they had found a place high on the first tier, he was dripping with sweat and his shirt stuck to his back.

"This is too far away," she said.

"No, we can make it work," said Seth. "Set this up and I'll change lenses."

The game was underway. Third game of the first set, on serve.

She took the aluminum tripod but didn't unfold it. "We're not here to film the game. We need emotional close-ups. What about those courtside blinds?"

"Yeah, that would be better," said Seth.

The crowd fell silent to see what was happening. Madic was at the baseline pointing his racket directly at them. The umpire reminded everyone to be quiet.

"We're moving," Charlotte whispered. "We were supposed to be courtside. What's the best entrance to get there from here?"

Seth liked how she'd phrased the question.

"Ground level K section," he told them.

They waited for the game to end and then went down. It was easier going up the stairs and Seth finally asked the question.

"What was up with you in the locker room? Were you teasing Bobby?"

"What do you mean?"

"The eye thing. Clenching shut like he'd done."

"Did I?"

"Yeah. Was it to make fun?"

"No. It wasn't. He was acting strange though, wasn't he?"

"Super psyched for the game? Some meditation we'd interrupted? I guess that might explain why the locker rooms are athletes-only before a match."

"Maybe," she said.

"So, you? What were you doing?"

She recalled the moment. She'd suddenly had a flash of a migraine. She'd had them before, so that's what she thought it was. It wasn't the debilitating kind. More of a humming. No, not even that. Less than a humming. Something she couldn't hear but could feel. And here too she corrected her thinking. She didn't *feel* anything. It was not pain, per se. Instead, she'd sensed it, and it reminded her of a migraine. She'd instinctively closed her eyes to retreat into the blackness which was her way when they came. It had passed in a moment.

"A passing headache," she said. "Like a brain freeze. Must have been the air-conditioning after standing outside so long."

"Did feel like a totally different world, didn't it?"

Charlotte didn't respond but wondered instead at the migraine that wasn't.

With the help of another usher, they found the hidden camera nests between the first and second sets. There was no room for them to set up a stationary camera and Seth had to shoot over and around the television men.

Charlotte looked worried, but he winked at her. This was guerrilla filmmaking like he remembered. Stolen shots.

By the third set, much of the crowd had left. The match featuring the number three seed was looking to be a barn burner two courts over. One of the TV guys left to see what he could get and Seth quickly set up.

It was hot in the camera blind, hotter than on court, he thought, since they didn't get the breeze. The walls practically sizzled in the bright sunlight. The air was thick with the smell of softening plastic and chemical sunscreen, artificial and pungent. Sweat poured freely down Seth and Charlotte fanned herself with a program.

"I can see Robert and Vanessa Weller," he said. "A good angle, right across from us. On the banister."

"Perfect. Get some reaction shots."

"Of course."

Charlotte looked over Seth's shoulder and found the couple in the box. There was the patriarch of the family, the head of Olympus Bank, stately and silver-haired behind sunglasses and a dapper white Panama hat. Beside him, with no hat but bigger charcoal-tinted sunglasses, was a tanned blonde-haired woman.

Seth filmed them as they followed the ball back and forth and then zoomed when he felt something was about to happen, hoping to catch the look of exhilaration or despair when their son played the point. He was disappointed. Their expressions hardly changed at all. The only smile he got was when Robert Weller Sr. was offered another drink, a mint julep, by the looks of it.

He mentioned it to Charlotte.

"You're not the only one who noticed."

"Well, sorry to bother you."

"No. Not me. I've been watching Bobby. He's glanced up at that box a couple of times now."

"That's not a good sign," said Seth, turning the camera to find Bobby Weller on the court. "That means he's distracted."

"He just lost serve."

"He won the first set, so he should be okay." He found Bobby at his chair resting. A young boy stood behind him holding an umbrella over him for shade, sweat running into his eyes. He had visions of servants waving fans, slaves picking cotton, serfs throwing mud into a pile while King Arthur and a coconut-clomping squire accosted them.

"What's going on?" said Charlotte.

Seth pulled himself back and found Bobby standing up and walking behind the umpire. "Bathroom break?" he asked.

Charlotte had that feeling again, weaker this time, but still that sense. She blinked it away, or rather to quiet, and watched in strange fascination as Bobby walked over to just under the box where his parents watched and said something.

The umpire announced a warning.

Robert Weller leaned over and replied to his son. Bobby tossed his racket over the edge and then jumped up and grabbed the ledge, hoisting himself up. "That's not supposed to happen, is it?"

"He'll be disqualified for sure," said Seth. "Unless the match is already over and he's celebrating. Did Madic quit or something?"

"He's still sitting there," said Charlotte. "He's surprisingly calm."

Talk and catcalls filled the stadium, breaking the silent tennis reverence. The umpire called a forfeited game, and then as Bobby crested the box and picked up his racket, a forfeited set.

"Maybe he's doing it for the documentary," said Seth. "Wouldn't put it past these types to—"

Charlotte heard the halt in Seth's voice along with the sudden silence of the stadium. It felt like a weather front of a blizzard snow, sudden, soft, complete.

She looked up just as Bobby raised his tennis racket above his head. She noticed the frame of it was bent, the strings broken. "Cough them up!" Bobby shouted. "Cough them up!" And with the final syllable, brought the racket down hard upon Robert Weller's head, splitting it open and spraying the box with brains and blood. A third swing into the mush and all was silent.

It was when he turned to kill his mother that the crowd found its voice and screamed.

Chapter Three

Charlotte wasn't much of a drinker, and Seth had sworn off it – mostly – but the second fifth of vodka was already open and Seth was in the hall refilling the ice bucket for the second time. They were on their last Fresca. The news was all the Wellers' murder. Unsurprising, due to the public nature of the event, the multiple camera angles and live feed when it happened, but it was disproportionate, she thought, considering all the bigger tragedies happening that day. The UN had released a report on depleted ocean oxygen levels that was called "a loud, screaming alarm of onrushing doom," and three hundred and eighty-seven miners were trapped and presumed dead from a deep silver mine collapse in Africa, the Democratic Republic of Congo to be precise. They were too deep to even presume a rescue. Scrolling the feed on her phone in a vain attempt to land on cat pictures or landscapes to brighten her mood, Charlotte had found a dozen similar catastrophes amid the thousand posts about the murders.

She put down her phone and picked up the remote control, pointed it at the TV on the bureau, but remembering how she'd just turned it off a minute ago, she tossed it onto the couch.

The maids had visited the room, left mints on their pillows, animal towels in the bathroom. The suite smelled of light lavender sprayed over snuck-in cigarettes. It was clean but she thought it looked wrong for her roommate. Seth struck her as the kind of guy who never made his bed, decorated with day-old clothes and Styrofoam take-out cartons. His jacket was over a chair, the camera gear strewn out on the table, an empty sideways Smirnoff bottle lay on the bar beside its upright brother, but this was all recently done, since returning from the Garden.

The word was 'mayhem'. That's what happened at Indian Wells.

That was the word they agreed on in the cab ride home. Mayhem. The screaming, the panicking, the security guards wrestling Bobby to the ground, him fighting back, clubbing one with his wrecked bloody racket, gouging another's face. Seth had watched it in stunned silence. After the initial shock, she'd resorted to a mantra of "oh god oh god oh god oh god," which she kept up even as they dragged Bobby away. When they lifted him bodily out of the bleachers, she had a glimpse of the athlete's face. His eyes were wild, his nose gushing blood where he'd been hit, his white tennis clothes spattered the hellish crimson of blood, nasal ooze, chunks of gray matter, hair and skin. A piece of shattered charcoal lens from his mother's sunglasses fell out of his matted hair and down his sleeve. Five fought to contain him, all the while he was literally kicking and screaming. "There are more of them! More of them!"

When the action was over and the court filled with people, the stands empty, Seth packed up their gear and they left. Neither said a word to each other, though Charlotte continued her mantra under her breath. Seth had the cab make one stop and bought mixers and two bottles of vodka. Whiskey was his usual, but he was thinking of Charlotte.

They walked straight to his room, unloaded, poured drinks and, after the second, turned on the television to wall-to-wall Weller murders.

Seth returned with more ice and saw Charlotte sitting in the quiet room. He nodded and poured himself another drink. "You can have the Fresca, I'll go on the rocks."

"I should slow down," she said.

Seth grunted and pulled the curtains closed. It was dusk and the light was angling into the room. He didn't like that.

"What now?" she said.

"Well," he said, "I'll go through the footage, make copies just in case. See if there's anything the cops need."

"You think they'll need it?"

"No. I suspect they'll have plenty of footage from TV, but it's good form to offer it, or rather, it's bad if they ask and you haven't already offered. The copies are in case they do ask and try to take the lot." He tipped the glass back and for the first time tasted what he'd call a drink.

"It is always like this?" she said.

He fell into a cupped, padded chair, pulled out from the writing desk. It was done in industrial floral, hydrangea on tawny background. One pattern to match most anything. It was nice, sturdy, and fitted the suite well. He liked the suite. He was sad to think he'd have to leave it so soon.

He took another sip and noticed Charlotte's earnest gaze. "What? Always like this? How the hell would I know that? You think I go to a lot of patricides, do you?" He'd been going for sarcastic to relieve the mood, but it came out aggressive and accusing.

"I just thought…filming…"

"Sorry," he said. "I wasn't a war correspondent. I snuck into places I wasn't supposed to, filmed parties that got crazy, people doing stupid things backstage, but nothing like this. Nothing. No one has. No one ever has."

"We saw history today, huh?" She offered him a wan smile.

"That we did." He smiled back.

"I'm still in shock."

"Try this."

"What?"

He took a deep breath, aimed his face to the ceiling and yelled "Fuck!" as loud as he could, drawing it out until all the breath was out of him.

Charlotte covered her ears.

"Well?"

"Really?" she said.

"Yeah. Try it."

"I don't—"

Seth's cold, unimpressed gaze cut her off. Charlotte took a deep breath, like Seth had done, aimed her face to the ceiling and screamed the profanity. It sliced at the ceiling like a saber and when she was done, she felt a little better.

"See?" said Seth.

"Yes." She giggled, then laughed, then choked. She fell into a fit of sobbing, rushed, uncontrolled and wild.

Seth came over to her on the bed and put his arm around her. She bent her face into his chest and bawled. He tried to think of what to say, maybe stroke her hair, coo something, but nothing was right. He kept his arm around her only, friendly, caring. Fatherly. Images of Bobby Weller braining his father with a ten-thousand-dollar graphite tennis racket made him jump as if he had felt a blow.

"What?" Charlotte managed to say between sobs.

"Nothing. Let it all out," he said. "I'll join you."

He didn't cry. Couldn't, but wished he could. He envied Charlotte the release she had. The best he could do was his obscene howl which he performed again, but not as loudly.

"You'll bring the maids," Charlotte said.

"Nah. This is a suite."

And he was right. No one came to the door.

After a while Charlotte peeled herself away. "You should get some sleep," Seth told her.

She lay down on the couch, tucked on her side in a ball.

"I'm going to turn on the TV," he said. "Sure you don't want to go to your room?"

"I'll be okay."

Seth toggled the remote and there was Ivano Madic with a bouquet of microphones under his chin. Seth turned up the sound.

"That's a pretty serious accusation," a reporter said to him.

"He killed his parents, and cheating is the serious accusation?" said Madic. "American journalism."

"What did he say?" asked Charlotte, sitting up. "Bobby was cheating?"

"Shh…"

The interview was frenetic, reporters jostling mics, action around the athlete, people moving like there was an evacuation in progress, but the man himself was surprisingly calm.

"He had a paid film crew stationed to distract me at set point in the seats. When I called him on that, you could see him begin to melt down."

"What? Us?" said Charlotte.

"This day gets weirder," said Seth.

"And that's why he killed his parents? Because he was caught cheating an hour earlier?"

"I don't know what he was thinking. Ask him. I guess he didn't like his parents. Maybe they were rooting for me." Madic smiled at the joke and a chill ran down Seth's back.

"Jesus…"

"What an asshole," said Charlotte.

"You just noticed?"

"I don't know the guy."

"No, but you know the type."

"Arrogant men?"

"I see what you did there," he said, happy to see her joking. "No, rich people. The beautiful people. Fuckers."

"I still don't agree."

He shrugged.

The broadcast went to the scene of Bobby climbing the wall to the box.

Charlotte rubbed her temples as if fighting a headache. "Turn it off."

Seth tapped the switch and took another sip of his drink.

"Did he hate his parents?" Charlotte said.

"Apparently."

"How did we not see that? We have hours of interview with him. Did you see it?"

"Never came up. I guess we should have been more hard hitting. Come at the class angle, ask him how much of his success he attributes to choosing the right parents."

"Maybe."

"No," said Seth. "That wasn't – isn't – the film we were making. We are focused on the tennis player. His skill, his work, his rise and fall."

"Do you think Madic was paid off to lose?"

"Where are you getting that?"

"Bobby was an underdog today. Madic was his first real competition. If he won, it would be good television."

"I don't know. Nobody seemed to care we were there."

"Robert Weller has been accused of bribery in the past. Several times."

"That's par for the course when you're that rich and powerful."

"Being accused?"

"Bribery. It's how they do it."

"'They' again. You're a little old for a hippie, aren't you?"

"Actually, I'm decades too young. History not your strong point, eh?" He was getting surly. The drinks had caught up to him. It took many to do it these days, but they still could.

"Maybe we should call it a night," he said. "Get to bed early. Reform in the morning."

"I can't sleep."

"Want a pill?"

"No."

"Okay." Seth stayed where he was, lifted his glass to his lips and then lowered it.

"There were times when I could have killed my old man," he said.

"God. Really?"

"Well, take a swing at him anyway. I think it's a guy thing. One of those rites of passage."

"My dad was always sweet. My mom too. Pushy, but sweet." It was her usual description of their family, but today it tasted sour.

"You're an only child?"

"How'd you know?"

"You seem the type."

Charlotte picked up her glass. "You got the whole world figured out. What type am I exactly?"

"The only-child type."

"What type are you?"

"I'm one of a kind."

She snorted in derision and reached for her phone. She had it in her hand and switched on before she remembered what it contained.

"I don't know what to do," she said.

"You should try to yell again."

"No."

"Did the crying help?"

"I think so. Sorry about all that."

"Hey, don't be," he said. "I get it."

"You have kids?"

"Got one boy. Travis. He hates me."

"Enough to kill you?"

Seth humphed at the bad choice of words. "No."

Charlotte, with a little laugh, "Sorry. I don't mean to—"

"No, it's good," said Seth. "You're dealing. That's good."

She wasn't so sure. She felt like her whole body had been injected with slow-setting glue, a resin to replace her cell by cell. It was setting, and when it was done, when the moment was absorbed into her, she'd be forever someone else. It was too late to alter, too late to be saved. The event had only to settle, she had only to accept the new form. The less she thought about it the better.

"Travis?" she said.

"Product of my second mistake."

"Marriage?"

"Yeah. I hardly count the first one, but everyone else does. A year of squabbling and a breakup. Neat and tidy compared to Ellen."

"Travis's mother?"

"Yep. She got the boy at six and since she hates me with the fury of a thousand suns, what chance did my one have?"

"Punny."

He winced. He'd used the line before, frequently, and hoped it wasn't obvious.

"We used to get along, see eye to eye on everything. Now she's with Kyle, the direct opposite of me."

"What does the opposite of a one-of-a-kind look like?"

"He's religious, upright. A teetotaler who never had to give it up in the first place. My son now takes after him, but with a more militant view."

He didn't like thinking of Travis. The boy was unrecognizable to him now, not that he ever got to see him. He followed him on social media, marveled at his growth and despaired at his ideology. He was a Second Amendment fanatic, played war games, waved Confederate flags as if his Maine ancestors had been with Lee. When he'd phoned him on his last birthday, Travis had asked him if he was still a 'bleeding-heart liberal' as if he were asking if he'd overcome an infection.

"I'm not political," he'd said. "That's a young man's sport."

"So what are you doing?"

He was barely hanging on with a part-time teaching salary from Commondale, and learning to like the bottom-shelf plastic-bottled fifths of whiskey. "I'm teaching."

"So, programming the elitists?"

"I prefer the phrase 'teaching college'."

It was enough of a retort to push the barely amicable conversation over the edge. "Whatever," Travis said dismissively, and made his excuses to get off the phone.

"The last thing I heard about my son, Travis," Seth told Charlotte, "was that he was arrested for pepper-spraying protestors."

"Oh."

"He got off with a warning. Hospitalized two people, and got a warning."

She didn't know what to say.

"One was a baby. Piece of work, that guy."

"Kids do stupid things."

"You have kids?"

"Hell no. Never. But I used to be one."

"Used to be?"

"Cute," she said. "Now you're calling yourself an old man."

"I feel that way sometimes."

"Sorry about Travis."

"Well, there were some good times," he said, trying to remember some. "What about you? You say you got along with your folks?"

"Yes and no," she said. "They're pushy." She heard the slur in her voice and it surprised her. "I'm getting a little drunk."

Her confession gave him permission to finish his drink. He raised his glass to her. "Welcome to the party."

He'd long since stopped tasting the alcohol. The familiar numbness crept through his limbs and he leaned back to enjoy it. "Like being home."

"What now?" she asked.

"Now we are drunk."

"After that."

"We fall asleep."

"Seth…"

"Don't think about tomorrow," he said. "That way lies madness. If there's one thing I've learned in my long, old age, is that our world doesn't reward that kind of thinking. It's now and nothing."

She thought about that but couldn't get a handle on it. Her mind was foggy, her vision blurred. It seemed important somehow. "You mean now *or* nothing, don't you?"

"Nope. It was right the first time. The mantra of the modern age: now *and* nothing."

"That doesn't seem right."

"No, it doesn't."

Chapter Four

Dreams came dark and sharp to both Charlotte and Seth that night. Charlotte's were filled with grim acts of violence, clear and shattering, set to mournful music, a witness to atrocities she was unable to turn away from. Seth's suffered from lower down, dreams forming in images of Travis and Ellen, his many lost weekends, his cynicism challenged in bile-biting arguments, relived and reimagined echoes from a time when he cared enough to try. These, unlike Charlotte's, were lost when he awoke.

He was in his empty suite. Charlotte had left a note for him to join her for breakfast. A glance at the clock and he'd call it brunch. No need to hurry now. He dragged his headache into the shower.

Charlotte sast at the hotel café watching her fourth cup of coffee grow cold, hastening it with the occasional slow stir. She hadn't eaten anything. She told the waitress she was waiting for a friend, but she hadn't been hungry. They'd let her sit and stare out the window at the morning with minimum interference. Charlotte was grateful for that.

The grant from Commondale, or rather Robert Weller's money, allowed them to stay in places like this. No use staying in a rat's nest to try to get into a mood for a penthouse later. Bobby Weller stayed in penthouses. Or he did. Now he was in a hospital.

She'd read the updates on her phone. Bobby Weller had been in a 'drugged frenzy' at the time of the killing, so said reports. He was being observed in a hospital. Police were investigating.

The explanation, though uncredited and unverified, soothed Charlotte. It was such a horror and she'd been near enough to hear the thumping of the racket, the cracking of the skulls, the slosh of viscera, that when the screams came, they were a welcome relief. She remembered a conversation she'd had with her mother when she was young. She'd been caught watching a gory movie, something her friend had recommended. Her mother had thrown a fit. At fourteen, Charlotte was already half a pistol, finding new ways to disappoint her parents even then.

"How can you watch such filth?" her mother had demanded to know.

"The violence is important to the story."

"There's already far too much violence in the world. If you need *that* to tell a story, you don't have a story."

"Different tastes."

"If you'd seen what I've seen—"

"I'd have fled the country and started again in America, putting everything I had into the success of my only ungrateful child?" she offered.

"Charlotte!" Her mother raised her hand to smack her.

Charlotte flinched but didn't move away.

Her mother dropped her arm, her dark face a palsy of expression, gray wiry strands of hair reached out like ivy over her forehead where they'd freed themselves from the tight bun.

"It's all fake, Mamma," Charlotte had said. "It's all fake and I know it."

"It looks like hell."

"But it's all make-believe. This is what happens here, Mamma, this is what they watch. If I'm to be the American princess you want me to be, I've got to be able to watch it."

"To be desensitized?"

"Exactly."

Her mother took her change of tack as a conciliatory gesture, glossing over the obvious and recurring dig with the 'American princess' line.

"I'll turn it off, Mamma," said Charlotte.

Her mother nodded once and then left the room, pulling the door shut behind her, which made it easier for Charlotte to finish watching her show.

Make-believe. Desensitized. Words that she thought had won her the argument a decade before now tasted dusty in her mouth. She tried to think of the event as a movie – actors, not real people. Not family. No. Not family. Stunts. Special effects. It helped a little. Maybe.

The waitress topped off her coffee mug and Charlotte thanked her for the quarter inch of new coffee. She reached for the cream and peeled back the seal on the single-serving teaspoon. She poured it into her cup and swirled the white with the brown.

It was a metaphor, she thought. Her parents wanting her to assimilate. Her parents going all-in on her to succeed.

The waitress had neglected to take the other three empty plastic cream cups she'd used. Left also the used blue paper packets of sweetener she'd piled up on a paper napkin. These things would have bothered her parents. She remembered her father, in a rare moment of frustration, bemoaning the waste of the world through Kleenex.

"What's wrong with a handkerchief?" he'd wanted to know.

Charlotte pulled another tissue from the box and blew her nose again. She tossed the wad at the wastebasket, missing, and piling up with several others.

"Not sanitary," she said.

"It's a waste. You know how many trees are cut down so you can blow your nose?"

"How many?" She couldn't remember her age, but wouldn't put it far from the fourteen when she'd been caught watching the movie.

"Millions," he said.

"Do you have their locations? I could maybe go replant them."

"Don't be smart with me," he'd said. The sharpness in his voice had called Mother into the room.

"Rajenbra," she'd said, using her father's real name, "don't be upset at Charlotte. She is sick. Let her alone."

"Lots of waste. Everything is disposable here."

"Yes, dear."

Strange she'd remember that now.

She poked at the plastic cups, pinched the foil top, dropped it back. He'd had a point of course. She'd known it then. Now things had only gotten worse. The environment was in shambles and there was always some new obstacle, some new debate, to slow anyone from even talking about the problem, let alone fixing it. It was the way things were. The way things had been her entire life. Normal. The Normal.

A million trees to blow her nose. Once. He'd neglected to say 'once'. That would have spoken to his handkerchief.

He'd bought her some handkerchiefs that year, monogrammed ones. Nice. But she never used them. They were out of style, which, she saw, now meant 'not normal'.

She wondered if her parents had seen the attack at the Garden. They probably had. Maybe she should call them.

"You're up early." Seth slid into the chair across from her. He took in the coffee and her faraway look, and thought she looked pretty good for a hangover.

"I feel terrible," she said for good morning.

"You get used to it," he said and signaled a waitress. "Coffee. Bring a pot. Water, four eggs over medium. Double toast and butter."

"Is that all?"

"Make it five eggs."

The waitress looked at Charlotte who said, "Cottage cheese."

"Whoa there, you don't want to bloat," Seth said.

"I'm not in the mood," she said when the waitress had left. "How'd you sleep?"

"The…" He was about to say 'usual', but that wasn't right. "Not great."

"But longer than I did."

"Is there an accusation there?"

Charlotte looked up. "Was there? Sorry. I don't know. I'm grasping at napkins here."

"Yeah," he said. "What's the news?" He gestured to her phone.

"New spin is that Bobby was on drugs."

"No."

"How can you be so sure?"

Seth stroked his beard absentmindedly as the waitress poured his coffee. "Leave the pot," he reminded her.

When she was gone, he said, "I know it's hard to believe looking at me, knowing something of my past as you do, but I am not unfamiliar with drugs. I'd have sensed drugs if Bobby had been tweaking."

"You don't know what drug it might have been."

"There are few drugs that can make someone do that," he said. "Hell, there's no drug that could make anyone do that."

"Bath salts," said Charlotte. "There was that story about that one guy who ate someone's face."

"I think we'd have noticed face-eating intent in Bobby before the act," he said. "He'd won several sets of tennis against a ranked player. Drugs that fuck you up that much don't tend to make you excel at tennis."

"What do you think happened?" It was the big question that had been unspoken the day before.

"I was thinking about that."

"Really? So was I."

"Oh, the sarcasm's back." Seth smiled. "It's good to see."

"You like my sarcasm?"

"I worried about you last night. You looked sick."

"I was."

The eggs arrived with his toast. A half cup of cottage cheese on a leaf of crisp green lettuce was placed delicately in front of Charlotte. She poked it. Seth swallowed one of his eggs in a gulp.

"Protein," Seth said. "Always good for the day after." He watched her taste her cottage cheese. "So, cottage cheese?"

"Cottage cheese." What else could you say about it?

Seth watched her, waiting for an opening. He had an idea. It was the second question, the more intimate elephant in the room, a situation that had literally been shocked out of their thinking the day before.

As if she were telepathic, she said, "It's amazing how quickly things can change. Alive – dead; filmmaker – unemployed."

"About that," said Seth. "I think we should carry on."

"A feel-good tennis documentary about a murderer?"

"We might need to make some adjustments."

"You're kidding?"

"I'm not ready to go back home. I like these hotels. This is nice. The Florida one was nicer. I say we stay on the hotel circuit and carry on."

"We don't have a subject," she said.

"I can understand that," Seth said. "But to come back to your earlier question, what happened? We could find out. Make that our movie."

She shook her head.

"Okay, we started about one thing, but who says we can't pivot to something else?"

"Our sponsor."

"Our sponsor?"

"You know," said Charlotte. "The one paying the bills."

"Would that be Commondale or Robert Weller?"

"What's the difference?"

"Well, the difference is in how we handle them."

She put down her spoon and sipped her cooling coffee.

"Charlotte, this is probably my last chance."

"At what?"

"At doing anything meaningful."

"What about all those other films you made?"

"Forgettable and forgotten and done long ago. I'm over the hill for the real working jobs. My only chance forward is to be executive. Cinematographer, DP – that kind of thing."

"Professor. You could be a professor."

"I was a professor. A couple bad decisions and I'm lucky to still be on the books."

"They'll forgive you eventually. You'll—"

"No, they won't. They're putting up with me, and I them. An overdosed undergrad in a hot tub doesn't go away. It gets buried at best."

"I didn't hear that."

"That one was buried. The drugged-out classes, the slurring videos, those you heard about?"

"Yes."

"Fuck it. Ugly shit and though not my fault, not really, my hands aren't exactly clean. My life is a wreck. Commondale has been decent to me. Too decent, but it's a dead end and I've dead-ended."

"You're being dramatic."

"When you get to be my age—"

"Did you really just say that?"

"Shit," said Seth. "Yeah, okay. That did sound terrible."

"It did."

"But listen, okay. This is your chance too. Trust me on one thing, know this from my experience of life, whatever that may be, opportunities are not as common as you think. Getting one now does not mean you'll get another later. And fucking up does not bode well for the future."

"Commondale isn't a dead end."

"Says the woman who'll be graduating."

"What does that mean?"

"I'll be stuck there, you'll be gone."

"You make it sound like I'm abandoning you. We hardly know each other."

"We've been working together for a month. I think I know you."

"Ha."

"Okay, then I'd like to know you."

"Now are you coming on to me?"

"Charlotte." His voice was sharp and she had visions of her chastising mother.

Seth saw the effect and tried to soften his approach. "Let's press on."

"How?"

"By not stopping."

"You're too much."

"No. It's that simple, if we don't make it harder."

"You're still drunk."

"Even if I was."

"Are you drunk?"

"I had a shot in the room."

"For chrissakes."

"Robert Weller won't say no."

"God, Seth, you're sick."

"Okay, we have a question about going on. Who do we ask about it?"

"The regents."

"Who'd ask Robert, and there we are again."

"It feels like stealing. Our mission is over."

"We got a grant. The grant is still good."

"Revocable."

"I don't know about that. Do you?"

"Well…come on."

"As I've tried to tell you, in this business, it's better to ask forgiveness than permission."

"And you want to be an executive?"

"Okay, in this business, at our level, doing what we're doing, forgiveness, all the way. When we have lawyers and shit, permission. Probably."

She studied him, her eyes a little sensitive to light, a distant ringing in her ears. "So…what?" she said.

"Well, let's take a look at the footage we have, see what it suggests. We have leads."

"Stay with tennis? Another player? Madic?"

"Fuck no. Well, maybe. Let's see. I think we have to dig deeper. Tennis may have to go and I'm pretty sure that after yesterday the feel-good story is out the window."

"This is all so morbid. Are you talking about some kind of event autopsy?"

"Maybe. That's a good idea, but we can't know yet. Our work will lead us."

She rolled her eyes.

"Charlotte," said Seth, "this is not a setback. It's a golden opportunity. We are perfectly placed. We have a team – you and I, we have money, leads, connections. We're close to the center of this thing."

"This crime?"

"Sure."

The sun was high out the window and Charlotte took it in. The world looked the same this morning as it did yesterday. The air, the sea, the trees, the furniture and grass all carried on as if one of the richest men in the country hadn't been beaten to death by his son on live television. Everything was just...normal.

"And, Charlotte, think as a journalist. Don't you want to get to the bottom of this? Find out what happened? See where it goes?"

A distant memory of sound rose in Charlotte's subconscious, a hum and a rhythm that stirred her blood. "Follow the music, see where it takes us?"

"What else can we do?"

Chapter Five

The first was a sickening thud that spread out into the hush he remembered. The arm raised and down it came again and the head split open with an echoing crack and a twang of breaking strings. Up again and down two, three, four more times until the air was a cloud of scarlet blood and gray matter. Still surrounding silence. Mrs. Weller, blood-splattered, her mouth agape, whimpers ever so little, a sound Seth had to crank up to be sure he heard. It must have been the sound, small as it was, that drew Bobby from his father and on to his mother. Up came the racket—

Seth turned away from the monitor, took off his headset and reached for his glass of bourbon. He was shaking. He'd watched the scene a dozen times and each time it turned his stomach. He was pleased at his work. His video was at least as good as the stuff the networks were airing. It was also from a different angle and had better sound. It would be a selling point if it ever got to that.

He was glad now that Charlotte hadn't wanted to go over the raw footage. When he'd offered it after breakfast, he'd thought her weak, and he'd worried because of it. He knew he was on thin ice with her. He liked to think that he'd nailed it in his talk with her, that chances are few and this is a once-in-a-lifetime chance, but he knew there was smoke up his ass. This was probably his last chance, but she'd have more. She was young, pretty, educated, driven, exotic. She filmed great. The camera loved her.

He switched to a scene with her in it as a palate cleanser. Boston suburb: Bobby, Kinsley and Charlotte. He paused the feed on Charlotte. Even when she didn't know the camera was on her, she looked great. It helped settle Seth's stomach.

He refilled his glass and looked around the suite. The sun was on its way to setting. It was an hour shy of magic hour, that time of day when Mother Nature blesses filmmakers with perfect light. The thought rushed his veins with adrenaline like of old as he wondered what shot he could get. Nothing today. A waste.

Another sip and he found himself calling bullshit on his speech with Charlotte. He'd won the 'debate' if that was what it had been, but he didn't feel good about it. He felt like he'd cheated. Not just because of Charlotte's real potential, but also because he wasn't so sure his own motivation was right. He wasn't sure he wanted to get back in the game. He'd been there, at the periphery at any rate, and it wasn't that good. Maybe Director of Photography would be, but it sounded like work to him. He wasn't sure about that. Seth poured soda into his glass to weaken the bourbon and thanked the gods for ice and bubbly water. The room was comfortable, big, nicer by far than his own home. The drinks were free, the food was free as long as their grant held out. This, he realized, was the real reason he didn't want to give up the film. The thought of his old life, his grubby rooms, freshman classes, and monthly trips to the laundromat hardly beckoned his return. Drudgery was home. He didn't want to go home. Maybe because he didn't have one.

"Fuck," he said out loud, recognizing the rut of self-pity he was falling into. "Not today Sether-boy."

He unplugged the headphones and let the tinny speakers of his computer provide the sound. He pressed play.

"Everyone should have a reason," said Bobby in Boston, "a purpose to be alive."

Bobby Weller, philosopher. Blond, blue-eyed, blue-blooded, American royalty talking about purpose like everyone has a choice. For film it worked. For the documentary they were making it work; for the one they were making now, it could probably be the centerpiece.

He played the clip again, without the sound this time, concentrating on the tan face and rugged chin of the young athlete. He was looking for clues, tics, suggestions of a double meaning behind what he was saying. Aforethought, in mystery terms. He saw nothing. Like Charlotte, Bobby Weller was easy to look at, warm, amiable. An obvious child of privilege, but once within his sphere, personable. Human. He turned the sound back up and played it again. The clip would be key for some part of the documentary, he was sure, an eerie uncontextualized moment of foreshadowing.

One more time through it, Seth set the scene in his mind as a cornerstone for future filming, cementing it subconsciously in his psyche to guide future direction. Listening to Bobby's voice, smooth, calm, collected, unhandled and unfazed by the film crew's interest, he was helpful and frank. The clip, used the way Seth intended – the way any editor would – was disingenuous, a lie to the intent of the words, a falsehood masked by the exclusive meaning of the literal letter. Unfair but poetic. It wasn't Seth doing it. Events had spoken. To see it any other way, looking backward to that moment with the knowledge of events, would now be incongruous. That is, the context had changed.

He flipped back to the film of the attack, thinking how he might intercut that with Bobby's talk about having a reason. He'd put the voice over the image. The sound of the attack was too much. The attack was too much, but showing it would be unavoidable. He reminded himself that the audience would already have seen the attack. The media was playing it to death. Poor choice of words.

He was getting ahead of himself. He had to find some direction to go now, some tangible next move to continue. Charlotte was on board at the moment, more or less, but she could easily sour and bail on him. Seeing someone stab the jagged end of a shattered tennis racket through his mother's eye could do that to a person.

He played the attack footage without sound from the moment Bobby went to the wall. This time he covered the center of the screen with a yellow sticky note, the better to observe the crowd's reaction to it. He wondered if, like him, they'd been unable to take their eyes off the ghastly gore. It was a strange thing. He could barely sit through slasher movies, he squirmed at the Karo Syrup splatter. He remembered in camp as a child having to turn his head when a friend lanced a blister on his foot. When he passed crashed cars on the freeway, he kept his face straight ahead. Last year he'd cut his finger in the kitchen. He'd rinsed it under the tap without looking at it and wrapped it in gauze and a bandage by feel alone. He was squeamish; not a good thing for a documentary cameraman. But there in the stadium, the most horrible thing he'd ever seen, he'd kept the camera steady, watched with a gripped fascination that was beyond uncharacteristic. Everyone had. Strange how it'd been then, but not now. Now he struggled to watch the footage at all.

The paper blind helped, and silently he watched the crowd's reaction, which exactly matched his own. They watched the murder of Robert Weller in stunned shock. Not a sound, not a reaction beyond wonder and witness. Near and far, old or young, everyone stared blankly as if mesmerized, hypnotized, or drugged. Still and silent, Bobby the only actor. The security guards might as well have been marble statues.

For distraction, he switched to his browser, and sought his son's social media. There he was in a recent picture, taken in some backyard. Ellen was there, and her new husband, and Travis in a camouflage t-shirt and canvas pants. A shadow spilling out from under his sleeve suggested a new tattoo. His brown hair was buzzed at the sides, yet sported bangs over his serious eyes. Seth tried to remember a time when his son wasn't so serious, a time when he played and laughed. He had to go back many years in his memory for such a scene, so far, in fact, he couldn't be sure it was a real memory and not a fantasy.

He read a few posts, followed comments, some links he thought his friends, whoever they were, would be interested in. Kyle was apparently now fixated on a group calling themselves Sons of Stone. The way Travis described the group made them sound worse than the despised Antifa. The exception here was that the SOS was a real group. He called them 'an existential threat', the members 'brainwashed', 'ignorant', 'puppets'. The usual slurs he threw at his political targets. The SOS logo was a cartoon rock with a bite out of it. Travis had photoshopped a picture of Calvin peeing on it and used it as his Twitter avatar.

He tried to blame Ellen and her new husband Kyle for Travis's fanaticism, but no matter the logic, he always found some blame for himself. He'd failed the child so much that he'd turned against everything

Seth believed in. It was like he sought to kill his father by fighting his ideas.

A random chain of connection sparked boozy synapses to a connection that sent a chill down Seth's neck.

He returned to his video, back to the attack. He lined it up, turned up the sound, but kept the sticky in place.

"Cough them up!" Bobby Weller had said as he bludgeoned his father to death. "Cough them up!"

Something Barney Faro had said in that freshman mythology class. Seth had sat through part of one waiting for his colleague to come drinking with him after. He remembered snippets from that lecture which was much, much better than what he could remember of that night.

He was woolgathering. Spending his limited energy in the wrong direction.

Time was short. Striking up another cigarette, he tried to find a lead that would interest Charlotte. He had to keep the project going.

He took in the opulent room, the auburn streaks of light sliding through the window sheers illuminated in the smoke of his bad habit. He could make out the smell of top-rate balsamic vinegar smeared over a room-service plate, a subtle satisfying scent just detectable below his cigarettes. He had half a bottle of whiskey and a phone to bring up another. He had all the ice he needed. Life was good for now. It was temporary, he knew, but it was enough. It would end if he couldn't convince Charlotte to go on. He had a little time, so he turned off the computer and watched the magic hour fill his stolen suite with rose-orange light, brilliant and warm. He'd worry about tomorrow if he got one.

Chapter Six

In the poolside spa, Charlotte's mind was as empty of thoughts for tomorrow as she tried to keep it from yesterday.

She'd signed up for the full signature experience. Three hours of pampering at a cost of only one of her paychecks. Paid for by the grant. Hey, better to ask forgiveness than permission. Seth was rubbing off on her. Another thought she didn't want in her head.

The appointment had been made by phone from the suite. There was a fast-dial button for it, in fact. They knew her name before she said it and promised her the very best the hotel had to offer.

At the door she met Tiffany, a slim brunette athlete in a miniskirt. Whoever had done her makeup could work the Oscars. Every flattering line was accentuated, every fault covered up. Her hair was casually perfect, falling past her shoulders over diamond stud earrings onto the navy-blue blouse, hotel insignia embroidered over the breast opposite her gold name tag. She'd welcomed Charlotte to the point of obsequiousness.

"Your day today will begin with a massage, then a full body exfoliation and facial. Afterwards you can relax in our Hawaiian lava pumice immersive mud baths for the full holistic experience."

"Lovely," said Charlotte, hoping she sounded less pompous than the word sounded in her ears.

"This way."

Tiffany led her to the first room, a massage room where she was offered a choice. "Steve, Patrick, Marci or Patti?" Four people stood in front of four doors in a short hallway. It was a buffet, she realized. Steve and Patrick were men, both beautiful and tall, Steve Black and built like a football player, Patrick blond and athletic like a cyclist. On the other side, Marci was a dishwater-blonde, a swimming champion if Charlotte had to guess, while Patti had sculpted cheekbones, tight cornrows and a skin color she could only match to soot or the best mahogany. Her features were classical and she could imagine her stepping out of a pharaoh's tomb, and then wondered at the grim image.

"Perhaps you'd like Patti," said Tiffany, guessing her preference.

"No, I'll take Patrick," she said. "Or Steve."

Patrick stepped forward and offered her his hand with a big grin. She took his hand, noting that his tanned skin was still ten shades lighter than her natural one. The other masseuses smiled as she followed Patrick into his room.

She'd had massages before, some better than others. Not many, really maybe six in her life. This immediately promised to be one of the better ones. There were soft lights, and moody synthetic music. Patrick warmed his hands by rubbing them together before coating them with heated oil. A dispenser in the corner puffed little clouds of light lavender.

She disrobed and for an hour had all the tension worked out of her. He never said a word beyond asking her to roll over, face this way or that. He kept the towel covering her and averted his eyes at the appropriate times. She sensed, however, that there might be other ways the massage could go.

The muscle work and tactile sensations up and down her back, neck and thighs relaxed her more than any massage she'd ever had. She found it easy to forget her troubles, her memories, her trauma. She found it easy to remove thoughts from her mind in total, concentrating on and relishing the contact.

It was over before she was bored of it, a first for an hour massage. Patrick left the room and told her to relax in quiet for a moment. Charlotte lay there thinking about how much cash she had to tip him before remembering the strict rules of the spa against tipping. She was about to check her purse when there was a knock on the door.

"Ready?" came Tiffany's voice.

"Sure," she answered, though she didn't know what for.

Tiffany opened the door and two Asian women came in with baskets under their arms. "This is Li and Yang, they'll take you through the wrap and facial."

"Okay."

Tiffany glanced at the two and retired out the door. Patrick, nowhere to be seen.

With whispers and hand gestures, no eye contact, they rubbed her body with a thick white cream that cleared with the rubbing. They moved up her thighs and around her chest with the attitude of nurses.

"What is this lotion?" Charlotte asked, if only to hear something above a sigh.

"Chupasangre cactus butter," said Li. "Very rare. Very expensive."

"Ten bushels in this one bottle," said Yang, holding up the jar.

They offered nothing more and wrapped her with industrial-weight cellophane, covering her body in a second skin. They pulled the plastic tight, and as they did, she could feel her skin tingle and numb beneath it.

They sat her up and then applied another cream to her face.

"This one?" she asked.

"Clé de Peau Beauté," Li said. "We use very little."

"Need very little," added Yang.

"Very expensive and very rare?"

"More than gold," said Li.

Yang nodded agreement.

At least the cucumbers were probably cheap, Charlotte thought as they carefully placed a layer of them over her entire face.

"Few minutes," whispered Li.

Charlotte, afraid of knocking off a slice, didn't reply.

She waited. She didn't know how long, but long enough for the magic of the massage to fade and release the thoughts she'd blocked away. It required real concentration to keep from worrying about where the movie would go now, what her future would be, why Bobby Weller would do such a thing, and how she could justify the expense of this spa.

Then the cucumbers came off and the women scraped her face with fine porcelain spoons. When they were done, she had to admit she felt fresh as a flower. She could feel the breeze on her cheeks.

Then they pulled the plastic off, or rather, they cut it away with surgical scissors. They'd used rolls and rolls of the stuff and it was all discarded into a garbage pail that overflowed when they were done.

Li and Yang bowed and excused themselves while Charlotte sat on the table. Before she could feel abandoned, Tiffany was there offering her a white terry cloth robe. "I hope that was delightful," she said. "Now follow me to the shower."

The robe went to the floor and felt as heavy as a bearskin cloak. It was warm and engulfing and she decided to wear it like she deserved it, reflecting the attitude she'd decided to have for the rest of the experience. Beyond bad thoughts of nightmare moments and coming uncertainty, she also put out of her mind self-consciousness, guilt, and questions of merit. This was her time. She'd relax and enjoy it. Spas were self-indulgence for the unrepentant.

Down the hall to the end door, Charlotte found a locker room. She was pleased to find no one else in there. The room could accommodate four people, judging by the number of lockers and not the square footage, which rivaled her entire childhood house. She was surprised to find her clothes and belongings already in one locker. She couldn't remember anyone taking them. What was that someone once said? 'You never see a good servant, only their good work.'

The shower had eight separate showerheads, digitally dialed temperature, pressure for each, and twelve steam settings. There was a bench, unopened shampoo and foreign soap she'd never heard of but which had to be expensive. The tile was pink and gray. Granite maybe, or marble. The shower was decadent and effective. She stood under the water jets for ten minutes before she thought to actually wash. With the help of a natural sponge luffa, she scrubbed the places she could reach and waited under the jets until she felt drowsy.

When she came out of the shower her robe was gone, replaced with a fresh one, neat and folded on a bench. Again, she hadn't noticed anyone come or go. Rather than be weirded out, she accepted it as par for the day.

No sooner had she put the robe on than Tiffany appeared at a far door with a big smile. "Time to get dirty!" she said with a giggle.

Charlotte followed her across a gray granite-tiled room with six sunken tubs of steaming black mud. The basins circled a central table upon which a dozen bottles of designer drinking water waited next to a silver ice bucket. The room smelled mildly of sulfur, fragranced with talcum. The air was thick and surprisingly cool.

Charlotte noticed one other person in the room: an elderly woman in one of the tubs, only her pale wrinkled face and yellow bathing cap visible above the muck. Her eyes were closed and Charlotte could not help but focus on the woman's lips, a firm, pursed pucker, wrinkled and over-engorged. Age, meet collagen.

Tiffany took her to one of the tubs, held up a towel and averted her eyes. The towel was large and concealed her from the other occupant who might have been asleep. Once naked, she moved into the tub. "It's a little deeper than a bathtub," Tiffany said very quietly. "Hold the railing to climb in."

"What should I do with the robe?" asked Charlotte.

"Oh, just drop it."

"It could get muddy."

"That's fine."

Charlotte hesitated. She imagined how hard it would be to clean that robe, how much water, soap and chemicals might be needed. How long it would be in a dryer. Terry cloth was soft but a pain in the ass. It's why she didn't own any herself.

Remembering her plan, she let the garment fall to the ground, a sleeve flopping into the mud with a softened splat. She immediately felt the cool air and goose-pimpled before descending the three steps into the bath.

"The steps are at your foot end." Tiffany was almost whispering. "Lie back and use towels for your head. I'll be nearby."

A stack of towels was at the end of the bath. Terry cloth. She hadn't seen anyone put them there.

"Do I do anything?" Charlotte asked.

"No. Just sit back and relax. I'll rouse you in twenty minutes."

Charlotte sat back and tried to relax. She cringed when her hand came out of the gloop to arrange the towels for a pillow, muddying them up to a level that would have brought a spanking from her mother. She reminded herself to be pampered, leaned back, and closed her eyes. The mud was warm and tingly. She could feel a throb through it, as if an engine had been placed underneath her and vibrated the tub. It was the strangest sensation, affecting every part of her body. Like the massage, but all-encompassing, engulfing her, like the heavy black sulfurous mud she was in. It felt strange but not unpleasant. No, not unpleasant at all. Freeing and ancient.

She became aware of music, soft and angelic, similar but with more bass than she had with her massage. The kind of thing you might hear underlying a church service, but with more martial rhythms. Not unpleasant. Nothing she owned, nothing she could identify, only classified as being beyond her general tastes.

If Charlotte chose to lift her head while the other woman did the same, they might have met eyes. Their voices would have carried. A conversation could be easy, but both lay quiet while the music played, and Charlotte relaxed in tickling grit.

There was something familiar about the sound and the sensation, her whole being a receptor to subtle vibration. Seeking a metaphor, she thought this was some approximation of a womb perhaps, or maybe, in a dark flash of unsilenced disquiet, an unsettled tragedy of a yet-to-be nightmare.

She slipped out of the moment and grew peeved, then angry at the day. The masseuse wasn't allowed tips? What's up with that? And all the invisible servants. How is that not dehumanizing? What kind of cactus did they say? Some precious endangered species, some plant harvested by slaves in a jungle, marked up to obscene levels and sold to people with more money than morality, more interested in their pores than anyone poor. And the plastic. Rolls and rolls of it for a few moments of mock mummification. She recalled the trash can full of the greasy plastic and her anger seethed to rage. Designer water in cut crystal bottles. How was that anything but ostentatious and wasteful? Then there was a woman in the other bath, the old woman, entitled and pampered. She was the kind of person who would take a spa day like this on a weekly basis, spending money she'd never earned, laughing over cocktails at the plight of the burning rainforest, paying for surgery with generational blood money. Tummy tucks and Botox to match her lips. She was an abomination. A curse. Charlotte's body shook with outrage at the audacity of it. She felt her hands squeeze into fists.

Charlotte opened her eyes to see Tiffany standing above her holding a robe. The room had gone quiet. The music silenced. Her mind emptied. The mud no longer throbbed, its temperature had become undetectable by acclimation, and yet she shivered with fright. The thoughts she'd had...

"Has it been twenty minutes?"

"Yes."

"Wow," she said.

"Would you like me to help you out and into the robe, or would you prefer to do it yourself?"

Charlotte looked for the muddy sleeve, but, of course, this was a fresh robe. Her third of the day. Terry cloth. A flash of anger, more easily put down, but still a flash.

"I'll do it," she said and took the robe, which stuck to her mud-covered body like lotioned plastic wrap.

"Time to hydrate." Tiffany offered her a bottle from the table. Charlotte took it, tasted water, just water.

She noticed the old woman was gone. It was just the two of them.

Tiffany said brightly, "You'll have a refreshing shower and then we'll talk manicure."

Charlotte recalled the space, recounted the eight showerheads and felt her jaw tense.

To make conversation as they walked out, Charlotte said, "I really liked the music. I liked how I could even feel the bass throbbing within the tub. What was it?"

Tiffany turned and smiled warmly, but confusedly. "The immersion mud baths are meditative," she said. "A silent space as much as possible. There was no music. You must be remembering something else."

Chapter Seven

It was no secret that Commondale University was an upstart in the academic world, a new riser vying for recognition among established Ivy League veterans. Originally a small college on the verge of bankruptcy, in the last decade it had been saved by benefactors looking to leave a legacy. Thus fueled by private donations, the Wellers leading the pack with a billion-dollar foundation, Commondale meteorically rose to international prominence by unashamedly poaching the best and brightest from other institutions. Its faculty could boast, among other things, two Nobel Prizes, a Booker Prize, two Pulitzers, six Oscars, a Tony, eight Emmys, an Adam Smith Award, a Turing Award, and a Grote Prize for history. None of these lauded scientists and scholars held regular classes. Most were too old, some in their dotage. One rumored to be dead. Most served as advisors and none lived within a hundred miles of the campus. Some even continued to work at other colleges. Nevertheless, their awards graced the Commmondale website and peppered all promotional material. It was an effective tool to lure new students and more money.

Seth did not begrudge these people what they were doing. If anything, he was envious. He understood that a Grote Prize didn't pay bills, an Adam Smith Award wasn't worth a cup of coffee. Royalties on textbooks and the odd speaking engagement didn't make up for the poor salaries of academia. Those that could, did, and cashed in all the more by associating with money-to-burn Commondale. Those that could, but chose to teach, those whose honors were half a century old, who knew well the flavor of week-old brioche, were more than happy to leverage their forgotten life's work into a better paycheck and a bit more fame by association. Commondale put all the awards together in its marketing and PR; an Edison Award next to an Oscar, a Pulitzer next to a Lyell Medal. Names and dates concealed in an endnote in microscopic type.

Charlotte found reason to be upset about Commondale's antics, as she called them.

"It's a bait and switch," she said on the flight back from Indian Wells.

"It was at first," Seth said. "Now, I think the school is actually living up to all the hype."

"Psh."

"I find it comforting."

"All those people prostituting themselves for the school. You know they have to sign a contract."

"And?"

"And it says that they can't promote other things without express written permission from the school."

"And?"

"It's selling out."

"What country at what time in history do you think you're living in?"

"You too? Really?" She looked at him like she'd just discovered he was covered in sores.

"Me what?"

"Psh."

"Oh, that."

"Seth Lian—"

"Don't talk to me like that. You sound like my mother."

"Your parents did that too?"

"Whose didn't? I think it was taught on some TV show."

"Sorry."

"I've been at Commondale for a long time. At times well respected. I was there back in the day when they called themselves the 'Compromisedale'."

"How?"

"Well, it's about halfway between the University of Oregon and Oregon State University. It wasn't liberal like the Ducks are thought to be, or conservative like the Beavers. You haven't heard this before?"

She shook her head.

"Well, also it's geographically centered between the two schools, and more inland, so we get neither the wet coastal slog of the west or the high desert barrens of east Oregon. It was marketed, poorly I admit, as the perfect school for the undecided. As a junior college in those days, it was cheaper to get your generals there. All you had to do was put up with blizzards and second-rate teachers."

"Are you including yourself in that group?"

"Oh yes."

"I was kidding."

"No, it's all right. The school worked for me."

Charlotte felt the pressure in the cabin change and tensed.

"What?"

"My ears popped."

"Yeah, mine too. But I didn't look like I was about to shit myself."

"Charming. You were saying?"

Charlotte was pleased to let Seth continue. The pressure shift felt too much like the eerie moment she'd been jarred out of her dark ideas at the mud bath. She quickly checked her memory to make sure she hadn't been fantasizing anything untoward.

"I should have decided one way or the other. Gone all in on film, or all in on teaching. I did neither."

"The school used to be something. Now it's a whorehouse."

"Ouch."

"Well, it is. Who knows who Josefa Rojaz is?"

"You do, apparently."

"He won something for growing cacti in Chile."

"Chile needs help growing cacti?"

"Some of them are very valuable," she said and felt her hair raise. "Anyway, he's one of the badges on the brochure."

"Look at it this way," Seth said, turning to her. "It's hard to get anywhere. If you're not connected it's all but impossible."

"A pep talk."

"Relax. And calm down. You're coloring."

"I am?"

"Yes."

"Sorry."

"Sometimes, the way to get there is fake it till you make it. Believe it or not, it works. You pretend to be successful, act the part, think the part, and sooner or later, you are the part."

"That's stupid."

"No, it isn't. Don't you believe in positive thinking?"

She shrugged. "Not all Indians are gurus."

"Is that some backhanded way of calling me a racist?"

"No. Of course not."

Seth looked at her, trying to read her face. As a representative of the empowered and privileged white male middle class, he had stepped in plenty of piles of his own ignorance to the point that he almost had a chip on his shoulder.

"Well, case in point. Commondale. It faked it till it made it."

"Money did that."

"That didn't hurt, but I'll point out that our business school is called the shark tank in the chambers of GreedCo."

"Is that real?"

"Yes. It's the nickname."

"No, I've heard that about the school. GreedCo. Is that real?"

"No. Just an easy way to type a certain kind of capitalist monster."

"I still don't like it. It bought its way into a fixed game."

"What would you have done?"

"I don't know. With the kind of money these people are throwing around, I guess I would have maybe tried something different. Maybe a college without grades, free tuition. Something egalitarian."

"Again, what world do you think you live in?"

"Is that now your go-to line?"

"It might be."

"I live in this one," she said. "I think it could be improved, okay?"

"If wishes were fishes."

"We'd all have castanets."

"What?"

"Something a friend of mine once said."

"That's funny."

"She killed herself."

Seth felt his grin collapse faster than it had arrived. "Fuck," he said.

"Her choice." She turned to look out the window. Clouds below and an unbearable blue brightness above.

Though it was jarring, Seth had to understand why Charlotte's demeanor was so different now. Gone was the light, breezy, excited new reporter of the flight out; now he had a critical world-weary companion. He didn't like mirrors.

"Anyway. Now they call Commondale 'the best of both worlds'. That's where it came from. The evolution of 'Compromisedale'."

"Both worlds?" she said to the window. "There are only two?"

"Binary thinking. The basis for evolution."

Seth waited for a question to explain his idea of the human means of understanding, but nothing came from Charlotte. Around her turned head, clouds floated beneath them in an endless plain to the horizon.

They remained silent for the rest of the flight, and it was only when they were in the cab heading back to the campus that Seth ventured the question.

"Are you going to ask permission?"

"I don't know."

"Nice guys finish last, remember."

"I need some time."

Seth was the first to be dropped off. He watched the cab pull away, taking Charlotte to what he imagined to be a tastefully furnished townhouse in the new suburb on the other side of campus. He was glad Charlotte didn't ask why he wanted to be dropped off at the university instead of home. He didn't want to dance around his depressing basement apartment in a gentrifying neighborhood. Mold, cold, skyrocketing rent.

He walked the snow-melted sidewalk to his shared office in the arts building. He didn't know Finn's schedule but doubted he'd see his office mate today. Pulling his bag along dry sidewalks, he remembered when there'd still be two feet of snow along the paths this time of year. It made him feel old. So he focused on the budding trees and the fresh notes of spring perfume in the afternoon air. The evergreens, the mountain chill. He liked the transitional seasons, fall more than spring, but still he could appreciate the promise of change, as long as the change was a familiar one. An oxymoron, he realized, but apt.

The flags were at half-staff and it took him a moment to figure out why. Of course, Commondale would mourn their biggest contributor.

Otherwise, the campus was as it should be. Distracted students absorbed in their phones, not even looking up at the permanent protestors by the Student Union building. A group had built an igloo back in December and had round-the-clock occupants handing out information and resisting the administration's attempt to remove it. Nature did the job the groundskeepers couldn't. It was now only a ring of melting ice, and a pup tent where it had been. Still, kids where there 'raising awareness' and not missing the opportunity to show comparative historical snow levels, like he'd just remembered.

"You read my mind, guys," Seth said as he passed them. "Keep up the good work."

It was meaningless. In his heart he knew this. College students weren't the cause of the problem so he doubted they could be the solution. Like so many of the disempowered and frustrated, Seth could support the cause but backed off from committing to its success. One trip down the rabbit hole, one imaginary journey into the possible – no, *probable* future, considering the problem's enormity and obstacles, and he'd retreated to the compartmentalized world of denial. It was the human superpower, he'd been told: compartmentalization. It was kind of like doublethink, Orwell's hellish concept of believing two contradictory things at once. This wasn't that. This was ignoring things when they were inconvenient. Not 'believing', per se. Avoiding.

Looking at the protestors, seeing how young they all were, thinking how the students got younger every year, every year more distant, he realized that denial goes a long way. There were demonstrations like this when he was a student. And look what happened. Awareness without progress. He remembered seeing a recent graphic of how many clean energy projects had been started – windmills, solar, tidal, each of them an accomplishment, but they didn't replace anything. They added to the net energy total. The old carbon plants were still chugging along. Clean technology was being proved but it wasn't taking the place of the dirty. Not a single plant had shut down for replacement. Some had shuttered, but for their own reasons. The world saw a net gain in energy. For the all-important carbon, they'd plateaued the poison at best. As these kids were well aware and struggled to do something about, plateau didn't solve anything. It was like putting on the cruise control while heading off a cliff.

He didn't want to think about it. He'd not live to see the worst of it and felt a perverse comfort in that.

"SOS, man," said a young man with snarled brown hair above a tan windbreaker.

"I hear ya."

"The revolution solution." He handed Seth a brochure.

"Printed on recycled paper?" he asked.

"Of course."

He took the pamphlet and pretended to read it as he entered the arts building. A big red 'SOS' bending around a blue globe. Trifold, letter-sized. Something printed off the internet.

Once out of sight, he stuffed it in his pocket and found his office on the third floor.

It was unoccupied and he dropped his luggage on the floor, pushed it under his desk, the only space with any room, and noticed the blinking light on his phone. Quaint, he thought, an old-fashioned land line with a message feature. It was cheap motel kitsch and surely meant that administration had sent out some global impersonal announcement, probably about parking.

He sat down in his chair and realized he had no room for his knees underneath. He pushed back, bumping the cheap metal bookshelf behind him. It held decorative books on film theory, coffee-table things to compete with Finn's bigger ones on sculpture. All for show. He never referred to them, and he assumed Finn, his art teacher office mate, didn't either. He meant to ask about removing the bookshelf to free up eighteen inches, but never got around to it. He and Finn had very different schedules; he taught most of the time, Seth didn't.

This office was a throwback to the days Seth was a student. The university had upgraded the offices of most of the other departments, but not this one. The business college and law office especially were fantastic. They'd appeared in architectural magazines and *Forbes*. The art offices, like all the Humanities, were left pretty much as they'd been for the past half century – rustic and in keeping with the school's view concerning the importance of the subjects.

He liked the little office though. It was nostalgic of a simpler time. Sometimes he wore jackets with leather on the elbows for the same reason. He couldn't bring himself to smoke a pipe, but that would be along the same line. The little window showing half a pine tree, a snow-matted lawn fading into a distant parking lot, sometimes allowed enough light in to compensate for the fluorescent bulbs.

He heard Finn's heavy footsteps coming down the hall and then the door swung open.

"You're here," he said, and sidestepped to his desk.

"You're looking particularly tired today," Seth said. It was true. The man was in his mid-sixties, but often carried himself like he was eighty. The thin atmosphere and harsh light had been unkind to him, and he wore his deep wrinkles like battle scars.

"I don't get them anymore," he said.

"Who?"

"The students. They're speaking a different language. They're…they… If art history wasn't an easy general education credit none of them would be there. They don't care."

"Why should they?"

"Not you too?" Finn said, melting into his chair. "Don't you teach film history sometimes? Or did?"

Seth knew that wasn't a dig, just a comment. "Yeah, but film hasn't been around that long. It's still in the imaginable past."

"Past is past."

"That's how they see it."

"God, Seth, remind me never to talk to you."

"What do you want?"

"Sympathy. Tell me they're wrong. That there's value in the history of our culture. That a rounded education is a good education."

Seth thought about this for a moment and didn't say anything. He agreed with Finn, of course, but it might have been in defense of the many hours he'd spent 'rounding' his education with classes and subjects that didn't interest him or help him.

"You're getting paid."

"You're missing the point. They're missing the point."

"Maybe it's history they're reacting to," Seth said, "as a comparative."

"To what?"

"The future."

"How so?"

"It's in vogue, isn't it, to think there is no future?"

"The typical immortal youth paradigm?"

"But worse."

"Worse," he agreed.

"Just keep doing what you're doing. I'm sure you're doing good."

"I don't know. If I were younger maybe they'd listen to me."

"You're not that old, for chrissakes. There are fossils roaming the campus."

He shook his head. "Maybe there is no future or maybe they just don't like what I'm selling. Nobody needs to know the different kinds of columns or tell a Manet from a Monet. Not really."

"But those who do know those things are better than those who don't."

"You mean smarter."

"Nope."

"Well, that's a positive sentiment in any event. Still, I tell you, every day I feel more and more obsolete."

"Don't let the bastards get you down," he said. "What's the worst they can do?" To change the subject, Seth took up his phone and pressed the message button.

"Hello, this is Oliver Christiansen with Christiansen, Bryers and Peters. I'm Bobby Weller's cousin and an attorney representing him. He asked me to contact you. He'd like us to take a meeting."

Chapter Eight

Charlotte slept the day and night and half the next day, waking at sunset with a headache. It was an unsettled sleep, full of dread and impotent action. She got up twice to pee and unknot her sheets, changed her pillowcase once for the sweat on it.

Her dreams were hers. Recognized. That at least was something, and strange, for within the dreams she was aware of authorship, that this was her doing. These were not lucid dreams in the way she'd experienced them before. Once as a child, she'd done it, recognized the moment and seized the opportunity. She had jumped off a swing and into the sky, her arms spread as wings, and she rose into the air. She could taste the wind, feel it on her face. She rose like a starling, controlled and quick, over and under, dip and roll, she soared until her grasp of the in-between slipped just so much to wake up excited with the lingering thrill of flight, a misplaced certainty that dream control was a feat she could repeat. She never had.

The dreams after Seth had left her to her thoughts and her lonely apartment were close but not those. She was present as an observer with only a single datum, that of origin and authorship, and this, terrifyingly enough, was only because of the comparative. It was the echo of the dread itself, the aftertaste of the horror of the killing, and the terrifying drift of her imagination from mud into murder. It was a blood rage she'd never felt before. Horrible as it was, as deep and primal and violent as she'd ever imagined, the greater horror was the feeling that it had not come from her. This paradox of privacy, her dream mind had embraced. She knew, in the dreams that were hers, that the rage had been birthed outside of herself. Those dreams which were hers that upset her were thus of two kinds: the one to be expected, to process and classify events, but another besides, one brooding and fearful, sensing a violation in the extrinsic nature of these dark and terrible thoughts.

There were two choices here: either there was a frightening darkness within her, a potential if not a permanence of homicide, or there was some mystical force luring her to violence. Mysticism was not an option. Charlotte did not work that way. Charlotte was a modern girl. Charlotte was not a believer.

Noting the time, too late to do anything now, she made a mental and then a paper note to call a doctor for possible neural illness. A distant relative had died of brain cancer once, she seemed to remember. Another had a stroke and a third, a head injury. All had undergone a personality change, if the stories her parents told her were true.

Somehow, thinking she had brain damage relaxed her enough to eat. She made herself some scrambled eggs and wheat toast. The milk had turned but the orange juice was fine. Any time is breakfast time when you live alone and she'd made a science of making it automatically, whatever condition she was in.

She cooked the eggs and spread the butter, poured the last of her orange juice before sitting down to eat. Out of habit she pulled out her phone to scroll the news.

She'd missed eight phone calls, had half a dozen voicemails, eighty emails and thirteen texts. The emails she could ignore, those were usually junk, the texts would get attention, but phone calls were novel and she went there first.

Phone scam, her mother, unknown, her mother, a Commondale extension, her mother again, and finally Seth Lian. She played the first.

"You must contact immediately us or policemans will come to you..." An easy delete that made her shake her head. Did anyone ever fall for that?

Next was her mother's. A long message. She hesitated. They didn't speak much. Not because they didn't try, but because Charlotte avoided them. A familiar pang of guilt joined her scrambled eggs in the recesses of her gut. The message could only be bad news. Good news could wait, bad news not. A call and a message, and another later, made her cringe.

She'd have to talk to her parents, but she was not in the right state of mind to do that just then. She might have a tumor, that would explain these feelings. Yes, a tumor. There'd been a time when she could tell her parents anything, but that wasn't now. If she didn't tell them about her suspected tumor, they'd see her as a terrible daughter, but should she tell them before she was sure? No need for them to worry. No need for her to open up, to be frank, to allow her father to project his disappointment, or her mother to ask about husbands and children. No thanks.

This was the kind of thinking a bad daughter did, the kind of behavior one might find in the thoughts of bad murder-fantasizing spa-goers.

With her self-esteem slid down low, she played her mother's first message.

"Hello Charlotte dear, it's me, your mom." Her mother always did that, as if Charlotte didn't have caller ID or that she'd somehow mistake her mother's long-lingering accent, still discernible as from New Delhi among those who knew the dialect. "I'm here with your father. We're doing well, though your father's back is grieving him and my arthritis hurts me much." She paused then, as if waiting for Charlotte to offer sympathy. "Father has been given his pink-list." She heard the sound of a hand cupping the phone receiver before her mother came back. "Slip. He's been pink-slipped. Retired. Like fired. The company is bankrupting. It is very sad. Father is strong and we will get by, but it is a shock and a concern and we thought you should know. Please call soon. Your voice is always a welcome delight. Goodbye."

As if to remind her it was a tumor, her first thought was as cruel as any she'd ever had. 'Good. They deserved to suffer. Rightly done.' Then she softened to 'that was their problem'.

She peppered her eggs and doused them in hot sauce, yearning for the burn as if in penance.

What was wrong with her?

Nothing.

She was independent, fiercely so. Her lack of a lover was a side of that, but so was her separation from her old-fashioned parents. It might not be kind, might not be ideal, but it was right. Normal. Her life choices were hers.

For consistency's sake, she forgave herself her reaction, but wondered now at her feeling of guilt. It had to be the murder. Patricide. No one could see the violence and not be shaken, no one could know the relationship between parent and child and not be shocked.

She finished her food and wondered if she had the mettle to be a journalist. She'd chosen a profession where she'd witness and report. Would it always rattle her this way? She wanted to go back to bed.

The next message, from Commondale, was Seth. "Hey Charlotte, I know you're still decompressing. I just wanted to let you know that I got a message from Bobby's people and he wants to talk to us. I'm going to go ahead and make the arrangements. I'll assume the expense cards are still active. If they're not, I'll let you know. I really think we have to follow up on this, if only for the scoop of the interview. And we have to do this fast before the news cycle forgets it. Already this is being pushed off the air by the De Lange thing. Maybe that's something we can use too, I don't know. I'll call you back later. Bye."

Oh, right. The job. She had a chore. Her schooling, her career. Her big chance if she were to believe Seth, which she kinda did. What was the De Lange thing? She didn't know. At that moment, didn't care.

What would be the point of checking to see if the funding would still be there? It was or it wasn't. They'd call her, right? And she had to admit they were in a cherry position to do follow-up on a news story, however tawdry and terrible it was. Bobby wanted to talk to them. Okay. Seth had come through with a direction. Good enough. Step by step.

Having a path gave her courage. She played the next message, the other from her mother.

"Hello Charlotte dear, it's me, your mom. Did we see you on the television? At least I think I did. Were you at a tennis match? That terrible one where that terrible thing happened? There was someone saying you were cheating or something? I don't understand. Who was that man with you? He was very handsome. We look forward to meeting him."

And just like that the world was back in place.

A text shook her phone. It was from Kinsley, Bobby's girlfriend.

Charlotte saw it was the newest of several from her. Scrolling up to follow the thread from the beginning, she saw that they'd started late last night.

Bobby said he'd like to finish the movie. Call him.

Are you still planning on coming to the Vineyard to meet people?

I don't have a problem with that but I'll check around.

Then this morning.

It's hard to get ahold of people. Lots happening.

An hour ago.

Just come.

And the one that just came in.

I'll put your names on the list. Send them to me when you get a chance. You'll have to dress up.

It was hard to gauge anyone's emotional state from a text message, nearly impossible. Emails were much the same way. Letter writing was a dead art and texts wouldn't allow for this kind of thing anyway. Immediacy was important. Remembering this, Charlotte tried not to read too much into it. She'd sensed that Kinsley was surprisingly calm at the murder. She remembered Seth zooming in on her placid face during Bobby's attack. Shock, right? People deal with shock in different ways. Look at her and her dreams. She wouldn't hold a few cold texts against her for that. Not remembering her and Seth's names was a little harder to justify. Maybe that meant that she was rattled, which was understandable. Cynically, Seth would suggest a classist interpretation: she'd not bothered to learn their names.

The other texts were prosaic reminders from her department about an upcoming meeting, a reminder from the pharmacy that her birth control pills were ready to be picked up. An amber alert, then canceled, and a campus stalking alert. More spam. The emails were all junk.

Rinsing her dishes in the sink, she played the last message.

"Hey Charlotte, I guess you're really out of it, huh? I got us reservations to California, and a red-eye the day after that for South Africa. Yeah, I think this De Lange thing is for us. The credit card is still working, by the way. Call me when you get this."

Chapter Nine

The De Lange thing was out of reach. South Africa required a visa and Charlotte wasn't even sure where her passport was. That was settled within five minutes of Seth arriving at her apartment that night.

"So we try to interview Bobby and then his friends. In that order?" she asked, cracking ice for drinks.

"Wait, you gotta know about the De Lange thing."

"I don't have any mixers," she said.

"Ice is fine."

She had whiskey, an old, unopened bottle of Wild Turkey she didn't remember buying. She set a pot of coffee to brew and brought Seth a glass of ice and the bottle.

"Aren't you having any?" Seth asked.

"I just got up."

"Don't mind if I do?"

"That's the first time I ever heard that as a question."

"I'm the soul of politeness."

"Go ahead."

Seth was thankful. He'd had a drink before coming over, several in fact. He needed them to keep going. Alcohol in his system was his normal condition. Charlotte seemed to understand that and didn't judge. He took a sip and reached for a pack of cigarettes. Noting the lack of ashtrays and the sidelong glare from his host, he put them back.

"Here. Let me show you." Seth opened his laptop.

"Just give me the highlights."

"Okay, so South Africa…" Seth clicked on links and struggled to find what he was looking for. "It hit the media last night. Our little nightmare is already out of the news cycle."

"De Lange? Is that a place?"

"No. Jaco De Lange is – *was* a mineral tycoon. Gold mines and diamond mines all over Africa. He's Afrikaans, one of the richest men in the country. His family stuck around after apartheid. Their houses look like fortresses. They have their own army. They can afford it." Seth showed Charlotte a picture of a huge house, men standing on the porch with guns. "This is their Johannesburg house. They have like eight of them in South Africa alone. More throughout the continent. That rich."

"Got it."

"Jaco is the patriarch of the family. He inherited everything and has expanded the holdings. Read 'colonial exploitation'. Blood diamonds, the kind of gold mines you see on documentaries where people climb out of a crater with a basket of mud trying to get enough money to eat for the day. Real fucker."

"And…?"

"His wife is Ineke. Also blue blood. Son is called Danyon. Three days ago they were all inspecting a mine, an old one. Big hole. He was going to buy it or something."

"Something? There's some journalism for you."

"Are you going to listen?"

"I'm waiting to hear how this has anything to do with me."

"Us. Our movie."

"Seth, I haven't showered."

"Thanks for the update." He smiled and refreshed his drink. "Danyon pushed both his parents down a mine shaft. Two hundred meters. That's a long way. Splat. Dead. Cleaning them up with spatulas."

"God, you're jaded."

Her reaction took Seth aback until he remembered. "Hey, I'm sorry. I know I'm callous. I just have the bit in my mouth here."

"Have you seen so much death that you aren't affected by it?"

"No more than anyone. Movies, you know. This one happened off screen so it's easy for me. As for the other one, I've calloused there. I've gone over the footage so many times now that I can actually watch it without wanting to run away. I keep thinking how the real thing is much cleaner than special effects. If Quentin Tarantino had—"

"Don't. Just don't," Charlotte said.

"Yeah, I get it. I'm sorry again. Your coffee is done."

Charlotte went to the kitchen to pour a cup. The milk was still bad, of course, and she poured it down the sink. She hated black coffee but thought with enough sugar, maybe she could choke it down. She dumped half a bowl in and came back.

Seth watched her return, noticed her heavy step, the big bags under her red eyes. The housecoat.

"There's been another family tragedy," she said. "This one half a world away."

"There are parallels, don't you think?"

She shrugged and sat down on her couch, tucked her knees under her for warmth. "Is that what our movie is about now? Are we to chase down every domestic violence case? Even our generous grant won't allow for permanent employment."

Seth looked crestfallen. Good, she thought. About time he calmed the fuck down.

Feeling bad for her jab, she offered him a bone. "Okay, so it might be worth a phone call, maybe Danyon will be as chatty as Bobby."

"Danyon is dead."

"Suicide?"

"No. Better," he said and instantly regretted it. "One of the workers there saw it happen, saw this kid push this hated man and his wife down the shaft and then ran up and slit his throat."

"How's that better?"

"It made headlines in the U.S. Talk of race war."

"There's always talk of race war in South Africa."

"Class war?"

"You're fishing," she said. "You just want a trip to Johannesburg."

"What else are we going to do with that money?"

"I'm not sure you have the right attitude."

"It's use it or lose it, right?"

"Where are you getting that? We don't even know if the money is still available. We start putting intercontinental flights on the Visa and I bet someone will notice."

"We should go slow. Milk it."

"Wrong attitude, Seth."

He smiled. "There is something here," he said. "And Bobby wants to talk. In fact, he's sending a plane for us."

"A plane?"

"Well, a jet, I'm sure. Waiting for us tomorrow."

"There does seem some momentum here," she said. "Kinsley said we're still on for meeting the friends."

"When did you talk to her?"

"She texted." She offered him her phone. He took it, scrolled up. She grabbed it from him when he left the text screen. "Rude!"

His grin was cute and playful. She squinted at him over a grin of her own. He could be fun, she thought, before she remembered her mother's message. Seth saw her harden suddenly. "Sorry."

"No. It's fine."

"Then give it back."

"No." Grin in place. She noticed his glass. "Do you need more ice?"

"I'll get it," he said. "If that's okay?"

"Sure."

He left her for the kitchen. Like the rest of the apartment, it was small and clean, though it smelled of spoiled milk. He found the ice and noted a dearth of groceries. She lived alone and cooked in. Chicken breasts and frozen peas each in a resealable bag.

Charlotte scanned the news feeds on Seth's computer. Bobby wasn't mentioned on any front page, neither were the De Langes. What a short memory people had, or was it that new tragedies were happening so quickly? More rainforest deforestation, a whole river gone toxic in Louisiana, fungal bloom off New Jersey, California wondering what was left to burn. Election coming up. Promises being made, taxes being lowered for some, raised for most. Normal.

"What do you see?" Seth had helped himself to a second glass and filled it with ice as well.

"Is that for you?" she asked. "The walk too far?"

"Trying to be a gentleman," he said.

His mustache twitched when he smiled like that. He set the glass down before her and poured himself half a glass. He lifted it but didn't drink. He sat back in his chair.

"Want to talk about it?"

"What's new to say? Everything is normal."

"Is it?"

"Hurricanes, pollution, fossil fuel poisoning, assassination, slavery – all regular-day news stories for forever. Now upper-class domestic violence. It's been normalized too."

She expected a quick comeback, but he just looked at her. Outside, someone let the world know that they had a loud motorcycle and the streetlight flickered through her third-floor window.

"What do you want to do?" he asked. "We're in this together." And then, under his breath, added, "We all are."

"Explain that," she said, and said it so that it wasn't a challenge, but a real inquiry.

"It's what you were talking about. The normalization of disaster. We're all in it together. It was a phrase bandied around for a while in my college days to try to get everyone to remember we're sharing the Earth."

"It's still used the same way," she said, disappointed he was referring only to a stale political catchphrase.

"You know what bugs me?" Seth said. "Selling out."

She watched him and didn't reply.

"I always thought that every artist would have a moment in their career where they'd be offered a chance to sell out. They'd license a song for a car commercial, attach their art to a beer brand, associate their face with some creep. It'd pay."

"You have to have something to sell before you can sell out."

"Right." Seth stared into his glass for an answer.

"Maybe what you mean is 'giving up'."

"That's probably it," he said. "Maybe. I'm having a hard time putting my finger on it. On why I want to follow this story. It's a shit story. It was shallow and shit to begin with, no offense, now it's dark and shit. It's all shit, but it's our shit. And we're lucky to have it. The world rains shit down on us and we're powerless to do anything about it. The best we can do is attach ourselves to a piece of shit and hope it carries us a little while."

"How many of those have you had?" she said.

He lifted the bottle, showing it a third done. "And half another of these at home."

"Shit."

"I'm used to it."

"How'd you get here?"

"Drove."

"Seth..."

"Thanks."

"I meant it."

"I know you did."

Seth sipped half his glass. Charlotte shuddered to imagine straight whiskey.

"We grab our turd and ride," she said. "Why not?"

"Unless you can think of a way to flush the whole thing, to power wash the toilet, what else can we do?"

"What is it the Joker said?"

"Which one?"

"The one with Jack, eh – *The Shining* guy one."

"Jack Nicholson. That one's ancient. What was the line?"

"This world needs an enema!"

"Close enough," Seth said. "I'll drink to that." He raised his glass.

Charlotte poured herself two fingers into the glass Seth had brought her and returned the salute.

"Cheers," she said.

"To the enema!"

They drank. Charlotte coughed, then giggled and wiped her mouth, leaving only an embarrassed smile. She was pretty when she looked that way.

Chapter Ten

The hired car split from the highway and wove them through unfamiliar neighborhoods they could only see darkly through tinted windows. They hadn't spoken much on the trip. Perhaps Charlotte was a little hungover, perhaps Seth was thinking how it would be to have your own jet.

Bobby's lawyer had told them that a plane would be waiting for them at ten o'clock. They'd arrived together in Seth's old Saab at nine fifteen and apologized for being late. It took a moment to realize there'd be no security rounds, no baggage check. They were the only passengers, and they could take off any time they wanted, or not at all. The pilot and steward smiled as they explained this. Seth felt stupid. Charlotte felt awed.

They were accompanied by a man from the law firm, Mr. Menalson, who was as taciturn as he was stiff. After they landed, they got into the car on the tarmac and Charlotte ventured a question. "Where are we going? This isn't Indian Wells."

"No. We're going to Bel Air," said Menalson. "The interview is there."

Seth took some footage of the jet and the stretched car. The private airfield with jets and catering. The pilot and steward standing like gargoyles by the door.

In the car, Charlotte asked why Bel Air, but Menalson would say only that Mr. Christiansen would brief them. She threw a glance at Seth, who shrugged. The silence lingered.

The roads became curved and tree-covered. The car slowed and Seth saw a large iron gate swing open, a man in a uniform waving them up a cobblestone driveway to the front of a stucco-sided mansion.

Seth got out and raised his camera, but Menalson was quick to cover the lens.

"No?" said Seth.

Menalson smiled politely until Seth put the camera away.

Charlotte stood by the car counting windows, guessing square footage, calculating floors. Three? Not including a basement? The air was warm and dry, a breeze kept the smog moving. The perfect, happy weather California was once famous for.

Charlotte's hangover intensified, and she grimaced against her throbbing headache. It'd been a dull weight that morning, rising during the flight. It lessened during the drive, but began again in the neighborhoods. Now, in front of this monstrous house, it spiked in her ears. Her thoughts turned amorphous and dark.

"You okay?" said Seth, coming over to her. "Head ache?"

Charlotte saw colors behind her eyelids, felt a wave of cymbal clash rise and fall as she fought it back.

"Hey, Mr. Happy," said Seth. "Can you get the lady some aspirin?"

Menalson smiled and waited.

"I'm okay," said Charlotte. "I have some in my bag. Get the gear."

Seth unloaded their camera equipment from the trunk. "Can we leave our bags in here?"

"Sure," said Menalson.

"Swell."

A tall, tanned man in sparkling white clothes waited for them at the door with a blank expression. He made no attempt to unburden Seth's load when he passed.

"Where to?" Seth asked once inside.

It was a huge room, formal and stately. A grand stairway flowed down from an upper, balconied floor. The wings extended out right and left; forward was space and doors. The furnishings here were sparse, with high-backed wooden chairs, little tables with flowers. A couple of paintings. Otherwise, it was all white marble and columns.

Menalson led the way straight through the foyer, past a door and down a carpeted hallway that was a drastic change from the echoing marble floors. He opened a door and showed them outside to a large, sun-drenched courtyard.

Seth had to cover his eyes. The sunlight was dazzling, reflected off white tile and the surface of a still swimming pool. The soft smell of lingering heat, chlorine, something floral. The soft murmur of a fountain trickling into the far end of the water like some Elysian reenactment.

Charlotte's headache pulsed in her temples and she missed most of the opulence behind her clenched eyelids. Inside, she'd noticed the columns and white marble with visions of ancient temples, sacrifices, and statues. Outside, continuing on the theme, it struck her as a bacchanal backdrop waiting for guests.

What they'd expected to find was not this. Seth had some idea of a lawyer in a mahogany office carefully laying out a PR campaign for his client's defense. Charlotte had visions of a wired glass wall and linked telephones in a jail visiting center. Neither expected to see Bobby Weller in a swimsuit, reclining by a pool, with a tall sweating umbrellaed glass.

A slender man in a shimmering tailored suit met them as they came out. His smile was too white, just a shade off natural, his skin too tan, just a shade off casual color. He was in his sixties, maybe seventies, though he wore it extraordinarily well, hinting at his age through his eyes and demeanor. His watch caught the light and sparkled in diamonds as he offered his hand to Seth. Seth could only nod, not having a free hand to offer him back, so the man offered it to Charlotte.

"I'm Oliver Christiansen with Christiansen, Bryers and Peters," he said. "I spoke with your cameraman on the phone."

"Producer," said Seth. "Co-producer."

"You're Bobby's cousin too, right?" said Charlotte.

"Yes."

His age would make him more likely an uncle. His attitude toward his cousin made him more likely a servant. "It is Mr. Weller's wish that you come here today."

"Very kind of you to send the plane," she said.

"It was nothing."

"Come over here!" called Bobby from the lounger, waving.

Mr. Christiansen stepped back and let them pass. Seth noted that he also didn't try to help him with his burden of equipment he carried.

"Thank you so much for coming." Bobby put his glass carefully on a side bistro table and stretched. "I thought maybe that table over there." He pointed to a round white wrought-iron table with four chairs sheltered under a broad gray umbrella away from the fountain.

"That'll work." Seth moved quickly to set up his equipment. In a fluid motion, he unloaded cameras and mics, tripods, tablets, receivers, laptop, headset. Then arranged the scene with a two-camera setup. It was a dance he knew well and could do in his sleep.

While he worked, Bobby said, "Can I get you guys anything? I'm having aspirin and whatever will wash it down. Damn headache."

"You have bourbon?" said Seth, half ironically.

"Of course." Without being asked, Christiansen stepped to the door, spoke to Menalson and then returned. He stood a respectable distance away, careful to be out of camera.

Charlotte stood and blinked, trying to make sense of it all. Her ears were still ringing, her head an echo chamber. Through this lingering buzz, she added the confusion of what she was seeing. True, a person is considered innocent until proven guilty, but how in God's name was Bobby Weller, his hideous act broadcast nonstop for days across every media on the globe, not only not jailed, but calm, smiling, and reclining like some Adonis in Bel Air?

The tanned man they'd seen at the door appeared, carrying a tray laden with bottles, glasses and an ice bucket. He carried it to the table. "How do you take your whiskey, sir?" he asked.

"Over rocks is fine."

"And the lady?"

"Water."

He poured Seth's drink and set it aside before opening a bottle of water and pouring it over ice for Charlotte. It was the same brand they'd had in the spa.

Bobby sat down in the chair Seth indicated. A throbbing in Charlotte's skull made her sit down before she was ready.

Seth noticed her discomfort, noticed also the butler waver in his stance, catching his balance on the table before straightening up and leaving them.

Seth arranged the second camera for a two shot. Two cameramen would have been better, but he'd guerrillaed this kind of setup before. "You guys remember not to move too far from how you're sitting now," he told them.

"Let me settle," said Charlotte, rubbing her eyes.

"Bobby, you need to take the sunglasses off. If you will."

"Surely."

His eyes were bright and untroubled. Seth started recording without announcement, just to get those eyes. He set up the microphones. Checked the levels.

Charlotte took a sip of water and pulled out a small legal pad with her notes from her bag. "Okay, Seth, how's this?" She straightened up, turned her best one-eighth profile.

Seth focused the camera on her, adjusted the tripod, checked the feed and timer. He began recording with this camera again without notice. "Remember I'm shooting over your shoulder, Bobby. Two inches right and you'll be in the shot."

"Fine. Are we ready?" said Bobby

"Are we in a hurry?" asked Charlotte.

The first unpleasant note came from Bobby as his smile fell a little. "No."

Settling onto a table to the side, with the feeds showing on his computer and tablets, Seth said, "We're ready."

Charlotte remembered too late that she hadn't checked her makeup and was about to ask for some time, when Bobby spoke.

"I know it looks bad for me," he said. "But I'm innocent."

Seth admired the earnestness in his face. Having watched that same face twist up into a grimace, tightening and tightening after each stroke into his father's skull, it was shocking.

Charlotte felt something similar, but controlled herself. Composure was at the heart of her theory of journalism. "I was there," she said. "I saw you do it. Many people saw you do it. The world saw you do it. How can you say you didn't do it?"

"I...I...I didn't say I didn't do it," he said. Seth thought it strange that he seemed unprepared to answer such an obvious follow-up and it got his hackles up. He was playing them. "I said I was innocent."

"You're innocent?" Charlotte let her face betray doubt.

"We're all innocent," he said.

Charlotte felt uneasy. Bobby's body language was now tense and alert, a stark contrast to the way they'd found him.

"Why are you home now instead of in jail?" she asked.

The question seemed to calm him and he sat back. "This isn't my place. We're leasing it. I'm not allowed out of the state. I got bailed out. I have to stay in the state."

Seth could only imagine what a lease on this place would be. Probably the cost of a middle-class house every week. Maybe two.

"You got bail?" Charlotte said. "Was it a lot?"

Bobby shrugged. "I guess so."

"You don't know if it was a lot?"

"We had it. Money really doesn't matter to people in my class."

The statement made Seth look up. Charlotte caught his reaction out of the corner of her eye.

"That's very blunt of you," she said.

"It's the elephant in the room, or one of them. We've been dancing around it ever since we started this movie. It's a dance we all know to do when we're around people outside our class."

"You're speaking about other rich people?"

"Yes. It's the same with powerful people. Power works differently there. It's not exactly the same. But we have to pretend."

"Why do you have to pretend?"

Bobby looked surprised. "So you don't figure it out."

"I think a lot of people suspect."

"Suspicion is one thing. It implies the all-important uncertainty."

"What would be so bad about being certain?"

"If there were two firing synapses in your heads you'd rise up and slay us."

He'd said it matter-of-factly, but the condescension was unconcealed.

Charlotte sat stunned. Seth zoomed in subtly on both faces.

"Because you're innocent," Bobby said. "We are not innocent."

"But you said you were innocent."

"I was then," he said. He looked at Charlotte earnestly, as if trying to get his point across with facial expression. When that didn't suffice, he turned to Seth a little ways off and stared at him.

"It's important," he said. "Innocence. Culpability. Blame."

"Responsibility?" said Charlotte chillingly.

"Yes!" said Bobby, leaning out of his chair and making Charlotte pull back. "That's it exactly."

Seth adjusted the automatic cameras, moving to wide. He regretted it because there was something wild and desperate in Bobby's eyes. He looked earnest and hard, his head bobbing as if matching some forgotten march.

"It's the ugly truth we can't let you know. It's why we don't talk to you. Never directly. We can't. You'll find out. We consider you another species, beneath us. And it's true. We're different. We have different rules. Different laws. For God's sake, I'm having cocktails by the pool and I'm a pariah. We are above you, but not because we're better. I don't think we are. No. I'm sure we're not. We've lost the plot somehow. Somewhere. Some time. Time. We're there now because we've been there. We got there. There was something before—"

"Mr. Weller," said Christiansen. "Perhaps we should end this now. I don't see how this could—"

"Quiet!"

The lawyer hesitated. "If only you'd let me have our guests sign the—"

"Shut the fuck up!" Bobby stood up and regarded the suited man hovering behind Charlotte. Seth couldn't get a two shot, but pulled back until he could see Bobby and the table, and Charlotte with her hands to her temples. Looking up from his monitor, he could see Bobby's wild eyes.

"You're part of it, Christiansen," Bobby said.

"I'm only a functionary, Mr. Weller. I'm here to help you."

"Like I need help."

The statement made the lawyer chuckle, returned some of his cool. "I assure you, you do."

"It's things like this," Bobby said to Charlotte, "that allow creeps like my father to do what they do."

"I'm your lawyer now, Mr. Weller – Bobby. I'll do as you direct, as I did with your father, as our firm has served your family for a century. I'm confident we can help you. We've helped your ancestors out of worse than this." He smiled triumphantly.

Bobby stumbled back, upturned the table and knocked over the camera filming Charlotte. Seth was on his feet in a flash to salvage the equipment. Bobby stood still and grim as Seth discovered everything was unhurt. He unlatched it to go handheld.

He framed Bobby as he knelt beside the overturned table, studying the broken glass, spilled ice, untasted bourbon on the white marble tile. Bobby rocked in imitation of Charlotte, who added the dramatic and disturbing element of hands to her ears. Mr. Christiansen stood stolidly, waiting.

"Mr. Menalson," the lawyer finally said. "I think I'll need your help getting this cleaned up."

Menalson stepped out and slowly walked around the pool.

Bobby lowered his hands and stood up. Charlotte watched him, her eyes wide and fearful.

"The sins, the untenable arrogance. The suicidal selfishness. The song. The song. A new song. To hell with it!"

Seth followed the sudden movement as Bobby stepped, then sprinted to the lawyer. By the time he reached him, the man's hands were out in defense, but it was not enough to hinder the athlete's momentum. Shoved, staggering, falling, the two tumbled into the serene aqua blue of the swimming pool. The air flavored a subtle moistness as the two grappled in the water.

Seth zoomed in. Across the pool Menalson stared big-eyed, confused, the same expression on his face as worn by the ten thousand people at the tennis arena.

The splashing slowed and stopped. Bobby held the suited man beneath the water until the clamor was gone. Seth, switching filters, glad for image stabilization, showed the stilling blueness of the depths streaking now with wisps of tendriled blood escaping Christiansen's nose and mouth, like smoke from a censer. Bobby's surprisingly steady breathing was the only sound.

"Witness," Bobby said into the camera. "See? I'm innocent."

Chapter Eleven

Anthony Bryers from Christiansen, Bryers and Peters was on his way. Menalson had called him before he had the police. He told Charlotte and Seth not to say a thing to anyone until Bryers got there.

"You don't need to tell me never to talk to the cops," Seth said, though in this case he couldn't see any reason not to. Except maybe the film. He quickly collected his cameras and equipment before the crime tape went up. Bobby drank Long Island Iced Teas by the pool, staring into the water from where servants had removed the drowned lawyer.

Charlotte, beside the pool the whole time, staring in, now only nodded.

The neighborhood meant that the cops were quick and they arrived in minutes, swarming through the door and around the house. Menalson said he had to stay with Bobby and a butler directed the filmmakers into a comfortable waiting room – a sitting room he called it – with high ceilings, low tables, plush chairs, sturdy couches, landscape paintings and showy bookshelves. No TV.

Seth tethered his phone to the cloud and quickly uploaded his footage in case the cops played rough. "How much battery do you have on your phone?" he asked Charlotte.

She didn't respond.

"Charlotte. Charly. Your phone? If mine dies, can I—"

She sat on a paisley settee, toward the center of the room, her back to him. The movement was slight, a jump in her shoulders, then it quickened; extended. Heaved as her head fell into her hands and she cried.

"Idiot, Seth Lian," he said to himself and quickly came over and sat beside her.

"Charlotte, I'm..." He leaned over and put an arm around her. She leapt off the settee.

"No." She was on her feet.

"Charlotte, I... Sorry."

"I'm scared," she said.

"It's over."

"No. I can still hear it."

"Hear what?"

She stared at him, tried to find the lie, but her eyes were unfocused and tearful. She tried to form the words, but hadn't even commenced the thoughts yet, and so sat down on another divan. And took slow, deep breaths as her mother had shown her, softening them until she could count them, in and out, count to ten. Start over, and again.

When she could focus her eyes, Seth was back at his equipment.

"What are you doing?" she asked.

"Saving our work. You watch. They'll take our stuff."

"How can you think about that right now?"

She noted that the sound had receded, and the realization of its movement, its flow, almost lifelike, shocked her, and she didn't hear what Seth had said. "What?" she said.

"This is one of them."

"One of what? I didn't hear you."

"I said, I don't have many moments when I can think beyond now, but this is one of them. So I'm preserving our footage."

"Preserving..." The word tasted strange in her mouth. Familiar and foreign.

"From the bastards."

"The bastards..."

"Charlotte. I'm sorry, okay? But I'll mourn for the shit-stain lawyer and entitled brat later. The world really isn't that worse off without them, if you must know. These people made me sick before they took up public homicide."

Charlotte shook her head, confused. She'd lost the thread.

Seth took a deep breath and said, "I know this sucks. I know it's affecting you. It's affecting me. You do you right now. I'm kinda in anger mode, if you know what I mean. What are the others? Denial? Bargaining? That shit."

"I wanted him to do it," said Charlotte.

"Hey." Seth turned on her. "I didn't say I wanted it to happen. I just meant that, you know, in the long run…maybe…" He ran his fingers through his beard and sighed before flopping into a chair. "It's a coping mechanism. I guess."

"Seth," said Charlotte. "I mean it. I wanted it to happen."

She watched his face change in waves as the statement took hold.

"No. You're just coping."

"Don't fucking mansplain to me!"

He stared at her, speechless.

"Seth, I know how it sounds. I hear it. I heard it. I'm sorry I snapped."

"I probably had it coming," he said.

Outside the door they heard voices and heavy footsteps, radio static, the distant lament of Bobby demanding to see his lawyer and then breaking into hysterical laughter.

"We've got about five minutes before the cops come in here," Seth said. "I think I'll just make it."

Charlotte took a chair across the table from him.

"Something's wrong with me," she said.

Seth watched her but didn't speak.

"When Bobby went for that man, his uncle, I was happy for it. I was excited. I wanted to see him die."

Seth pretended to adjust the cabling and said, "I don't suppose you met the guy before, did you?"

"The lawyer? No. Not at all. Just met him today. But when Bobby started talking, when he got mad, got up, then, all of a sudden, and totally – all-consumingly – I hated him. I really hated him."

"It might be shock."

"It's happened before."

"When?"

"At the hotel in Indian Wells. I hated — I wanted to kill this old woman in a bathtub."

"The spa day. That was also shock. You're stressed and I feel bad now for twisting your arm in continuing this."

"Didn't you hear it?"

"I heard him," said Seth. "Nothing I didn't know, but damn interesting to hear him admit it. Interesting. Something I haven't cared about in a long time. When I was younger, younger than you, I would have been all over that somehow."

"You're talking about Bobby's speech."

"Yes, it was great. I got it all."

"I'm talking about something else."

"The killing. Yeah, I got that too. God—"

"Seth. There was a sound. A hum. Music. You didn't hear it?"

"No."

"I think Bobby did. I think he heard it better even."

Seth didn't know what to say that he hadn't already said, so he said it again. "Charlotte, you're in shock."

"Maybe. But I don't think this is that. I heard it before Bobby killed his parents. Remember when Bobby mentioned tinnitus in the dressing room?"

"Fungus? I'm sure he had a cream."

"Are you trying to make a joke? Because I'm not laughing."

"I remember," he said. "I watched the tape."

"I think Kinsley heard it too."

"Why?"

"A feeling."

"And you heard it, but I didn't?"

"Think. How did you feel when Bobby was killing Christiansen?"

"I was filming. I was on autopilot."

"I felt happy. I wanted to jump in and help Bobby do it. If Christiansen had managed to slip away or get the upper hand, I think I'd have dove in and tried to drown him."

"I don't know what to tell you. I got the feeling that Bobby had something against old Oliver. The attack looked pretty personal. Maybe he and Bobby's father had done something to piss him off. Probably about a will or something. Abuse, maybe?"

"That's right, they were cousins."

"Good to see that domestic violence isn't reserved only for the po' folks."

"God dammit, Seth, I'm trying to be serious."

"And I'm trying to cope," he said. "Not just with the shit the Wellers are throwing, but also you. You're scaring me."

She began to shake again, her shoulders announcing coming sobs.

"Charlotte…"

The door opened and two men stepped in. They were cops, plain clothes, but with badges hanging around their necks on chains.

"You two the filmmakers?"

"Yeah," said Seth.

"She okay?" He gestured to Charlotte.

"No. Not really."

"Get the medic in here," he said over his shoulder to the other cop, "when he's done wrestling that maniac."

The other man left.

"You guys got names?"

"We do. Do you?"

The policeman smiled. "Hill. Detective Hill. First initial H. Detective H. Hill."

"Harry?"

"Henry."

"I'm Seth. Seth Lian. Commondale University."

"Glad to meet you." He didn't look glad to meet them.

Charlotte was bawling into her hands, beginning to hyperventilate.

"Breathe, Charlotte," said Seth, putting his hand out to her.

"Charlotte what?" asked the detective.

"Sakshi."

"Is that Paki?"

"She's American."

"No. The name, is it Pakistani?"

"Charming," said Seth.

"Is it?"

"No. It's Indian I believe."

"Is she Muslim?"

"No."

He nodded as if that settled something.

The officer returned with a bottle of designer water and passed it to the detective, who passed it to Seth. He offered it in turn to Charlotte, who curled a lip at it before finally taking some.

A moment later a paramedic came in, red-faced and wild-eyed. "He seemed so calm at first," he said to no one in particular.

"Check her out." The detective pointed to Charlotte.

The detective inspected Seth's equipment on the table, when his phone rang.

"Hill." He listened, glancing around the room at the other people. Menalson had appeared in the doorway. Hill kept his gaze on him for a while before saying, "Understood," and hanging up.

"I've got to take all this," he said. "Phone too."

"What? Why?" said Seth. "I need a phone."

"Orders."

Seth looked at Menalson for support, but the lawyer's lackey was stone-faced.

"You did this," Seth said.

Menalson didn't respond.

The detective called in uniformed policemen with Tupperware boxes and loaded it all up.

Charlotte was barely aware of the proceedings. She felt the medic touch her neck and forehead, open her eyelids and shine a light into them.

"Have you suffered any kind of injury?" he asked her.

"I don't think so."

"Head trauma?"

"What?"

"Do you feel dizzy?"

She nodded. "Headache."

"We better take you for a look," he said.

Seth said to Menalson, "I assume Christiansen, Bryer and Dick Shit will cover the cost?"

Menalson gave him a curt nod.

"Swell."

Chapter Twelve

Originating deep in Charlotte's skull, seeping down her back to pool in her legs before they rose again, the tremors had their own volition. She watched them bleed out to her arms, biceps, elbows, wrists and fingers, where they shook her hands with a palsy that alarmed the ambulance staff to turn on the siren and run red lights.

She was taken right in and given a bed. She didn't even see a waiting room. Doctors and nurses swooped in and measured her blood pressure, pulse, temperature, pupils. They asked her questions which she didn't know how to answer, and stammered. She felt herself go in and out of the moment, looking now at herself as if from a distance, then locked inside a cell, all the while remembering Bobby and his words, his acts. Their shared headache, which she still had in the back of her eyes. This she mentioned and they rushed to her a magnetic machine and told her to be still while they slid her in and out like a key testing a lock.

Vaguely, through the rush of tests, she understood that she was a 'VIP'. Who said it, she wasn't sure, but assumed it was the Wellers' law firm. Hadn't Seth arranged for them to handle everything? She asked if she could go home and they moved her to a private room for observation.

The day was growing long in the windows when she asked for something to eat. It came quickly, a pork chop and potatoes, Jell-O – it was a hospital after all – and two kinds of juice.

"The doctor would like to talk to you," said a nurse, peeking in. "Is now a good time?"

"Sure," she said.

"I'll go get him."

"Isn't he busy?"

"Be right back."

There was something decadent about the doctor waiting on her instead of the other way around. Then she remembered she was in Bel Air.

A young man who looked like he'd stepped out of a soap opera pilot beamed with a tender smile. He had light brown eyes, surfer-blond hair, parted but stylish. A slight tan. He smelled of antiseptic, clean with an edge of bleach.

"I understand that you had a shock," he said. "You saw something terrible."

"And I have a headache," she said.

"Oh?" His concern was clear, or maybe just well faked.

"It's just a headache," she said. "Probably stress. It's not a tumor," she said in her best Schwarzenegger in a reference no one ever got.

"Miss Sakshi, may I call you Charlotte?"

"Okay."

"The psychological is every bit as important as the physical. A problem in the mind is a problem, and I'm here to fix problems."

"That's very…"

"Enlightened?"

"European was what I was going for."

"Well, most American programs don't appreciate the issue the way they should."

She thought he was talking about insurance, but since he was skirting around it, so would she.

"I'm a psychiatrist," he said. "I heard from your friend some of what happened."

"Is Seth here?"

"Seth? No. It was a Mr. Menalson."

"Oh."

"I've already scheduled you for some therapy sessions. I understand you'll be staying in town for a little while."

"I don't know about that."

"Well, I can make the referral for anywhere."

"It's been pretty terrible, the things I've seen. All at once. In my life. I mean, terrible things keep happening right in front of me."

He pulled up a chair and sat down, bending close with a practiced, caring bedside manner.

"Is this a session?" Charlotte asked.

"If you'd like it to be. I have time."

She knew the doctor had trained to appear sympathetic. His dashing good looks didn't hurt either. This is what the rich and famous got to have. She remembered Seth telling her to live it up in the suite while they could.

"Terrible things happened right in front of me. I was at Indian Wells for that…thing."

"I see."

"And again today."

He nodded. "That's pretty terrible, but it wasn't your fault. I want to put that out there right now."

"I didn't think it was. I…maybe it was a little bit."

"Tell me about your headache."

"My headache? It comes and goes."

"Make you dizzy? Your mind drifts? Gets dark?"

"What? Yes. Yes, that's it. It's not like a regular headache. It's like a sound."

He nodded. "You're not crazy," he said. "I've been seeing this for weeks. I suspect there's a virus going around. We're trying to contact trace it."

"Like COVID?"

"Not like that. Not deadly. Just a headache." His smile wavered. "We've seen it in young people around here. I'm sure that's where you got it. Very recent and localized. Nothing from the inner-city hospitals around L.A. that I've seen, though Johns Hopkins may have some too. We're cross-referencing to find out."

"What are you prescribing?"

"Sedatives. The usual for the super stressed. It seems to help here. We can treat the symptoms. Get lots of sleep. Avoid sharp objects."

"Is that a joke?"

"Some patients report dark thoughts."

She felt her face warm. "That's the best news I've heard all week."

"Because you've had them too, you're not alone?"

"Yes."

"I won't put that on your chart," he said, "but these should help." He had a bottle in his pocket and offered her a pill. She swallowed it with a shot of apple juice. He took his dry.

"Get some sleep," he said. "That'll help. We'll talk tomorrow."

★　★　★

Seth couldn't get updates on Charlotte, except that she would be an inpatient for a couple of days. That seemed pretty excessive, or maybe very concerning. He left a message for her to call him.

For a moment he'd entertained staying at the Bel Air house, but Menalson was quick to tell him no on that. In lieu, he arranged for a hotel room for him while Charlotte recovered. It was nice of him, Seth thought, nice of his firm, but of course he knew there were ulterior motives. He suspected it had to do with potential litigation. Didn't everything in that world? They were protecting themselves, and apparently Bobby Weller, still.

The hotel room wasn't as grand as the suite they'd had in Indian Wells, but it was nice, a place near enough to the rich enclaves that visitors could dash in and out. Without a car, he doubted he'd be doing that, so after learning that the bill was taken care of, he made use of room service and the bar.

It was an old routine now; recovering from the horror of a murder in a luxury hotel. The only difference was that this time he was alone. Had he handled the incident that much better than Charlotte? Why wasn't he a basket case now?

Forty-six years of American culture, most likely. If it wasn't a movie dripping with blood, it was the news doing the same, but with inferior special effects. He'd often remarked in his film classes how America censors sex but not violence. Europe tended to go the opposite direction.

In the U.S., we were apparently prudish about the beginnings of life, but enthralled with its rapid end. And so, like most of his culture, he blushed at bare breasts and yawned as someone was cut in two with piano wire.

And yet he felt there was more to it than that. Perhaps the water had had something to do with it. An echo of the past, an inevitability. A permission.

He put his feet up on the railing of his eighth-floor balcony and sat back with an ice bucket and a bottle of Crown to consider. He sipped the booze, tasting the cold, liquid smoke of an aged whiskey, letting it calm him, soothe him into a normal condition. He didn't want to get drunk, at least not yet, but he needed some to maintain control. Now was not the time to risk withdrawal. He figured his functioning alcohol blood level was about forty proof. That line usually got a laugh, even in AA meetings. It wasn't far off, though the meetings now were. A year he'd been required to go to them, get tested, be someone else, in order to keep his job after the incident, after the girl died, after she'd been with him. A stupid thing among adults, but college students weren't adults, were they? Not when someone called themselves a professor.

'Legalize adulthood' was a slogan Seth held close to his heart. He used it to justify drugs mostly, but surely it went beyond that. It went to the idea that everyone should be free to live their life as they wished. Or to end it.

Gina Breeves might be the reason that this new horror struck him so differently than the last one. The girl at the center of his troubles, the event that highlighted his drug use and laissez-faire attitude toward adulting. The undergrad who'd overdosed in his hot tub asking him, before she nodded off, not to wake her. He hadn't.

Her death was ever so more beautiful than Christiansen's. No thrashing, no blood, no outside agent. A surrender that was a lifetime in coming. Not sought after, maybe, but not resisted. Her body never getting cold in the water as he slept it off on the couch to find her the next afternoon.

He hadn't saved Gina. He hadn't tried. He'd done more for the dead lawyer, but not much more. He'd aimed a camera and witnessed. He'd never even gotten splashed on. Never got that close.

Another strong shot of drink to blur the connections his mind was trying to make.

"This isn't about you, fucker," he said, quoting his son's parting line last Christmas.

He couldn't feel bad for Christiansen. He could for Gina, a little for the lost potential, but the lawyer? Good riddance. Wasn't he involved in that Oklahoma thing too? Had he heard the name?

He fetched his laptop and refilled his ice bucket.

The Oklahoma Poisoning. *Fracking Gone Bad* was the headline, as if fracking ever went well. A third of the state's water supply poisoned and undrinkable. The last part was important. People could taste the poison, unlike in Flint Michigan, which had water nearly as bad but residents didn't notice. In Oklahoma, every glass of water tasted like hydraulic fluid and was flammable out of the tap. Hundreds of people had died from it and the loss in livestock was felt in the national GDP. Tent cities were still up in Texas and Arkansas two years later. The Choctaw nation was on life support, a new trail of tears as they moved away from their lands, their lakes greasy with a reflective oil sheen, unbroken among the floating fish. The lawsuits were many but no one had yet to be held accountable and nothing had been done to fix it.

Yes, Christiansen, Bryers and Peters were all over the case, representing oil companies, corporate investors, and of course, Olympus Bank, which was said to have buried not one, not two, but fifteen separate environmental reports about the project while working hand in glove with in-house investment brokers. Robert Weller was named in several early articles, but later ones had been less specific. Recent ones mentioned only the faceless, unaccountable, too-big-to-fail corporations. *The Worst Environmental Disaster Ever on American Soil – So Far*, claimed one forward-looking headline.

A day in the life of America.

The current headlines were full of such things, maybe not to that degree, but not far off. This was how it is. Another ocean dead patch discovered in the Gulf of Mexico. Not the two already discovered, but another one, heat related, not pollution. Same difference. The Amazon is still on fire. Always on fire. Methane from Siberian permafrost melt compounds the coming crisis. Coming? Another war in Africa. Rebels in Central America. An Alt-Right march in Albuquerque claims three lives. No arrests. An acclaimed college professor, who'd been fired for using a racial slur which hadn't been a racial slur last year, had her house set on fire and burned to the ground with her, her father and her daughter still inside. No arrests.

Around the world, an Asian dictator was murdered. The prince is suspected. A royal and exchequer on holiday together in Scotland die when their hotel catches fire. A dozen others died too, but who's paying attention to them? Terrorism suspected. The article noted that the line of succession would be changed again. Again? Prince Harold died suddenly last week. Who the hell was Prince Harold?

Business pages. United Aerotech shares plummet as CFO goes missing on family holiday. Another retailer facing bankruptcy. Gold at an all-time high. Sun Valley Airport reported a plane crash yesterday.

Seth paused and regarded the picture of the jet wreckage somewhere in Idaho. The plane was a corporate jet that held maybe ten people and could literally fly circles around airliners. No mention of who was inside, but remembering that Sun Valley was a retreat of the rich, he figured somebody who was somebody was no more and a new line of succession would need to be adjusted.

The Sun Valley crash had happened yesterday. The royals, the day before. Prince Harold a couple of days before that. The Asian monarch about the same time. Seth jumped back in his browser history and correlated dates. All these high-profile-trying-to-be-low-profile deaths had happened recently, since Bobby killed his parents.

He went back to earlier weeks to see if he were making things up. Nothing. The social pages were full of notices, but no one who wasn't scheduled to die, like from being one hundred and four years old, had died. Was this significant? Was he seeing a pattern where none was? Were they coincidences? Accidents? Could he use this?

Indian Wells, South Africa, Scotland, Thailand. The rich and famous dying. No, he corrected himself: the rich and powerful. Already, news of Bobby's most recent incident was making the news though it was shrouded in uncertainty. Fewer witnesses to this one; unless their recording slipped out.

What would be the purpose, though? He laughed when the word 'justice' came to mind. Justice was as tiered as a mountain rice farm. The world would be lucky if Bobby got actual time for his murder – *murders*. Laws were for all, but punishments were for little people. The prince in Siam, or wherever the hell it was, would say oops and take the throne.

Meanwhile, a homeless guy selling cigarettes by the puff in New Orleans is beaten to death by uniformed police. No arrests.

Half a state was drinking toxic sludge. No arrests.

Justice delayed is justice denied and the tiers were many and far between.

Bobby Weller, who committed the most viewed murder in history, got bail and killed again within a week.

He'd walk.

That was how the world was. The best anyone could do was take the ride as far as it would take them. Don't look back and hell no, don't look forward. Hell no. Now is the moment. "Now. Let me have this now," Gina had said. "Don't wake me."

What else was on offer? What else could there be?

He threw the ice out of his glass over the railing and listened for the clink on the sidewalk below. He heard nothing. In the light of the dying sun, he poured himself a straight glass of whiskey. Golden brown poison. Pure contaminant. Not even an ice cube to dilute it. He drank it like a man dying of thirst in an Oklahoma desert, mad with it, disregarding the horse corpses around the watering hole, the buzzards casting circling shadows from above. He could no longer taste the alcohol. He phoned down for two more bottles of their top shelf to be brought up, charging them to the room. They came double quick. He tipped with a signature and took them to the tub, which steamed in the air-conditioned room. Naked and sweating, he lowered himself in, lay back, drank and soaked.

"Don't wake me," he said to the air as he cracked open the next bottle.

Chapter Thirteen

The hospitals of the rich were day spas with blood-pressure cuffs. They kept Charlotte two days and gave her medicines for stress, encouraged relaxation with music and soft, colored lights, provided as much therapy as she wanted, physical, mental, drug rehab options if that was her thing. They tested her for everything – blood in a hundred ways, x-rays, magnetic resonance scans, even brain waves were looked at. When she asked about costs, she was assured that it was all taken care of. In between medical moments was the pampering. They gave her a manicure and brought a hair stylist to prepare her for her discharge the next day. Shampoo and color, a cut and style. And of course, she did not turn down another full-body massage.

The headache was gone, or at least retreated to a level she could ignore. The thought of it, the memory, the pain and strange obsession only returned to her in any force during the massage, when she found herself falling again into a rage.

"You're going the wrong way," her masseuse said, an Asian woman with big hands and wiry muscles. "I swear, since I've begun you've become more tense. Just try to relax."

The soothing, accented voice brought Charlotte out of her stupor of physical senses and mental diversion. The headache returned, a burning hum flitting behind her eyes, hiding at the base of her skull, chasing down her spine as her consciousness tried to identify it. The hands found her shoulders and kneaded them from stone to clay to sand and as they weakened, she caught a glimpse of what, or rather who, she raged at – herself. Who was she to have access to all this? Who was anyone? The servility, the lack of reciprocity. To calm down, she told herself that the masseuse was surely well paid. The obsequiousness was an act, a caricature of a bygone…

The idea slithered away, replaced by the numbing dirge of the doctor's pill, and she let her muscles absorb the unentitled energy of another so when she came back to herself, startled awake by her own snoring, she found herself bleary and untethered, in a bed with metal bed rails to keep her from falling, but the headache had receded.

Back in her private room, festooned now with flowers and stuffed animals from a law firm in damage control, she felt out of place and wary and ready to go home that afternoon. When the doctor came in with a jar of the magic pills for her, she felt her headache rise as he took each step closer. It was a booming thing but distant, a march of drums, the steps of soldiers in clanking armor. A music of war.

"You all right?" the doctor said. She still didn't know his name.

"My mind is wandering. Getting poetic."

"That's why I brought you these." He gave her the bottle.

She read the label and noted that her name did not appear on it, only the hospital pharmacy and the drug name, which she didn't even try to pronounce.

"Thanks."

"Don't mention it." And he left. She was free to go if she wanted to.

She wanted to. There was something about the place, something beyond the regular hospital vibes that bothered her.

She reached for her phone just as a call came through. Feeling strange, she decided to take it.

"Mom," she said.

"No, darling, it's your father."

"Oh, hi Dad."

"Your mother called you the other day, didn't she?"

"I meant to call her back, it's just been so crazy out here."

"Terrible business. I'm sorry you're involved in it."

It was probably just an honest statement meant to sympathize and connect, but Charlotte heard accusation and disappointment in it, as years of experience had taught her.

"I was lucky to be there," she said. "It'll make a great story."

"You've missed that boat, haven't you?"

The last time he'd used that metaphor her womb had been involved.

"I don't think so," she said.

"The news had it for days and now it's gone. Snooze and lose."

"I'm making a documentary."

"Did your mother tell you about my job?"

The change in direction reinforced her suspicions.

"Yes."

"Your mother is very concerned."

"And you're not?"

"I am. Of course I am. Why wouldn't I be?"

She took a breath. "Why did you call, Dad?"

"We were waiting for a call from you."

"Been busy. You have me now. What do you need?"

"Charlotte, Charly," he began.

Her gut tightened. The double naming was a recognized pattern that brought up long-conditioned fear.

She tensed. He hesitated.

"What is it, Dad?" she said into the long, grave pause. "Do you need money?"

"It's worse than your mother told you," he said.

"How much?"

"No. No. Not money. I'm not calling you for money. What kind of man asks his child for money? Do you think I'd be that kind of father? You know me better than that. I'd never—"

"Then just tell me what you want to tell me. What's worse?"

He sighed into the phone, a quick gust followed by a winded speech. "I lost my job and with it our insurance, and I'm sick. There. I said it. I'm sick and we don't have insurance anymore."

"What is it?"

"Cancer. Lymphoma. Known for a year. Been in and out of the hospital."

"Why didn't anyone tell me before?"

"We didn't want to worry you."

"Jesus Christ, Dad."

"Don't blaspheme."

"Really? You're not Christian. You're not even Hindu anymore."

"I still revere the names of God. Why would you take such risks as that?" In her father, a nonpracticing believer of any creed, blasphemy, like several other superstitions, had old and firm roots.

"The risk that a god will strike me down?"

"Yes," he said matter-of-factly. "I know it's unlikely, but it is not impossible there is a deity."

"Did you want to argue religion?"

"No, Charly, I didn't. I just wanted you to know about my condition so it wouldn't be a surprise."

"You mean a surprise later?"

"Yes."

"Wait, what's happening later?"

"I'll get better or I won't."

"That's bleak, Dad."

"Call your mother. She worries about you," he said. "I do too."

"I love you too, Dad."

"We think about you all the time, you know? We've been thinking about you forever, even before you were born."

She didn't know how to respond to that. The melancholy in her father's voice was unusual. Deep and suddenly frightening.

"Is there something else, Dad? Something else you want to tell me?"

"No," he said. "Take care of yourself."

"Of course."

And he hung up. The headache was back, not the recent one, the old one. The one about disappointing her parents. The one about guilt and pressure, water over the bridge.

She called Seth.

"I've been spending Weller money like it's stolen," he said.

"That's funny. I guess the law firm is paying for my hospital."

"No. That's Weller money too. Bobby arranged it."

"When?"

"The day you went in. The law firm is just the middle man."

"They're still talking to him?"

"Hell yes. What's a little murder among rich people?"

"The world is sick."

"And we're on the cutting edge of it."

She heard something there. "And...?" she said.

"I hope you haven't changed your mind about the project."

"Frankly, I haven't even thought about it."

"Well, I have and so have other people. There's more here than before."

"You have more leads?"

"And more money. I heard from Bobby, or rather his law firm. They trebled our grant. Sent me an American Express card to use."

"Trebled?"

"It means three times."

"I know what it means, I'm just wondering why."

"Public relations, I—"

An orderly entered Charlotte's room bearing a ream of papers. Seeing her on the phone, she paused and waited.

Charlotte covered her phone. "What's that?"

"Just the paperwork for your visit. Your copies." She placed them on the table. "Doctor says you can leave any time."

"Thanks."

"...a cult."

"Sorry, Seth," she said. "I didn't hear that."

"I'll tell you in person?"

"Any time."

"I'll pick you up on the way to the airport."

"You bought us tickets?"

"Actually, Bobby arranged for us to use his jet."

"Where are we going?"

"Martha's Vineyard. We've been invited to a party, remember?"

Half an hour later they were on their way to an airport in the back of a hired car.

Seth was explaining his earlier phone call. "It was Anthony Bryers, the middle guy from Christiansen, Bryers and Peters, Attorneys at Law."

"Uh huh." Charlotte traced palm trees through the window.

"He said, 'Mr. Weller, Robert Junior, wishes you to continue the project. He apologizes that he might not be available to personally assist, but has financially backed the project to treble the original grant amount.' That's where I got the word. Treble. Who says that?"

"Treble?"

"Right?" Seth laughed, but Charlotte's mind wandered as her attention, what little she had, was focused on California as it passed by in scenes of freeway gridlock. She read the billboards but they meant nothing, soulless, smiling faces, bold script, objects and things. All a static blur.

"My dad's sick," she said.

"Shit. I'm sorry to hear that. Maybe after Massachusetts we can take the jet and visit him."

"I'd rather not."

"Okay."

The car took them straight to the tarmac, where uniformed pilots stowed their baggage before entering the plane. Inside, Seth found a complete bar, even ice. He poured himself a bourbon.

"Are you going to drink the whole way?" Charlotte asked, putting on her seat belt, though no one had suggested she do so.

"Yes."

"Make me one."

"Same?"

"Sure."

Seth poured her a whiskey in a same cut-crystal highball glass he had, but only noticed now. It was superb – handwrought, heavy as a grenade.

"Here ya go."

"Bobby's gotta know that the tennis angle is off. Why would he do this?"

"Because he needs our help. I think he wants us to make him look like a nice guy."

"Did anyone say that?"

"Not exactly." Seth slid into the plush chair. "This is more like an RV than a plane. Cheers!"

Charlotte sipped and glared. The plane rose into the sky. "We're spending all this money and we can't even promise anything will come of it."

"Hey, what's wrong with lapping at the tit of opportunity."

She stared at him. "That's a phrase."

"You know what I mean."

"It's mercenary, and morbid. This is supposed to be about a rising tennis star, not a serial killer. You think it's some kind of spending spree. People have died and you think it's all a party."

"I don't think it's a party, but if you're trying to guilt me into regretting spending Weller's money to sleep comfortably, get a good meal, you're going to be trying for a while."

"You feel entitled?"

"There's a loaded word." Seth sipped his drink. He was going slow with it, finding equilibrium, not intoxication. He should have put in soda. He got up to do just that.

"Weller's a creep," he said, admiring the crystal clear ice cubes. "His bank is fucked. These people are assholes to a person. Bobby was right when he compared them to another species. They didn't earn their money; they stole it or inherited it. If inherited, it was the ancestor who stole it. If I can wedge a piece out for our lowly selves, eat well for a while, replace the camera we lost – and need – I'll remind you, good for us."

Charlotte noted then the new equipment on the seat.

"Replaced and upgraded," Seth said, raising his glass. "And delivered. Want to help me unbox it? Half the fun."

"They'll eventually discover the missing money—"

"They won't even look. This is loose change to them. And if they did – you want soda? No? If they find out, like a true American capitalist, I'll ask forgiveness and dare them to do anything about it. Remember Trump?"

"This is a political crusade?"

"It always was. It started as propaganda for the ruling class. Show Bobby, who couldn't guess how much a loaf costs for both his testes, as a regular guy, aspiring to greatness in a sport that requires stupid time and money to get good at. Working people can't join the tour. They gotta keep jobs to have houses, health. It was all a show to begin with."

"What are you going to do with this new camera when you get the other one back?"

"Donate it to charity?"

She rolled her eyes.

"Sell it and pay rent for a while."

She rubbed her eyes. "This has been a week from hell."

"Tar tar," said Seth and laughed under his breath.

She sipped her drink and winced at it. "Tar tar?"

"Inside joke," he said. "I've been thinking about Barney Faro. Do you know him?"

"History professor."

"Classics. Yeah, he's cool. Probably my best friend, though I never see him."

"What about him?"

"I was thinking about him the other day. At Indian Wells, in fact. There was something in the air, a hum or something, and it reminded me of his classes. Tartarus is Greek hell."

"I think I will have some soda."

Up again like a jack-in-the-box, Seth was back to the bar.

Charlotte popped her ears and listened for the haunting sound, and not hearing it above the hum of the engines and the pressure lock of the cabin, leaned back and relaxed a bit.

Seth said, "I think there's a pattern here. Remember those South Africans I told you about? Well, they're not the only ones. I've found a bunch of similar incidents all in the last week or so. Big, powerful people. Rich people, kings. And it looks like their children are doing it."

"What are you talking about?"

"What we've seen of these people – this class of people – suggests that they're very insular. It's a small group. Though the killings—"

"Killings? All killings?"

"Sudden deaths, some more suspicious than others."

"Deaths."

"Fine, these deaths are happening all over the world, and I bet we can do two degrees of separation between each to Bobby Weller and his clan, if not one."

"Reaching."

"It's an angle. It might pan out, it might not. I'm talking about the new direction for the film here. We can show Bobby is just one of a bunch of people doing this. It only has to carry enough water to connect the film together. Gives us new places to go, new people to talk to, to continue on."

"This is below tabloid shit."

"Tabloids are already on it," he said. "They're calling them copy-cat killings, but they have only found one or two so far. I've found dozens."

Charlotte scowled. He smiled and it was contagious. She wasn't sure she liked him, suspected she disliked him in fact, but still she felt safe here now with him. She paused and considered options and couldn't at that moment find a place she'd rather be that she could conceivably reach.

The alcohol misted her mind. She closed her eyes. "We can't just film without knowing what we're looking for."

"Sure we can. It'll be harder to edit, but I see no reason not to press on. We'll see what we find, and then, like a great book of literature, we'll deconstruct it and figure out what it all means. And that will be our movie."

"And while we do, we live the high life."

"No day but today," he said.

Chapter Fourteen

The plane had Wi-Fi and Seth showed Charlotte the links he'd found and suggested possible narrative devices to connect them. "It doesn't have to be true," he said. "Only interesting."

Charlotte read the articles, only half paying attention. Behind her eyes there was turbulence, her father's situation, her mother's, and the ethics of journalism.

Charlotte had been told by more than one person that reality was much different from academia. They were two different worlds. One full of highlights, good intentions and gold, the other dirty and shadowed, compromised and wanting. One was unobtainable, the other inevitable.

Ethics was one of the reasons she'd chosen journalism as a major and now a career. She'd had visions of Woodward and Bernstein, Upton Sinclair, thinking she could stand against the power in this age of propaganda and sound bites. She could be trusted. She would be the new Walter Cronkite. Reality didn't take long to muddy that idea. Journalism wasn't a political entity today; it was a branch of the entertainment industry. It had been like this for a terrible while. Bleeds and leads, clickbait, sensationalized and one-sided. Infotainment was the closest she was likely to get to making a difference. CGI approximations and a cut to the bones of an extinct species. What we might have looked like, what we are. Where you will be soon.

Intellectually she knew she'd eventually have to face the sloppy side of journalism, the sensationalism, fluid truths and alternative facts. Making shit up to justify what you needed to justify. An idea, or a goal. The documentary was over. She had no business pursuing this anymore. She'd written a thesis, sent in an official proposal, been awarded status and money on the basis of the promises she'd made. Bobby Weller, rising tennis star. To continue now, without the express permission of her superiors at Commondale University, was unethical. Seth's idea of jury-rigging another film was plainly and obviously – and to his credit, confessedly – a self-serving ploy to keep the expense money flowing in. Looking around the opulent interior of a twenty-million-dollar private plane, the high-minded journalist in her cringed with shame.

Seth showed her another murder in a rich family, this one in Japan. Three children confessed to killing their two parents and four grandparents at a picnic. There were scores of witnesses. No one had lifted a finger as each was strangled to death with a cord.

Charlotte turned away. "It could be a form of confirmation bias," she said. "You've found things that support your theory."

"Not a lot of sense in looking for anything else is there?"

"In journalism, you're supposed to be fair and balanced."

"I'm aghast, Charlotte," Seth said. "To use that phrase, which has not only lost all original meaning, but been completely usurped by liars."

"Still."

"I guess we could google rich people who didn't die recently. Try that."

"You're hilarious."

"I'm glad you're coming around."

She regarded him with his drink, the light shining in the window off clouds low beneath the plane. His eyes were bright, a wry smile was on his lips. He looked like he was just enjoying the moment, enjoying it much more than she was.

She leaned back and shut her eyes, concentrating on the sensations of flying.

Seth watched her face in the stark sunlight, thinking he was old. "My wife got sick of me," he said.

"Wasn't it mutual?"

"What do you mean?"

Without opening her eyes or shifting position, the light warming her cheeks, she said, "It's hard to be around someone who doesn't like you. If she got sick of you, you surely got sick of her being sick of you."

"There probably was some of that," he said.

"What happened?"

"She found someone who could offer her the life she thought she wanted." He shook his head. "Could I use any more modifiers?"

She didn't stir.

"Key word there is offered. He's conservative in the bad way. A racist fuck. Drives a big white truck and sells lawn equipment. He makes a good living. Ellen doesn't have to work. Travis is taken care of."

"Travis?"

"My son. The reason we got married in the first place. He's nineteen and wants nothing to do with me. He thinks I'm a radical."

"Why does he think that?"

It was interesting how she would not open her eyes to look at him. He considered how the light fell on her face and knew his face was a poor substitute for that.

"His mom set him against me."

"That sounds pitiful."

"Well, he hasn't tried to find out who I am now. I was once the kind of guy to march in protests, but that was many moons ago."

"So you'd call yourself conservative now?"

"Who in their right mind would call themselves that?"

"Just asking."

The plane banked and drew Charlotte into shadow. She remained still.

"I'm convenient for him – them. I'm the boogeyman, a local fear that unites them into a loving family unit. My son collects assault rifles like he's going into business. Ellen...I don't recognize. I guess she's happy."

"Does that matter to you that much?"

"I know the answer here is, of course, I'm a friendly caring fellow, but I guess I'm nonplussed. Is that the word?"

"Sure."

"I try to reach out to Travis once in a while, hoping he's grown up enough now to see through the mud screen of first marriage, but it hasn't been easy."

"Did you pressure him to be something he didn't want to be?" she asked. Her eyes were still closed and her chin upturned as before, as if she were soaking up the shadow as much as she had the light. Seth smiled at the simple beauty of it, and was embarrassed, glad she hadn't seen him do it.

"No. They left me when he was eight and I was painted as the villain in the divorce. I wasn't around to pressure him to do much, except finish his vegetables, clean his room, turn off lights. That kind of thing. I'll tell you though, I'd have resisted his later direction if I'd have been there."

"It would have just forced him that way even further," she said.

"What's the issue with your parents?"

"I thought we were talking about your family."

"I was. You weren't."

She smiled at that.

"Generational disconnection." She opened her eyes, squinted and blinked. She looked around the cabin, sipped her drink. "My parents are from India," she said. "They were refugees from one of the wars they had over there. I forget which one. Started as one, ended in another. A couple in between. Still happening."

"Shit show with Pakistan."

"Internal stuff too. Place is a boiling pot. In more ways than one." She took a deep breath. "Well, anyway, they fled, got naturalized, had me. Named me Charlotte to make me sound more American. My father, Rajenbra, calls himself Ralph for the same reason. My mother, Kusum, is just Kusum, though she forces herself to wear heels."

"Only child?"

"Yes. Exactly. Upon me have they put the dreams of their line." She said it as if she were quoting. She might have been, but she couldn't recall from where. Might have been her own mind.

"Time is different in the old cultures, I think," she went on. "They look so far ahead, remember so far back. It's intimidating. I'm a link in a long, long chain. My purpose, as they see it, is to build new chains and carry on."

"Are you describing romantic pressure?"

"Yes. And more. They're like Christians."

"You better explain that." Seth pulled out his cigarettes, patted one halfway out and then thought better of it. "Something to look forward to." He put them away.

"Dream big," she said.

"Your parents aren't Hindu?"

"Oh, they are. I guess. You know there are varying degrees of religious. Holidays and lip service, but they've fallen away from all that. They want to be American. They really see this place as the ticket to happiness."

"They're happy?"

"Hell no. It's not their happiness they're looking for."

"Yours?"

"Farther ahead," she said. "What I meant by the Christian thing is how that whole religion relies on trading happiness now for more of it in the future. Suffer on earth, get treats in heaven."

"I don't think the Christians have a lock on that one." Seth again remembered his friend Faro and channeled him a little. "It's all about sacrifice," he said. "Give God a little taste of this lamb or that incense. It's tithing, it's a bribe."

"No, it's beyond that," she said. "My parents have this idea that their lives don't matter. I think it may even be a conscious thing, something they may have discussed before coming here. I don't know. I could ask, but I haven't. Won't. Something happened to them, or they got some idea that the meaning of life is not their life, but some future life. Their goal – their lives' goal – is to get some descendent to that happy place. It's focused. It's surgical. It's calculated and it has fucking failed."

The plane banked, and a soft announcement over actually good speakers announced that they would be landing soon.

"They failed?"

"I failed."

"Whoa, Charlotte. How many of those have you had?"

"*I* don't think I failed. *They* think I failed." She finished her drink and splashed a little more in her glass. She didn't fill it. Seth admired that. Anyone who could pour a drink without topping the glass was a moral saint, as far as he was concerned.

"They put all their attention to me," she said. "Only child. By design. Going against tradition. Going against…I don't know. Common sense? All eggs in one basket. Shower me with praise and opportunity. All their money, all their prayers, all their ambitions."

"You're doing great."

"I haven't given them a grandchild, the next link."

"Yet."

She glared at him. Seth raised his hands in surrender.

"The pressure is too much," Charlotte said. "Too much. I'm not interested in kids, or marrying. Or putting this kind of pressure on someone else. Besides, have you seen the state of the world?"

"I have, actually," said Seth. "And I for one completely – and I mean completely – understand." He raised his glass.

"You can't know."

"I said understand. Not know. There's a difference."

"What do you understand?"

"Carpe diem, baby. Reality is the exact opposite of your parents' creed. The promise of a future has been mortgaged for short-term loans and disposable water bottles."

She thought about this for a moment and sipped her drink. She couldn't taste the alcohol. "Don't call me baby," she said finally.

"Sorry."

"You've got a kid."

"And boy, has that ever been great."

"But you love him." It was a statement.

"I know I'm supposed to," he said, "and I feel the pressure to agree with you, but I honestly don't know. It's like what you said before, hard to like someone who doesn't like you. Children or no. I really would like to have a good relationship with him, and I've tried, and I'll try again, because that's what I'm supposed to do."

"But?"

He shrugged. "No promises."

"That's a motto for the ages."

"This one at least."

The pilot's voice came on over their heads. "We're on final approach to Martha's Vineyard. You may want to put your seat belts on and stow any splashables. It should be a smooth landing, but ocean winds can be unpredictable. We hope you've had a nice flight."

Charlotte looked around the cabin, not at all like any plane she'd flown in before. This was a luxurious living room with little windows. The pilot's obsequious announcement brought her back.

"This is unreal, you know," she said. "Traveling like this."

"Like different worlds, right?"

"Yeah," she said. "For a different species."

Chapter Fifteen

They were met at the plane near dusk by a man in a tan suit and narrow-rimmed glasses. He introduced himself as Mr. Halluk, assistant to the Carreau family, traveling with Kinsley this week. That was all the information he offered as he led them to a waiting car and drove them from the airfield.

Though they'd had the most luxurious and comfortable transcontinental flight of their lives, the two were tired and rode in silence as the trees flowed by their window. They'd smelled the sea air when they'd gotten out of the plane, the scent of salt and raw fish, seaweed and diesel. Inside the car it was air-conditioned and stale. They were on a small island. They'd noticed it from above but neither had spoken about it, though it had impressed them both. It was a famous place to those back west, a familiar one to those in the east. They both felt like the tourists they were.

Seth had finally broken down and lit a cigarette on the tarmac and carried it past Halluk to the car. When no one told him to put it out, he allowed himself a second. He tried to keep the smoke away from Charlotte but didn't roll down his window because the early spring air, scented though it was, had a chill.

Charlotte's mind wandered, softened by the jet lag, stirred by the conversation, churned by events. She regarded Halluk in the front seat, traced his quarter profile from her vantage point. He struck her as a taciturn stoic, someone with something on his mind. She tried to imagine what it might be: relationship problems, 401(K), a father who was ill. She imagined having a drink with him, letting him open up. She pretended in her mind that they were friends, and she could talk him through the lease renewal that so perplexed him. Then she remembered.

They could not be friends. He was not an actual person. At least not now, not as she'd ever see him. He was a functionary. A servant. An attendant attached, possibly by birth, to a house. Her visions of friendly beers became nightmares of serfdom and slavery.

"What?" said Seth.

Something she'd done had betrayed her emotion and had alarmed Seth.

"Spinning in my head," she said. "I need a nap."

Seth nodded and put out his cigarette. "You ever been here before?" he asked.

Charlotte cast a glance at Halluk, as if telling Seth to be quiet. He looked at her confused.

She felt self-conscious, out of water. Tourist didn't describe it. She felt like a spy behind enemy lines.

"Never."

Seth said, "*Jaws* was filmed here and I've seen that movie so many times, this feels like I'm back at summer camp. Or did, in the Seventies. It's changed a lot since then."

"Since before you were born?"

"Yep."

"It's hard to go home again," she said.

"Ain't that the truth."

There was no beach yet for Seth to get his bearings. From the plane he'd tried to see the *Orca* battling Moby Dick's little cousin, but in the brief moments of sand and sea, he saw only unfamiliar places. The island was wooded, more so than one would think for so old a settlement. That was the East Coast for Seth, an old place, stodgy and historic, at least by American standards, which were a complete joke to anyone in Europe. Europe is a place where a hundred miles is a long way while America is a place where a hundred years is a long time. Distance and history. The new world vs. the old vs. the old new world on a wooded island.

The car stopped in front of a colonial four-story building; white columns, a turret on top. A widow's walk. White and gray with scarlet accents. Cleaner than new, with shaped shrubs and wicker furniture on the porch. It was more than a house, less than a mansion. A fake. Modern interpretation of a classical design. The Cozy Visit Bed and Breakfast Inn. Any promise of an informal stay was immediately erased when two uniformed porters jogged out to help with the luggage.

"Mr. Lian and Ms. Sakshi," Mr. Halluk told one of them.

The luggage disappeared through large wooden doors.

"When will we see Kinsley?" Charlotte asked.

"Someone will be in touch," Halluk said. He waited for a moment, offering a short window of conversation, and when none came nodded curtly, got in the car, and left.

The lobby was big and kept with the illusion that this might have been an actual residence once. Soft couches and nooks and tastefully mismatched furniture filled the space. Tall plants with fleshy leaves, ferns, bright flowers in pots. Paisley in red and blue, frills on the lampshades.

"Welcome," said a man in a flannel shirt, with a gold pin over his heart: Innkeeper James. "Here are your keys. You can take the stairs to the second floor, or there's an elevator down that hall. You shouldn't be bothered. It's the off-season."

"Food?"

"We have room service and a café. There's also our bar, Quint's Place."

"Pictures of the *Indianapolis*?"

"Actually, yes." The concierge looked appreciative.

"I'm Seth. This is Charlotte. Care to join us for a drink?"

The concierge looked around the lobby, the empty lobby, and back to a corner table which doubled for a desk in front of an unmarked door that smelled like office space. "I really can't."

"I insist," Seth said.

"No, I—"

"Really," said Seth, looking him in the eye. "I insist. Unless you have more important people to talk to."

A dark look passed over James's face, the briefest shadow that evaporated quickly into the warm, floral-scented room.

"Of course," he said. "Sure. I can give you a good Martha's Vineyard welcome."

Charlotte didn't like this. She sensed a scene brewing that she wanted no part of. "Seth, I'll—"

"I won't let you drink too much. She's a lightweight. Last time she literally danced on a table."

That wasn't what she was going to say. Of course it wasn't. She was tired and wanted to see their rooms, charge her phone, sit and think. Seth's insistence, though, was not to be ignored. He'd hard roped the reluctant staff; how could she refuse?

"Just one."

"A couple," Seth said. "You brought your tap shoes, right?"

She shook her head to James, who smiled and seemed to understand.

The bar was upscale but still touristy. The theme was, of course, Quint from the movie *Jaws*. Fishing nets hung in swooping curves; yellow barrels were placed conspicuously by the door. Charlotte noticed framed photographs of the film production on the walls, faded amateur snapshots probably taken by the locals. In a place of honor, above the bar, illuminated by two aimed lamps hanging from the ceiling, was a framed black-and-white autographed headshot of Robert Shaw himself.

Innkeeper James led them to a prime table with a window overlooking the dark grounds. A floating candle flickered in a dish of water in the center of the distressed wood tabletop.

A waiter appeared before they'd settled and took their orders. James included an appetizer: oysters, the house specialty.

Seth offered a longer introduction for him and Charlotte, explaining their mission and dropping the names Weller and Carreau. James nodded as if they were mentioning shared friends.

"The Carreaus were the ones who arranged your stay," James said. "They have an account. Here, and every other five star on the island. They all do."

"They?" asked Charlotte.

She caught Seth glancing at her sidelong, an approving smirk on his lips.

Innkeeper James downed his drink and signaled for another vodka rocks.

"Nothing," he said.

"No," said Seth. "I'd like to know what you mean."

James just laughed. His drink arrived. Before sipping it, he rubbed his temples and offered them each a smile.

"Our project has changed since we started," said Seth.

"It's becoming a story of different worlds," put in Charlotte. Wasn't that what Seth was getting at? Or was that her own construction?

James, a glow in his cheeks, said, "I got a job here."

"Off the record," said Seth. "We're just looking for angles. You'd do us a solid if you could point us in a direction."

James looked conflicted.

"Or would you just rather talk about *Jaws*?"

Before he could answer, Charlotte pressed. "Who'd you mean by 'they'? Which group?"

James took another sip. "There are only two groups," he said. "Them and us."

"Them being...?"

"We're us," he said.

"They are the rich folk?" offered Seth.

"Yes, sir."

"Bet you have stories to tell."

"Too many," he said. "I've lived on the island my whole life. It's been tourist based forever, but lately it's been a specific kind of tourist. The obscenely wealthy. They'll call themselves that. Really. They think it's funny." He shook his head.

Seth downed an oyster, upended the shell and let it just slide down his throat.

Charlotte cringed. To James, she asked, "How long have you worked here at the inn?"

"After college I came home. My father was the innkeeper then. I took over when he died suddenly."

"I'm sorry," said Charlotte.

James looked positively pleased at her. "Thank you for saying that."

Charlotte's thoughts flitted to her own father and made a flash mental comparison between her life and James's.

"He died of cancer. Treatable, but expensive. Too expensive. He was fired from the inn when…" James stumbled and blushed. "When he got too sick."

Charlotte put her hand on his and he blushed again. A tear was in his eye. Charlotte felt one developing in her own.

"He was fired when he asked some of the guests to contribute to his medical bills. He had one of those internet calls for money, a website people could contribute to. Lot of locals had pitched in. He made a comment to some guests, just a comment about it, you know."

Charlotte's gut wrenched.

"It was untoward, he was told. He was required by management to take it down. Not just stop soliciting contributions from the guests, but actually to take it down because it reflected badly on the inn."

"Shit," said Seth.

"The insurance maxed out and that was that. Buried him in the rain. They wouldn't let scheduled staff attend."

Another vodka had appeared on the table just as Seth finished his first. Charlotte's wine was untouched.

"You know, three of the board members of that insurance company have houses here. They come here all the time. I see their kids. This place is liked by the kids – Kinsley Carreau, Bobby Weller, Devin Thorpe – those guys. We're a favorite hangout. Their parents prefer The Reef or the Hilton. It's a generational thing, I guess."

"Why the fuck do you work here?" said Seth. Charlotte cringed at his bluntness, but the question was on her mind.

James sighed. "I once had an idea about that." He shook his head. "The pay's good."

"Different generations. That's got to make it easier," said Charlotte.

"Yeah, some of them have real daddy issues."

"We were there," said Seth. "When Bobby Weller went berserk."

"Weren't we all?" James said. "I kinda liked him. He'd put up his tennis buddies here sometimes. Good tippers. He put up that SOS guy for a while here. No. Wait, it was Carreau who did that. I'm not sure she actually met with him, but for a weekend he ate lettuce and walked around the island."

"Who?"

"Kinsley Carreau. She likes to invite weird people here for parties. 'A living conversation starter,' she calls them, though the group is so tight, I wonder why they bother. Maybe it's for the shock factor. I don't know."

"You're losing me," said Seth. "Plus, I think I've been insulted."

"For being a party favor? Why not? Pays good."

"You said SOS. What's that?"

"The current internet sensation. Or was it last month? Month before?" James's speech was beginning to slur. He signaled the waiter, who appeared with another drink. "Aspirin," James said.

"And a water?"

"No, this'll do." He lifted his fresh drink.

"Maybe you should slow down," said Charlotte. "You're on duty."

"Yeah?" said Innkeeper James. "But I'm the boss unless the boss is here and he's dead. And fuck him."

"Dead?"

"Drowned off the cape three days ago with his family."

"Rich?"

"He was one of *them*," slurred James. "Hotels and accommodations."

Charlotte mouthed water to the waiter, who nodded and brought over three glasses with a jar of aspirin. James took four with his drink.

Seth saw that Charlotte was uncomfortable, worried about James. To be fair, the innkeeper did seem surprisingly easy to get talking and couldn't take his drinks the way Seth was taking them. These things Seth saw as his advantage.

"SOS, right," said James as if suddenly remembering where he was. "Sons of Stone. Brazilian group to save the planet. Environmental tree huggers or something like that. Mark Sosa. A Black guy. The leader. He came here last year. November or October. Ms. Carreau invited him, but like I said, he didn't get to go to a party."

"Canceled?"

"I think he got too controversial. It's one thing to call for an end to clear-cutting in Brazil. It's another to call your hosts 'leeches', 'lampreys', and 'conmen'."

"Oh my," said Seth, inciting a laugh out of James.

"I haven't heard of him," said Charlotte.

James looked at her, his eyes unfocused. He rubbed his temples and squinted. "I know about him only because of *them*. They talked about him. I met him when he stayed here."

"Nice guy?"

"He was really intense, but a nice guy."

"You tell him about your father?"

James shook his head. "I don't know why I told you. Can you just forget about that? Maybe forget about everything else I said. I probably will." And then he laughed.

Seth joined in. Charlotte felt nervous. Smiled. Noticed a knot in her stomach, sensed her headache circling the periphery of her skull. She finally tasted her wine.

It was full dark outside. The oysters were gone, Seth had eaten them all.

"Let's see our rooms," said Charlotte. "I'd like to freshen up before dinner."

Seth gave her a look of objection, but her glare won the argument.

"Thanks, Innkeeper James," Seth said, standing up. "Put the drinks on the room and know you're a hell of a host. I'll leave you a super Yelp review. I hope we talk again."

"Good to have one of us to talk to," he said.

Chapter Sixteen

"This could be a good angle," said Seth. "Mark Sosa is a character himself. He could have his own documentary."

"How do we know he hasn't?" asked Charlotte.

They were in the inn's café for breakfast. After the interview with James, as Seth demanded it be called, Charlotte had gone to sleep. Seth had stayed up to do research. It was only now they'd met again.

"Doesn't seem like it," said Seth. "A bunch of YouTube vids and a dozen websites devoted to him and the Sons of Stone."

A waiter brought them each a cup of coffee. "I'm charging it all to the room," Seth explained. "The menu doesn't even have prices."

She ground her teeth as Seth poured cream and sugar into his cup, while a plate of breakfast meats appeared next to his open computer, a new computer, she noticed.

"On a hunch after what James said about his boss," Seth explained, "I googled recent deaths at Martha's Vineyard."

There were other guests in the café, but not many. A couple in their late thirties, a group in their twenties. All white. All clean. All stank of wealth and privilege. Charlotte remembered the old lady at the spa, imagined her blood dripping from her fingers in a vivid flash.

"Four noteworthy hits," Seth said. "A CFO died in a hit-and-run. A 'Wall Street Executive' went missing after a walk. An aged heiress died in a mugging with her young athlete boyfriend. No suspects. A family drowned in what they're calling a boating accident. You know what I say?"

"What?"

"Boating accident? This was no boating accident." He grinned.

"How do you know?"

"I'm quoting *Jaws*."

"Oh. I should watch that."

"You haven't seen it?"

"It's so old."

"It's great. It made Spielberg. The conflict is between society safety and the economy. Sacrifice people to keep the shops open and tourists coming. Thinking about it now, it was a preview for the American COVID response."

"I thought it was about a shark."

"The shark isn't the conflict. The shark is a complication."

"Are these some kind of official terms? Film jargon?"

"Not just film, but yeah. You don't know what I'm talking about?"

"Journalism doesn't think that way."

"You mean there's no theory behind your work?"

She smiled. "That sounds a bit snobby. The kind of thing an unemployed writer says to a working newspaperman."

"Ouch."

She looked around the room again, smug in her retort. The couple had gone, the twenty-somethings were glancing back at her. When she met the eyes of a young man, he held her gaze. It surprised her. Usually – no, always – when she'd catch someone out like that, they'd instinctively turn away. She turned instead, a murmur in her ears.

"Lots of deaths on the island this last week. More than the last three months combined," Seth said. "Also, the people dying were somebodies."

The group across the café, the cluster of somebodies she was sure, broke out into a communal laugh.

"What about Sosa?"

"Right." Seth closed the laptop and tasted his coffee. He made a face and poured more cream in. "He's originally American. From Philadelphia. Son of a radical who either fled the country or was exiled, depending on who you ask. The father is dead. Sosa calls Brazil his home, but where in Brazil, no one knows. Sosa's a wanted man there. He's sure El Presidente Valera is out to kill him, claiming he's a terrorist."

"Melodramatic much? And it's Portuguese, not Spanish."

"Brazil is a mess," said Seth. "There are always stories coming out about rainforest activists being killed, villages of natives massacred. It sucks down there. Varela is worse than Bolsonaro ever was. From what I read, the word 'fascist' doesn't even begin to cover him, and frankly, Sosa probably is a left-wing terrorist."

"Judgmental much?"

"You're on one."

"Sorry. My attempt at humor. Go on." She noticed her coffee then. It steamed and shone with a colored film she'd never seen in a beverage before. Smelling it, she detected the hints of ripe nuts and blossoms in the aroma.

"Sosa's Black."

"So?"

"So guess who's coming to WASP dinner? This crowd doesn't look like they value diversity. Remember Indian Wells? Why invite a Black person to anything?"

"You know prejudice goes both ways, right?"

"You mean why would he come here?"

"No. I mean you need to check your own thinking. So what if he's Black?"

Seth jabbed a sausage with his fork and took a bite.

Charlotte said, "Could there be another reason he was invited besides being Black?"

"Well, yeah. Of course. He's political. A radical. Famous in an underground sort of way, but not really the somebody these somebodies would approve of."

"You're prejudicing again. Obviously some did, or he wouldn't get invited."

"Maybe they didn't look too deep then, because the things he has to say about the ruling class are pretty harsh."

"He's a socialist. Everyone goes through that stage when they're young."

"Your wisdom is uplifting," said Seth. "Sosa used to be an advocate of reparations for slavery. Very vocal about it. That alone should make him unpopular."

"But he's changed his mind? He used to be an advocate you say?"

"He probably still is, but he's taken it a step further. He's for bloody revolution. No. He's worse than that."

"What's more?"

Seth finished his sausage, sipped his coffee, glanced at the group in the corner who were getting loud on mimosas. "Revenge," he said. "He doesn't say that, but his new manifesto kinda implies it."

"How many manifestos does he have?"

"I know, right? I thought the rule was you were only allowed one. He has four or five. The first was written when he was in junior high school. I didn't read that one, but it's available online. Do you want to see it?"

"No."

"I'm not sure how they got a hold of him, or why he agreed to come. Or how he came. He says the U.S. is looking for him too."

"He sounds really paranoid."

"His father was assassinated."

"Are sins inherited?" Charlotte's impatient gaze again found the group in the corner. Three girls and three boys. She couldn't bring herself to call them men and women. They were children playing adult. You could smell the carefreeness about them. Not the kind of carefree that brings freedom, that her meditative parents strived for, but the natural state of not having any real problems.

Her stomach twitched, a ringing pierced her ears and then faded. "Prejudice is a hell of a thing," she said.

"I'm not one to speak," Seth said, "being in the privileged class of white, handsome and male, but—"

"Handsome?"

"Fuck yeah."

She smirked and rolled her eyes. "You were about to display more of your arrogance."

"It's automatic behavior, prejudice is. Some of it is learned, some of it we are born with."

"Born with?"

"Yeah, like snakes. Spiders. There seems to be some innate fear of those things in most people."

"We're talking racism, not instinct."

"Are we? Say way back in the day, a bunch of our friends were killed by snakes. Before language, the fear of long, slithering things was planted in some genetic code – or maybe some cultural or even special memory. It transferred to dependents, and they were born with that knowledge."

"Knowledge?"

"Sure. Like how a cat knows to hunt, a dog to howl. Take either from their animal parents and they'll still show their instinct. Sex is like that."

"You've spent a lot of time thinking about this, have you?" she said.

"Sex?"

"Arrogance."

"Okay, so the truth is not every snake is dangerous. Some might even be helpful. I know people who've kept them as pets. They had a spider too. Big hairy thing that she'd let walk all over her."

"You have great taste in women."

"Ha, there, you see? You're judging this woman only knowing that she liked snakes and spiders."

"And she was with you," said Charlotte playfully. "That's three points of information. Ought to be enough to base a conclusion."

"Cute."

"I know I am."

Seth liked the sparkle in her eye, her wit and playfulness just now. Here was a side of her he'd not seen. He pressed on. "Okay, now let's talk about the 'Other'." He made air quotes.

"Other with a capital O?"

"Yes, you know it."

"I do have a college degree, you moron."

"I wasn't sure they're still teaching that."

"Gender and ethnic studies are required these days."

"Well, that's good."

"Dinosaur."

Seth stuffed a whole sausage link into his mouth and chewed it loudly with his mouth coming open.

Charlotte chortled. The group at the other table were getting ready to go, standing up, collecting coats.

"You know to trust your group and have, dare I say, an instinctive distrust, if not fear, of the *other*. Other tribes have raided your stores, made slaves of your people, stolen your women – and men. I don't want to discriminate."

"Why stop now?"

"Hey."

"Go on."

He gave her a playful squint. She returned it. He went on. "It's a shortcut, hardwired in the brain."

"That's the mistake."

"It can be. The tribe might be nice. Might be friendly, but caution at first is always safer. Always. We have history to prove that, the same history that has given us the prejudice that has kept us alive."

"It still doesn't wash. Racism has been shown to be taught. Racist parents, racist kids."

"But not always."

"Not always. That's my point."

"Remember that humans are fat-heads. Really. Literally. We're fat-heads. It's why our females give birth to such useless, helpless blobs as they do. Other species drop their children onto the grass ready to play, run, fight, follow the herd. Much of our development – most of it, happens outside the womb. Parenting does that. Who's to say that a parent's instinctive teaching of race prejudice isn't just the delayed genetic imprinting? We can look at it as a polishing of instinct or triggering it. Fear the other, but in our case the other is the big hair people or mud folk with frog jewelry."

"Now you're just making shit up. I'm not even sure you can compare genetics to nurturing. No. I take that back. I'm sure you can't."

"I always say that we don't have enough time on the planet to learn all the lessons we have to learn. That's why we read, listen to stories, slow down and gawk at freeway accidents, ask our friends why they divorced. We're learning from other people's mistakes. Prejudice is a flavor for that."

"Saying that some race is intellectually inferior is learning from other people's mistakes?"

Seth hesitated. Chewed, watched the group finally exit the café. "In that case," he said slowly, "it's about justification. Making the other inferior to justify your hatred. It's the intellect rationalizing a decision the subconscious has made."

"That sounds more like it. The subconscious is wrong. It's up to the intellect to deal with it."

"Okay. People can change their views. The good ones anyway."

"Another prejudicial remark."

"Aren't they all?"

"Cheap line."

"No. We could get into the whole idea of semantics, the barrier between reality and what we think it is. It's all very deep. Have you ever done acid?"

"Wow, that was a shift."

"Was it? Well, okay, forget I said that. I don't want you to think any less of me."

"You don't have to worry."

Seth grinned at her. He held it as he drank coffee. Charlotte smelled hers and noticed changes in the aroma. She tasted it and found flavors that weren't even suggested by the smell.

"You know how a lot of people don't like white cisgender men these days?"

"I've heard of such a thing."

"It's because we're a bunch of bastards, right?"

"Go on." Every sip of the coffee was different. Charlotte put her cup down to keep it from distracting her.

"Historically speaking, we deserve it. We've been in power and we've been assholes. Entitlement is a thing. White privilege is a thing. Male, straight, blond is a thing. I get that. I'm a member of that class, and though I'm an ally to the opposition, and have never consciously abused the system—"

"Much."

"Much. Okay. Not abused it on my behalf much; I admit I've benefited from it. I doubt I'd have kept my job at the university if I'd have been Black."

"You might have. They'd have been afraid of race lawsuits."

"Hm. Well, what I'm saying is that the people who've been discriminated against by prejudice are now prejudiced against people who look like me, regardless of who they really are, what they do, or what they think personally. I'm lumped in with the villains."

"So now you're playing victim? That tracks."

"Charlotte, are we having a deep philosophical conversation here or what?"

"What."

He shook his head as a fresh cup of coffee appeared.

"Don't doctor the coffee," Charlotte said. "Smell it. Let it sit, then smell it again. Then taste it. And again when it's cooler. It changes."

He looked at her incredulously and deliberately raised an eyebrow. Then the other. Then danced them.

"Do as I say."

Seth smelled his coffee.

"Take a deep sniff."

He did. "Hmmm," he said. "That's…different."

"I know, right? Taste it."

He did. "Wow. Okay. But you're distracting me."

"The coffee is."

He put down the cup. "Some of the most prejudiced people I've ever met have been minorities. Blacks who despise gays, women who would like to murder all trans people. The lack of self-reflection is staggering."

"Smell it again."

He did. "Wow."

"It evolves. Taste it now."

"Hm."

"How does it taste?"

"Different."

"From what?"

"It's the weirdest thing," he said. "It's different from what it tasted like before, it's different from coffee."

Charlotte took a fresh sip with closed eyes and savored new sensations, the warm but cooling dusky flowers and saps. Nuts. Citrus? Earthy tones that reminded her of meadows and bitter roots. Distinct and swimming together.

"It's unfair to stereotype people by the way they always act."

"What? Oh. That's dark."

"It's a shortcut. Lazy to be sure, but who has time to form an opinion on everything? The best we can ever do is be aware of it, because it'll always be there. People who say they're not prejudiced, or don't see race, are a bunch of fucking liars."

"All of them?"

"Yes. All of them."

"Try it now."

Seth sipped his coffee, remembering the time he'd tried to learn to drink it black, how he'd hated it then, hated himself for trying to be something he wasn't. An odd thought, he mused. Then the flavors warmed his tongue. One combination now, changing and sparkling as he swished it in his mouth. Different in aftertaste. He tried to give them names – almond, grapefruit, cinnamon.

"Well?" asked Charlotte.

"It's coffee, right?"

"What else?"

He shook his head. "This isn't what I'm used to."

"No. This is *good* coffee. It answers an old question I've had."

"What's that?"

"Why, or rather how, people ever drank coffee to begin with. What was the attraction before you had acquired the tastes?"

Seth nodded. "This is an experience. What I drink every morning is fuel. Both are called coffee. They share a name and little else."

"You're reading too much into it. Just enjoy it. I'll ask the waiter where they get it. I bet it's rare and expensive."

"Ah, that's it then."

"What?" asked Charlotte.

"Which should get to keep the name 'coffee'? Ours or theirs?"

"You are in a mood, not me."

"I can't help thinking that we get to keep the name coffee, due to its ubiquitousness and simplicity to market, and they get 'gourmet coffee', or some other adjectival adornment to differentiate theirs from ours and them from us."

"You're a class bigot."

"The Other is dangerous. Haven't you been listening?"

Chapter Seventeen

Seth wanted to see the yacht club, it was a landmark, but they were to be met at a pier on the other side of the island. It was a beautiful place though, not a bad place to wait. Not half as crowded, not a tenth well known. Behind the shelter of a fishing shop they could absorb the moment, enjoy the scene, wind-battered and bright. Their eyes naturally followed an aged pier reaching out into the blue water like a pale finger pointing the way.

Kinsley had deigned to call them herself. Charlotte hadn't put it like that; Seth had. They'd planned a mellow day of sightseeing leading up to the party at the inn that evening. Seth was anxious to have some time to coordinate plans, sneak in a camera if necessary, wire themselves for sound, planning all along to ask forgiveness before permission and that only if caught. The yacht trip was unexpected.

"She sounded upset," Charlotte said.

"Do you think she knows what we're trying to do?"

"The spying? We're not really doing that are we?"

"There you go, still doing journalism like it has Marquis of Queensbury rules."

"It's just a rush to the bottom with you, isn't it?" Her patience with him was thinning. "But no. It was something else."

"Bobby?"

"Maybe. Anything new online?"

"I didn't get any alerts. They can really block the news, can't they? Total blanket over the most witnessed murder in history. If only there were some plucky journalists out there doing the good work."

"We were hired to do a feel-good documentary about sports. Now you're WikiLeaks."

"The good work."

"If *Jaws* is a social commentary against capitalism," she said, "how much money did it make?"

"Several moneys," he said. "I wrote a paper on it as an undergrad, trying to find deeper layers in a blockbuster. I suggested that the reason it resonated so well was that people instantly understood the politics."

"Yeah?"

"It was total bullshit. I made the case, got a good grade, but always felt sheepish about it. Not that I was wrong. Those layers are there. Politics played a part, in the script and the novel. It holds it together, but the reason it was a hit wasn't that. People really don't give a shit about that. It was because it was an excellent movie. Great actors, great director. They overcame a famously temperamental mechanical shark to start the wholesale slaughter of an entire species."

"Have you always turned everything to politics?"

He pointed to a sign on the front of the fishing shop. *Catch and release or kill. Fish from this area are deemed unsafe for human consumption.*

Charlotte compared the somber sign to the bright trim on the storefront, the carved sign with a happy fish on a hook that spoke of summer seasons and family outings. Suddenly it looked like a bygone era, a mythical age when fish weren't poisoned. She listened for birds and heard none. She listened for human voices and found none. The wind blew gently and cold.

Then in the distance, a ship. It was less than she imagined: a sailboat, one central mast, two triangles of white sail. Nothing like the yachts on the internet with a waterline garage for another boat and jet skis, a helicopter pad that could double as a lacrosse field.

Seth looked disappointed too, but didn't say anything.

Slowly, carefully, the boat maneuvered toward the pier and the pair made their way toward it. They weren't sure it was Kinsley; it was the only thing on the water. And the water was poisonous, Charlotte remembered.

"Ahoy!" called Seth.

Kinsley looked up, saw them, but didn't react. The sails dropped and a motor kicked in with a cough and a cloud of blue smoke.

Diesel exhaust now mixed with the rank breeze from the ocean. Seth could see green algae bobbing in big patches like carrion oil slicks; a strange over-organic scene for dead water, the new fumes appropriate.

Kinsley slid her boat expertly alongside the pier and tossed a rope to Seth, who figured he was supposed to tie it to something. He did, and then she threw him another and the boat was secured. Kinsley paused for a moment, scanned the horizon behind her, around the coast toward the club, held her gaze into the distance before jumping off the boat.

"Thank you both for agreeing to meet me here," she said, strangely formal. "Have you heard from Bobby?"

"Not since... No," said Charlotte.

"I have," she said. "We need to talk." She scanned the pier down to the parking lot, then turned back and took in the boat and the coast around the island. "We'll walk and talk, okay?"

"Good with me," said Charlotte.

Seth nodded and let the women lead. Behind them only a step, he arranged a hidden microphone under his jacket, found the recorder in his pocket, and switched it on.

"I don't know why I'm talking to you," Kinsley said, shaking her head. "It's not like we're friends."

"Sure we are," said Charlotte.

"Pfft," was her response.

"What did Bobby say?" he asked.

"He says he doesn't remember doing it."

"Pfft," was Seth's reply. Charlotte shot him a harsh glance. He ignored it. "Going back to the insanity defense, even after California?"

"Maybe if you two could lose the film you took then," she said.

"The cops took it."

"You have a copy though, don't you?"

"The cops took our film."

She stopped and looked hard at Seth. "You have a copy though, right?"

"So?"

"You could lose it."

"But the police – oh. So, the fix is in then?"

"We're friends."

Seth looked at Charlotte, who didn't react. They walked slowly off the pier, onto a path by the dead beach. The cool wind was constant from the sea. Charlotte fastened the top buttons of her coat.

"Tell us what happened," Seth said. "You suspected something would happen at Indian Wells."

"This between us?"

"Sure," he said.

They stopped at a bench and sat down. Charlotte sat in the middle, so Seth leaned forward for better sound.

"None of us like our parents. It's instinctive. Children are born, and then wait for them to die. They're in the way. It's a question of independence."

"And inheritance," Seth said under his breath, adding louder, "You all feel this way?"

"Of course. Everyone does." She gestured to take in the whole species.

Charlotte thought of her own parents, how she'd broken away, demanded to make her own way, dreaded contact with them, but she didn't want them dead. Of course, they had nothing to offer her dead.

"It's a gag. We joke about it. Everyone does." Again with the wave of inclusion. "Bobby was just so stressed, you see? The joking became real. And he had those headaches."

"What about the headaches?" said Charlotte.

"Stress headaches for the tournament. He said he couldn't hear right."

"But you had it too."

"Not the same, but sure, I was stressed for him. I like Bobby. I care about him. We've known each other since we were children."

"How can you be sure they weren't the same?" Charlotte asked.

"Well, for one, I didn't kill anyone," she said flatly, then added, "but you wouldn't—"

They waited for her to continue but Kinsley instead scanned up and down the walk as if expecting to see someone coming. A car pulling into the parking lot kept her attention, until a family tumbled out and ran to the beach with chairs and sand shovels.

Charlotte, speaking in the soft tones of an intimate friend, asked, "What is it, Kinsley? What's bothering you?"

She looked up and down the paths again. They waited. She took a deep breath, let it out.

"They got it into their heads, you know?"

"Who?"

"My parents. After Bobby, I guess, and Scott, they got it into their heads that I'm trying to kill them."

"Who's Scott?" said Seth.

"A friend in England."

"What happened?"

"Does it matter?"

"Yeah," said Seth with some indignation.

"Seth, chill. She's opening up." Charlotte's glare was dark.

Kinsley said, "His parents died in a hunting accident."

"And he was there?"

"It was an accident," she said. "Shooting birds on the moor. Very gothic. An accident."

"Both—"

"I'm trying to tell you about me," Kinsley said. "My parents. They're freaking out. They think there's a conspiracy. They think I'm going to kill them."

Seth bit his tongue and didn't ask the obvious question.

Charlotte stepped in. "What are they doing?"

"They're following me," she said. "It's why I took the boat. Easier to see if I am being followed."

"Were you?"

"I don't think so, but they may have drones or something. I turned off the GPS."

"Your phone?"

"I have the privacy settings on."

Seth knew those could be broken, but he didn't say anything.

"What are you going to do?" asked Charlotte.

"Stay away from them. I'm flying to Rome in the morning. It'll give them time to come to their senses."

"Is any of this related to Mark Sosa and the Sons of Stone?" said Seth.

"What about him?"

"I heard your gang invited him to a party."

"Who told you that?"

"Did you?"

"Yeah, but it didn't happen."

"Why did you invite him?"

"I didn't. It was Bobby's idea. He thought it would be fun to put a socialist in the middle of us all."

"Bobby's idea?" said Charlotte.

"What happened?"

"We took him out boating and he pissed us off. I mean, he was our guest and he wasn't polite. Real asshole. Called us leeches, among other things. We disinvited him. He went home."

Seth, playing the 'bad cop' in the interview, pressed on with the pointed questions. "Was part of the attraction in having him here that it would piss off your parents?"

Kinsley watched a man walking slowly toward them.

"Was it?"

"Sure. Always fun to do that," she said. "Let's head back to the boat."

They headed back toward the pier.

Seth said, "Are we still invited tonight?"

"Of course."

"Even if we don't lose the tapes we have of Bobby drowning his lawyer?"

Kinsley smiled. "We all do favors for each other. You guys want to come to Italy with me?"

"Really?" said Charlotte.

"Why not?"

"Did you really talk to Bobby?" Charlotte asked.

"Yes."

"I don't think you did," said Seth. "I think you talked to his handlers. Bobby gave us a speech before his show. He seemed to want everyone else to hear it too."

The man following them on the path stopped and sat on the bench they'd vacated, stretching his legs out and tipping his hat over his eyes.

"It was insanity," Kinsley said. "Madness. He didn't plan to kill his parents. It just…"

"Happened?"

"Dammit, Seth, what is your issue?" said Charlotte.

"Sorry," he said, more to Charlotte than Kinsley.

"No, but that's right," Kinsley said. "It just happened. What he told you at the pool – yes, I talked to him – was his later rationalization."

They arrived at the end of the pier again. Kinsley's boat bobbed on the low, wind-driven swell, an orange pennant whipping atop the mast.

"And the second murder?"

"He's not well," said Kinsley. "He needs help. Have you shown the films to anyone?"

"No," said Seth.

"Good. Let's just leave it alone for now. It'll be worth your while. Italy's fun in the spring."

Seth looked at Charlotte. Kinsley followed his gaze.

Charlotte realized then that Seth must be recording all this. He was not making conversation, he was interviewing – no, he was interrogating their host. She felt stupid for not figuring it out sooner. Before she could even think what it meant or how to react to it, she realized too that they were now all waiting for her response to the bribe. Kinsley, who Charlotte actually liked, who for her at least broke the stereotypes of standoffish elites by being warm and approachable, looked on her with caring eyes. They'd all suffered from the horrible events. Bobby was her friend, if not lover. This request was a human reaction to affection. Didn't that count for something? But looking at Seth as they walked, seeing the cynicism in his eyes, she knew he saw it as a test of her journalistic principles.

She was spared the chance to answer.

The flash of light was brief, just enough for them to turn their eyes seaward. Then the noise hit them with a searing shock wave, and knocked them all down.

All was smoke, dust, and din.

Charlotte was slow to rise. She called to Kinsley and then to Seth. Seth was some ways away, staggering toward her through the falling debris. She called again, heard no answer from either and no sound from herself. Her ears were deafened, ringing from the trauma. She covered them but only pushed the noise in closer – a painful screeching she felt in her jaw.

She bent over and helped Kinsley stand up. Her hair was singed.

Seth said something, but she couldn't hear it. Charlotte tried again to speak and heard her voice as if from far away.

Seth was in front of her, combing her hair back, touching her skull, pacing around her in circles, inspecting her.

Kinsley stared at the smoking pier. The foremost of it was gone, the middle, splinters and debris. A cloud of smoke hung in a miasma over the place. Of her sailboat, nothing remained.

Kinsley's chin dropped and raised as if an assent, then again, as if bobbing to an agreeable tune.

Seth turned Charlotte to look at him, held her face in his hands and peered deep into one eye and then the other. He looked relieved and said something, but she still couldn't hear it, distracted as she was by the deep, long, lingering sound that underlaid the blast echo.

Chapter Eighteen

The party would go on.

That was the message from Kinsley. The message had arrived via James, the innkeeper, received by telephone and delivered to them while they sat together in the lobby staring into middle distances.

They absorbed the news in silence, ice melting in their glasses.

Charlotte was the first to speak. "I don't think I've ever seen you ignore a drink for so long before."

He was different. The EMTs said he was in shock, and wanted to take him in for observation, but he'd waved them away. Kinsley had done the same. They didn't offer Charlotte the trip. She might have taken it, but was glad she hadn't. Her insurance wasn't good and if she went, she might have missed the party. She laughed at the thought of it.

Seth turned to look at her.

"I wasn't laughing at you," she said. "Just at how the party must go on."

"What have we gotten ourselves into?"

"The lifestyles of the rich and famous."

"Did you see Kinsley? She was deadpan. Lucid. Clear. Like boats blow up around her all the time."

"Shock. Don't judge."

"Maybe."

"Of course it was."

"What have we gotten ourselves into?" he said again, looking past her to a vase of flowers near the desk.

"Did you get good sound?" she asked.

So she'd sussed it out. "Haven't checked yet. I think so."

"Kinsley will kill you if she finds out you recorded her."

Seth turned to her again, his eyes now sharp.

"Figure of speech," she said.

"What about Italy? Are we taking the bribe?"

"What do you think?"

"I think I asked you the question."

"But I want to know what you think first."

"The Artful Dodger," he muttered.

"Yes."

"So why have a party?"

"Good question, but who's dodging now?"

He knew the question of the bribe, of the party, of Kinsley, and even the near death were all dodges. What was really eating at him, what had surprised him, was Charlotte. Blown in the air, sliding across the asphalt, rolling on his knees, he hadn't thought of himself at all. Finding his feet he'd rushed to her, and the relief when he saw she was alive, when her eyes dilated and she called his name, felt like an orgasm. He'd held her chin, looked at her soot-smeared face, found her deep brown eyes and without thinking told her he loved her.

Thank god she hadn't heard.

"With precious few exceptions, no one even watches documentaries," he said. "With even more precious few exceptions, no one gets rich making them. If we were one of the precious few exceptions, with all that fame and glory and treasure we might hope for, we might be able to afford a trip to Italy."

"A pragmatic answer," she said. "I honestly thought you'd tell me to finish the film."

"You thought I'd forsaken my get-it-while-you-can attitude?"

She shrugged. "I guess so."

He shrugged too, but not dismissively; uncertainly.

"But I will do what you decide," he said. "It's your show."

She met his eyes, saw them still moist. He turned away and found a new window to look out.

"I don't want to decide now," she said.

"Okay."

They had four hours until the party started. Somewhere in the inn, probably in the back clubhouse on the other side, preparations were being made. James was in and out of the lobby frequently, riffling papers, mumbling on a phone, the business of catering.

"An accident?" said Charlotte after a while.

"That'll be the report," Seth answered. He picked up his drink, looked at it, watched a bead of water slide down the glass and put it back. "Faulty fuel line in an old boat. Happens all the time."

"Even when the boat's engine isn't running and it's been moored for an hour."

"Not a whole hour," Seth said. "A little less."

"Oh. Okay, then."

After the initial disorientation, Charlotte had pulled herself away from Seth and ran to Kinsley, picked her up and led her to a patch of grass beside the path. There they sat, watching the smoke swirl and disappear, the ruptured world forgotten in sea breezes and scents of new spring. After a while, the blast-cleared air was again full of noise, another din this, one of wailing sirens and men talking over each other. Charlotte hadn't noticed it, but once her attention was drawn by Kinsley, the sound rushed in on her like water through an open lock.

EMTs threw blankets around them, led them to the back of an ambulance. Gave them water, peeked into their pupils. Firemen wandered up and around, picking up debris, chatting with each other. There were no flames to extinguish, nothing to do really. The tide would do most of the work.

Eventually police and the fire marshal visited them. They were each asked what had happened. None had anything to say except they were talking and the boat went boom.

The fire marshal nodded and said, "Fuel fume ignition. An accident we see all the time. Small craft are known for it. Get a few jet skis going up every year. This one was just bigger. Bigger boat. Good thing you weren't on the boat when it happened. Why weren't you, by the way?"

The question startled Charlotte; it literally made her jump. Seth's hand found hers and squeezed.

Kinsely ignored the question, her eyes on the horizon, her head tilted as if listening for a distant sound.

Halluk pulled up in the Mercedes, got out and stood by the door. Charlotte tried to read his face. She had a hard time focusing and he was wearing sunglasses. She turned to look at Kinsley, who made the thousand-yard-stare look fashionable.

"Halluk is here," she said.

Kinsley turned to see the car and the man.

"I'll call you," Kinsley said before getting into the car and leaving them.

And she left them sitting on the grass, wearing thermal blankets on a bright brisk day.

"Can anyone give us a lift back to the inn?" said Seth.

"I'll get someone," the fire marshal said.

Charlotte forced herself to smile at the official, noting his wrinkles and gray temples. She put him in his late seventies, early eighties perhaps. Old. Healthy, but old. Somehow, that made her queasy.

"The fire marshal surely knew what he was talking about," said Charlotte, her mind returning to Seth at the table. "I mean, he's probably had that job for decades. Half a century, maybe."

"He knew something all right," said Seth.

"Would we feel this way if Kinsley hadn't been paranoid?"

"I'd like to think so," said Seth. "Being journalists and all. Contrary to what the guy said, I don't think explosions happen all the time."

"Maybe he was just trying to keep calm to avoid a panic? Not worry Kinsley."

"Like in *Jaws.*"

"But for real."

"In the book, the mayor had a personal financial interest in downplaying the danger, not just the good of the town. In the movie, he could almost be forgiven for thinking of the townsfolk's bank accounts, but in the book it's all clearly mercenary."

"You're seeing everything on this island through that book."

"And movie. Saw the movie first. I liked it better."

A white panel truck pulled past the window 'McGrath's Fresh Seafood and Catering'.

"Looks like it's going to be a good party."

"Still planning on going?"

"The ride's not over. Or is it?"

"Are you going to sneak in a microphone again?"

Seth nodded. "You should be wired up as well."

"What about cameras?"

"We don't have any sneaky ones. Security footage later perhaps. If there's any. Be nice and gritty."

"Have you thought of just asking Kinsley if we can film?"

"No."

"Do."

"You do it."

"I will."

"So do it."

"What? Now?"

"Party's coming up fast. See how's she's doing. See if the party really is still happening."

"Fine." Charlotte produced her phone and dialed.

Seth took a deep breath. He wasn't sure about the party, about being here, about anything. He felt unmoored. Confused. He was going on, going on hard because it was the open way, the way the momentum had pushed him. He wished Faro were here. He'd be able to put events into some order, probably find some tragic ancient equivalent, find Oedipus in his worry, Lysistrata in his angst. Odin in his unease. The man saw patterns repeating like he was a weaver instead of a reader. Whatever. He wished he were here. He thought to call him. See how he was doing, tell him about boats that go boom and lawyers that don't float. A shark circling them when they needed a bigger boat.

Charlotte rang off her call.

"Not there huh?"

"I talked to her."

Seth hadn't heard a word.

"And?"

"She said she expected us to bring a camera. Wondered at the call."

"Huh."

"It's why the party's being thrown. To get interviews about Bobby."

"I don't think they need a reason to have a party."

Charlotte sighed. "We've got to stop treating these people like they're aliens. Like they're enemies."

Seth didn't answer, but finally tasted his drink. It was watery.

"How's your head?" Seth said finally.

"Ringing is gone," said Charlotte. "Mostly. Yours?"

"Same."

Another truck rolled by. A florist. It disappeared around the building.

"I got the explosion on tape. Also the fire marshal."

"Let's leave that for now. Get our heads straight. We're here to talk about Bobby Weller. What a wonderful guy he is, what might have made him snap."

"Okay. What are you going to wear?"

"Coast casual. You?"

"Jeans. Blue sports jacket. Boating shoes. Might see if I can find a hat with an anchor on it. Blend in."

"Nice."

"Before we get to Bobby, let's consider asking a few questions about Mark Sosa."

"Why do you think he's still involved? He was here for a joke and the joke didn't even happen."

"A hunch." Seth would like to say more, but didn't know himself. The activist's name had cropped up both in his personal and professional life. His student, his son, his friend, and his subject. "A counterpoint maybe? Or the source of Bobby's insanity?"

"You just want a trip to South America. Isn't that where Sosa is?"

"Somewhere down there, yeah. Could take a long time finding him. We'll need our shots."

"Glad to see you back to your normal self."

"Oh yeah, no amount of murder and attempted murder can divert me from my selfishness."

"And why do you think that is?"

"I am a modern man."

Chapter Nineteen

The smell was of exotic and living things, fleshy plants, rich earth, floral perfumes. Seth knew not their names, but recognized they were all beautiful, all colorful, all out of season, and all out of place in New England. What he'd have called a clubhouse that morning was now a ballroom, transformed by the tasteful use of money in decoration and ambiance. A band played modified chamber music in a corner but was ready to rock later if the waiting strobe lights and warming fog machines were any clue.

The partygoers were all young. Seth measured them between sixteen years old and twenty-eight. This was the crowd once made infamous by Paris Hilton. She'd aged out of it, but this was them now. Represented here were the richest and most powerful families in the country, if not the western world. Their faces were unknown outside themselves, their worths unspoken for etiquette, their power felt across the globe. Their families' power at least. Seth was by far the oldest guest there, though some of the waitstaff were older. He'd never seen such disciplined servers in his life. They moved like whispers between the guests, delivering drinks and shrimp and vanishing before you looked again. They were invisible functions among these powerful children, for that's how Seth saw them. He hated to feel old, knew he wasn't, not really, but compared to this crowd of the powerful and beautiful people in their prime, he felt like a fossil.

Charlotte moved freely among them, though she was as out of place as Seth. For her it was not the age – she fit in perfectly – but her color that set her apart. She was beautiful, chestnut dark, but even against the most expertly tanned among the elite, she was a shadow. A more Caucasian party Seth had never been to that was not some kind of Mormon family reunion. Speaking of which, Seth could not help but notice certain similarities in the features of these people. Many of them were surely related, cousins once, twice, thrice removed. The aristocracy is an incestuous group in every sense of the word.

Still, Charlotte, beautiful Charlotte in the prime of her life, lovely and bright, the day's horror behind her, smiled and warmed these strangers with her eyes. They knew to expect her, talked freely to her, though Seth could not tell about what. He hoped she was getting good material, and hoped also that she wouldn't be hurt by these people. Seth instinctively feared them, saw them perhaps through the lens of his own failures, or maybe through some Marxist book or tragic headline. Whatever it was, it showed them to him clearly as spoiled little shits, the peak of self-centered entitlement. Sixteen-year-olds with martinis. Double-murdering athletes who're sure to walk, even after the crime was televised to the galaxy.

"Get me a drink," he said to a passing waiter. "Something strong."

"Flavor?"

"Whiskey."

The waiter left and Seth hated himself instantly. He'd promised himself he wouldn't drink. He'd be sharp for this visit into the lion's den, this class dance he had to make. He had to be alert to lies, find the seams, get the proof for whatever it was this was.

The drink came before he could complete his self-loathing, an unfamiliar but excellent bourbon. He wanted to ask what it was, but stopped himself. Act like you've been there, he told himself. Don't show how common you are.

As the heat found his veins, he felt much better. To have an edge, he needed a drink. He was a drunk after all; not an alcoholic. Alcoholics go to meetings. He giggled to himself at the old joke.

"Enjoying the party?"

It was Innkeeper James.

"Not really."

"I'm sorry. Anything I can do?"

"Not and stay out of jail," he said.

James smirked. "After the hors d'oeuvres, we'll have a light salad. Anyone who wants more can order off the menu."

"Salad, eh? Just like my old frat days."

"You were in a fraternity?"

"Fuck no," said Seth.

James nodded. "They like salad. This will be a rare one. Some of the ingredients are as hard to find as dodos."

"The extinct bird?"

"Taste it while you can." There was no mirth in James's voice.

James made to leave, but Seth leaned in and spoke softly to him. "Tell me who are the real fuckers here," he said.

The innkeeper pulled back. "I wouldn't—"

Seth's stare cut him off.

James shrugged. "The cluster to the right of the stage. Those are the children of the insurance company I told you about. The tall one and his sister are the children of the owner of this establishment."

"What are their names?"

"Chad, Mercer, Devlen, and the siblings are Theodore and Theodora."

"You're kidding."

"No," he said. "Enjoy your drink. It's Miller and Son's Kentucky bourbon 1855. Only two barrels left in existence after tonight."

★   ★   ★

Charlotte had a splitting headache and Seth was making it worse. There he was across the room talking to James. His job was to get close to the guests, not the waits.

"Bobby would never do anything like that," said a woman called Aristra with a soft Southern drawl. "I wonder if the whole thing wasn't some kind of *Star Wars* special effect."

"I think he was drugged," said David Joseph, heir to a real estate empire. "That guy he was playing was some kind of foreigner. I bet he poisoned Bobby's water."

"He played Ivano Madic," Charlotte said. "But I think they tested everything for drugs."

"You can bribe people to cover that up. Or maybe it's a new drug. I know Russians. They play dirty over there."

"And we don't?" This was a girl called Priss who wore a pink-sequined dress that flared out in Fifties style and nearly found her knees. She seemed to be the rake of the bunch, playful and teasing. "Remember when those three boats sank before the regatta?"

David Joseph gave her a stare and a wry grin. "We're talking about tennis, Priss. About Bobby. We have to help out our chum."

"Chum? Like in *Jaws*?" Seth had arrived just in time to embarrass Charlotte.

"Oh, he has arrived," said David Joseph.

"You hear what happened to Kinsley?" was Seth's retort.

"Shameful," he said.

Priss stepped back and made a show of looking Seth up and down, squinting and turning her head as the music found a faster tempo. "You're not half bad in a rugged artist kind of way," she said.

Charlotte felt her face grow hot and then caught herself noticing it.

"Thank you," said Seth. "Are you eighteen yet?"

She laughed. "I will be soon."

"One year or two?"

"Two. But who's counting?"

"What do you think happened to Kinsley's boat?" Charlotte said directly to Priss.

"Her parents blew it up," she said without missing a beat, but her gaze fell away from Seth.

"Why?"

"They think she's trying to kill them."

"Why would they think that? Because of Bobby?"

"My old man thinks the same thing," said David Joseph. "He's written me out of the will if he dies by any unusual circumstance."

"Oh my God," said Aristra. "What if he falls off a bridge or his arches fall?"

"I'm not worried," said David Joseph. "It's hard to argue when you're dead. If possession is nine tenths of the law, living is ten tenths over the dead. Hard to get good council from the grave. Or a cell."

"A cell?"

"Daddy's recent paranoia proves he's out of his mind. I'm having him committed."

Charlotte waited for the punchline. It didn't come.

Aristra smiled. "You'll inherit early then?"

David Joseph winked at her. Charlotte felt her skin crawl. She looked at Seth, who downed his drink. Held it up and had it replaced in a moment.

"Seth, you had a question," she said.

"Did I? Oh, yeah, could some of you sit down with us for a chat about Bobby after dinner?"

"Absolutely."

"Of course. But you'll have to dance with me," said Priss, adjusting her top. A nipple flashed in Seth's direction, causing her to giggle.

Charlotte felt her hands begin to shake.

"Is this new?" said Seth to David Joseph. "The paranoia?"

"With Daddy? Assuredly so."

"What about the desire to kill your parents?"

Charlotte had to turn away. Between the strange jealousy she was feeling toward Priss and the social savagery of Seth's demeanor, she felt adrift.

Aristra and David Joseph stared at Seth. Priss cocked her head and said, "It's something to do while we're waiting for them to die. We don't act on it, well not usually." She giggled and pantomimed a backhand tennis stroke. "But we do talk about it. Not much else to do with the old farts but talk about them. They live too long. Sometimes they spend all the money. Remember Barb? Ponzi-schemed to middle class. Wonder what happened to her."

"Sounds like she fell into the middle class," said Seth.

"Yeah. I guess that's it."

"Did you talk about this with Bobby?" Charlotte asked tentatively.

"I think so," said Priss.

Aristra said, "We definitely did, right before Bobby went to California. We all suddenly had the same thought. All of us at once. It was strange. Morbid. We laughed about it. Forgot what brought it up."

"Was there a sound involved?" asked Charlotte. "Maybe a headache?"

"You know—"

"There's our host," said David Joseph.

Kinsley was on the threshold, a step inside the room. She'd gone formal in a long scarlet dress that lapped her heeled ankles but slit up her left thigh. Paisley-patterned sparkles caught the light near her calves, as did the diamonds around her throat, framed in a plunging V neckline, all this held up by spaghetti straps over smooth bare shoulders. Her hair was done simply, accentuating her diamond-studded ears. Her lipstick matched her dress, red and deep; her eyes drew others to them in lines and shade.

"Leave it to her to say casual and come like that," Priss said, shaking her head.

Indeed, all eyes were on Kinsley. Stealing a glance, Charlotte saw that the men all wore smiles, the women, smirks. The staff, stone. James, the innkeeper, from where the food was being laid out, stared. Charlotte tried to read him; his expression was intense and sad. As if sensing her looking at him, he turned to see her, and when their eyes met, she jumped.

"Seth," she said, pulling his gaze from Kinsley.

"Yes?"

"She looks great, doesn't she?"

"She is pretty, but that's not what I'm looking at."

"What are you looking at?"

"A different woman. This is what? The fourth Kinsley we've seen?"

Charlotte shook her head.

"The first was who we initially met, second was the paranoid one this morning, third the shocked girl at the pier. How would you describe this one?"

"Pleased with herself?"

Seth nodded. "She glows. Who has that kind of confidence in a normal situation, let alone one like today?"

"We all handle stress differently," she said. The music slid to dinner-worthy background and conversation slowed.

Kinsley melted into the party, smiles, quips and laughs.

Seth went over to her. "You're looking well," he said. "We were worried about you."

"No need to worry."

"Any news on the boat?"

"Oh, it's totaled," she said and laughed.

"Kinda figured that when it was vaporized."

"Have you met Chad?" she said, introducing a tall blond child to him and then floating into the crowd.

"Hello. I'm Seth Lian."

"You want to talk about Bobby, isn't that right?" He was probably twenty, maybe twenty-five, with miraculous skin care. "I knew him."

"Yes. I'm trying to get a feel from where he came from."

"He's not your everyday kind of bloke," he said. "We went to—"

"Excuse me." Seth left Chad midsentence and caught up with Kinsley before she joined the line for food. He took her arm and pulled her aside. She stared at his fingers like they were mold.

"Something's happened," said Seth to her. "What is it?"

Charlotte was by him now. "Are you making a scene, Seth?"

He removed his hand, but kept his eyes on Kinsley.

Taking in the two before scanning for anyone nearby, Kinsley whispered, "Self defense."

It didn't register until Charlotte saw the expression on Seth's face.

Kinsley gave them a little pucker and then melted into the crowd.

"Oh God…" said Seth.

"Who's—?"

"Time for another drink," he said. "You hungry?"

"I don't know."

Seth collected a salad plate for her and raised his empty glass above his head. It was taken by a waiter who said simply, "The same?"

"Yes, please."

"Charlotte, Seth." James came around the table to them. "I want to show you something."

He took Charlotte by the arm in some formal pantomime of dance, set her plate aside, and promenaded around the table. Seth followed.

He led them outside behind the hall and down a path through dark trees, the night air moist and chill. Charlotte shivered through her dress. Seth took off his jacket and draped it over her shoulders. A waiter tracked them down and gave Seth his drink before returning up the path.

"This is superb whiskey, by the way," Seth said.

"Glad you like it."

They arrived at a small greenhouse and James threw open the door. The fall smells were breezed away by warm fragrance flowing out of the greenhouse like a breath. James switched on a light and fluorescents flickered alive. They shuffled inside.

"Here's where I cope," James said.

Here was the source of the beauty in the other room. Though many stalks were bare, recent cutting for the current party, some blossoms remained. Vines snaked over lattices in blue and yellow cups, spikes of flowers, orchids, and clusters. Beans and peas. Potatoes and lettuces – rare and unidentifiable.

James behind them, the two stood for a long moment taking it all in, smelling the succulent sweetness, the earthy bitterness of soil and fertilizer, the strange moving air that wafted it all around.

"What are those?" Seth pointed to several potted saplings under a bench.

"That is a Honduran Rosewood. The other is Florida Yew. The yew's doing a lot better."

"Are they edible?"

"No. They're endangered."

"And these?"

"Rare lettuces. Those came with the house. My dad grew them. I added the trees, the Calibar beans, the yellow jasmine, white baneberry, and horse chestnuts. Aren't they lovely? I've been waiting for the right time to—"

His watch went off in a bright alarm.

"Oh. Here. Help me with this," he said. He pointed to a crate by the door. Seth opened it. A large bronze gong lay inside.

"Would it be too rude of me to ask you to hold that for me? It's a special surprise for the guests."

"Sure," said Seth, shrugging his shoulders. He drained his glass and set it down and took up the gong. It was pounded copper, bright and orange, and hung on light chains from a horizontal bar, about eighteen inches wide.

James collected a padded mallet from the box and rubbed his temples before leading Seth and Charlotte back toward the hall.

The pain had not appeared in Charlotte's head, but it registered. She felt the makings of a migraine. The edges of her eyesight closed in ever so much and a distant humming could just be imagined beyond the silence of the night.

James arrived at the door first and held it open.

"Your luggage is all packed," he said. "There's a car waiting at the front door that'll take you to a plane." He waved them in.

They entered behind the serving table, Charlotte first. Her head swam in a rising hum, a throbbing chord, rising, rising. Her eyes were hazy and only slowly could she focus upon the salads, upon the beans and leaves, the blossoms and seedy dressings. The noise at once crested and fell away. It was this inner quiet unreplaced by any outer that made her look up. She was five steps in before she halted.

"Hold it up high," James said to Seth, who stood dumb beside him.

The waitstaff all stood stock-still, trays in hands, unfocused stares, expressionless faces absorbing the scene. There were twelve of them. They were easy to count. They were the only ones upright.

Beneath them, sprawled in clumps of sudden death, were the children of the aristocracy, their bodies twisted in paralysis, their breaths stilled in silent shrieks, their eyes unbelieving and dark.

James swung the mallet and the gong resonated across the room like judgment itself.

"Time's up, motherfuckers!" he announced.

Part Two

Events

Chapter Twenty

The regents had asked to see them, but in the week they'd been back at Commondale, returned to Oregon from the 'dead coast' as they'd called it in their stupor on the plane home, their appointment had twice been moved. Charlotte suspected it had something to do with the Weller family. Seth was sure it was because the police were looking for them and the powers that be were waiting for greater powers to be done with them.

The mass killing had not gone unnoticed. It was a cause célèbre for a couple of news cycles, more than most mass murders. It brought out herds of gun nuts who basked in having a slaughter not be linked to their fetish. 'Young people killed by disgruntled workers' was the main headline. The pain this caused the powerful was private, a thing not for public consumption, their existence as a class was practically a state secret, only occasionally sliding into fashion or gossip magazines teasing the rabble with their opulence. At least that's how Seth figured it. They'd mourn in their own way. If they mourned at all. Seth wasn't so sure.

Among the victims blamed on James the Innkeeper were the Carreaus, Kinsley's parents, whose bodies were found the next day along with their private secretary, Mr. Halluk. All had been shot point blank with a small-caliber weapon that had yet to be found or identified.

The innkeeper was locked away and undergoing psychological examination. His staff all claimed ignorance, though Seth knew better and bet the authorities did too. They claimed to have been shocked and watched in horror as it happened. None had moved to help. No one had called the police, an ambulance – anything. It had been a delivery man with fruit tortes who'd done that well after Seth and Charlotte were gone. The eyewitnesses all said they'd been too 'dismayed' to act. Who says dismayed?

The shock went beyond the emotional. The clearest indication that the murders at The Cozy Visit Bed and Breakfast Inn were a bigger deal than eight score dead children – Seth still saw them as children – came in the form of a major sell-off of stocks. An unprecedented crash in the market requiring five interventions was chalked up to randomness, Reddit, and general unease as the leadership of venerable institutions fell into doubt and fund managers bailed as fast as they could in the uncertain future. Seth read the financial sections of a dozen newspapers online, and tracked names that few in his income bracket had ever heard of. He found two alarming things. First, most of the huge corporations in the country – hell, the world – had a sick incestuous relationship between their boards of directors. Magnates from one billion-dollar concern would sit on the board of a dozen others, while their own board was populated the same. Many entities with just a few hot bodies running them all. The second thing Seth realized was there were decidedly fewer hot bodies now than there had been before. Cold they were now, cold. And dead. Recent. Killed. In keeping with their paranoid privacy, details were scant, but the pattern was clear and the shaken financial world reeled from it whether they could pinpoint the cause or not.

Charlotte for her part retreated and sought not to think about anything. She was just glad to be home. Glad she didn't have to see Seth every day, though she wasn't sure why. She was not at all surprised the regents wanted her head. She'd be happy to give it to them. She didn't feel well. She was eating aspirin like they were Tic Tacs and not sleeping. Her ears rang constantly. She tried to get an appointment with a psychologist at the school clinic, but was told they were unusually busy, bizarrely so. The soonest appointment was three weeks away. There was a waiting list if she wanted on that, but it too was quite long.

She was raw. Her emotions were a mess, her feelings and sensibilities dragged across gravel. The nightmares she'd been witness to had been the shock to stir up the unsettled muck of her mind. Her father's illness had only occupied a corner of her thinking, a dark spot of guilt amid the horror of death. She regretted the relationship she had with her parents, but couldn't think of what she could have done differently. The tension gripped her, and with some swirl of the mud which was her life now, she saw that her ignoring Seth was directly related to her parents.

It wasn't the man personally; it would have been anyone. He was just the only man in her life in any capacity. Her parents naturally looked for it to be a romantic relationship, or on the way to one. It's all they wanted for her. Success and offspring. They were old fashioned, in an eighteenth-century mentality. They vexed her. She never understood how they could have lived their lives in the twenty-first century and still hold such archaic values. It was retrograde. It was simple. Biological. It was the lowest common denominator and she knew, though her parents would deny it – had denied it – that if she had been male, their goals for their offspring would have been greater than reproduction.

Their years of pressure, subtle and engulfing, defined her relationship with them, so that she now had a marked aversion to any romantic adventures at all. She'd even considered becoming a lesbian but learned she didn't lean that way. Abstinence was the course. Maybe one day she'd have a mate, but children were out of the question. This world didn't need another person, and that person sure as hell didn't want to come down here.

And so she'd pushed Seth away, consciously at first, for want of healing, and subconsciously of late, because of her parents.

Seth, on the other hand, thought about her a lot. He worried that he'd broken her. He was not upset when the regents postponed their meeting for yet another week until after midterms. Not having any classes to teach, Seth could have stayed home but the place was oppressive and he drank too much there.

It was two weeks since they'd been back that he ran into Charlotte in the cafeteria.

"So, next week for the regents?" he said.

"Looks like."

"What have you been up to?"

"Working on my alternate doctorate thesis."

"Your what?"

"For graduation."

"You think they'll kill the project?"

Charlotte made a surprised face. "It is killed," she said. "And that word is most appropriate."

They ate in silence a while. Charlotte ate unselfconsciously, Seth chewing and thinking.

"I've been doing a little digging, by the way. Seeing what's what, researching possible—"

"The project is dead," she said. "The documentary was done the minute Bobby went into the stands."

"I know. I just don't want to give up yet."

"There's nothing to give up. It's not our choice."

"It might be."

"No."

"I bought this lunch off Bobby's credit card," Seth said. "It's still working."

"You're too much."

"Poor man's gotta get by. And this…project still has places to go."

"Maybe it does, but I'm not sure I want to go there to find out."

"I get that," Seth said.

"But…" she offered.

"But…?"

"You want to say, I'm not acting very journalistically."

"I was just going to say that we have more leads."

"Sosa?"

"He's a big one. But we could at least do background on the island thing."

"The island thing? That's some soft-pedaling there."

He said, "I'm trying to keep it in perspective, trying to be detached. I can do that sometimes. I'm kinda shocked I'm doing it as well as I am now."

"Good for you. I'm not so evolved."

"Sorry, I'm pushing again."

She shook her head. "It's all you do." There was a finality in her voice.

He took a bite of his sandwich, picked a sesame seed from his teeth. "How goes the alternate thesis?"

"Sucks. I haven't even decided what it'll be on. I'm committing myself to another year while I figure it out."

"Charlotte, even if we don't get any further footage, we can still put together something they'll take."

She shook her head.

Seth tapped his finger on the table for emphasis. "After what you've been through, they should give you the degree on principle."

"That's not how it works."

"That's exactly how it works," he said. "You think there's some objective criteria for this shit? It's all political. We have only to get ourselves out there a little more and they won't dare—"

"We?"

"We. We can edit what we have. We don't even have to leave the campus. We have hours of footage. We can conclude at Indian Wells, if you like. Show the sudden…incident, and leave the viewer pondering after seeing all the background on pure Bobby Weller."

"Kinsley would have liked that." There was a hitch in her voice.

"Hell, we can take it to Sundance."

She stared into her salad.

"Don't make any decisions now," he said. "Let's see what the regents say, then we'll decide what we can do."

"Don't you mean the regents will decide what we do?"

"No. I don't."

She chased a tomato across her plate with a fork. "You're a pain in the ass."

"Thanks."

"I didn't mean it as a compliment."

"Too late."

A little smirk, it was all he could hope for.

"Hey, you know what? We need a party. Tomorrow night, let's invite a few friends over to my place and we'll drink good beer and bad whiskey and play faculty team building."

"Faculty? So we get the school to pay for it?"

"That's a good idea."

She made the sour face again.

Seth said, "I want to invite Barney, Barney Faro. You haven't met him and I want you to. He's the most interesting person in the room, but still cool."

"Being smart can make you uncool?"

"Can't it?"

She smiled. She liked being with Seth.

"Okay," she said. "Why not?"

"Good. It's a date."

She blanched.

"A date for the party. Not that kind of date."

"Okay."

"Unless you wanted that kind of date."

She gave him her *very funny* look, but he held his serious one. Her heart skipped.

"Really, just a faculty bender. I used to be famous for them."

"What happened?"

"Someone died."

Chapter Twenty-One

Seth sat in his shared office knowing that he should go home and clean up the place for the party, but he tarried. He looked at the wall of books, the papers Finn had left ungraded. He listened to a bird sing outside the building, remembering when there'd been a cacophony of them and not the single one now. He'd found himself in a place of woolgathering, and damn it all, creeping self-pity. He felt old. He felt every one of his forty-six years on him like mud, thinking of the young Charlotte and her life ahead of her, wondering if she'd go as far astray as he had, thinking he should leave her alone and free her of his influence.

So many years of blur, drink and blur, hiding and blur. Chances squandered, not for failing them, but in failing to even try. He lit a cigarette and glanced at his watch, ready to calculate how long it would be before someone followed the smell and reminded him of the no-smoking building policy.

Travis came to mind. The next step of his biological existence. As he was an extension of his father and his before, back to Adam, or the slime in the pool, so Travis was his. Biologically, Seth had done all he had to do. He was theoretically exempt now, retired from the species. Anything he did with himself now didn't really matter since he'd fulfilled the procreative imperative. It was an old thought, an old dodge, and it didn't release him from his thoughts as it had in the past.

Missed opportunities with Travis. Missed time. He'd lost the child, but maybe – and here he knew his thoughts reached to fantasy – drew him into some hallucination of hope he had no business to believe. Maybe he could know the man that was his son.

He dug his phone out of his pocket and found the number. Before he could stop himself, for some part of him knew to stop, he'd dialed Travis's phone.

It rang and rang and went to message. He ended the call and called back, letting it ring again to messages, and then did it again. On the third try, his son picked up.

"Hello, Travis. It's Dad. How goes your journey?"

For a response he got a disgusted groan. "Only people who are really fucked up use that phrase."

"Yeah?"

"It's like a last ditch effort to frame their poor choices."

"I see."

"The kind of thing a burnout fresh from rehab might say."

"I thought I heard it somewhere."

"I'm surprised you knew my phone number. I didn't give it to you."

"No," Seth said. "You didn't."

"Then how'd you get it?"

"We know some of the same people, you know?"

"Yeah, okay."

"How goes it?"

"My journey is fine. And none of your business."

"I'd like to hear about it?"

"Why?"

Seth took a deep breath. It was going as it always went, and yet he was once again surprised.

"Travis. I'm your father."

"I think it's great that you think you have to tell me that."

"It seems like I do."

"My life is my own business."

"Fine, your life is your own business. I respect that."

"Then why are you calling me?"

"I just wanted to hear your sweet voice."

That got a laugh from the other side and for a moment Seth had hope, but the laugh turned mean in a hurry.

"Really, what do you want? Money?"

"No. Why would you think that?"

"One of the steps, is it?"

"What— Who do you think I… Travis, just for no good reason, tell me that you're all right."

"I'm doing all right."

"Tell me what you're doing? Are you in school?"

"Are you kidding?"

"You mother didn't tell me."

"You talked to her?"

"No."

"You're too much."

Another sigh escaped Seth. "Travis, how long are you going to be mad at me?"

"How long you got?"

"I'm not even sure why you're so mad."

"Then you're an idiot."

"I did the best I could."

"With what?"

"With everything."

Seth did not think he'd been a 'bad' father. He'd not beaten his son, not deprived him of necessities. He'd been, if anything, lax and let the boy do as he would and find things out for himself. It seemed to be going well until the divorce, then it all fell in on him.

"Fine, you did the best you could. Whoop-de-do. No problems there."

"Then what is it?" He'd take him at his word.

"Just because you're my father, raised me 'the best you could', doesn't mean I have to like you."

"No. But how about love?"

"Typical left-wing drivel. The best thing you ever did for the family was leave."

"No school?" He needed to change the subject. He'd actually heard all this before.

"Throw money at the ivory towers of mental conformity and liberal bias? Hell no. I'm a soldier, not a pansy."

"You've joined the army?"

There was a hesitation. "No."

"What then?"

There was no answer.

"Travis, we can have differences and still be friends."

"Typical."

"Is it politics? Is that the issue?"

"Everything is political."

"What if I told you I wasn't political anymore? Couldn't care less. Not even sure who my senator is."

"I wouldn't care."

"Could we be friends then?"

"No. Hell no. Ignorant and uncommitted is worse than wrong."

"How's that?"

"It's people like you that fucked the world up for me and my generation."

"What about Kyle? He's my generation."

"He fought to stop people like you."

Seth's heat was gathering. "He fought for corporate shills and con artists. I wouldn't say he did your generation any favors."

"Are you kidding? He fought to keep illegals out, stood up to terrorists and the lame-stream media."

"At best he made a political donation. I marched."

"You are an idiot and you make me sick. Nothing is going to be better in this country until we take our country back from the bleeding heart social scum who stole it."

"That sounded rehearsed. Did you learn that at army camp?"

"Fuck you, Seth. Lose my number."

He hung up.

Seth knew what army his son had joined. He'd seen mention of it on his social media. They called themselves a rifle club, but it was a militia and probably on a government watch list.

It was Ellen, of course, and her new husband Kyle that had turned Travis against him. It made the transition of her remarriage easier.

Scapegoats do that. One day Travis would grow out of it. He was still a child. Just barely nineteen. He was still in mourning for the divorce, and the economy, his prospects, the future. People grew out of that, right?

He thought of his own father. Had he ever forgiven him? No. But he'd been a completely different man – abusive, mean. Violent. He had once come looking for money and beat Seth up to get it when he was in college. A different man than he, a different man entirely. The father he swore he wouldn't be with Travis so his son wouldn't have cause to hate him. But hate still happened. He thought of Barney Faro, who he remembered he had to invite to the party. The classicist would tell him, he was sure, that Travis was acting out Oedipus in some psychiatric, if not mythological, sense.

There was nothing Seth could do but wait, hope time would heal whatever wounds Travis thought he had. It might, or it might not. He had to let him go. Son or no, it was out of his hands now.

He put his phone down and tried to think if Barney would be in class or not, then thought it didn't matter. That's what answering machines were for.

"Barney, Seth here. I'm throwing a party tomorrow night. You have to come. I haven't seen you in forever and I have much to tell and need your sick insight. Come at seven. If you can't come, come anyway. Seven. Tomorrow. My place. Party. Ciao."

He hoped he'd put enthusiasm into his voice, thought he had. Barney grounded him. Travis, his son, was a fucker. Sad to admit, but it was true, and Seth said it out loud just to test the veracity. "Travis, my son, is a fucker." Yep, checked out. He laughed, pretending that the matter was so easily dismissed.

He went down his phone contacts looking for prospective partygoers, faculty from the old days who used to come. Students, grads and undergrads. He balked, knowing that they'd probably all moved on. He rifled through a drawer looking for the last faculty extension list the university put out, a quaint printed book with advertising for pizza joints and copy centers. He'd lost his.

He moved to Finn's desk and looked among the papers and mild clutter that his office mate had left.

He thumbed through some of the ungraded sketchbooks. Each was called 'Caravaggio interpretation, David with the head of Goliath', and each had some reimagining of a similar scene of a young boy holding up a huge, severed head. He didn't know the original picture but judging from the similarities, the boy was practically naked, the head was in the left hand, and blood was everywhere. The pictures were upsetting sketches and watercolors, some acrylic, a couple printed computer graphic renderings. All were bloody and red and horrible. He put them down and found the directory in a side drawer and slid it into his pocket, before putting on his coat. The pictures unsettled him, having been already upset by Travis.

Before he left the office, he noticed a big coffee-table book of Caravaggio on Finn's shelf and took it down. From the index he found *David with the Head of Goliath* and turned to it.

The painting, dated 1610, was currently housed in a museum in Rome, which made sense since the painter was Italian. Far from being red, as the students' pictures all were, the original was black with deep Baroque shadows. The boy's body was not naked but had an open shirt exposing half his pale juvenile chest. The head was indeed in the left hand. The youth held a sword, and the head was surely dead with glassy eyes and mouth agape, but there wasn't a speck of blood, not a hint of gore beyond the artistry of stillness. The original was powerful; the students' interpretations, at least the ones he'd seen, didn't even try for the power of the picture. Theirs were more like storyboards for some new slasher film. Glancing back at the sketchbooks on the desk, Seth grew more uneasy and left the office just as a janitor arrived to tell him to put his cigarette out.

"Twelve minutes," Seth said, glancing at his watch. "Getting slack."

"Not a lot of call for enforcement lately," the man said. "Most people understand the rules and abide by them."

Seth glared at the janitor, a young man, middle twenties, short hair, clean overalls. Boots. His eyes looked back at Seth accusingly.

"Sorry," Seth said. "I guess I forgot."

"Of course," he replied. "Could have happened to anyone. It explains why you timed me."

Seth fought an urge to light another cigarette, blow the smoke in the kid's face. Instead, he gave him a curt nod and locked the office door behind him, before finding his way out of the building and into the open air where he chain-smoked all the way home.

Chapter Twenty-Two

Seth texted Charlotte that she should invite anyone 'cool' she knew to the party. She thought about it and couldn't pull any names but then, in a mercenary move that Seth would appreciate, remembered Susan, a nurse friend of hers she'd been meaning to reconnect with. They'd gone through orientation class together back in the day, and hung out for a while, connected by skin darker than the snow that was on the ground then. She dug up the number and sent a text, inviting her to come, offering her vodka and cranberry juice, the classic Cosmopolitan. The reply came back quick, seeking the address and asking if there'd be any eligible non-medical men there. Charlotte promised there would be and agreed to pick her up.

Both Susan's address and Seth's were places she'd never been. Charlotte had never explored the little city. She knew where her place was, the university, shopping. The airport. The rest was just a ways from the other. Seth lived in an old neighborhood, some distance from the school. Susan in a newer one, even farther away.

She pulled into the driveway at seven fifteen, a quarter hour late. She texted she'd arrived and a moment later Susan came out of the right duplex in a tight, short, white dress with plunging neckline and heels that threatened to topple her as she approached. She'd accentuated her dark latin eyes with expert shadow, and teased a brighter than normal lipstick that was a bit untidy just then. As she got in, Charlotte could smell alcohol on her breath under a breath mint, which helped explain the lipstick.

"I am so glad you texted me," said Susan, leaning across the seat to hug Charlotte. "This was looking like another wasted Friday. It's so good to see you."

"It's been a while."

"Too long. Friends are too precious not to hang out with." Susan beamed with rosy cheeks and adjusted her straps. Charlotte pulled out and headed to Seth's.

"I'll tell you something, Susan," said Charlotte.

"Seth Lian? I know all about him. Got the short end of the stick."

"You've met him?"

"Bend is a lot smaller than people think it is, and he used to be very social."

Charlotte always thought the town was pretty darn small. "It was another thing. I contacted you partially because I have a medical question."

"You didn't need to bribe me with a party for a question. God knows I get enough of those from my family. Cousins I never heard of call me up to ask about moles and tummy aches. What do you have going?"

"I tried to get into the clinic at school and they were full up."

"Everyone is full up."

"What?"

"Yeah, you can't get an appointment with most providers right now."

"Headaches?"

She nodded. "I even got one. No one knows what it is."

"Affecting everyone?"

"No. But, you know..."

"What?"

"Enough to worry people, enough to worry about letting the news out for a panic."

"Who's getting it?"

"Younger people mostly. We thought it was flu being spread on campus, but it's everywhere. Take some aspirin. Get plenty of sleep. Relax," she said and drew out the last word in a playful way.

"No idea at all what it is?"

"Well, people are looking into it. The funniest theory I heard had to do with the Taos Hum, if you can believe it."

Charlotte shook her head and squinted at road signs.

"Why don't you just use your phone?" Susan said.

"I'm trying to learn to be more self-reliant. Can you read that sign?"

"Stop."

"Cute."

She made a left onto Pinecrest. "What's the Taos Hum?"

"It's a phenomenon in New Mexico. Some people swear that the town gives off a low hum. Not everyone can hear it. The Emergency Research Center is pursing that idea."

"Emergency Research Center?" said Charlotte.

Susan blanched. "I probably shouldn't talk about that."

"Now you have to."

"Well, I don't know much about it, except our hospital is helping them compile data on the problem. It's some government agency and we're all sworn to secrecy, but really, everyone knows. There's something weird going on."

"The headaches like I have?"

"Some kind of virus, I'm sure. Probably a COVID variant. They say COVID broke the blood-brain barrier. I think that's the direction they should be looking. They probably are, maybe. Just in bigger hospitals and such."

"Should I see a specialist?"

Susan blinked and regarded her friend. "How bad is it? You're driving. Can't be that bad."

"It comes and goes."

"They can't help you. They'll tell you to treat it like a migraine – sleep, drink. Dark rooms. It's a pain in the ass because everyone's freaking out."

"I'm not freaking out."

"No, not you, but I mean if they'd just let everyone know that something was out there, people could self-diagnose. It'd be useful just for people to know they're not suffering alone. Secrecy in a problem."

"Why are they doing it then?"

"The usual. Afraid that people will panic. Want to get a handle on it before it gets complicated."

"A sound, huh?"

"Or orbital mind-control lasers," she said. "But it really is probably just a COVID variant. Get your jab."

"I got it."

"Good girl."

The house wasn't much to look at but there were more cars on the street than the street wanted.

They parked, got out, and snaked their way through the line of cars to a sidewalk which they followed down a carport to a basement door on the side of the house. The main floor was dark and silent. Light and music seeped out from below. Charlotte went to knock but Seth opened the door before she could.

"Hello," he said. His face was bright, ruddy. The sweet smell of sinsemilla wafted around him, the music was low and soothing, the vibe immediately welcoming. "And I know you."

"Susan Alvarez," said Susan, offering Seth her hand.

"Of course. Come in."

Seth stepped aside to reveal a surreal scene of hippy flashback. Colored bulbs had replaced regular ones and made kaleidoscope pools on what had to be tawdry furniture. A black light on one wall lit up a kitschy felt poster of a galaxy. The place looked and smelled like a hippy den or retro head shop.

"Beer, wine or punch?" said Seth. "Herb is in the convo-nook."

"Jesus, Seth," said Charlotte. "Even you are too old for this Sixties stuff."

"Consider it an homage, a pastiche, an act of reverence to a time before when young people sought to change the world."

Susan said, "What's in the punch?"

"Just alcohol," Seth said. "No electric Kool-Aid tonight."

In the kitchen, a bearded man with glassy eyes filled a red plastic cup with red beverage.

"What does that even mean?" said Charlotte.

"Acid in the punch bowl."

"God," she said. "People did that?"

"A dollar a drink."

She hugged Seth like old friends re-met, all made up. They both held on to each other a moment or two longer than necessary. Both recognized it, and both approved.

They broke reluctantly, but then each took half a step back. Seth had a gleam in his eye and color in his cheeks. Charlotte looked past him into the small apartment. "Introduce me," she said.

"Sure thing," he said, offering her his arm. "I'm Seth. I'll be your host tonight."

"Cute."

"You know Susan."

She waved and smiled behind her cup.

"That's Finn and...Jannis, is that right?" She nodded. Seth said, "I share an office with Finn. He teaches art history or some such nonsense."

"I heard that," he said.

Jannis stood up from the couch and approached. She had long, straight brown hair and a pale European complexion. "I'm studying political science," she said. She couldn't have been twenty-four.

"Hello. I'm Charlotte."

"Maybe you can help with the argument."

"What is it about?"

"Patriarchal hegemony."

"What else?" This spoken by the last man to be introduced.

"That's Barney Faro," said Seth. "The guy I told you about."

The man nodded at her and lowered his gaze to look over his thick-rimmed glasses. He looked every bit the stereotypical academic, mussed curly hair, graying, jacket with actual leather elbows, comfortable shoes with worn soles. He even had a pipe in his mouth. Charlotte had to smirk.

"And that is Lucy with Barney."

A short girl with short hair and squinty-framed glasses waved from beside him. Charlotte figured her to be barely drinking age, but even sitting down Charlotte could see that she carried herself with a certain confidence that spoke of experience and hardship.

"What are you studying?" asked Charlotte. She accepted an offered cup of punch from Seth.

"I'm working," she said. "I manage Which Brews on Pine Avenue."

"Getting a jump on the job market?" said Jannis in a tone that quieted the room.

The awkward moment was broken by Seth bringing more cups of punch into the parlor.

"Now, now," he said. "Let's not let the booze do the talking."

Charlotte hid behind her drink. It was double-sweet punch with a kick of something strong. Not vodka. Something else.

"What's in this?"

"Don't you like it?" said Seth.

"Don't answer a question with a question," said Barney.

"My conscience has spoken. It's Kool-Aid and Everclear. For old times' sake."

"What times are those?" asked Susan.

"Misspent youth," said Seth.

Jannis and Finn exchanged a look that made Charlotte a little angry. She was quick to see condemnation in it, a judgment of the event that defamed her friend. It was rude, especially since they were his guests.

"What did Seth tell you about me?" asked Barney.

As a counterpoint, she found Barney and Lucy pleasant and real.

"Just that you'd have some insight into…"

"What?"

"What's been going on," said Seth.

"What we saw," corrected Charlotte.

She found a ripped padded chair at the head of the little group. On her right were Finn and Jannis on a settee. On her left Barney and Lucy on a sofa. Seth pulled out a couple of kitchen chairs and took one near Charlotte. Susan planted herself next to Finn but watched Seth.

"It's bigger than what we saw," Seth said.

"What did you see?" asked Jannis.

"The tennis thing," said Charlotte.

Jannis shook her head.

"The murder at Indian Wells."

"Oh," she said. "Everyone saw that."

"They were at the stadium," said Barney. "And they were also in Cape Cod."

Jannis shook her head again.

"I was telling Barney and Lucy about what we'd been through," explained Seth. "Before you got here."

"Are we going to finish our earlier conversation?" asked Jannis.

"No," said Seth.

Jannis responded with a sulky smirk.

"So?" said Susan. "What?"

"All the violence," Seth said. "It's everywhere."

"Welcome to patriarchal America," said Jannis.

Lucy rolled her eyes.

"There's violence everywhere. It's nothing new," said Susan.

"This strikes me as something new," said Seth.

"Not new at all," said Barney.

"No, there's something about it. It's not the run of the mill."

"I didn't say it was run of the mill," said Barney. "I said it's not new. In fact, it's so old we have myths about it."

"What do you mean, Professor?" asked Charlotte.

"Oh, god. Call me Barney. Please."

"Of course."

"Who has fire?" Barney lifted his pipe. Seth tossed him a lighter.

Barney lit the bowl, took a deep puff, and passed the pipe to his left. Lucy took a hit, offered it to Jannis and when she wouldn't even look at it, gave it to Finn who took the embers and gave it to Susan. "Well, this party is off and running," she said, and took a deep drag before finding herself in a coughing fit.

Charlotte passed the pipe untouched to Seth, who took a small toke, out of politeness she thought.

"It's myth. It's legend. It's religion," said Barney, knocking out the ashes onto a paper plate. "Let's begin with Cronus."

Chapter Twenty-Three

"You've been to the mountaintop," began Barney.

"You're going to appropriate Martin Luther King, now?" said Jannis.

"Chill," said Finn. "Seth, bring Jannis another drink."

"Double," she said.

"I'm on it." He retreated to the kitchen but kept his ears open. He'd told Barney about the killings, explained in quick detail the horror and the repetition. First the tennis match, then the house in Bel Air and then the mass murder in New England on the heels of the killing of Kinsley's parents. He'd invited his friend over early for just that reason. He desperately wanted to have his input, but after he'd finished his descriptions, before he could respond, Finn and Jannis arrived and then Charlotte and Susan. Barney had listened intently, asking no questions but absorbing the information like a collating computer. Lucy had listened to the whole thing with interest, asking a couple of notable questions, like how they expected to get away with it, and who raised these kids.

Seth regretted telling him once the party got rolling, the drinks served, the conversation open, and had thought to leave it alone for the night, just try to relax, give Charlotte some respite, but it wouldn't leave him. Jannis's earlier feminist rhetoric had opened the night up to heady subjects and it was at the center of Seth's thinking, so he'd brought it out and was pleased to see Barney prepared, as he knew he would be, to answer in the professorial fashion his friend was famous for.

Jannis's drink arrived and Finn said, "Now behave. Barney has the conch."

"No, it's all right," said the humanities teacher. "She's right. It was a shit connection. What I meant to imply is the seats of power.

The mountain being where the rich and powerful lurk, not the noble mountain of enlightenment, which I assume was MLK's vision."

"Apology accepted," said Jannis.

Charlotte cringed. Susan gave Seth a look. Charlotte cringed some more.

"That's where I got the idea, anyway," said Barney. "The places of power. Parliaments and Congress supposedly now, before that royal courts, before that, temples. Then, dare we go back as far as Olympus?"

"Why not farther?" said Jannis.

"Okay, let's do that. Before Olympus. What was before Olympus?"

"You're not going to do the *ask questions of the class to keep them involved* schtick, are you?" said Lucy. "Read the room."

Barney said, "Everyone's got my number tonight."

Lucy bent over and gave him a peck on the cheek.

"Was there anything before Olympus?" asked Charlotte.

"Yes. There was a whole group of gods, or god-like things bigger than gods before Zeus, Apollo, Hera and the gang showed up. The Titans."

"Were they big?" said Susan.

"I guess so. They were the only show in town. Rulers of everything, but they were overthrown by their children, this even after being warned that it would happen."

"Who warned them?" asked Finn.

"I think it was Gaia – wait, which reminds me. We didn't go back far enough. I blame the smoke. It's fogged my brain a little."

"Who knew it could do such a thing?" said Jannis. "What?" she said in reaction to the looks she got. "It's why I don't use it."

"Okay, so the Titans were actually the second generation, the gods the third. The first was Uranus and Gaia, the sky and the earth. They had lots of kids, not just Titans, but monsters and stuff. Nymphs and things."

"You haven't connected it to what we saw," said Charlotte. "Seth was pretty sure you could."

"I can," said Barney, taking a sip. "It's good too. You'll like it."

"I'm not sure we will," said Seth. He'd heard a tone in Charlotte's voice that said they were on thin emotional ice. He wondered if he should change the subject.

"Okay, get this. Gaia, as I remember it, didn't like how her husband ran things, so she got her son Cronus, the biggest Titan, to castrate him and take over rulership of the universe. This he did with a sickle, an unlikely weapon today. A tennis racket seems more modern."

"What? You're suggesting that Bobby Weller's mother set him up to kill his father? She died too."

"Okay, it doesn't fit right yet, I just thought I'd start drawing connections."

"You're high," said Susan. "But I like it. I always thought ancient history was quaint."

"The thing is," said Barney, "after you study it for a while, after you get decades under your belt, you realize ancient history was last week. Much closer than you imagine. It's kinda spooky."

"Cronus," said Charlotte, keeping him on task. "The god of time?"

"Yeah. He'd have some connection with Kali too then."

"What brought that up?"

"A book I just read. *What Immortal Hand*. Kinda hinted at all this."

"Stay with the Greeks," said Seth.

"Gaia cursed her son to suffer the same fate as his father, to be overthrown by his children. I guess she had second thoughts about the change. Cronus took the curse literally. He and Rhea, who I think was his sister – would have to be, right? – had kids, but every time she gave birth, Cronus was right there and he ate them up. Nummy nummy, ate all his children. Gnash gnash, gobble gobble…"

"I'm glad we're talking myths here," said Jannis.

"Myths are always based in reality."

"Let's not go there."

"The idea, though," said Seth. "That's what you're getting at, the overthrow of the father."

"Exactly. Rhea got sick of having her offspring served as hors d'oeuvres, and with Gaia's help, finally swapped one of the kids out for a rock. Zeus was that kid. Cronus swallowed the swaddled rock, not noticing that it wasn't meat, and went on his merry way. Rhea hid Zeus away and when he grew up, he teamed up with a bunch of monsters, and made Cronus puke up the others he'd eaten, and then exiled old dad to Tartarus where he and the other Titans lay imprisoned probably to this day."

"Surprised he didn't just kill him," said Finn.

"Why didn't he?"

"Well, now that you mention it, let's look at that. I think it plays into what I'm talking about. First, we could say that Titans being so close to the source couldn't be destroyed. Like Uranus and Gaia, their existence was necessary. But I don't think so, because Zeus showed mercy in what he did, which suggested that he could have done worse. Which brings us to the Old Testament."

"It's like following a drunk fly," said Jannis.

"No, he's making sense so far. I think," said Seth. "Sure you don't want a hit, Jannis?"

"No. I'm good."

"Okay."

"Thank you, though."

Seth was pleased she was at least trying to be more agreeable.

"Go on, Professor Faro," Jannis said.

"What's the first commandment?"

"God. Can't have any other god," said Susan. "I know that one."

"Which always begs the question, why? Followers of the Judeo-Christian philosophy believe that there is only one God. If that were the case, this rule would make no sense. The obvious answer, and one historically validated, is that when the Old Testament was written, there were other gods. Baal was big at the time and in region, not to mention the pantheons from other cultures. Thus, it was a practical prohibition to a very real problem. The first four commandments are all about staying true to Yahweh. Depending on your denomination, no other God, no graven images, don't use the Lord's name in vain, and keep the Sabbath. All these are to conform to the creed because, like I said, there were other gods in the race. What's the next one?"

"Killing?" said Finn. "Because it was so violent back then."

"As opposed to today?" said Charlotte.

"Point made," said Barney. "Nope, not killing. That's six."

"Parents is five," said Susan. "Honor thy father and thy mother."

"Exactly. So what was the threat there?"

"You're going to say this is a rule against pulling a Zeus?" said Lucy.

"Yes. It's telling that after the establishment of a conservative God, then it's don't mess with the people who put this god there. It smacks of a problem that needed addressing."

"There was a rash of kids slaying their parents?" said Charlotte.

"Yes, I think so," said Barney. "Frankly, I often think that the world was designed for that. Young blood fights the old leader and takes over the pride."

"That still happens because people die," said Susan.

"That's too slow," said Seth. "We live in a gerontocracy. Rule by the old."

"Well, I don't know how to measure it that far," said Barney, "but I think there is a natural impulse in younger men to overthrow their fathers. It's Oedipus on an instinctive level."

"Why would Zeus keep Cronus alive?"

"So when his time came, maybe they wouldn't kill him?" offered Susan.

"Something like that, I think," said Barney. "Maybe in the real deal, the archetypal event that Zeus and Cronus represent in some pre-history, he did kill him. Exile was usually a death sentence."

"You're talking cavemen now?"

"Sure, archetypes."

"Pretending that there is a true story behind the myth?" said Lucy.

"Yeah, why not?"

"Okay," said Jannis. "You're saying older people later realized that how they got their power, i.e. killing their parents, was a bad precedent for them, and so made taboos about it for their kids?"

"Bingo!" said Barney. "Jannis gets it."

"Jesus, Barney, you're feeling your oats today," said Seth.

"It's been mulling around in the back of my brain for a while. You asked me if I could find a parallel. I could, even after the histories have been whitewashed to protect the guilty."

"The old people?" said Charlotte.

"The old rulers," said Barney. "The taboo against killing elders has often been overlooked by the aristocracy. It's almost normal on those levels."

"This is all cute and even interesting," said Charlotte. "Well, not cute, but interesting, but I still don't see how it reaches Bobby Weller. He could take nothing over. He sacrificed himself."

"I'm only pointing to the idea of generational displacement as an archetype."

"There have been other incidents that more closely follow the 'kill the father, take the throne' theory, ones where the removal wasn't so obvious."

"It's in our DNA," said Barney. "And we know it. Think of wolves chasing young males out of the pack to keep from being challenged. Horses too – most mammals. We're the aberration in the animal world. I don't know fish."

"We're all still living under Gaia's curse?"

"Yes."

"What happened to Zeus?"

"He survived several coup attempts," said Barney, "but ultimately hung on long enough to be replaced by other religions."

Charlotte glanced at Seth, who met her eyes. "It's interesting background, but not really useful," she said.

"Maybe it's a through line," Barney offered. "Something to link the pieces."

"I think it must happen all the time," said Jannis, "but we're just hearing about it now because it's the new crisis. Media is always looking for new crises to shill."

Charlotte smirked at Seth. "Aren't they, though?"

"Hey, I think what you guys are doing is worthwhile," said Barney.

"What are they doing exactly?"

"We're following a thread of upper-class murders to a possible cult."

"We are?" said Charlotte.

"We're not done yet, but that's the best guess now, don't you think?"

"And if it isn't, we can still go there?"

"Shape the facts to fit the narrative?" said Jannis.

"We'll have something to say, if that's what you mean," said Seth. "We're making something."

"Art is never objective," said Finn, "and all things that man makes is art."

"Sexist quote."

"All things people make is art. Better?"

"Yes, actually."

Charlotte nodded.

"I understood what you mean," said Susan. "We all did."

"Another one," said Jannis.

"Stop picking fights," said Finn.

"I have to," she said. "How else can anything ever change unless the old, bad ways are challenged? Like Barney says, the new, younger ideas should rise up and fight down the old, wrong ones."

For the first time that night, no one had a rejoinder for Jannis. Charlotte nodded in agreement, liking that the night's lecture could be applied to something other than the gruesome events of her life; while in Seth, something clicked, a confirmation of what Barney had said, he'd seen, and Jannis felt.

"What now?" said Lucy. "Are you in between interviews or what?"

"We're waiting to hear from the regents," said Charlotte. "Our funding is at stake."

Seth wasn't so sure. Bobby Weller's credit card had bought the booze that night.

"The regents are a mess," said Finn.

"Always."

"No, I mean it. The deaths."

"Robert Weller was a big deal to be sure," said Charlotte. "I'm not optimistic they'll continue the project."

"Not just him, but Kate Claysman and Paul Abernathy."

"What about them?"

"They're dead."

"What? How?"

Finn nodded. "Paul last week, Kate this week. Natural causes."

"Eh-hem," said Susan. "Not Claysman."

"What?"

"She was admitted to my hospital."

"You're a nurse?" asked Lucy.

"Yeppers."

"Then you're under HIPAA limitations."

"Shh," said Seth. "Let the woman talk."

Susan slugged back another drink, finishing her cup. "Won't leave the room?"

"Promise," said Seth for everyone.

"She was strangled by her druggie grandson."

"There's another one," said Seth.

"That doesn't count," said Jannis. "Male violence is endemic, as is elder abuse. This is confirmation bias. The only reason you're thinking along those lines is because you're in that mindset. Everything that happens to you will speak to that or you'll ignore it. Even tonight."

Charlotte nodded. "True."

"Doesn't mean we're wrong," said Seth.

"I wonder if we could find out if there's a real wave of something happening or it's just perception."

"No," said Jannis.

"Yes," said Lucy. "Facts don't care about feelings. We can do searches, compile info. Use math."

"Research will uncover newspaper articles and other media which may or may not be similarly bent," said Jannis.

"Is it all perception?"

"That's the world we live in," said Jannis.

"I don't know," said Charlotte. "Things seem more acute now, like there's an event happening. Not a rediscovery of an event, not really. Not new light on an ongoing thing, but an acute rise. A spike in the behavior, maybe even a new one. It all seems so…"

"What?" said Lucy.

"Connected."

"Delusional," said Jannis with a wave of her hand.

"But what if everything just keeps lining up?"

"That's confirmation bias at its best."

Seth shook his head. "Don't you see it, Charlotte?"

She had an inkling of it. "It makes sense," she agreed. "Human behavior is human behavior. Barney just found it imprinted in myth."

"But we're living it. Or, rather, witnessing it. It can't be a coincidence."

"Coincidence is what the psyche calls the bias," said Jannis. "I think you're missing the point."

"No, there's another term isn't there?" said Lucy.

"The Baader-Meinhof phenomenon," supplied Barney. "Not a fan, but there it is."

"What is that?" asked Charlotte.

"It's like confirmation bias. It's believing there is a higher frequency of something after you first notice it. Say you want to buy a red Dodge. Suddenly you see all the red Dodges driving around."

"Why aren't you a fan?" said Lucy.

"It's the world we live in," he said. "Perception is all we have. By giving it a medical condition-like name, it makes it sound like an ailment, when in fact it could just be heightened awareness."

"It is an ailment. It's delusion," said Jannis.

"Yeah," he said. "It has been linked to schizophrenia, but what hasn't?"

"The distance between a mystic and a madman is a hair's breadth."

"Who said that?" asked Finn.

"I did," said Lucy. "There's another quote – a couple, I think – but I don't remember them."

Barney gave Lucy a warm smile and a wink. "Yours is better."

Jannis looked up from her phone. "The frequent illusion," she said. "Key word is *illusion*."

"The world is flat," said Barney.

Jannis gave him a confused look, but Barney just smiled and sipped his punch.

Seth regarded Jannis, then he raised his hands. "These are explanations, definitions of events people experience, it doesn't mean they're wrong."

"It kinda does," she said. "It suggests that it's delusion."

"Doesn't matter," he said. "It's like you said, this is the life we live. The water we swim in. Therefore, I see connections. Maybe it's just my mind trying to make sense of what's happening, maybe it's my desire to keep on the project, but I can't escape the coincidence. Cronus, Zeus and that rock."

"What coincidence exactly?" said Lucy. "Barney talking here? You asked him to. That was your making. You can't say that came out of the blue."

"I'm not, but still it fits. Maybe I knew it before, but I don't think so. In any event, the story he told – see the connection, Charlotte? Our next stop."

"The regents—"

"Forget them. Regardless of what they say, we have to keep on."

"To Central America?"

"South America," he said. "It's clear, isn't it? We have to follow Sosa now. All roads lead to him."

"What the hell is he on about?" said Susan.

Charlotte understood it then, and a shiver went down her back. "Mark Sosa. The Sons of Stone."

Chapter Twenty-Four

It took Seth another week to convince Charlotte to go on with their project, and then a week to arrange it with the university. During that time Seth threw himself into research and tracked the elusive Mark Sosa down to an email which garnered a vague promise to meet them in São Paulo, Brazil. The regents were otherwise distracted, a third of their number suddenly dead, another third possibly in hiding. Their appointment was officially canceled for now. Charlotte's time was spent worrying, until she found the permissions she needed to continue their project and reframe it.

"A university exchange?" said Seth when he'd called to give her the news of the meeting promise.

"Three departments are sponsoring us. Film, journalism and international studies."

"And?"

"And we can continue our official sabbatical and get some financial assistance. The flight and a house on campus."

"That's impressive," he said.

"We do the same for their students."

"Whose?"

"Oh, sorry, São Paulo University. Biggest in Brazil. One of the biggest in South America. They send people out here every year, and since the partnership program started, we've sent all of two students their way."

"Didn't even know it existed."

"I did."

"So it seems. Is there a catch?"

"None that I see yet. They might expect us to take some classes, but that's kinda up to us when we get there."

"I doubt we'll be there very long. A quick interview and home."

"But now we are academics, see? We're intelligentsia."

"That really matters to you?" he said before he could stop himself.

"Yeah."

"It's a good idea. Well done."

"Jannis had a point," she said. "At your party."

"She was just spouting opinions and aphorisms."

"The media is involved," she said.

"By shining its spotlight on these crimes, thereby making them seem more prevalent now than before?"

"That and maybe by encouraging copycat killings."

"I think both those ideas are wrong."

"You just don't want to think that we're in the wrong business."

"Wrong?"

"Unethical?"

"Don't flatter yourself. We've done nothing."

"Yet."

"Okay, but there's more. I've been doing a lot of research this week. Not just Sosa and the Sons of Stone, which are tricky to find by the way, real dark web stuff. Hard to even find a good photo of Sosa. Should have asked Kinsley for one."

"Missed opportunity," Charlotte said flatly.

Seth heard the tone, but pressed on. "Similar killings are happening all over. Places where our media can't touch. Places where there is no media."

"How did you find them?"

"I've been using the deep academic search engines, getting leads and then digging."

"You didn't seem the type."

"I've needed something to do." Seth didn't mention that he'd used up half his supply of emergency Adderall during the last week to power his descent down the rabbit hole. The previous night had been his first real rest in three and a half days.

"I've found sudden violent deaths all over the place. Asia, Canada,

Africa is losing their elders at an alarming pace, and half of Chechnya's ruling class is AWOL."

"Confirmation bias. Did you research how many didn't die recently?"

"Cute," he said, "but there are real academics who are cool, right? Real academics who are following this thread. We're not the only ones to notice it."

"Anything about the noise?"

"No. So you think they're related?"

"I don't know."

"I know that you're thinking about it. This proves to me that you're at least open to the idea, if not secretly sold on it."

"Am I?"

"Yes." He let the word hang.

"And I'm just playing devil's advocate?"

"Yes," he said, hanging the word again.

"Why?"

"Because it's spooky."

The line went quiet for a moment.

"We're leaving next Wednesday," she said.

"Excellent work. Good on the Wednesday. That works perfectly."

Charlotte had the feeling that Seth hadn't told her something. The feeling remained that weekend as they prepared, packed, and finally left for the airport midweek. He was taciturn, but at one point he grumbled about his son, before quickly changing the subject. Since her mind slipped regularly to her own family, she imagined she understood.

They did not sit together on any of the three planes they flew on. They separately endured the twenty-two-hour day of traveling, the last leg through the red-eye hours until the dawn light stabbed through unshaded cabin windows.

The trip was exhausting, and by the end of it Charlotte ached in places she hadn't thought about in her life and was as short-tempered as she'd ever been. Seth had managed to sleep for much of it, thanks to his liberal use of the drinks cart. He stank of booze.

"Cab?" Seth said after they'd gotten their luggage and passed customs and immigration.

"I think there'll be a car," she said. "Don't bump me."

"I didn't mean to. Some jackoff hit me."

The man who'd bumped Seth wasn't there to hear the insult, having disappeared into the swarming throng of people.

"Could it be any more crowded?" asked Charlotte.

"Let's get to a curb or something. I'm for taking a cab to a Hilton and spending a night."

"And how would we pay – oh, you still have that, do you?"

"Bobby's credit card? I do. I checked. It was even paid off. We have the whole enchilada."

"How much is that?"

"Open. Who knew there was such a thing?"

"You make me sick sometimes, you know that?" She heard the tired in her own voice.

"That was harsh."

"It's like robbing a grave."

"Bobby's not dead."

"It's not his money."

"No one's using it."

She shook her head. "I have a headache," she said in explanation or warning.

"The sound?"

"No, just sick of pressurized sock-stink and cold rubber chicken with plastic forks."

Seth nodded. "We'll get you some orange juice. Here's some pain pills."

"What kind?"

"Over the counter. Advil. Generic."

She took two. Seth gave her two more. "You'll feel better after a day at a Brazilian spa. You could get a wax."

"Seth, I will punch you."

Seth smiled as she squinted at him, but then broke into a grin herself.

"There'll be a car," she insisted.

They made their way to the pick-up area. The airport wasn't as security conscious as the American ones, but instead of checkpoints, they had more than their share of machine-gun-wielding guards who looked to have no sense of humor at all.

"Pity we flew over the Amazon in the dark," he said. "I'd have liked to see it."

"There was nothing to see. I had a window seat. There was nothing but clouds," she said.

"Smoke, actually." A young Black man in a teal guayabera shirt and a sign that read 'Commondale' offered his hand to them. "I assume you're Charlotte Sakshi and Seth Lian from Oregon?"

"Well met," said Seth, taking his hand. "I'm Seth."

"I figured." He had an American Midwestern accent. "I'm Davi."

"You're Brazilian?" said Charlotte.

"An ex-pat. There are a few of us. You can call me David if you'd rather."

"No, Davi's fine," said Seth. "It's cool."

"Glad you like it."

Davi led them through the crowded airport.

A cab would have been more comfortable, safer, much more stylish. The beat-up Corolla harkened to the last century and was literally held together in places by wire. Charlotte remembered the limousines and hired cars of last month and sighed, as Seth stretched bungee cords over their luggage on the roof that wouldn't fit in the trunk or cab.

"Where are you from?" Davi asked as he was pulling into traffic.

"Oregon," said Seth.

"Your people. Originally." He looked through the mirror at Charlotte sitting in the back seat. Seth had the passenger seat.

"Oregon," said Seth again.

"India," she said.

"Then your people knew the struggle."

Seth noted the use of the article and raised an eyebrow.

"Sure," said Charlotte.

"There's a little house off campus you're using."

The freeway led through a modern cityscape of steel and glass skyscrapers, suggesting the size of the vast city. It felt enormous, expansive and engulfing. Seth was immediately lost and uneasy as they exited at the freeway detour sign that closed the entire route. Circumventing the heart of the city, the modern area of commerce and finance that the city was famous for, Davi took them through what could be charitably called the environs.

Commercial structures moved quickly by, and then through their windows came varying scenes of poverty. Even the nice buildings showed signs of decay, neglect, misuse and despair. Seth could see the favelas rising up on distant hills, see the beggars and the gangs eye the car, which for all its rust and age was a trophy in these neighborhoods.

Charlotte's mind reeled at the sensory overload, the sights, colors and smells, none of it inviting, all of it cruel. Already, from the view from the back seat, she had culture shock. Imaginings of her parents fleeing similar squalor back in India. They'd barely talk about it, barely acknowledge their origins. For a while she thought there must be some crime involved, some terrible shameful thing that they had fled and would never conjure for her, but seeing this city, tired as she was, irritable, raw, she saw the shame of poverty and hardship, the anguish and hopelessness, and knew there needn't be a murder to never want to return to this, even in stories, even in thought.

"I've never seen anything like this," she said to herself.

"You should have seen it before."

"Before what?" said Seth.

"Well, COVID, Bolsonaro, the uprisings."

"What was it like before all that? Was it a paradise?"

"Not this bad," Davi said. "Disease and capitalism run amuck. Can't tell you how many died."

"Sure you can."

Davi gave Seth a sharp look. "It's in the millions; uncountable because that would require social services of some kind."

"And I thought the U.S. was bad."

"It'll get there," said Davi. "Unless something drastic happens."

"Like what?"

"Like that." Davi pointed out the window to a broken wall that once might have been part of a post office, but now was a ruin. Upon the peeling paint was spray-painted *Filhos da Pedra*.

"What's that?"

"Children of the Stone."

"No shit?"

"No shit."

"Who are they?"

"A revolution," said Davi.

"Another uprising?" said Seth, remembering the reports from a few years back.

"No. I said, a revolution."

The pulled up to a checkpoint and three men with automatic rifles in their hands and fingers on their triggers leaned in and spoke to Davi. The young man responded. Seth and Charlotte could guess some, but only some – 'Estados Unidos', 'universidad', 'professora'. Neither one spoke a language besides English.

Davi said, "Show your passports."

They handed them over. The guard took them and Davi's ID to a Humvee parked on one side of the concrete barrier. The other two guards held their rifles and waited.

For five long minutes they waited, until the guard returned, handed Davi the papers back, and waved them around the barbed wire and barricade.

Finally, they were through into what Charlotte might consider a depressed neighborhood back home, but here was the best she had seen. Small houses with driveways. It was a good imitation of American suburbia. It could have been Florida.

"This is the faculty compound," Davi said. "Your house is just there." He pointed, but passed it. A little ways farther in he pointed to a vacant pool and modest clubhouse. "You can use this. There'll be a key inside the house."

"How do we get around?" asked Charlotte.

"There's a bus that takes you to the campus."

"What if we want to go somewhere else?"

"Where?"

"Groceries?"

"I recommend you order them in. It's more expensive, but much safer. Kidnappings, you know."

"No, I don't know," said Charlotte.

"Lots of them," said Davi. "Foreigners are prized for ransom deals. They don't often turn bad, but they can. At best it'll be an expensive detour on your trip. Just order in. Again, there'll be instructions inside the house."

"What if we want to go sightseeing?" said Seth.

Davi circled around and pulled into the driveway of their pink stucco rambler. "I wouldn't recommend it."

"Nevertheless."

"You can call a cab or maybe rent a car."

"But we're not furnished with a car?" said Charlotte.

"No," said Davi. "You shouldn't need one. That's what I'm saying."

"Well, we'll get out here," said Seth. "Thanks for driving us and welcoming us to São Paulo as only an embittered ex-pat can."

Seth opened the door for Charlotte, got their bags out, and carried them to the door. It was unlocked. He opened it and they went in.

Davi watched them from inside the car.

Chapter Twenty-Five

The house was comfortable but small. A single person would find it cozy and wonder about the second bedroom. As it was, they were content to have walls and power to charge their cameras and equipment. Charlotte retired right away and fell asleep in her room. Seth, still working through the chemicals he'd ingested – alcohol and caffeine in abundance – cycled through the television channels for an hour and then spent a couple more on his computer surfing news sites that left him uneasy. He fell asleep with the help of a pill.

Charlotte was the first to rise sixteen hours later. Seth an hour after that, roused by the smell of coffee and bacon.

"You went out and bought food?" he asked on his way to the coffeemaker.

"No. I found supplies in the front room when I woke up. A gift basket too. Some cheese and wine. Crackers. Plus basic provisions for a couple days."

"In the front room?"

She nodded.

Seth found the sugar bowl empty and held it up.

"Not something that came. It's not bad black. It's actually pretty good coffee."

"As good as Martha's Vineyard?"

"On par."

"Close to the source." He sipped it and felt the warmth on his tongue and followed it down his throat. "Front room, though?"

"Yeah. Did you go out?"

"Nope."

"Forget to lock up, then?"

"Nope again. I checked before turning in. Our Good Samaritan grocer has a key."

Charlotte blanched and changed the subject. "So what's our move?"

Seth grabbed a piece of bacon and got a slap for it. "Can't I have some?"

"When it's done."

The moment was déjà vu to Seth and he paused to recall whether the domestic cliché was a personal memory or just a TV trope he'd recognized.

"We're supposed to check in with the administration on campus at some point," Charlotte said. "How do you like your eggs?"

"Over medium."

"I'll assume I'm good to cook in bacon grease?"

"Assume correctly."

She broke two eggs into the sizzling skillet. "Three?"

"Yes, please." A third went in.

"They'll need an agenda of what we're doing. Get us into classes if we need any. It occurs to me I don't even know if they're on semesters or what? Where are they in the year?"

Seth shrugged. "I emailed the contact I had for Sosa, said we're here, but nothing back yet. We're going to have to think of something to tell the university to buy time until we hear back," he said. "What did you tell them already?"

"Nothing. It's wide open. Do you think they'll have a problem with us making a commercial documentary?"

"No. But Sons of Stone could be a hot spot."

She plated his eggs and put the greater share of bacon on it. "There's juice."

"I'm good."

Two eggs for her. "No SOS because of what we saw yesterday?"

"And what I saw on the news last night. The country is on high alert. There're rumors of coups and the Filhos da Pedra were mentioned."

"You mastered Portuguese overnight, did you?"

"The internet isn't bad here. Pulled up local news. I saw burning cars and concerned anchors – plastic smiles, scared eyes."

"Davi's revolution?"

"Maybe, but the SOS is getting the blame. Or maybe credit. The news was accusatory but chatter on the net was mostly supportive."

Charlotte's stomach turned. "God, more violence."

"Yeah."

"I just wanted to film some rich brats playing tennis, graduate, get a good job. Now I'm a murder magnet."

"Violence is everywhere. Or maybe it's that frequency illusion."

"Or it's the world we live in and I'm just seeing it clearly for the first time."

"Yeah," he said with a sigh.

"God. How did we get here? Who did this to us?"

"Evolution?"

"God," she said exasperatedly.

"Zeus?"

"I didn't mean it like that."

"Still a good guess."

"Do you think it's getting worse?"

"Violence sells. It's probably just a media thing."

"I dreamt such shit last night."

"I have pills for that," he said. "What were they?"

"I forgot them the moment my eyes opened, but I had the residue, you know? I woke up anxious."

"It's in the air." Seth poked his eggs and stomached black coffee, waiting for its effects. Charlotte plated her eggs and joined him at the little table.

"Is there actually a threat here?"

"Probably not. Last night they were reporting on Paraguay. The 'Corporals' Coup' took over there." Seth used air quotes.

"I guess I'm an American, since I don't know what we're talking about."

"I didn't either," said Seth. "A sudden coup in Paraguay. That's what happened. In a day. A terrible, bloody coup led by a bunch of corporals, practically new recruits. They not only took out the government, publicly shooting them on the steps of parliament, but they're saying they killed anyone they deemed a threat in the military as well. They say there's not a general left in the country and only a couple of colonels, probably in hiding."

"Tell me this is usual for Central America."

"I say yes, but the U.S. is incensed. It wasn't our coup. Usually it's ours. CIA and all that. Lots of them, but this one has more threat than the Bolivian one."

"I thought Bolivia elected theirs?"

"Did they? I can't remember."

"Well, I guess shit happens."

"Something's happening in Moscow too."

"Come on, Seth. You're making Jannis look sane."

"You didn't think she was?" asked Seth.

"You know what I mean."

"I'm just telling you what I did last night. Lots of news outlets in Moscow are either silent or mentioned a new workers' revolution."

"Now you're reaching."

"One outlet linked it to a rash of high-profile murders among the oligarchy in the last couple weeks."

"This is why I got off social media," she said.

"And then there's—"

"Don't," she said. "Just don't."

"Okay."

"Just not right now. We have an interview with someone who might have some information about Bobby and Kinsley and the Martha's Vineyard thing. That's the angle."

"I'm good with that. I get it."

She sipped her orange juice and noted a different flavor than she was used to. She moved her eggs around, and still looking at the plate, said, "It's not just dreams, Seth. I hear a song in my head."

"I get that all the time. Someone said it's bad sleep cycles. Over-tired."

"I don't know the song."

"Maybe you picked it up from here. Does it have a tropical beat?"

"Seth, I know you're trying to help, but it's the buzz I mentioned before. It's the same feeling. Half there, half not there. It's more persistent. I can forget it's there for a while, but it's never really gone now. It sounds closer."

"Since we got here?"

"I think so."

"Hmmm."

"What?"

"Could be the flight still. I have a low-grade headache," said Seth. "Might be the same thing."

"In the back or front of your head?"

"Uhm, the back."

Charlotte nodded.

They both jumped when the phone rang, a loud, ancient bell harkening back to days before their births. The phone was an antique, a faded-gold wall-mounted beast with a dial instead of numbers. Charlotte was closer and picked up the receiver.

"Hello?"

The woman on the other end spoke clear, concise English with a slight accent. "Welcome to São Paulo," she said. "My name is Talita. Come to campus this afternoon at one, and I'll show you around."

"Sounds wonderful."

Seth watched as she listened, her eyes clenched shut, her fingers massaging her temples. "Oh, let me get a pencil," she said, and then took down some instructions before hanging up.

They dressed, collected some gear, and found the bus stop on the corner. This late in the morning, the buses ran only every hour, but they got lucky and one came in short order. It was a cross between a school bus and an airport shuttle, adult-sized seats, but no place for luggage. The driver gave them a quick glance before closing the door and driving on without a word. They settled into a seat together in the middle.

"I've never been on a project like this before," said Seth, lighting a cigarette. "Everywhere we go, we've been welcomed. Not my usual way at all."

"Maybe it's your manners," said Charlotte, nodding to the 'no smoking' sign.

"Shit. I thought we were away from that noise." He took a deep drag and stubbed the cigarette out under his seat. He exhaled and held up the butt, looking for someplace to put it. Charlotte rolled her eyes.

"They are rolling out the carpet. The house would have been plenty, but the basket and now the tour. I wonder which department is doing it."

"Our choices being what?"

"Same as Commondale's sponsors, so journalism, film and international studies."

"It's the last one if it's any of them. Journalism is a dirty word in current politics, film eats their own. International studies has the promise of money."

"Or maybe it's just the university being nice. I'm sure we do something similar for visiting professors in Bend."

"You told them we were professors?"

"You are. That's enough. I'm a grad student, which is close. We're here to meet peers."

"They must be hard up for visitors."

"Maybe they are." Charlotte pointed out the front windshield.

Seth followed her finger to the skyline over a diminishing row of trees, and saw a pillar of coal-black smoke rising up straight, disappearing behind the roof of the van. Farther away was another and several more to the sides. Most were as black as the near one, but several others, some in huge billowing clouds far off to their right, were tawny brown and yellow.

Seth opened his phone.

"I have no signal."

"I have no bars either."

"But do you have a signal? Anything?"

Charlotte saw *no service* in the menu bar.

"No," she said.

"Let's get you mic'd up," he said. "This could be an interesting day."

"Why do I feel suddenly scared and sick?"

"Because, my dear Charlotte, you are an intelligent woman, an experienced professional who has a supernatural knack for being in the right place at the right time."

"Just me?"

Seth checked the sound level on a mic. "Put this under your blouse," he said.

"You do it," she said.

"Me?"

"If you cop a feel, I'll kill you," she said distractedly. "Just do it. We're here now. This is where we are and what we're doing and, goddammit, Seth, you have a point about us being in these places."

Seth carefully clipped it on the inside of her blouse. He could feel the heat of her skin on the back of his hand. "How's that?"

"Fine."

Seth chose a light camera to hold in his hands. He held it up, tested the focus, panned around the inside of the van, and just happened to have it pointed to the north as an orange fireball rose into the sky.

"Charlotte…"

He filmed its slow rise, its churning and turning in on itself, drawing a black trail of smoke beneath it, mushroom and high.

"Seth—"

The shock wave cut off the rest of her sentence.

Chapter Twenty-Six

"The black smoke is tire fires," said Seth. "That big one was something else."

"An industrial accident?" asked Charlotte.

"I read something about a planned general strike, but I didn't think it was today. Or here."

"Are we in danger?"

Seth looked up at the driver, who carried on as if nothing had happened. "That's a good sign," he said, pointing. "The locals aren't fazed. Neither should we be."

Just then the driver turned his face to profile and spoke. "I'll take you to the university gate, but let you off there. You be safe. I must go home."

"Do you know what's going on?" Charlotte asked.

"Filhos da Pedra," he said. "Those bastards making trouble."

The trouble seemed to be contained to farther areas of the city and the traffic moved smoothly as could be expected. Quickly they pulled onto the campus and the driver opened the door.

"Have a nice day," he said.

Charlotte thought to ask about a ride back, but didn't. There would be a bus or there wouldn't.

On the curb, as the bus turned around, Seth checked his phone. "Signal," he said.

"Is this how life is down here?" asked Charlotte.

"Apparently."

"Where are we meeting this person?"

"Clock tower."

Seth consulted his phone and gestured. "That way. Check out this satellite picture." He passed Charlotte the phone as they walked.

"What about it?"

"See all the green on the map? Trees. See any here?"

There was indeed a disconnect between what the phone showed from the net and what they saw. Charlotte remembered seeing pictures of the campus and it had appeared green and lush as any tropical paradise. Now, walking the sidewalk, the trees were gone.

"What happened?"

"My guess is the fuel shortages from a few years back."

"And the satellites just haven't updated?"

"Probably intentionally. Bad publicity to remind people of the troubles."

Charlotte scanned the horizon in every direction and could see the rising plumes of smoke surrounding the campus. Most were toward the center of town southeast of them and the big one, the one from the explosion, was now a clog on the horizon to the west. It dominated the sky that way, a vast black smear reaching as high as she could look in the bright Brazilian sunlight.

"Let's get a shot here," said Seth. "Just describe what's happening." He stepped back and got his partner into frame. Charlotte shook off a look of confusion and then, in a moment, put on her professional face.

"We're in São Paulo, Brazil," she said. "We may be witnessing the rise of a new revolt in this country." She turned to profile to suggest to Seth to pan that direction. He held on her a long time, medium close-up trying to read her expression through the lens, then he panned to the smudge in the sky.

"We're here in search of Mark Sosa, the alleged leader of a group called the Sons of Stone," Charlotte said. Seth panned slowly around the horizon, taking in all the black lines connecting earth to sky, the lack of trees, and yellowed grass in the once lush city.

"We were led here by a series of tips originating around our original subject. Somehow, this new direction seems correct, if not unavoidable."

He ended the three-hundred-sixty-degree pan back on Charlotte, whose eyes carried in them the weight of what she'd said. He held on her a moment, a beat, and then one more, and then he lowered the camera.

"You work great under pressure," he said.

She shrugged. "Come on, I can see the tower there."

They followed the sidewalks past quiet buildings and dead lawns. "Not a lot of people here," Seth said.

"This could just be the wrong side of campus."

Green tufts were rising here and there, but it was clear that water had been a problem. The drought part of the recent problems was yet to fully pass.

"I don't know about this meeting," Charlotte said.

"Why's that?"

"It's very nice of the university to have someone meet us and show us around, but it seems wrong also. Particularly today."

"Maybe refinery explosions are a way of life around here," said Seth, lifting his phone. "They're saying it was an accident."

"Who's they?"

"Official sources."

"Anything about the tire fires?"

"Usual unrest in the favelas," he quoted. "Do you have anything else that suggests this meeting is fishy?"

"That's a word," Charlotte said, rounding a building and seeing a large dead square with a gray slab monolith in the middle. The clock tower. She noted the strange sidewalk arrangement, it didn't make a lot of sense to her. It wasn't symmetrical, didn't look organic. Looked false and wrong. There was a woman waiting on a bench near the tower.

"My mind screamed when I took the call from Talita."

"A hunch?"

"That noise."

"Huh…" said Seth. "Thus, your line about unavoidable."

She didn't respond.

Seth took a camera out of his bag, adjusted it to film ahead, turned it on, and carried it casually as they approached the woman.

The woman stood up. She was a tall, slender woman with medium-length black hair pulled back from her face with an elastic band. Her face was bright, tanned. She took off her sunglasses as she extended her hand to Charlotte.

"Talita?" said Charlotte.

"Yes. Welcome to São Paulo."

"Who sent you?" said Seth. It was a simple question, but Seth had said it with such a blunt inflection that it was either caricature – an inside joke, quote from some well-known movie – or a cold interrogation. Talita looked at him with a surprised grin, which faded as she realized it was the latter.

"Mark Sosa sent me. It's him you're here to see, right?"

"It is."

"Jesus, Seth," said Charlotte. "That was a leap."

"Was it? My father, who was not really the kind of person one could learn from except in the negative, said once, 'The best way to check on a coincidence is to expect it. When it doesn't happen, you'll see it was bullshit all along.'"

"You're saying you're with Sosa, not the university?"

"Can't a girl do both?" Talita's smile was cold but present.

The humming in Charlotte's head rose a notch. It wasn't uncomfortable, but it was difficult to ignore.

"Walk with me," said Talita.

She headed toward the center of the campus and the two Americans followed behind her, falling into step together to the same unbidden rhythmic beat in Charlotte's throbbing skull.

Seth turned the camera off to conserve battery. He had Talita's reaction, had all the establishing shots they'd need. Filming from such a crap angle below the waist was always, well, crap. He heaved the heavy backpack up on his shoulder to balance the weight, and followed Charlotte a few steps back, listening to the quiet of the campus and the distant melees in the city. It was like they were in a bubble of silence while the world around them screamed.

He wondered at the sudden memory of his father's quote, a long-forgotten piece of his childhood that he thought he'd long-since abandoned. How had he phrased it? 'The kind of person one could learn from except in the negative.' How true that was. The thoughts of his father were always bleak, painful and quickly to be buried. How he'd sworn he would never be that man and hadn't been, but still he'd failed in much the same way.

He recalled when his father had given him the coincidence line, a line of his own creation. Seth had never seen it anywhere else. Give the old man credit for one original thought, at least.

Seth had been stealing liquor. He was thirteen and wanted to try it. Had tried it. Was trying it. His father had suspected him, so he'd moved from the whiskey to the vodka. His father would begin on the whiskey and move to the clear liquors afterward, probably because he bought decent bourbon but cheap vodka. After you're drunk you really don't notice. With a start, Seth realized he'd done the same thing. Does the same thing.

His father had walked in on him refilling the Smirnoff bottle with tap water and nodded his head in disgust, not shook it, but nodded it, as if he'd suspected all along what a lousy son Seth was.

"I should make you drink that whole bottle," he'd said. "To teach you a lesson, but I suspect that you already have, and that water there would only help your hangover."

He'd whipped him instead with his belt. Another beating, indistinguishable from all the others except for the line about how he figured it out. The coincidence of him not getting as drunk as he usually did.

When Seth had drank then at thirteen, again and beyond, for most of his youth, he thought that booze was wasted on the old. Like good health and beauty. When he was young, it made him happy, silly, funny. When old people drank, like his father then, like he'd caught himself at times lately, it made one surly, melancholy. Violent. He'd not gotten there, but he saw how it could come.

It almost made him want to forgive his father. Almost.

The problem was that his father was not a forgivable man. He was not particularly bright, accomplished or thoughtful. The quote Seth thought of most often consciously was 'spare the rod, spoil the child, and my damned child won't be spoiled'. The final syllable of the statement was usually accompanied by a blow, so much so that when Seth quoted the line in his mind, the classic version and his father's addition, he invariably added a 'swat' as the final beat. It stood in place of the period.

He hated his father, and fate, to be just, had made his own son hate him in return. He shook his head at the thought of it, shook it hard – so much so that he found himself stopped on the sidewalk, watching the pair leave him behind. He quickened his pace to catch up, grateful no one had noticed his inner storm blowing his physical body into stupor.

They were different though, thought Seth about himself and his damned father. Both had drug problems, but Seth had never laid a hand on anyone. He might have shown disappointment at a bad grade, nudged Travis this way or that, but not at all like the authoritarian manner of his elder. And yet the reaction was the same. Seth wouldn't cross the street to save his father's life, wouldn't visit him in the home as his organs failed one by one, liver, pancreas, brain and heart.

Seth had gone to the funeral, but kept apart. Everyone gave him space thinking he was grieving, but he wasn't. He was just there to see it through, to know that the man was gone, out of his life, safely buried, to be forgotten. But he hadn't been forgotten. Travis once asked him why he hadn't cried at the funeral. He'd been so small then, a child. They still had some kind of rapport then. Travis was concerned that the pain would 'blow him up', something his mother had told him, to be sure. Seth had told his son, and here maybe he'd made a mistake – but it was one sentence in a childhood of experience, how could it be so important? He'd said, "I did all my crying a long time ago." Travis had accepted the answer, but he knew he didn't understand. It was the kind of remark a smart college-educated artist might say in a group meeting, pithy, deep, accurate. Forgiving. But to a five-year-old, it was confusion. Years later, he remembered wondering if he'd given Travis the idea that everyone has a finite amount of tears. Years after that, he saw that Travis had come to understand that Seth had hated his father, a man Travis had never met. There was his legacy to his son – a hatred of the father. Oedipal. Zeus hating Cronus. Barney would be pleased with the simile. Or was it a metaphor? In any event, Seth knew it was unjust. He had not sinned against Travis as his father had against him. He had scars, cigarette burns, a fractured arm – real scars to correspond to the mental ones. From this beginning, Seth had risen to be the man he was. Not perfect, far from it – hella far from it, he thought with a smirk, but a goddamn positive step of evolution to be sure. He'd ended the cycle of abuse as he'd vowed to do.

But it hadn't mattered.

His son hated him now.

It would pass, he told himself. It was one of the few bits of faith Seth held on to, maybe the only one.

It would pass.

Talita paused as a low concrete and glass building came into view across a full parking lot.

"That is the Salsbury Institute of Aging Science," she said.

"I've heard of it," said Charlotte.

"What have you heard?"

"It's internationally famous for medical advances. It was mentioned in an article I saw about stem cells."

Talita nodded. She was younger than Charlotte. Maybe twenty-one. Her accent was clean but present, a definite foreign tone but one Charlotte couldn't have placed before this trip.

"They're making people immortal in there," Talita said. "How do you feel about that?"

Charlotte sensed a test question. Talita's look and Seth's sudden tenseness behind her put her on edge – more on edge. "It's what we do, right? 'Fight the coming of the night,' and all that."

"They already have treatments, organ cloning, stem-cell rejuvenation."

"I hadn't heard about that specifically."

"Of course not," she said. "That's what I'm saying. These advances are not for us; they're for them."

"Them being the rich people?" asked Seth.

"Yes."

"It's good to be rich."

"For them it is. For us – for the world – it is not. They're thieves and liars. Killers and monsters. The least they could do is die out, but even that is too much to expect from this abhorrent species."

Seth realized he should have been filming this. He unslung his heavy pack. "Could you say that again?" he asked. "You put it so well."

"Mark will," she said and glanced at her wristwatch. She gestured to a bench. "We'll wait there."

"Will Mr. Sosa meet us here?" asked Seth.

"No, but in a few minutes you'll see what I'm getting at."

"Film?"

"Sure," she said. "That's why Mark brought you here."

Charlotte took a seat on the bench and wished she'd brought an umbrella or a fan. The heat was exhausting.

Seth fidgeted with his camera, taking an establishing shot of the two women on the bench, panning around the scene, framing the Institute between buildings and lampposts, all the time thinking about all the work he had done to arrange a meeting with Sosa, and wondering if, perhaps, it had been Sosa arranging to meet them. He couldn't rule it out; he'd lucked into quite a number of leads. Such coincidence. So many, he should have expected them by now.

"Get the building," said Talilta to Seth.

"I did."

"No. Get it now." She gestured to her watch.

Seth trained his camera back on the building just as the windows blew out.

Chapter Twenty-Seven

They were close enough to feel the gust of heat as the building burst with fire. Orange balls of flame like some breaking fungus ruptured every weak orifice. Doors, windows, ducts, nightlights, all a bloom of churning fire. Seth kept the camera aimed, tense and taught, smelling his hair singe as the flames receded, turned to smoke.

"Were there people in there?" asked Charlotte.

"Oh, yes," said Talita.

"We should go," said Seth over his shoulder.

"Another moment."

The first was a distant pop, a child with a finger in her cheek. Strange. Out of place. A second later came another, and then a rapid set of eight or ten. The last ones were punctuated by gray puffs of smoke shooting out of the sides of the building in regular array like some choreographed geyser show.

A half breath behind them, after a sickly pause, came a deep plaintive rumbling and then the building collapsed upon itself, the roof falling through the six floors, crashing into some basement, and all was a cloud of gray smoke.

Seth filmed until the cloud engulfed them and he couldn't see. He quickly shoved the camera back into his bag to protect it from the fine concrete dust that even then clawed at his throat and sent Charlotte into a coughing fit.

"Come on," gasped Talita. Charlotte felt the woman take her hand and lead her away. "This way."

They stumbled over a low rise and then came to a sidewalk on the other side. Charlotte could barely make out her shoes beneath her as she felt herself being led along. She could hear Seth behind her, coughing and wheezing.

"This way," said Talita again. "We're almost there."

Seth followed the sound of their footsteps, Charlotte's coughing, Talita's hacking. His eyes were barely squints, watering down his face to where he could taste the moist concrete on his lips. All was murk and dark, an early unnatural nightfall.

"Here," came Talita's voice.

Charlotte felt a car door, opened it and ducked inside. Talita was right behind her, entering through another door. Seth, hearing the doors, staggered and tripped and split his lip on the curb. It took him a long moment to get his bearings. Crawling on all fours, blood dripping from his lip onto the ground, his hands fell upon a car tire. Through streaming eyes, he recognized a late model silver SUV and heard Charlotte coughing within. Standing up, he found a handle and pulled.

"Get in," came Talita's voice.

Seth let himself in the back, clambered inside, pulling the door closed behind him, and fell across a leather seat.

"Here." Someone pushed a wad of moist towelettes into his hands.

The wipes had done little for Charlotte; in fact, the alcohol in them had hurt her eyes, so when Talita put a water bottle in her hands, she poured it straight over her face before drinking the rest. Her coughing finally subsided with her last swallow.

"Is there more water?" she rasped.

"Here." Another bottle appeared in her hand.

"I'll take one of those," said Seth from the back.

He felt the plastic bottle drop onto his lap. He too poured it into his eyes before drinking.

"We'll wait here a minute until the cloud dissipates. It shouldn't take too long. I hope."

Outside the car Charlotte could see darkness with occasional flashes of light seeping through the churning dust, illuminating tawny particles of destruction.

At least here, she thought – as horribly accustomed to murder as she was – she hadn't seen the bodies. These were faceless strangers whose cries never rose to her hearing, whose dead eyes would never judge her for her silent observation.

Talita started the car. The dust cloud had cleared to allow an all-pervasive glow around the vehicle. She switched on the headlights and windshield wipers before pulling away.

"You're bleeding," said Charlotte, pointing to a red streak down Talita's cheek.

"Oh," she said. "I guess we were too close."

"I'm sure you'll get it right the next time," said Seth from the back seat.

Talita turned halfway to give him a look, but turned back to the road. Charlotte didn't know what to think. She remembered her microphone.

"You set that up for us to see?" she asked.

"No. It was always scheduled for today. The riots are part of it. You just happened to be here."

"Lucky coincidence," said Seth.

"Lucky."

Talita navigated slowly through the streets until they suddenly came out of the cloud and found themselves on a paved street. Charlotte didn't recognize where they were, couldn't tell which side of the campus they'd come out on.

Talita sped up and away.

"Where are you taking us?" said Seth.

"Still with the spy-talk?" said Talita.

"Seems appropriate."

"You wanted to see Mark. I'm taking you to Mark."

Fire engines, police cruisers, armored vehicles and ambulances sped past them going the other way in waves of wailing sirens. Charlotte saw the cloud still in the side-view mirror, hovering like a soft pillow between her and the horizon. In that blankness, another smear in the sky, she imagined the people who perished there. People who would miss them, regret not making peace with them before they couldn't, whose lives would continue so much the worse for the loss. The faces she created looked a lot like her parents.

"Mark will explain it all," Talita said. "You'll see what we're doing is right."

"I'm not judging," said Seth.

"I am," said Charlotte.

"Then you, Miss Sakshi, are honest, while in the back seat sits a liar."

"Where did you learn your English?" said Seth.

"I'm a scholar," was her reply.

The stream of official vehicles abated.

Charlotte's father stayed in her mind; the link was made from several angles. She'd researched cancer and cures after hearing of his diagnosis. It was there that she'd surfed internet waves to stem cells and the Salsbury Institute. It was one of the places promising a real possibility for a cure to cancer. In the cloud, beyond her sight now behind her, but still in her mind, lungs and lashes, was possibly a last chance for her father.

"They made medicine there," said Charlotte.

"But not for us."

"Some of it."

"If you could afford it."

"What price life?"

"Life is a privilege, not a right."

"What does that mean?"

"It means they lost their privilege. The privileged class is evil."

"Easy to say that from the outside looking in," said Seth, remembering Charlotte's microphone was still hot.

"Exactly," was Talita's response.

She pulled the vehicle into a full-service corporate gas station.

"I'll fill up. There's a good washroom around back."

Charlotte got out of the car.

"Get a key first." Talita pointed to the kiosk.

Seth followed Charlotte inside. The man behind the counter said something to them in Portuguese.

"Key?" said Seth, miming turning a lock.

"Yes," came the response in English.

"Hard day?" he said, handing them each a key on a long fob connected to a three-inch steel nut. Some things are the same everywhere, Seth thought.

"Yes," said Charlotte.

The bathrooms weren't special, typical gas station toilets like in the States. If these were good, she shivered to think what others were like. At least it had a locking door.

She looked at herself in the mirror and thought she was seeing a corpse. She was caked in the grayish-tan dust from the demolished building. Her face was streaked with lines where the water had run down. Her eyes were red. She coughed again and shook a cloud of dust out of her hair.

She ran the water and, with a wad of paper towels, tried to make herself camera-worthy. She ended up stripping and shaking her things out the door, hoping no one was standing right there.

Putting herself back together and despairing at how little she'd improved herself, she was struck by how mundane and meaningless it was, how quickly her own selfish concerns about beauty and presentability had erased a mass murder and her father's plight. "People are selfish," she said to herself; then, recalling her mother, not a phrase per se, but an idea, amended it to, "I am selfish. I will work on that." Indian philosophy in a Brazilian gas station restroom after an act of international terrorism. The world we live in.

She found Talita sitting in the SUV, Seth cleaning dust out of his camera at the compressed air station, a roll of coins broken at his feet.

"You cleaned up pretty well," said Talita. Charlotte noticed the new Band-Aid over her right eye.

"Not really. Where are we going?"

"It's not far now."

Charlotte helped herself to another bottle of water and took the passenger seat again. Seth, seeing the other two waiting for him, put his equipment away, and checked his phone. He had bars for a moment, went to check news, but lost them before anything loaded.

"Thanks," he said, giving Talita the half-used roll of coins. Seeing Charlotte, he said, "You cleaned up nice."

"Funny."

"No, you look better than you did."

"Not saying much."

"No. Probably not." He got in and Talita took them onward.

Soon they were out of the strangely middle-class suburb where the gas station had been. They passed a group of industrial parks that made Seth nervous, feeling they were going to be blown up at any minute, then they turned down a steep grade between smoldering tires, billowing black smoke, and the road became rough.

Talita took the speed down to avoid the many people crowding the narrow streets of the favela where they found themselves. Charlotte's nose was assaulted as much as her eyes. She could smell the poverty, the desperation in spicy food, tire smoke, body odor and excrement. Designer shirts, stained and colorful, thrown-offs, scavenged, were a jarring panoply of color. Bright yellow, green, blue, red. Stripes and corporate logos adorning accusing eyes that tracked the vehicle like a passing predator. Charlotte was taken by how many children there were, and she wondered if the mutilations many of them had couldn't have been intentional, a means to be a better beggar. What if, like the old stories that had conjured this vision, they'd been disfigured by their family for that purpose?

But they weren't begging now. They only watched, and Charlotte felt herself judged, recalling her decision not to burden anyone else with life. She wondered how much a tubal ligation cost and hated herself for thinking it.

They bumped and rattled across paths that were more gutter than road, and then just stopped. Seth looked around expecting a roadblock, a gang attack, but he saw only the street. Talita turned off the car.

Seth's phone beeped once, then went quiet as whatever signal he'd had left as fast as it'd come.

"We walk from here," Talita said and got out.

Charlotte followed. Seth triggered his camera, brought it up and got out with them.

The road ended in a pile of smelly garbage, citrusy and rotten. They followed Talita around it into a narrow alleyway with a stream of sewer water running in the middle. Fifty paces on they took a right, thirty more, a left. The path was pedestrian and narrow. A scooter could make it. A motorcycle, maybe, but nothing wider. People watched them from within doorways of scrapped-together homes. Some had brick, mud, metal sheeting, but most were plywood and plastic. There was a sense of crowdedness, but they passed only a few people, dark-skinned natives who kept their gazes down and clutched their possessions while they waited for the party to pass. Noises – talk, unknown music from grainy speakers and footsteps on the rooftops, splashing and a child's laughter – these were the alien sounds that broke the silence of their march through the favela.

Charlotte didn't know how long they walked. The day was warming and the air was thick and still. Only twice did the sunshine touch the ground and only once did a breeze find them. Abruptly, they stopped.

"Here," said Talita.

The space looked like every other ramshackle home they'd passed, identical in its hodgepodge of materials, lingering organic smells of waste and food and rot from unseen places. Taking a step back, until he brushed the wall behind, Seth filmed it, took in the walls of discarded boards, street signs, planking, corrugated roofing. It was part of the block, connected to its neighboring dwellings with shared walls. A blue tarpaulin moved eerily in an unfelt breeze. A dark orifice, hidden in shadow, suggested a way in.

After a long moment, just as Seth was about to lower the camera, a man appeared in the doorway. No, not a man, a boy. A teenager. He waved at them agreeably and stepped out. He found the camera and nodded to it.

"Seth, Charlotte, hello and welcome," he said. "I'm Mark Sosa. We should talk."

Chapter Twenty-Eight

He was American. African American to be more precise, but definitely a Yankee. Charlotte figured him for younger than twenty, maybe eighteen. Maybe younger. He was medium build, medium height, with a medium-dark complexion to match his eyes. His hair was cut short. He wore an old, blue basketball jersey – the 76ers – and dirty khaki shorts. Upon his feet were dollar-store flip-flops.

"I see you brought your camera, good. I didn't know how to alert you."

"I had a hunch," said Seth.

"Why not just call us?" asked Charlotte.

"Not that easy. At least not at the time. I had Talita and I have backup contingencies. I have another camera inside if you want to use it." Sosa stepped aside and gestured for them to go in.

"Is it okay I film?"

"Are you streaming?"

"No."

"Then it's fine."

"I doubt I could stream anyway. There's no kind of signal here."

"Yeah. Who'd have guessed?" Sosa's smile was genuine and warm, a little playful. Seth felt like he'd entered some kind of fable and here was the prankster character, Loki or Coyote perhaps.

They followed him into the hut. The change in lighting was dramatic as the brightness of the Brazilian sun was replaced with the thick murk of unseen spaces. Seth paused inside the door to let his eyes adjust. Charlotte took his arm.

"You okay?" he asked her.

"That question…" she said.

"We're here now."

"I know," she said. "I'm good. Don't worry." Seth could hear the resignation in her voice, but strength in it as well, and was glad of it. He himself went forward because he knew this was what he had. Nothing else. This.

The house was two rooms and a back area open to the sky. The indoor spaces showed signs of dense occupation, though now there was only an old woman regarding them suspiciously. She sat on an upturned orange five-gallon bucket with a hardware store logo on the side. They passed her for the next room, which held cooking supplies and a cradle that looked recently vacated. Talita pushed Charlotte forward as her eyes lingered on the empty crib.

Outside, Seth was not overly surprised to see Davi there, the man who'd picked them up at the airport. He gave Seth a quick nod and readjusted the assault rifle hanging from a strap over his shoulder. Behind Charlotte, Talita picked up a similar rifle from beneath a crumpled towel and followed them out.

It was an enclosed patio, high walls made of plywood scraps reinforced by the living spaces abutting it on all sides. Small but cozy. There were several potted fruit trees Charlotte couldn't recognize, and a cannabis plant Seth did. There were two kitchen chairs set at a nice angle for an over-the-shoulder-style interview. An older but adequate video camera sat atop a tripod, poorly aimed between the two. The light was good, indirect and clear. Open sky, sound-dampening debris. A good place for a conversation. Seth moved to the tripod and got to work.

"Like I said, we weren't sure how you'd arrive," said Sosa. "You're welcome to use our equipment or your own."

"Both?"

"Sure."

Seth produced a memory chip and fitted it into the new camera.

Charlotte said, "I feel manipulated."

"Things worked out," Sosa said.

Seth said, "Let's get into position for checks."

Charlotte was taken aback by how quickly he'd fallen into professional rhythm. Did he not feel the same outrage, or was he only compensating better?

Mark Sosa sat down in the chair Seth indicated, Charlotte in the other. He angled the camera askew of Charlotte to take in the rebel. "Look left and right," he told Sosa.

"Why?"

"To see which is your best side."

"Of course." Sosa gave him three-quarter profiles and Seth decided the left was good and so the seating was fine as it was, which was best, because Charlotte's best side was her right. He moved to the other camera and positioned it for her.

"Do I look all right?" she asked.

Seth turned to Sosa. "What do you think?"

"We were too close to the Institute," said Talita.

"Oh," said Sosa. "We could probably find some water for you to freshen up."

"What do you think, Seth?"

"You always look great," he said. She gave him a smile and adjusted her microphone. Seth put one on Sosa. He checked the levels.

"What are the rules?" Charlotte said. "The limits to the interview?"

"We'll find them when we find them."

"It's an interview, not some kind of statement?"

"An interview, but I may have long answers."

Charlotte nodded. Seth checked the focus and said, "We're good to go."

Sosa gave a thumbs-up. Charlotte nodded.

"Go," said Seth.

Mark Sosa turned to look directly into the camera facing him. "I'm Mark Sosa of the Sons of Stone. We're in a favela somewhere near São Paulo, Brazil." He gave the date. "I'm talking to Charlotte Sakshi and Seth Lian, documentarians from the United States who've asked to talk to me."

Charlotte took a deep breath and got into character, wishing she'd had notes. Truth be told, she knew very little about Sosa or his organization. Seth should be the one talking here. She'd do what she could, trusting that her training and her genuine curiosity would suffice. The audience would learn with her. It was a cop-out for failure to plan, but it was a straw to hold fast to.

"Today is an interesting day," she said. "We've come here directly from the destruction of the Salsbury Institute of Aging Research. Did you have something to do with that?"

It was a blunt question under any circumstances, but right out of the gate, it was dangerous. Sosa took it in stride. "I did. We did. It had to be destroyed."

"Did it have to be destroyed with so many people inside it?"

"Oh yes," he said. "If you're going to strike at the ruling class, you have to disrupt their supply lines."

"Can you explain that?"

This was the opening he'd been looking for; she could tell. It sure hadn't taken long to find it. Such is the power of blunt questions.

Sosa smiled knowingly and settled back in his rickety chair. He looked so young in the camera, Seth thought, and wondered if Charlotte saw the child there as he did.

"Let us consider two things," Sosa said. "The state of the world and the idea of immortality. Within one are truths, in the other threats."

He paused, letting the statement settle or perhaps offering Charlotte a chance to respond. Seth watched her calm gaze through his monitor, admired her firm chin and clear eyes in the face of everything.

"The world is a mess," Sosa said. "I don't like working in understatement, but to put it in proper proportions would require screaming. The most compelling mess has to be climate change. That should have been the wake-up call. It was for a few, but mostly it was just bad news, an inevitable problem to ignore since the state of the world was incapable of doing anything about it. Some tried. Word got out about melting glaciers. Dying oceans. There was a push to conserve the Amazon in the name of the planet. Remember that? Someone figured out that oxygen was a good thing. Benefit concerts and chain emails. Minimum political pressure. But it was too little. Too late. Too many compromises. Jobs being so important, money being everything. Promises were made to protect the forest. Made and ignored. Made and compromised away. The day they found titanium in the woods, that was the day the forest was doomed."

"You're fighting for Brazil then?" said Charlotte.

"What? No. It's just the front line. Varela, *el presidente*, is a fucker and his time will come. Is coming," he corrected himself. "Maybe it's today. I hear good things."

"A rebel force, with you at the head?"

"Guerrillas maybe. We're small. A handful that inspire others. But it's not us. Not me. Oppression is like squeezing soap. I'm a bubble or two, a bit of water, lubricant. It's the squeezing that brings the sudden shift. Brazil, like the world, is in for trouble. The only questions are when and how much, and which side will win. Contrary to fables, and more in keeping with reality, the good guys lose. A lot."

"Tell us where you're from," said Charlotte.

"I'm from Philadelphia, United States of 'Merica!"

"How old are you?"

"I'm seventeen." Seth could see that Sosa was getting a little irritated. Charlotte apparently saw it too.

"That's pretty young."

"Are you going to let me finish?"

"Your rant? Sure, but I just thought it would be better to get a little information on you. Manifestos can be dull. A little human interest goes a long way."

Sosa looked shocked, then softened. "Yeah, guess I did fall into that mode pretty quick. Sorry."

"Can you tell me the story from your point of view? I promise to give you time to complete the lecture later."

"Lecture is a strong word."

"I saw people die today. I'm cranky."

Seth noticed Davi shift his gun on his shoulder. Sosa saw it too and raised an eyebrow.

"You're something else, Ms. Sakshi."

She smiled only. God, she was cool, Seth thought. Where had this steel in her come from?

"I was born in Philadelphia. My father was Loughton Sosa. You might have heard of him. He was an author and activist. He was murdered by police when I was six. My mother fled down here to avoid the same fate."

Seth remembered the name. He'd been shot to death in his bed, eighteen bullets through his blanket. Police said he'd drawn a gun on them. Never mind that the gun never turned up, he was naked beneath the blanket and the shots were in his back. He was called a terrorist, and there was some evidence to support that, something involving gun purchases and cyber currency. His death wasn't mourned outside of the political fringe. If he'd been white, Seth remembered thinking at the time, things might have happened differently.

"We traveled around," Sosa continued. "I learned a few languages, saw plenty. Learned more. Woke up and screamed one night and here we are."

"That's pretty dramatic," said Charlotte.

"But that's just how it happened," he said. "I was dreaming of music, clear as day. Some ancient tribal sounds, deep and urgent."

Charlotte felt a chill go up her spine, glanced into the camera, looking for Seth in the lens somewhere.

"It rose to a crescendo, and when it broke, I did that god-awful cliché of sitting up in bed and screaming." Sosa shook his head, looking embarrassed. "I saw it all then. I knew what had to happen. I'd been told."

"A religious epiphany?"

"I know how I sound. Maybe I should have stayed with the manifesto, but that's what happened. I knew as clearly as if someone – something, had come down and spoke it." He laughed at the word.

Charlotte offered a little grin in reply. She could feel her heart pounding in her chest, hear her blood throbbing in her ears. She'd seen Davi shift his gun when she'd pressed. She knew these people were murderers. The world was full of them apparently. There was no hiding from them. They sought her out. She'd seen so much of it that the thought of dying herself was losing some of its power, just enough to make her reckless.

"I don't believe in God," Sosa said. "Not as it's been sold. That being is a blatant lie. The state of the world proves that. But I know there's more than just this. And whatever touched me that day was more than me. Call it the old gods – those who were more honest than Yahweh. Call it fate, the planet, the collective consciousness, I don't know. Hell, call it my own idea, if you have to – my own intuition. Call it a global alarm. Whatever. Fuck the source – it's right and it's loud and I hear it still, and it demands action."

"You hear it still?"

"Yes," said Sosa. Then he paused and looked hard at Charlotte, studying her. Seth watched him through the camera. His eyes bore into her. She shifted uneasily.

"I'm not the only one," he said after a moment.

Seth could see the gooseflesh rise on Charlotte's shoulders.

Sosa settled back, calmer now. He took a breath. "Ocean reefs died," he said. "Entire swaths of the ocean dead. Dead, nothing. No life. A die-off in the Gulf of Mexico the size of Texas. Barely reported. Out of sight, out of mind. A million dead polar bears over there somewhere. Water polluted and warmed beyond the ability to grow anything more than toxic algae blooms. This was a problem for tourism. No worry. People can ski in Alaska. They still have snow there, right?"

"Last I heard," said Charlotte.

"I remember watching a Louisiana fisherman beside himself with the state of things. He had a creole accent, I remember. Interviewed on some news show. Maybe it was online. I remember the look in his eyes, the helplessness. Talking about how things have only gotten worse and worse. His grandfather, his father, and now him. He tried to blame oil spills, Mexican fishermen, but that was flailing. 'The oceans are dying,' he said. 'The world is dying.' That's what I remember." He looked at Charlotte, studying her. "Do you hear it?"

She jumped. "Hear what?"

"Do you hear it in that? The passive voice? The ocean isn't dying. The world isn't dying. It's being killed, and the people murdering it have names and addresses. Let us talk now about immortality."

Chapter Twenty-Nine

Charlotte forced herself to keep an impassive face, to keep her breathing in check, her emotions out of this. But it was hard. There was horror, shock, despair from today and these weeks all spinning together like a cyclone in her head. Then there was the sound – or maybe just the memory of sound – the thing that haunted her even now and which seemed akin to something this young man, this young murderer, was using as justification.

"There's a tension between new and old," said Sosa. "New things replace old ones. Things wear out. They're supposed to. That's progress. That's how evolution works. It's coded into our very cells. Death. Time limits. Do the best you can, then get the hell out of the way. Where it doesn't happen, there is stagnation. There is poison. This is a fact of nature which has been grotesquely reflected in our society. Capitalism has run its course. All it does now is perpetuate a parasite class to the doom of the planet."

"Those are some jumps," said Charlotte. "Linking cell biology to politics. Capitalism to the murder of innocent scientists this morning."

"Well…"

"Those people had families," she said.

"I'm not going to quibble about individual lives," said Sosa. "I could go into the idea of class traitors, enablers and so forth, but it's moot and there isn't time."

"I got nowhere to go today." Charlotte kept a placid face, but wondered, if he'd have seen the destruction would he still be so cavalier? Probably, she thought. That event, unlike the others she'd attended, was distant and faceless. Almost theoretical compared to a room full of young, rich dead children, a drowned lawyer, a bludgeoned family.

"I know how it sounds, but listen, the usual timings are too slow as they are in the current...climate. Adding a level of endurance to that *class*," he spat the word, "is beyond obscene, beyond immoral. It's suicidal. The Salsbury Institute you're so upset about is a perfect example of what I mean. Two billion dollars a year were spent there."

"Past tense is accurate," said Charlotte.

He gave her a look now. He was losing patience.

Sensing trouble, deadly trouble perhaps, Seth said, "Maybe we should—"

Sosa waved him off, his eyes staying on Charlotte. His face softened. He put his hands before him, making a bowl in some gesture of explanation. "Are resources being used to feed people? House people? Restock the fisheries, replant the forests, improve the planet in any way that doesn't directly impact the ruling class? No. Not at all. All those resources, all those stolen, hoarded resources – money, manpower, thought power, political power – all that that class has amassed, goes instead to reinforce their place, entrench themselves further, for longer. Maybe forever."

"You believed the Institute was actually going to create immortal beings?"

"Probably not. No. No, I don't think so. That wasn't the worry. Because if they did, the wheel would turn on them eventually and one sect of that vampire race would turn on the other. That would happen eventually. But too late. No, the threat was that they'd find something that would extend their lives. Which has already been done. They sell decades of more life. There's a brochure."

"How?"

"Why do you think that facility was down here in Brazil, a third-world backwater instead of Switzerland or somewhere?"

"I'm sure there are such places in other countries."

"There are, but there they have some oversight. Here it's the Wild West, as the media loves to say. Here there is carte blanche use of stem cells or clone organs, they harvest them from embryos, or from peasants."

"That's quite an allegation. You're saying the Institute was killing people?"

"Yes."

"Do you have any proof?"

"Yes."

Charlotte waited; when he didn't continue, she said, "Will you share it?"

"I don't see a reason. If you want to grab onto that to justify the destruction of the facility and the maggots within, to hurt the monsters without, that's fine. Those are just some of the crimes, there are many, many more. Bigger ones with consequences larger than organ harvesting to order."

"You have an easy way of dropping the humanity of your victims."

"Maggots?"

"Monsters. Vampires before."

"When you give up your humanity, you become something else."

She had to smile at that, him a murderer.

"Did you have anything to do with the incident at Martha's Vineyard?"

"No."

"I don't believe you."

Seth tensed. Was she fearless or rash?

"They invited me to talk a while ago, but they sent me packing when it became clear that I was talking about them."

"Looks like something you might have done, all things considered."

"I'm not going to mourn it, but I didn't plan it or order it. It was organic. That's what's happening."

"Organic? Now you're ducking responsibility?"

"It was never mine. I'm an agent. It's that wake-up call I told you about. I wasn't the only one who heard it. The peasant uprising in Martha's Vineyard was a response to what that class was doing to the world."

Charlotte rolled around the word 'peasant' in her mind for a moment, trying to put it to Innkeeper James and his cohorts. Sure, why not?

"Marxist revolution? Some kind of Hundredth Monkey thing?" she asked.

"It doesn't matter. However the signal arrived, the message is clear."

Charlotte put on an incredulous face. Seth could only admire it. "And that message is 'Eat the rich'?" she said.

"Exactly."

The moment sat like a stone on the path.

"Why are you giving this interview if this movement is organic?"

"To give the children a nudge. A banner, if you will. An organization. To show that they're not alone."

"How big is your organization exactly?"

"Wherever there is a poor person, we are there. Wherever... I can't remember the rest."

"How cliché."

He held up his hands in surrender. "True, that was a little much. Even for me, but there's nothing new."

"Global revolution is new."

"No, it's not."

"What are you comparing it to? A world war?"

"That's not far off. It looks like synchronization but we're all fighting the same pressures and injustices. It's in our cultural makeup. Our cultural DNA. It's in the stones."

"Explain that."

"It's a myth. Do you know your Greek mythology?"

Charlotte's face was still as granite, but Seth felt new sweat down his back.

"Zeus was the king of gods, but he didn't start that way. Before him was his father, Cronus. These guys were all gods so they were immortals."

"Cronus was technically a Titan."

"Oh, so you know the story?"

"For the benefit of our viewers, please continue."

Seth's chest heaved with his heart but he had to admire Charlotte's calm. Then wondered if what he was seeing was really a bad thing, a crassness and scarring of a tender person he had cajoled to be here.

"Well, when the king is immortal, how's one ever to inherit? Cronus was warned that he'd be overthrown by one of his children, so whenever he had one, he'd eat them straight away. The same way our kings and rulers are eating us now."

"Please…"

"No. The parallel is exact."

"Zeus," she said, telling herself that this was a created coincidence. Sosa and Barney Faro had just read the same old books.

"Zeus's mother, Gaia, the earth goddess. Note that, Gaia, like the spirit of the planet."

"Noted."

"She saw that Cronus was an evil bastard, so when Zeus was born, she replaced him in the cradle with a rock. Cronus ate the stone thinking it was Zeus and Zeus with Gaia's encouragement grew up and overthrew the tyrant king. That's what we're doing. Overthrowing the evil bastards hindering creation at Gaia's bidding."

Seth felt his phone vibrate in his pocket but ignored it. Probably some distant ricocheted signal telling him he had an ad for cheap Viagra by mail order.

"For someone who doesn't believe in religion you seem to use gods pretty easily."

"It's the language we speak. These are the archetypes our species uses. They're recognizable and understandable. The rich know who they play, the poor their role. This is a fight for supremacy."

"Was Zeus so much a better leader than Cronus?"

"Yes. Hell yes. Absolutely, hell yes. By all measures."

"History, or in this case mythology. is written by the victors."

"It's a metaphor, Charlotte Sakshi, an easy-to-remember label. We're fighting for the planet, because if we don't, the planet – the whole fucking planet – dies. We don't have time for half measures. There can be no compromise, no slow transition to alternative fuels, no new, progressive directors leading leeching corporations. No smooth transition to more just societies. The time for that shit is long gone. Now there's only violence. It's the only sane decision. The meek will inherit the Earth or there won't be an Earth to inherit."

It was as if the entire world paused to consider Sosa's words. Not a sound leaked in from beyond the garbage walls. The bustling favela stopped its frenetic chaos to consider, and even the breeze held back.

"What do you want to say to the world?"

He nodded slowly, as if in respect for how things had gone. A nod to Charlotte's method? Seth hoped so. He'd like to think their exit would be as easy as their arrival.

"I want to tell everyone who hears what I hear, to listen."

A long moment ticked by.

"I'm listening," encouraged Charlotte.

"Not to me," he said. "The sound. Listen to the sound – the call, the planet's song."

"What does it sound like?" said Charlotte. Seth tried to hear snark in the question, but knew it wasn't there. She was asking.

"It is a chord of calling, a low murmur of distress only some can hear. A scream. An image, an idea formed in rhythm. A horn across a mountaintop, a drum from the valley."

He closed his eyes in concentration and then slowly, as if catching some faraway song on an errant breeze, nodded to the rhythm.

It creeped Seth out a bit. What a strange person, he thought. Obviously crazy, not just for his immoral acts, but how he played all sides – political and spiritual. Asserting one, denying the other, then this, an affirmation.

He studied Charlotte in the other monitor, wondering if she saw the intellectual dishonesty on display, but instead he saw only the slightest bob from her own head, a nod synchronized to Sosa's.

The young man, Sosa, his face looking younger than ever, opened his eyes to show they were red and wild. Tears formed in their corners, and slipped down his cheeks. "The old must die," he said.

Charlotte didn't respond, giving the line the weight he wanted, but also to take a moment to compose herself. She'd heard something in the silence of before, that lingering sound, recognized and rising, as if she had summoned it. A virus. Susan had said something about that. COVID's revenge in stereophonics. The implications of it being otherwise were too terrifying, so she moved on.

"So this is a class war," she said. "What about the sympathizers you have in their ranks?"

"Who?"

"Bobby Weller," she said.

"How?"

"We talked to him." Charlotte gestured to Seth behind her shoulder; he saw that her hand was shaking. "He explained that he murdered his parents for the same reasons you're giving."

"News to me."

"And the event at Martha's Vineyard."

"That was done by an enlightened soul who took necessary and appropriate action."

"Killing children?"

"Until you can get to the root, go for the fruit." He smiled. "Hey, that rhymes."

There'd been moments when Seth had considered Sosa to be a prophet of some kind, a revolutionary icon to be, but making light of the massacre of children convinced him they were dealing with a full-fledged psychopath.

"No thoughts on Bobby Weller then?"

"He's rich scum who had his own motive for what he did. He's ducking blame. He can rot in a grave along with the rest of the vampires of his class. Fuck him."

That was a usable quote, thought Seth. Charlotte had found a way to link the entire documentary from beginning to here. She continued to impress him. His phone twitched again in his pocket.

"Let's get back to that sound you mentioned," Charlotte said. "Have you—"

It was unmistakable. Gunfire. First the shot that silenced the group, then a second and a burst and more. And then again, from another direction. Near. There, and on the heels of a machine-gun echo, came the whirl of oncoming helicopters.

Chapter Thirty

Seth was quick to move, nearly as quick as Sosa and his people, who immediately took up positions by the door. Sosa armed himself with a rifle from behind a bush, while Seth removed the memory card from the borrowed camera and pocketed it. The other camera he removed from the tripod and readied the hand strap.

Charlotte was caught in surprise and remained seated, dumb and stunned, not even thinking of moving yet. She remained calm, dispassionate, watching the frenetic action erupt around her as a necessary replacement to the calm conversation of before. Approaching noise above and without filled the once-cozy space with menace. She absorbed it all from afar, likening the din to that which had already vexed her mind for weeks, too distant and unreal for real care. It was only when a breeze, hot and untraced, brought the cloying smell of cordite into the patio that she thought to stir.

"Seth?" she said.

"We're leaving," he said, as much to Davi as to Charlotte.

The guard didn't respond. Seth panned the camera to him for an instant, catching the scene, syncing the noise, his breathing. He picked up the rest of his gear, filming as he went, grieving for the amateur footage the motion would yield. He stopped filming to save battery and memory, but switched on image stabilization for next time. Charlotte followed him into the house.

In two steps they were outside again. The sound of gunfire echoed down the narrow streets. Seth filmed right, Charlotte looked left and saw Talita disappearing into a house a few yards away. She tugged on Seth's arm and led him in that direction.

"Are you sure?" he asked.

"I saw them go that way."

"Are you sure we want to follow them?"

"They know the way out."

She was right. They were in a maze. Every street looked alike, they'd been turned around a dozen times – no sense of direction, no landmarks, not even the sun. Violence was approaching and one direction seemed as good as another.

They sprinted toward the door. Charlotte stumbled once, fell to a knee in foul, brackish gutter water, righted herself quickly with Seth's lifting hands, and moved forward.

The sound of helicopters was loud and ominous. Pops of gunfire – from where, Seth couldn't tell – were answered with a roar of automatic weapons and then an explosion.

Ducking through the doorway, they found themselves in a dark passage – not a house, but a tunnel. They could hear footsteps and yelling above them, clumping on the rickety boards. More shots. A smell of smoke from somewhere just below the sickly sweet of the neighborhood. Light leaked through cracks in the walls and led them around two corners to another hall, ending in a torn shower curtain with daylight beyond.

Out the other side, they were in a crowd on another road, this one hard packed and dusty. People shoved and rushed, panicked, in both directions. Seth caught sight of Sosa's blue t-shirt to the right and led that way. Charlotte was right behind him, holding on to the back of his sweat-stained shirt, wondering where all these people had come from.

Seth came to a plank door and found it barred. He shook it.

Behind them, Charlotte saw Davi emerge from the tunnel. Gun in hand, the throng fled from him, disappearing behind slamming doors or down the branching paths. He jogged forward toward them.

"Seth…"

Hearing the warning in Charlotte's voice, he turned and saw Davi, the gun held at the ready. He tried to read if he was a friend or foe, then remembered his camera. He brought it up to his eye just in time to focus on Davi's face, to hear the burst of gunfire, to see his chest burst open and him crumple to the ground.

Seth threw his shoulder into the door and it gave in a splintering crash. He fell through, camera first, but pulled Charlotte in behind him. This time it was she who helped him up before they ran farther in.

It was a house, crowded with frightened people. Two old women held blankets in front of them like they were shields. A handful of children clung to a woman in a flower-patterned dress like she was a lifeboat in a storm. The mother the same, holding on to the children by neck and shoulders as if they alone gave her the strength to stand. Charlotte saw their frightened faces, all eyes and silence – clinging, hiding.

No one said a word as they rushed past and into a patio behind. It was like the one before, but with three exits. Seth panned the camera to each like some kind of game show blocking and then he found Charlotte and framed her face as she slowly turned from the scene in the house to outside. There was written more than fear, more than tiredness. Upon her face was written regret. It was a shock to him, that drew him from whatever adrenaline-fueled uber cameraman he'd been, to companion, friend. To more. He became afraid then, realizing it was just him in this hellish danger.

Gunfire from the next street sounded through the house, close and loud. A child began to cry. Prayers in Portuguese traced upon their echo.

Seth made a choice and bolted to an exit, the one that promised the most distance from where they were now.

Another house. Another cowering family. Another street. Another tunnel twenty yards beyond. Doors closed and boarded. No other way to go.

Helicopters from above. Shooting from behind. Clomps of heavy feet on rooftops coming nearer.

Sosa signaled them to get back. Seth held the camera on him, zoomed into his panting, Talita's smeared makeup, the rifles at their sides.

From the next street over, sounding nearly on top of them, came shouts and orders. Screeching radio static. Seth's phone came to life for a moment, a vibration and buzz in his pocket. He dared a glance at it. No caller. No message.

On the other side, people huddled together. Some distance now, the gunfire was several streets behind them. The narrow streets of the favela were labyrinthine. Seth had visions of *The Shining*. Charlotte recalled rats seeking cheese.

Not running now, but still moving fast, they followed a path to the left which grew steep. Another tunnel and a wider street, still on a hill. Now for the first time they had some navigational reference: up and downhill.

The shooting had not abated. It had only grown, but it was more distant.

Seth found a ladder leading to the rooftops. "I'm going up to look around," he said to Charlotte. "You stay here."

He expected her to object, but she sat down in the dust, found a piece of cardboard and fanned herself with it. She was breathing hard, catching her breath, keeping her eyes closed as she did. Seth noticed then that he too was a lather of sweat. He climbed the ladder feeling his shirt stick to his back.

Atop the shack, he could see reinforced paths leading around. He could see higher dwellings only reached by these catwalks. The hill rose behind him, ladders climbing to keep pace. The buildings were as ragged here as below. No uniform height at all. Three stories, four. Gaps in the buildings suggested roads or just low dwellings. There was a child's plastic pool with chairs around it a few yards away. He crept low and took up a position looking down the hill. He triggered on his camera and took in the scene through the viewfinder window.

There were three black helicopters circling and shooting. He could see the muzzle flashes from barrels of the machine guns, tracer bullets like shooting stars, and their reports a breath later, a roar in his ears. He saw a dozen plumes of smoke, some black like he'd seen that morning, tires burning for beacon and cover. Some were sickeningly white, and the breeze confirmed his suspicion of what they were: tear gas. But more alarming were the many plumes of light tan smoke, rising in steady, billowing clouds veined with black and gray. These made by spreading fire. Houses burning, but this place was all a single structure and made of kindling. The favela was burning. He saw flames leap from one plume, stretching into the sky, ten, twenty, thirty feet above the roofs. A half mile away, a sister to that terror replied in an explosion of some kind.

He saw soldiers in useless green camouflage uniforms roaming the streets, flinging grenades, flash-bangs, shrapnel and phosphorus. He saw black-clad snipers sneaking over the rooftops. Seth zoomed in on one of those before he found cover and saw no insignia of any kind. He saw also resistance, men and women, their guns the iconic Russian AK-47s against the army's American brand. The sounds were different, but the results the same. For each soldier he saw, he counted two armed civilians – guerrillas, insurgents – what have you. When your home was being invaded, was there a difference? For each soldier he saw, he saw also a dozen bodies.

He filmed for a few minutes, unable to guess what was happening. He'd thought it had been for Sosa, a quick response for his morning atrocity, but this was more than that. This was a slaughter. Maybe it was both. A wholesale slaughter of this class in retaliation for the murder of theirs.

And the shooting went on and the smoke rose higher, and the fire, uncontained and encouraged, spread.

As if a gust of wind had directed them, the soldiers all moved to his left. Seth hurried across the rooftop, careful to stay on the boards so as not to fall into something. Twenty feet on the other side, lying on his belly, he could see down into a courtyard. It was maybe two hundred yards away. He steadied his camera and zoomed in. There was Mark Sosa and Talita, his blue shirt unmistakable next to the tall woman.

Blood stained the front of her shirt. Head wound, neck maybe, he couldn't tell. The two ran across the courtyard and disappeared into a doorway. A moment later they emerged again, Talita backing out, her gun blazing behind her. The sound was delayed enough to give the whole thing a surreal feeling.

They bolted for another opening, but three soldiers emerged from that one.

Talita's gun stopped firing. She dropped it. Sosa fired two shots with a pistol and then dropped that.

They both raised their hands.

Seth framed them between the roofs, a high-angle perspective shot, stabilized and 10K putting Seth right in the courtyard. The three soldiers emptied their guns into the surrendering young rebel and his companion.

It was good the stabilization was on because Seth's hands began to shake. The shaking rose up his arms into his shoulders, and chest, and he put the camera down. In his mind he had seen the face of Travis, his son, dead in the dust. He'd made no kind of connection between the two before, not until the one was killed, murdered in surrender. How he'd made the leap, he couldn't tell. Maybe because the two were roughly the same age, maybe because life was valuable. Maybe because he felt his own mortality finally, and the regrets of his life rose to be reckoned with.

More soldiers collected the corpses, two more remained to set fires. Seth crawled back to Charlotte.

He was pleased to find her where he left her.

"What happened?" she said. "Are you crying?"

"Tear gas," he said.

"What did you see?"

"I'll show you. But first we have to get the hell out of here. I think the fastest way out is that way." He pointed in a direction he'd scoped from above.

Charlotte reached out and pulled him to her. It was not a sexual embrace, but a human one, a need they'd not known they'd had. He returned it in kind, needing it, feeling the comfort of her body; sweaty and shaking as it was, it was comfort.

They separated; their hands met. They shared an awkward moment, a weakened smile, then all was white and deafness.

Charlotte regained her vision first just in time to see three men in black fatigues drop a bag over Seth's head. She made to say something, scream perhaps, but couldn't hear her own voice for the ringing in her ears. She stopped trying when a bag came over her head.

Chapter Thirty-One

Time had lost relevance, but Seth tried to reason it out nonetheless. It had been a bright day, then the bag, and the plastic cord around his wrists. He could remember the sound of the zip tie tightening. The forced march through the maze. Stumbling, wailing, hearing Charlotte weep somewhere behind him. Turning to move toward her, a slap on the head. Walking, stumbling. A vehicle door opening. Trying to move away. Men forcing him down. A jab in the ass. A drug. Burning pain from the deep plunge. Men still atop him, consciousness receding into screams and smoke penetrating the bag. He couldn't breathe. Slipping away to be teleported here, to a windowless concrete cell. Naked on the floor, sitting in a pool of his own piss. Single light bulb, no blanket, no towel, not even toilet paper. Sink with cold water. Enough to wash.

Was that day one?

How long had he been there before the first talked to him? Six meals. How long was that? Time measured in calories – beans on a paper plate, a tortilla. White bread once, but always beans.

Six meals and he was asleep on the raised platform, coiled for the cold, when he was again bagged and dragged and fastened to a chair in another room. Cold steel braces around his ankles and wrists. Cold metal bands up his back, his butt, thighs. Cold chair. Cold room. Stinking of wet, cold wet and stale cigarettes. His body still shaking from withdrawal. Alcohol and cigarettes. Pills. All of it cold turkey to match the ambiance. He thinks that it could be an accurate clock, his body melting down from withdrawal abuse, timed. Regular, milestones of want, but he's never been here before. Once he quit smoking for a month, drinking for a week, pills a fortnight. But never all at once. No.

Hell no. This was a new experience in pain and regret coupled with fear. What a world.

They didn't ask him anything he could answer. Why they wasted their time he didn't know, but for the first five or six or seven interrogations, they spoke only Portuguese and that usually in volumes and sibilants that compounded his pain. He'd answered as best he could, guessing the questions. Sosa, the favela, his identity, his purpose. Each time he was cuffed across the head, face, back, side, cuffed until he just sat quiet, listening to the ranting, offering only a single question in return – some form of "Where is Charlotte?" to which he received no answer, hardly a recognition that he'd spoken at all, except a blow across an ear. He'd try twice and go silent, listening, watching, offering nothing, his ears ringing.

He'd tried to guess at the identities of his tormentors. Some wore uniforms with insignia, others wore uniforms without a mark on them. Some came in suits, one group in guayaberas – three of them, one might have been non-Brazilian, German maybe. He didn't know. That one never talked. A stream of faces and people, short visits. Ten minutes, fifteen, two questions from him, rambling and yelling, and back to the cell. There was sense to it somewhere, he knew, but he couldn't fathom it.

Then those visits – interrogations – stopped. More meals alone in his cell. No more visits to the concrete room. Quiet. Cold. More plates of beans. Sixteen, seventeen meals. One meal a day? Two? One every eighteen hours? There was a regularity to it he'd discovered, one that he couldn't consciously measure, but his body, feeling a Pavlovian pang of hunger, could discern.

And in between the meals, in the always-bright of the caged bulb, in the three-pace-by-three-pace cold concrete cell, he put his mind to other things, other times, other problems. Freed from his drug-induced, amnesiac denial, the tremors withdrawing as well, taking away that distraction, he had to face his concise mind. Though he slept as much as he could, it was not enough and his thoughts returned for reckoning. Barney had once said that people cannot live in the now, they live in the future or the past, planning or regretting. As a history teacher, he joked that he taught regret. That was the place where Seth dwelled now. It seemed the safest place. The future was terrifying, the present was unbearable, the past was painful but firm.

Of course, he thought of his marriage and his son. He tried to remember good times, but the past was regret and whatever good there'd been hadn't stuck the way the bad had. There was a psychological reason behind that he knew, learning from failures, assuming success so its presence was invisible. It was a recipe for regret. He imagined happy times with Travis, playground visits that never occurred and moonlight walks on a soothing beach with Ellen along, the three of them holding hands in a greeting card cliché which stabbed him for never having happened.

He thought also of Gina. The young coed dead in his hot tub. 'Don't wake me.' She knew what she was doing. He was sure of it. She'd killed herself and he'd let her. That was his sin, he knew, and the consciences of the world knew, but luckily they couldn't imagine a young pretty woman intentionally checking out and him letting it happen. Too horrible.

She'd had a right to leave. There's a time to leave even if there's nowhere to go. She was independent and firm-willed, so said her obituary − he'd hardly known her − and so she'd taken control of her own life and extinguished herself. Nirvana meant 'to extinguish' didn't it? She'd reached nirvana. And he'd let her. How he wanted to talk to her now, to ask Gina Breeve to verify it had been a choice, to absolve him for doing nothing.

But of course he should have done something. The permanent solution to a temporary problem. He was authority, a teacher, a leader. Father figure perhaps. But responsibility had evaporated like the steam from the pool. She'd overdosed in his hot tub with him there. The only reason to do that in public was the desire to be stopped, perhaps by someone wise, caring, giving, charitable. A father figure. A failure he was. He had regrets.

And that always took him to Charlotte. Like an iron filing to a magnet, he'd flex back to what he'd done to her. She'd wanted to stop and he hadn't let her. It was the reflection of Gina; there he should have intervened to stop and hadn't, here he'd intervened to continue. Both would have the same results. And he was in the present again. And the present was unbearable. He longed for the torturers to return.

★ ★ ★

In another cell, Charlotte endured much the same. The cold, the damp, the inscrutable questioning. In deference to her gender and the mores of a once-Catholic land, she was allowed to cover her nakedness with a tan jumpsuit. She was given pads for her period when it came and sometimes she could hear music through the door.

She cried. She cried a lot, and the guards would check on her when she did, one even sliding a box of tissues through the little door in the base of the steel wall they took her through.

She cried for herself for a while, but quickly cried also for the dead who visited her in her cell, imprinting on her the responsibility of witness. Then she cried for the burden and likened herself to Christ, bearing a weight too heavy on the way to certain death. Then she cried for blasphemy. She cycled through her losses, the friends she missed, the opportunities passed and potentially forever out of her reach. For she had decided that she would not get out of the cell alive. She was not certain if they would kill her but suspected they would eventually. She had been disappeared. That terrible descriptor coined by traumatized survivors to describe the kidnapping and vanishing of loved ones. One could never be certain if the government had done it, or a bandit, or just a slip into a sinkhole walking home. It was a double blow of loss coupled with uncertainty, a cruelty compounded.

And she cried over her parents. Not for, not to. About. Guilt and anger intermixed. Gratitude and hatred. They'd born her and raised her and therein was the rub. Gratitude and hatred. Who were they to condemn her to this? To life which is suffering. And more subtly, but not less damning, to burden her with expectations. She'd been born into a debt to parents whose experience was not hers, whose goals were not hers and yet they'd made them hers. They were of an earlier time and place. Primitive by her standards. They couldn't raise their eyes above their plates, their hopes beyond lineage. Shallow. Animalistic. Misogynistic. Demanding she give up her best years to curse another soul? Sell herself to a man? Backwards. Devolved. They'd spent their lives' potential accepting the lowest goals life could offer. Her life was greater than that. Her goals loftier. She could understand her debt to them for allowing her these things, but that didn't mean she had to discard her goals for theirs. It was the opposite. She should embrace them. Be somebody. Make a real difference, or at least get the most out of her life that she could.

But she was locked in a cell somewhere in Brazil and had been for – she didn't know how long.

She imagined her parents shaking their heads at her, the usual cemented expressions of disappointment and 'we warned you'. The vision only enraged her. She'd tried. There was nobility in that. Tremendous nobility. Seth was her conscience and he'd been right to push her; hell or high water, she had to go on. There were only two mistakes she could make: not starting and not following through. If it killed her, she'd make herself accept it. She'd make herself understand she'd tried her best and had just fallen short. Quality versus quantity. That was the thing her parents didn't get. They saw only more life; she saw better life and the adventure which was her existence now went far beyond that. They'd had their own, to be sure, but this was hers. This was hers. This was hers.

She wondered how much footage Seth had of her. The story was changing all the time. It had started one way, went another, then turned and jumped and turned again. She saw herself as the protagonist now of the documentary they were making. This was a story of her journey to…to…something. That made her reconsider her doom. She felt the miles she'd come in her body, the shifts of perspective, understanding and insight in her mind. She was the hero. The story wasn't over.

And she stopped crying then, strangely confident of at least another act. And in this calm quieting of her mind, she heard again, consciously, the distant sound that had followed her. It brought to mind cicadas, though she had no personal experience with them. Was there not a sound around those insects? A drone? Or a buzz? An underlying yet overwhelming siren of sound set to a seventeen-year cycle? It was like that, but rhythmic. One could almost dance to it.

Her calm alarmed the guards more than her weeping. The slit in the door would open more often. Disembodied eyes peered in at her. They took her blanket, doubtless to stop her from harming herself. Her plastic spoon was discontinued, but her rations increased and white bread began appearing and once, a plastic-wrapped Twinkie was on the floor when she woke up.

Days stretched by, timeless, as unmeasured as a dream, and then her door opened and a white man in a blue Panama shirt called her by name. "Miss Sakshi?"

From her bunk, knees to her chest, waiting, she regarded him.

"Come with me," he said.

She followed him down the dank concrete hall she'd passed through dozens of times before but had never seen. They walked around a corner where men waited on the other side of a thick glass window. A buzzer sounded; the latch retracted.

"We have a car waiting," said the man.

A short walk through a police station. It was quiet, looked to have been evacuated recently and quickly. A skeleton crew with blank disinterest remained to watch them leave.

A door to the outside and sunlight found her face for the first time in weeks. It felt oppressive and sizzling and she guarded her eyes with her hand.

The man opened the rear door to a black SUV and waited for her to get in. She did. He got in beside her. He signaled her to buckle up and the driver pulled away on unfamiliar streets without a word.

"What is happening?" she said.

"I'm an American," said the man.

"I figured that."

"It's no longer safe here," he said.

She stared.

"I'm just collecting you," he said. "Allen will explain."

"Who's Allen?"

"The man who'll explain it."

"You CIA?" she asked.

He surprised her and said, "Yes."

"Why isn't it safe?" she asked, and as if the universe had heard her, gunfire erupted to her left and riddled the sides of the vehicle with dull, deadly staccato strikes. Her window, tinted dark nearly to obscurity, burst into a spiderweb of cracks. One, two, three centers, three termini of jagged lines testing the bulletproof glass. The last one spit splintered shards into Charlotte's cheek, which bled immediately down her chin.

The vehicle sped up. More gunshots. Thumps on all sides. A heavy splash on the hood. A man's face momentarily seen through the windshield – surprised, twisted, enraged. Young. His body broken and careening over the top of the vehicle to land in a crashed mound of flesh and torn rags behind the vehicle as it sped away, a cloud of dry red dust behind them.

Chapter Thirty-Two

Seth regarded Mr. Allen across the airport lounge with curious contempt. This he demonstrated with a cold, lingering stare that was unceremoniously broken by a hard cough from his strong cigarette. He hadn't had one in so long that now they tasted foul. They had always tasted foul, he realized, but now he was aware of it. He forced himself to keep smoking. They'd gone to the trouble of getting him a carton of them, after all.

The man he was staring at was Mr. Allen, the new man, not the man who'd woken him out of a shivering sleep in his cell with the words, "Seth Lian, come with me." The voice had come on a thick Southern drawl, west Texas and proud of it. The kind of twang that never went away because the speaker thought it an art form.

Seth had studied the man that matched the voice. Cowboy hat, jeans, boots. Button-down shirt, sweat-stained. He signaled for Seth to get moving, impatience shown by his tapping foot and how he scanned the hallway both ways as Seth got up.

"Get dressed," said the man.

Seth shook his head. "No clothes," he said, but it was more of a croak, his voice unused for many meals.

The man noticed Seth's nakedness then. "Shit. These fucking savages," he said. "Hold on." He disappeared to the left of the door, the direction they'd never taken him.

The door was left open. Seth stepped forward and looked around. The halls were concrete, cold and empty. He took a couple steps after the man, wondering if he shouldn't be running, when a different man returned with a handful of clothes.

"Put these on for now," he said. "Mr. Allen will find you something better."

It was a police uniform. More army than cop, but that's how things were now. He put them on and was surprised by how well they fit, though the boots were snug. He was a corporal now, he noticed.

"Let's go," said the man.

Seth followed him through a door to a parking lot, then into a black SUV without plates.

"Where're we going?" Seth asked.

"Airport, then home. You want to go home, don't you?"

"Do you always ask stupid questions, or does it come with the accent?" said Seth.

The conversation kind of died after that.

The man brought him to the airport lounge, introduced Mr. Allen with as few syllables as possible and left. Mr. Allen nodded, gave him a carton of South American cigarettes and sat down by the window.

"Your man said you'd get me new clothes," said Seth, taking a soft drag on the cigarette, practicing his smoke rings.

"He did?"

"Yeah."

Mr. Allen was a tall man, slim. His suit was institutional and did nothing to hide his shape. He had short hair, trimmed to stubble around the sides. In his fifties. He was distracted and kept looking out the window to the airport tarmac, maybe counting smoke plumes over São Paulo, maybe thinking of golf. It was hard to say.

The airport lounge was deserted except for Allen, Seth and a man at the door with a machine gun. A small German thing. Automatic firepower that could be hidden beneath a sports coat. The lounge was upscale, could fit maybe fifty people. The bar was wide and hardwood, the windows could be dimmed by some electronic alchemy that seemed out of place in South America. The lights begged to be lowered, the candles on the tables lit, but neither was the case. It was bright with clear light from the window, ceiling cans filling the room with clarity that suggested disinfectant and cleaning crews.

The airport outside the door was a panic, people fighting to get onto planes and get out of the city. The noise of the mob seeped into the lounge from up three floors and two hallways.

"Can I have a drink?" Seth said. "While we're waiting?"

"Miss Sakshi is in the building," said Mr. Allen. "They'll be here momentarily."

Seth didn't know how this bit of information had come to Mr. Allen, but could guess there was some radio in his ear, or maybe implanted in his skull. Such things existed, right?

"The drink?"

"Help yourself."

He didn't need the drink. He was seventy-one meals sober. Strange how already that measurement faded with the revelation of daylight. He made himself a neat whiskey for something to do, pouring from the best behind the bar – a nineteen-year-old Jameson. A drink older than his son. The bottle went for one thousand, nine hundred dollars in the duty-free. He took the C-note worth of alcohol back to his table to stare at it.

He was aware that his bravado was put on, a theatrical armor paper-thin to hide his fear and frustration. He'd put himself into his 'I don't give a shit' façade that was always vulnerable to reality. Thinking of Charlotte now, knowing he'd see her, fearing what they'd done to her, weakened it the more. He'd leave his drink. After so long dry, it might actually make him drunk and then he'd lose more control. Like he had any.

Charlotte was rushed through back hallways of an airport, past crowds of fleeing refugees. Down a hall and up some stairs, they paused to look into a large room filled with people. By the looks of them, by their voices, by their separation, she knew them to be Americans. A handwritten sign on the door proclaimed, 'This space is sovereign to the United States of America.'

While her man talked with another, she stayed by the door and watched as numbers were called. People stood up and shuffled out a back door toward the tarmac, where she assumed a plane was waiting. When the numbers stopped, people looked around dejectedly. Some found her standing among them and looked her over with aversion, perhaps even hate. Her color and clothes set her apart from the white-skinned business class around her. There was money in this room, fleeing money, scared money. One woman clutched two carry-on bags to her chest like they contained jewels. They probably did.

"It's Saigon all over again," said the man returning.

"I don't see Seth," said Charlotte.

"He's with Mr. Allen upstairs. Come on."

She followed the man out and the looks receded with another call of numbers.

Another flight of stairs and she was brought to a guarded door proclaiming 'Beach Club, Members Only'. The guard stepped aside and let them in.

She didn't recognize Seth. His clothes first – a uniform, then his face. Sunken cheeks over a wiry salt-and-pepper beard. Then the eyes, sunken but warm, brightening to see her, and then she saw him and found herself smiling for the first time in a long time.

They met in the middle of the room in an embrace. No words, just tight grasping, squeezing as if to test the reality of flesh and presence.

"We don't have a lot of time," said Mr. Allen.

"Charlotte," said Seth. "This is Mr. Allen. I think he's CIA."

"Me too," said Charlotte.

"Want a drink?" asked Seth.

"Juice?"

"Why didn't I think of that?" Seth went to the bar fridge and searched. Charlotte sat down, pushed Seth's untouched drink and smoldering ashtray aside, and waited.

"I am CIA," said Mr. Allen. "And Allen isn't my real name."

"There's no ice," said Seth.

"I don't want any."

"I'm sorry," said Mr. Allen.

"Not your fault about the ice."

"I'm talking about your last two months."

The two stared at him.

"I was trying to save you," he said. "From the favela raid. Kind of a thank you for services rendered."

"You're going to have to unpack that," said Seth.

"We tracked your phone."

"To Sosa?"

"To Sosa," he said.

"You were working with Valera?"

"Yes."

"How did you know to…" Charlotte didn't finish her question. Her mind was racing to catch up. She looked at Seth admiringly, glad he seemed all there. She wasn't sure she was.

"We've been tracking you since before New England."

"Fuck," said Seth. "How?"

"Does it matter?"

Seth thought about that.

"Did you know about the Institute? Before it happened?" Charlotte asked.

"We knew something was going to happen. Had we known it was the Salsbury, we'd have done something. That target has importance beyond here. Many people are upset."

"Mass murder will do that," said Seth.

"Anything would have given Valera the excuse he needed. He even asked us to do something to trigger it."

"This is sick," said Charlotte.

Seth brought her a glass of orange juice and sipped his own by the table, remaining on his feet.

"There's a lot of people *very* upset," said Mr. Allen.

Seth laughed. "Looks like."

"About the Salsbury."

"But not the favela?"

Allen shook his head.

"Sosa picked well," said Charlotte, choking down a sip, trying to taste the sweetness, the luscious smoothness of refrigerated juice. It could have been bile for all she could appreciate it.

Mr. Allen shrugged. "I'd think a courthouse or army depot would have been a smarter choice."

"Haven't you watched our footage."

"I did," said Mr. Allen. "Most of the world has." He signaled to the man at the door, who went into a back room and returned with their luggage. Among it was Seth's camera equipment that they'd had that day. The man put it on the bar. Seth regarded it like it was an alien body.

"Your money is all there. Your phones didn't make it." He said it in a way that discouraged follow up. "You have a good eye, Mr. Lian."

Seth didn't know what to say.

"And you have a good camera presence, Ms. Sakshi."

"Thank you," she said quietly.

Mr. Allen sighed and looked out the window. "This was a powder keg for a long time."

"Was a powder keg?" Seth gestured out the window to the fires, the panic, the now discernible approaching gunfire. "Yeah, well. Boom."

"Valera fucked up," said Mr. Allen. He produced a remote control from his pocket and activated a flat-screen TV on a wall. The windows immediately dimmed a little as shock waves from a distant explosion rattled them ever so much.

"State television took your film and showed it. They edited it, but not enough."

"Is this live?"

"Yes," said Mr. Allen. "On a loop. We think the station broadcasting it was set on autopilot and abandoned. Or maybe the rebels got it and liked the feed. We could jam it, but what's the use? Not like anyone is home watching TV."

Charlotte squinted up at the monitor and tried to make sense of the Portuguese voice-over. It made her skin crawl. That language would forever be associated with her confinement. Sosa appeared; subtitles scrolled beneath his chin. *"There's a tension between new and old,"* said Sosa. *"New things replace old ones. Things wear out. They're supposed to. That's progress. That's how evolution works. It's coded into our very cells. Death. Time limits. Do the best you can then get the hell out of the way. Where it doesn't happen, there is stagnation. There is poison. This is a fact of nature which has been grotesquely reflected in our society. Capitalism has run its course. All it does now is perpetuate a parasite class to the doom of the planet.*"

Mr. Allen said, "President Valera thought this would incite anti-communist sympathy."

"Did it work?" said Seth.

Mr. Allen gestured out the window in the same way Seth had done. "No," he said.

Charlotte's own voice came from the speaker, faceless but clear over a scene of the smoldering building. *"Today is an interesting day,"* she said, Portuguese text scrolled in tandem at the bottom of the screen. *"We've come here directly from the destruction of the Salsbury Institute of Aging Research. Did you have something to do with that?"*

The scene faded to Sosa's smiling face. He nodded and said, *"I did. We did. It had to be destroyed."*

"Did it have to be destroyed with so many people inside it?"

"Oh yes. It you're going to strike at the ruling class, you have to disrupt their supply lines."

Some big, bold letters appeared in the center of the screen. Sosa held in freeze-frame.

"What does that say?" asked Charlotte.

"'Murderer of innocents'," said Mr. Allen.

"Are the subtitle translations accurate?" asked Seth.

"They're pretty good. There are too many English speakers in the country to bend it too far. They do refer to the Institute as a hospital, however. I'm not sure that's accurate."

The scene changed to the favela and the battle there. Seth recognized his own footage and some he didn't take. Then the scene of Sosa gunned down, the sound of the gunshots a moment delayed for distance.

"They showed that? Why?"

"A warning? A threat to coerce the population?"

"How's that working out?" said Charlotte, watching an orange fireball rise slowly in the sky, the shock wave rattling the window at the end of her sentence.

Seth turned to see the rising cloud.

"I know that gas station," said Mr. Allen. "There was a good taco stand by it."

Seth turned back to the TV where more of his footage flowed by. "That footage was mine, you know? Ours. There was a paycheck there. News services would have paid top dollar. I've been robbed."

"You can sue Varela, but I doubt he'll be around much longer."

He thought about it. "Was it stolen?" he said.

"Your footage is all there with your cameras," said Mr. Allen.

"What?" Seth finally moved to the table to inspect his gear. It was battered a bit, but intact and the files were all there.

"We thought to wipe them, but why bother?"

"You thought...so you gave them to Varela's goons?"

"Me?"

"You know what I fucking mean."

"You got it back. You're alive. You're even being flown home. You're welcome."

"Thank you," said Seth. "Or should I be thanking someone else? The *they* we hear about."

"No, this was me."

"Then thank you," said Charlotte. "I'm not sure I understand what's going on."

"You were taken and imprisoned because that's how things work down here. You were freed because we're pulling out and I didn't want to leave you to rot."

"That's nice of you," said Seth. "You're real decent."

"You're not on the plane yet, Seth," he said.

Seth looked outside the window at the smoke, the tarmac, back at the door. "Okay."

"But why?" asked Charlotte.

"It was the decent thing to do. You're Americans. Plus, you don't seem to have a political agenda. You're just witnesses who keep finding themselves at the wrong place at the wrong time."

"You know what we've been doing?" said Charlotte.

"Yes. Since Indian Wells."

"Why?"

Allen cupped the side of his head and turned aside, obviously listening to something from his earpiece. "Government house has fallen, Planalto Palace. Valera is…" He paused, nodded, said, "Valera is dead. What's left of him is being carved up."

"I had no idea the Sons of Stone were this powerful," Seth said.

"They weren't until Valera in his infinite wisdom attacked the favela, martyred Sosa and bragged about it. Now everyone with a grudge is a Filhos da Pedra and then with the, uh…current milieu."

"Who's the leader now?" said Seth. "Maybe we'll stay and get an interview."

"Shut up, Seth," said Charlotte.

"No leader we have found yet."

"Good for them."

Allen gave a wry grin.

A man poked his head into the door. "Valera was butchered by his own daughter," he said. "The palace—"

"I know," said Allen.

"Time to go, sir."

Seth collected his things. Charlotte finished her juice.

"Seriously, Mr. Allen, why let us go? Why give us back all this footage? It can't be in the interests of…of the people your organization usually caters to. You know we'll talk. We're reporters."

"Seth…" Charlotte warned.

Mr. Allen shook his head in surrender. "I honestly don't think it matters anymore," he said. "When you two get home, you can catch up on current affairs."

Part Three

Holocaust

Chapter Thirty-Three

Charlotte didn't know the type of plane they were herded onto with a mass of other Americans who were desperately fleeing the burning city. It was a famous plane, propellered and with a big door at the end. Didn't Tom Cruise jump out of one of these once? Famously doing his own stunts? Nothing so sexy now. It was drab and cold and felt like a cattle car. Seth looked at her at one point and mooed at her, making her smile and confirming her theory.

They were among the last to be brought in, escorted not by Mr. Allen but one of the men by the door. Mr. Allen had sent them off with a nod but didn't watch them go, his gaze instead fixed on the growing chaos outside the window.

Charlotte tried to identify some of the passengers from the crowd in the terminal, but all the faces blended together and the main characteristic, fear, had faded, replaced with relief. Seth found them space on a bench by butting his hips into the overweight, gray-haired man taking up two spaces. And then again, to ripple it down the whole row, finally freeing up space for four. They were joined by a bottle blond in sunglasses and an old, round man in a shirt more wrinkled than his face. Neither acknowledged them.

Their bags were kept on their laps. There were no seat belts. The space was sweltering.

Explosions could be heard as the door closed. Shouts. Gunfire, far and near. Really near. Without windows, Charlotte felt claustrophobic. The packed-in people didn't help. Seth put his arm around her and kissed her head.

The plane shook and the air pressure changed. Blast or speed, Charlotte couldn't tell. Then the telltale feeling of lifting off, her own weight pushing her down, resisting. Giving up. Her ears popped.

Seth leaned in to say something, but whatever he tried to say was drowned out by the sound of the plane. She shook her head and pointed to her ears. He nodded.

Their rise was steep and long, nothing like a commercial jet. Then it leveled off all in a moment. The noise was thick, the air cold. A man in an army uniform passed out yellow foam ear plugs. Seth handed the first pair to Charlotte, then took his own.

She had no watch. She had no phone. She didn't know the date, but knew she'd been gone a long time. Her parents would be beside themselves with worry. No one had told her how long the flight would take, or even where it was going. She wondered if any of the others knew. Some would, for sure, but there'd be no communicating with them. Though egalitarian in their seating, they were separated by noise and might as well have all been on different planets. She nestled up to Seth and tried to sleep.

He'd been strong, he thought. His wall of bravado and cool had won the day. Hadn't it? He'd acted like he'd been thrown into solitary confinement all the time, tortured, starved and tormented for years on end. Same shit, different day. Lie or resistance? Who was he performing for? Mr. Allen didn't care. His agenda was unmoved, never questioned, never threatened. To him, they were grist in a fabled machine everyone knew about, but few had seen up close. The machine should have chewed them up and shat them out, but hadn't. This was a miracle made possible by the pity of a single broken man behind a pseudonym.

Seth had gotten them into it, but Mr. Allen had saved them. There was shame in that, but still Seth had to be strong, for Charlotte if not him. There could be no others. His pride made him act that way, his guilt made him keep it up. He didn't know what she'd been through, but anything short of a holiday on a beach was on him.

He decided that when they got home, he'd make a clean break with her and the project. How long could they swirl around the drain of destruction before being sucked in? This time they had barely escaped the current. Next time – and he knew if they went on, there'd be a next time – they wouldn't be so lucky.

He tried to sleep in the rattling plane, blind beneath clenched eyes, deaf behind the earplugs, but his mind would not be quiet. Guilt and fear beat like the vibrations from the fuselage rising through the bench, into his legs, up his spine, neck and skull, manifesting in his ears as a hum.

He was guilty of the sin.

The realization was as a dream, or more to his experience, like a moment of drugged clarity. There was a sin being punished. Connecting the dots, the motives, the world, the air, the fire – he saw the sin of short-term thinking. Ironic that the sin had not a better name, something catchy. Evil. He lit up on greed. There was a word that came closer to what was happening, what he had done. It was a better word containing within it the sin in the sin: selfishness.

Sensing the theme of the fabled song, he listened for the sound that Charlotte had told him about, that others had reported, that Sosa and referenced, but he heard it not. No matter. He didn't need that source to know the problem. His experience – which was the purpose of age, was it not? – had taught him.

Greed.

He'd heard it said that karma does not punish you for the act, but by it. He liked that, but didn't understand it. He liked that it took reincarnation out of the equation. He didn't buy into that. He liked that you got slapped now for being an ass, got tortured for going where you didn't belong, got killed in an imploding building for hubris against nature.

Greed and short-term thinking.

The entire ongoing ecological collapse of the planet could be put down to those motives. Every bubble in finance, every government bailout, every polluted river, every piece of plastic, every distraction and delay fell into the same. He'd read forecasts and realized that he'd be dead before the worst of it. Hell, everyone would. He'd noticed how so many studies ended at the century and didn't think to continue into the next, as if the ruin would halt in the year 2100. The few places that went into the next century made the predictions of this one look pleasant.

Another word came to him: capitalism. But that sounded hollow and dry. Ash on his tongue. This was not the work of a philosophy, system, or idea. This was the fault of people, people who had names and addresses.

But it didn't matter, did it? Wasn't it all moot? The world was as it was. His view of carpe diem was reinforced but now he felt dirty for it. Now, he saw how his actions had hurt someone he loved. And he did love Charlotte. He put his arm around her and drew her in. She jumped in fright, wide-eyed and panicked, but after blinking and looking around, seeing Seth's smiling face, forced as it was, and his watering eyes not forced, she went back to sleep.

He thought of the unnecessary suffering he'd put her through and hated himself. He thought of the unnecessary suffering of all the people – of the murders of the innocents in the favela – and grew angry. The feeling rose to rage and focused on the rich and powerful as only the mind of the powerless can. He shook with hatred at the rich, smug assholes whose children had died at a party, suddenly happy for their demise, glad he'd seen those generations ended. He felt honored to have been there when Bobby Weller dispatched the stain of his parents, the slime of that lawyer. They were the people who did evil things. They were the thieves who had nothing to lose because they would be gone before the bill was due. They would be escaping their karma and find justice only in an afterlife. Heaven and hell, divine justice, karma beyond this life – those were lies. He heard it clearly in the sound. Lies from the powerful to mollify the weak. Convenient. 'Suffer now, because later you'll be rewarded; suffer me now because later I'll be punished.' And the rage rose up in him to a point that he had to stand. Charlotte woke and watched him file out to the walkway.

"Stretching my legs," he mouthed to her.

Bleary and half-awake, she seemed to understand. "Karma," she mouthed to him.

"What?" he said.

But she curled up and closed her eyes.

Had she said that?

The rage slipped, replaced with wonder that she had shared his thoughts.

He shook it off and moved toward the front of the plane, where he thought he might find a bathroom. He glanced at the other passengers and felt the hatred rising up in him again. Only the setting, crammed together in this plane, kept him from…what? Had he met one on a golf course just now, or in a boardroom, what would he have done?

For weeks he'd done nothing but sleep, but now he felt more tired than ever.

An armed soldier eyed him suspiciously as he approached.

"American," he said as best he could. "Bathroom." He exaggerated the words to be understood.

The soldier pointed forward.

It was nothing grand, as utilitarian as anything the military might conceive, but it wasn't the disgrace of a hole he'd been shitting in for weeks. He relieved himself, wondering if he had dysentery. There was water and he washed his hands, splashed his face, but held back drinking any.

The face that stared out of the tiny mirror was unrecognizable. He'd lost a lot of weight. It showed in his cheekbones. His hair was long and a mess. His beard was the tragedy it always was when he tried to grow it. He suddenly felt ashamed that he'd kissed Charlotte's head with this face.

Remembering her sitting alone on the bench amid a sea of vampire sociopaths the world called 'the elite', he hurried back to Charlotte. He pushed his way back to his seat, daring any of the other passengers to give him a look or resist him retaking the space they'd already spread into, his equipment on the floor. A glance from him and they made room.

Once seated again, he shifted the bags and pulled Charlotte into him, wrapped her in his arms. She snuggled back, not waking, but saying something he could not hear.

He kissed the crown of her head. Loved and hated at once.

Before the plane landed, he wondered if Sosa shouldn't have left the Salsbury Institute alone. Giving the ghouls the chance of continued life might have changed their thinking, made them pay more attention to the future. The thought was short-lived, however, for the drumming in his skull told him that things were a certain way. Though his own transformation suggested it was possible to change ideas and values, the march of reality, the wars, the theft, the murders, the short-sighted greed of their reality in the face of certain doom, proved it was not a viable strategy.

And thus the revolution.

The Sons of Stone battling Cronus for the dominion of creation.

A story as old as time.

The meek shall inherit the world and he had watched them try in Saõ Paulo.

Chapter Thirty-Four

They landed in Arizona at an airbase ninety minutes from Phoenix. The temperature on the tarmac when the door opened to disgorge the privileged refugees was one hundred seventeen degrees Fahrenheit. It was mid-June in Arizona, and the weatherman had called it a nice day.

The heat stung their chilled bodies, stopping them on the ramp before they were pushed on by those behind. They'd known heat in the last day, but Brazil was moist and flavored with flowers, tire smoke and fear. This was dry as kindling, dusty as death. It made Charlotte imagine buildings, planes and people spontaneously bursting into fire.

They were led into an air-conditioned building where they were offered sandwiches and coffee in a lifeless cafeteria, closed and empty, but for plastic furniture and the pile of plastic-wrapped ham sandwiches and carafes of cooling coffee. Seth and Charlotte found a table and tried to eat. Seth looked terrible. It was clear he hadn't slept.

Seth, catching her looking, said, "That bad, eh?"

"You need a shave."

Two military policemen and an officer approached them. "Who are you?" they said to Seth. The menace in the voice was unmistakable.

Seth told them. They believed the borrowed uniform and not him.

"Ask Mr. Allen," he said.

"Who?"

"Of course." Seth had to chuckle. "I'm Seth Lian. My ID was lost. As were my clothes. And money, come to think of it. I was lucky to get these." He tugged at his shirt for emphasis. "The rest of the story is surely above your pay grade."

He eyed the film equipment. "But you didn't lose that?"

"No. Looks like I didn't."

One of the MPs took Seth by the arm, lifted him out of his chair like he weighed nothing.

"Leave him alone," said Charlotte. "We're American citizens. Saved from two months in damned Brazilian prison. Give us some slack."

The officer looked around at the rich and powerful who watched them. Charlotte realized then why they had been singled out. They didn't match the group. It was more than the uniform, though that was a lot of it, but they were of a different class, a different race, a different age.

"We're trying to get back to Oregon."

The officer weighed something in his mind that took his glance around the room twice and then landed on the MPs, who released Seth. "Someone will be by to help you arrange that." He left with the two guards.

Seth sat down at their table and looked. "Thanks," he said.

"Fuckers," Charlotte said, with real venom.

"Was it really two months?" Seth asked.

She pointed to a muted TV in the corner. The date and time were in the upper right. Scenes of violence and chaos, mobs rushing police, dead bodies in squares, cars afire.

"Another news cycle we could have been a part of," said Seth. He caught himself before he said he'd wished they'd stayed.

"That's not Brazil," said Charlotte. "That's Berlin. And that's Ankara. Where's Ankara?"

Seth turned back to the TV and squinted. His eyes were weakened from the cell. "Turkey," he said. "Is that Thailand?"

"Yes."

"Can you read it?"

"*EU officials will meet today to discuss declaring an international state of emergency, but Greece…*"

The picture changed to a baseball game.

"Was that L.A. at the end?"

"I don't know," said Charlotte.

The Red Sox were up against the Rangers, losing by two in Texas. The stands were all but empty.

"What did we miss?" he said.

The room, which had been at a low murmur, silenced to ice with the sound of gunfire outside the building. Three rapid shots and one burst, then a lingering silence which was almost worse than the guns.

"We're in America, right?" said Charlotte.

A voice from an unseen speaker proclaimed, rather calmly Seth thought, that, "Buses for Phoenix International Airport are boarding now at the front gate. Taxis and limousines are in short supply. First come, first serve."

The MPs with their white gloves waved everyone forward. The crowd moved as one, not quite in a panic, but neither mannered nor gracious, with some pushing hard to be served first.

A sign at the curb welcomed everyone to Patterson Air Force Base. Beyond the curve up the heat-miraged highway was a gate behind a double line of high, barbwire-topped fences, surely sizzling in the heat. The other way lines of building stood, their purposes unknown, barracks perhaps, offices, hangars and whatnot. Probably an armory too, thought Seth.

There were not many cars in the parking lot. The buses were in a line.

While Seth stowed their equipment in the cargo space, Charlotte found herself pushed past that bus and into another. When Seth boarded his bus and found Charlotte not there, he turned to leave and find her, but he was quickly and firmly pushed into a seat by the onrush of people. The door closed and the bus was moving before he could try a second time; more gunfire had erupted from the direction of the tarmac and the bus pulled away quickly.

Charlotte snaked through the third bus looking for a seat, watching as people spread their legs a little wider when she passed, scooted the wrong way with their eyes averted, filling the free space. Finally, she found a young woman sitting alone toward the back who couldn't pretend there wasn't room. Charlotte was acutely aware that her skin, soft brown and soothing, as it had been called, was the darkest natural shade on the bus by a mile.

The bus lurched forward to follow the others ahead of it, the bus behind too close, she thought. She heard shots but this time they didn't bother her. It was becoming ambiance, she thought, and laughed.

"What's so funny?" the woman asked.

Charlotte turned a kind smile to the woman, a girl really, about seventeen or eighteen. She had short brown hair, unnaturally blue eyes – surely contact lenses – a healthy figure and a loose sports watch she bet cost more than this bus.

"I've been away. I'm just reacting to the way things are. Reacting inappropriately, probably."

"Yeah?" said the woman. "I heard you inside. Were you really in prison?"

"Yes."

"Why?"

"I'm with the media," Charlotte said.

"Oh?" The woman lit up. "I'm something of an influencer myself. I have a quarter million Insta followers and four times that many on Twitter."

"I'm Charlotte." She offered her hand and was surprised to have the woman take it warmly in hers.

"I'm Meagan. Meagan Carlisle. You probably know me as 'Meg's Mind'."

Charlotte tried to place the name, link it to someone she'd heard of, but came up empty. "I think I've heard of you," she lied.

"It's okay if you haven't," she said. "Strange times. Do you get headaches? Ever heard of tinnitus? I swear modern life manifests in the brain as noise. I love that word. *Manifest.*"

The moment caught Charlotte in awareness – not of the coincidence, or rather synchronicity, Meagan's admission of the same ailment that seemed to be happening everywhere, but her own numbness to the news of it. The buzzing in her own head she'd partitioned away to a safe distance. Time in a concrete cell had given her time to reflect and organize. Solitary confinement for her might have made her stronger. Might have. She'd not have thought of that yesterday. And that was the strange thing. She had armor now. She was not falling apart. She was even surprised. The hellscapes she'd witnessed, the horrors and murders, slaughter and exposed underbelly of the world her species had created, were clear and, if not accepted, tolerated by her. She'd let go of something that had linked her to believing – even wishing – the world was another way. It was acceptance, but it was dark acceptance. A resignation and surrender more than enlightenment. All this in a flash as she noticed herself calmly regarding Meagan, wondering how she'd have fared in Varela's cell.

"I'd show you, but the network is crap. Daddy said the base has jammers. I'm not sure. The whole internet's been shit lately, don't you think?"

Charlotte noted an adult woman referring to her father as Daddy, and said, "Actually not. I've been locked up."

"Oh, right."

"Can you fill me in on what I've missed?"

"Uhm," said Meagan, looking out the window at a passing desert. "How long you been gone?"

"I was there when Sosa was killed."

"Who?"

"Just start anywhere."

Meagan shrugged. "Remember the Arab Spring? Or the Baltic Uprising? No? No one does, but they were like this, Daddy says. A spontaneous revolt against authority, but this time it's against the good guys too."

"And the internet's been down?"

"Some say it's Russian hackers fucking around with it. Others say it's the government, to keep the rioters from organizing."

"What were you doing in Brazil?"

"Daddy has interests there. I came down with him thinking I could talk him into letting me jet over to the Caribbean to see Phil and Lara. No soap. Saint Kitts has troubles too. Haven't heard from them in a week." She produced a big phone from her purse and moved it around as if trying to catch a signal on the breeze.

"Sosa was the guy killed who started all this," Charlotte said.

"Was he?"

"I was there."

"Shouldn't the cell phone still work even if the internet is down?"

"What were your friends doing in Saint Kitts?"

"Partying. Having a good time. Hanging out with the gang."

Charlotte envisioned a group of privileged young people, white, tan, beautiful people – cavorting on a beach in bikinis and shorts, tight abs, sculpted hips. Mai tais and martinis. Baggies of drugs in beach bags with towels. Laughing, ignorant of the world, killed to a person by waiters and peasants, locals and serfs. The generation cut down. Did they have their own film crew to witness it?

"Oh, there's a signal."

Charlotte watched as she tapped away on her screen. The desert, brown and stark, stretched in all directions, broken by brush and craggy peaks. The bus was air-conditioned but she could feel the heat from the window of the bus seeping in.

"No word from them," Meagan said.

"I'm sure they're fine," said Charlotte. A white lie or just a lie?

"Well, when we get home, I'll have quite a story to tell. Rebels attacking the airport. The fall of what's-his-name. I'm glad we didn't land in Mexico." She didn't elaborate. "Here's my feed." She passed Charlotte her phone.

She scrolled through pictures of Meagan on Brazilian beaches in elaborate houses that wouldn't have been misplaced in antebellum Georgia. She saw pictures of private jets and open champagne bottles, hashtags. #dreamithaveit #livingthelife #blessed #deserved. Faces of young people she imagined lying dead on a beach in Saint Kitts, their blood seeping down into clean white sand, sucked and absorbed. Spreading. Feeding the Earth and She lapping it up. Crabs would nip at their flesh. Gulls would take their eyes. No one would bury them. Eventually a tide would take them and fish would feed and algae and the world would finally be made better for their presence.

"What do you think?"

"Wonderful," said Charlotte. "Could I ask a favor, Meg?" She'd seen several comments use that name.

"What?" Charlotte thought she sensed her neighbor clutch her purse a little tighter.

"Could I make a phone call? I want to tell my folks I'm all right."

"Okay, but make it short. Phil might call."

No, he won't, she knew.

She called her parents' number and got no answer. She wasn't surprised. An unknown number never got picked up.

When the message beep finished, she said, "Hey, Mom and Dad, just calling to say hi." She passed the phone back to Meagan.

"Where are you from originally?" she asked Charlotte. "Was that a call to Pakistan or something?"

"I'm an American. My folks live in Florida, but I'm second-generation Indian."

"Indian?"

"Like Ghandi."

"Oh."

Meagan's phone rang.

Charlotte could see her eyeing the number warily. "Is Saint Kitts 786?" she said.

"That's Miami," said Charlotte. "Florida."

Meagan picked up. "Hello?"

She listened for a moment. Charlotte waited, knowing who it was, seeing Meagan's face fall from disappointment to annoyance as she handed Charlotte the phone. "It's for you," she said. "Tell them not to call my phone again, 'kay?"

"I will," she said.

"Hi, Mom."

"Charlotte?"

It wasn't her mom. "Yes."

"Charlotte, my name is Ernest Diaz, I was your parents' lawyer."

The words were but a pressure on her armor. Not piercing, not bending. Pushing only. She was intact and unfeeling.

"Was?"

"Sorry," said Diaz. "Yes, I am so sorry. I have bad news for you."

They'd told her about his cancer, but apparently they'd misrepresented the hope, either because her mother was too optimistic or her father didn't understand. The cancer had taken her father in the time she'd been in Saõ Paulo.

"I'm sorry to tell you – I've been monitoring this line waiting for you to call. Your phone—"

"My father's dead?" she said.

"Charlotte, both your parents have passed away. It was peaceful. In their sleep."

"Both? What?" Curiosity, not panic. The armor sound, her skin a mass of scars beneath it. No pain. Distant interest only. Maybe a bit of confusion, but that was all for now.

"Pills," said Diaz. "They killed themselves."

Chapter Thirty-Five

"The Little Rock riot started out as a race thing. Another stupid-ass cop got himself filmed shooting a minority and there goes the neighborhood. You'd think they had those people controlled better down there, but whoosh, up went the courthouse. Some people are calling it worse than the Tulsa massacre, or the reverse Tulsa massacre, but it wasn't like that. Just a typical race riot. L.A. and Chicago get them like clockwork. Now the shit that's going down in the Balkans…"

The man hadn't shut up since he'd got on the bus. Seth may have asked a question, responded with a word, agreement, nod or a grunt, but that was just punctuation to the man's never-ending monologue. His name was Roger. He was from Ohio. He was a promoter with interests in South America. Lumber related. He'd resisted leaving the continent with his claims unsecured, but then figured that the people he was fighting with for the rights to cut all the timber on the eighty-eight parcels he'd lucked into were the very people the rebels would push up against a wall. He was one of those too, he realized, and so took the last plane out of Saigon, as he called it.

Seth had mentioned he'd been out of communication for a while. Roger had taken it upon himself to fill him in, "American to American."

Seth tried to listen, to catch up on current affairs as Mr. Allen had suggested, but his guts were a pool of acid and his thoughts were all worry for Charlotte. She'd become his focus, his gravitational center, at least until she was safe. That responsibility might have been over once they'd set foot on American soil, but apparently that wasn't the case.

Part of him knew that Charlotte was fine, that she could take care of herself, but the guilt, the hatred for himself, and recrimination for their imprisonment, put such thoughts aside. He had to do something.

He had to save Charlotte. It was all he had. That would be his only redemption: that she be okay.

"My son was in San Francisco and he said it was a Marxist uprising, the October Revolution in May. The media weren't reporting it, but he said that gangs of people went door to door in some of the better neighborhoods and pulled people out of their beds and killed them. Real purge stuff. No one believes me that happened, but I believe my son. He's a straight shooter. He said the gangs were mixed-race, headed by mid-level managers." Roger laughed. "Isn't it always them? Captains and majors and colonels behind a coup. The generals are too comfy, the enlisted too weak. In corporate America, that's mid-level managers." He laughed again. "Can you see Harriott from HR storming the barricade with a clipboard?"

"TPS report in hand?" said Seth remembering an old comedy.

"Right?"

"Nothing. You said the media were lying?"

Roger ran his fingers through his brown hair. Seth noted the gray roots and then the crow's feet around his eyes. The dental work needing touch-up. He had money, Seth determined, but he wasn't born to it. A man who'd made his own money, lost it, and made it again. He had that look. The easy way he took things suggested it. He was no Horatio Alger. He was the sharp-toothed pioneer who tried to get there first. A cattle baron who'd lost his herd to a blizzard and then stole more from across the border. He'd never be accepted by the blue bloods whose children he'd known at the beginning of this nightmare, but his children's children would, provided the money remained. In the realm of the powerful, Roger would fall somewhere in middle-management.

"Some of the media is honest, but not much of it. I used to get my information from Newsvine, but the internet in Brazil was shit to begin with. After the Sosa thing, it got worse."

"Tell me about Sosa?"

"Made to order, Hollywood-worthy, bona fide martyr. Valera was a stupid man, but killing Sosa, and the razing of that slum – Jesus, the man must have been out of his mind. He was what? Eighty? I guess the Alzheimer's got him."

"I heard his daughter did," said Seth.

"Ha! That she did. Hopefully our boys will put a smarter man up in his place."

"Our boys?"

"Our boys. You know our boys? Our boys are always shifting around governments down there. I don't know what Valera did to piss the boys off, but it must have been something or they would have stepped in."

"Those boys," said Seth, remembering Mr. Allen. "Maybe it was a real revolution. A true October Revolution in May."

"That was— Oh, I see what you did. Third world is different," he said. "Sure, yeah, but if the boys didn't want it to succeed, there'd have been more 'advisors' than mangos down in those jungles faster than you can say 'not so fast'."

Seth noticed his own hands shaking. After so long of nothing, he knew now he was having a kind of sensory overload. His emotions unbridled, his mind untethered, his conscience uncovered.

Roger shrugged. "I dunno," he said. "Maybe you're right. Maybe our boys were distracted someplace else. Those African mines got advisors last month. Need that shit for computers. Brazil could wait. Our boys probably figured they'd see who took over and make a deal with them. If not, the country is now used to coups. Easy sleazy."

The line caught Seth by surprise. "Sleazy? That's not how it goes."

"It's exactly how it goes."

He was in his late fifties, Seth figured. Maybe early sixties. He wore it well. He was friendly and warm. A born salesman. "You married?" asked Seth.

"Unencumbered. Thank god," said Roger. "Only my son and he's grown and doing great. Just have myself to worry about. Greatest feeling in the world. That's freedom. A man travels best who travels alone. Ain't that the truth?"

The bus slowed and lurched to a stop. They were at the airport. With a hiss, the door opened and the bus was filled with the smell of smoke.

"Smell that?" said Roger. "That's California."

"Could be Montana," said a young man in the aisle. He was young, a high-schooler, acned and lanky. Tan hair. Tall. A black t-shirt advertising some band Seth had never heard of.

"Wind doesn't blow from the north, boy," said Roger, standing up to join the queue for the exit.

Seth winced at the name. A gaffe like that could get him called into the dean's office. The kid seemed unfazed, maybe even amused.

"No," the boy said, smiling knowingly. "It didn't used to blow from the north, but all bets are off now, aren't they?"

"What?"

The line moved and he moved beyond easy conversation. Roger pushed his way into the aisle. Turning back to Seth, he waved. "Good luck…" He faltered for Seth's name.

"You too, Roger."

The air was brown and hazy and smelled like wood fire, a nice change from the sooty oil smoke from the favela.

Seth immediately looked for Charlotte, but couldn't find her. He collected the gear and then thought how stupid he had been for not having a camera on him. He dug one out, found a battery with life, and tried to frame the buses in some kind of tableau, thinking of the best way to contrast rich people and Greyhound buses. The smoke went a long way to help.

"Seth!"

He panned across the faces until he found Charlotte coming forward. The bus he'd been in pulled away, leaving a black cloud of diesel fumes to comingle with the smoke.

He zoomed in, thankful for the image stabilizer, feeling the smile he wore behind the camera, joyful at seeing her. She was not smiling. Charlotte's face was pale, her eyes searching. Something was wrong.

He lowered the camera.

"Seth…" she said.

"Charlotte?"

"I…they…" She moved her mouth trying to remember how it worked, pushing her tongue to her teeth, bending her lips, willing them to form the words she couldn't conceive but had heard.

"Daddy!"

Charlotte turned to see Meagan behind her. The girl was nice enough, had lent her her phone, but was quick to take it back, and though the news was surely visible on Charlotte's face, had not asked about it.

Just as well. Meagan was not someone she could share this with. Only Seth would do. Seth was here. He'd been here with her through these terrible months, in person, pushing and prodding, but still there. Demanding and reckless, but still with her in spirit in the prison. She knew, and it was confirmed by his expression, that he would know what to do, to say, or not to say. He would hear her because she had to tell somebody.

"Daddy!"

Meagan ran up to a rotund man on the curb. He had a cane, was probably in his seventies. Bald on top. Immaculately dressed. He opened his arms to receive her.

The buses had gone, the curb was thinning. Traffic flowed as normal.

The chime was not a bell that she had heard before. It was not bright and welcoming, but mournful, low and brooding. Dark, if a ringing bell could be so. It made her jump. And she thought that Meagan too had heard it, because she jumped as well. She was about to ask Seth if he'd heard it when Meagan let go of the man she'd been hugging and nonchalantly pushed him off the curb into the path of an oncoming yellow cab.

The man was silent, surprised, confusion writ clear on his face. Into this quiet came tires squealing in brakes and swerve. In that screech, with the fading echoes of the chime still in her head, the right front tire rolled over Daddy's head in a sublime and terrible pop.

"Daddy!" Meagan said again, no change to her voice, volume, or excitement.

Of all the sounds of that moment, that was the most horrible.

Clear-eyed and calm, Meagan turned to Seth, who held a camera. "Did you see that?" she asked.

"Yes."

"Did you film that?"

"Yeah."

Noise from behind turned Seth around. Down the sidewalk, half a gate away at a taxi stand, the boy he'd seen in the bus, the high-schooler, was strangling an old woman. A bellhop tried to pull him off, but the boy swung the woman around like a sack and knocked him down, his hands clenched deeper into her throat. His eyes were clear, hers clouded. Before the bellhop could right himself the sound of breaking pretzel burst from beneath the boy's fingers and he dropped the dead woman onto the concrete.

New screaming from Seth's right. He panned the camera, having never turned it off, and framed Roger staggering out of the terminal door, his hand held to his throat, blood spurting between his fingers, staining his shirt. He paused, looked around. Saw Seth. Gargled the word, "Help," and slipped in a puddle of his own blood.

Removing his hand from his neck to stay his fall, Roger's throat erupted unrestrained into a spray of gore that painted the sidewalk red in an instant. He collapsed after a moment's pause and was still.

A teenage boy, brown skinned and wearing a shirt and jeans, followed him out of the terminal. In his hand was a steak knife. He stood over Roger, not menacing, but curious, watching him bleed out.

Screams rose from the curb and sirens from the distance.

A policeman burst through the door, his gun drawn.

The boy turned to face him, his face calm if not innocent.

The policeman shot him three times in the chest and he crumpled atop the bleeding Roger, his arm flopping on the concrete, the knife clattering away.

Seth followed the knife in the camera, watched it tumble to the curb edge, then teeter before falling into the gutter just inches from the lifeless body beneath the wheel.

Charlotte heard the screaming; the curb was alive with it. The noise filled her, resonated and harmonized with the diminishing ringing from before.

"Seth…?" said Charlotte.

He turned the camera to her, focused on her face, seeing clearly the shock.

She was aware of the camera falling from Seth's hand, knew he was rushing to her. These things she was conscious of, but lost track of as an insensible darkness engulfed her.

Chapter Thirty-Six

EMTs were called, lots of them. Six ambulances appeared, but there were few people to be saved. Only Charlotte, in fact, could use attention. The rest of the eighteen victims were dead. There were, however, many arrests to be made. Police cars outnumbered ambulances four to one. Charlotte refused to go with them to the hospital, accepting their care in an airport office just off the main concourse where they laid her on a couch, checked her vitals, took her history, gave her oxygen and a tranquilizer. They charged Seth four figures on an offline iPad. The networks were down again. He paid with Bobby Weller's credit card, which might or might not go through when the internet was back up.

While she slept, Seth looked for a flight home, but the airlines were full. Charter planes were booked and hired cars and rentals were all taken. After an hour on his phone with an antique phone book, he lucked into a bottom-rung car rental agency in Phoenix with a single remaining car. He instantly agreed to take 'the beast', as they called it, the last of the Lincoln Town Cars. A relic, its gas mileage so bad it would be illegal to make now. He pledged a hefty deposit and they agreed to the one-way trip to Oregon, giving him the name of another rental agency who'd pick it up at the other end. If it made it. For only five hundred dollars more on Bobby's credit card, they'd deliver the beast to the airport.

Seth talked an EMT into helping him load the drugged-out Charlotte into the car when it arrived. New incidents were keeping them busy, but he was amenable, eager to get out of the building for a while. They set Charlotte on the back seat. Seth improvised a pillow, found a jacket in her bag for a blanket. He threw everything else in the trunk except a camera that would ride shotgun with him for a while until Charlotte came to. With that, he aimed the car out of Phoenix and put the airport in his mirror as new smoke pillars rose from the city's center.

Charlotte had been angry at the attention. The EMTs had been clumsy. They'd failed three times to get a reading on her blood pressure, having forgotten the first number before the second arrived twice in a row. One had taken blood from her, an older woman, stern looking, strangely out of place. The needle had been big, intrusive, painful. When Charlotte asked if she shouldn't ask about taking blood samples, mentioning HIPAA like she knew what she was talking about, the woman only looked at her and pocketed the sample.

There were police everywhere. One had followed them into the little room where she was treated. His gun was in his hand, the hammer back on the pistol. His eyes studying her, looking for sudden moves, she thought. She almost laughed, and probably should have, seeing Seth the way he was. She could see fear in his eyes. Concern. A fidgety pacing as if the outside panic had found its way into his legs. There was more in his gaze. She recognized it for what it was, but wouldn't name it.

"I have a headache is all," she'd said.

The old woman leaned in then and shined a light into her eyes. The EMTs had done that once already. "Ringing in your ears?" she asked.

"Yes."

And out came a hypo and a shot into her arm. It worked fast.

"What was that?" said Seth. His fist was clenched.

"A sedative," said the woman. "Get her to a hospital." She spoke the last to an EMT, who pulled Seth aside with a clipboard. The woman regarded Charlotte a second as the medicine began to slither through her. She stood up, spoke into her sleeve and left.

"No hospital. Home," Charlotte said. Her voice was soft and faraway but her intent was clear and Seth wouldn't let them take her.

Coolness eased over her and she perceived herself falling into a deep-sucking sleep, slow but picking up speed. She imagined falling into a well, gravity accelerating the plummet. Nothing beneath.

She had a quick flash of fear – of helplessness – but it passed in Seth's anxious face and the tightening grip of stillness coursing up her neck.

Her last conscious thought was that the sleep, however dark and empty, would be better than being awake.

The traffic was thick on the freeway. Seth snaked past creeping cars to an exit to use side streets for a while. It was a good call. From across the valley, he could see I-17 had become a parking lot.

"How about we go west for a while," he said to sleeping Charlotte and turned toward the desert.

He fiddled with the radio, looking for music, landing on a news station.

State of emergency declared in St. Louis... Fires in Manchester England have shut down rail service... Switzerland has declared a state of emergency... Contact from Asia is sporadic but consistent with reports of military atrocities being committed across Thailand, Myanmar, Vietnam, Laos...

"The world's gone insane," said Charlotte.

"Oh, you're up." Seth turned off the radio.

"I have been for a while. I was listening to the world collapse."

"I should have found music. I'm sorry."

"Don't apologize," she said. "We've had a front row seat." She stretched and tasted her mouth. "We got water?"

"No. I'll stop."

"How'd we get in this car?"

Seth told her about the lines and crowds, the limited avenues of escape he could find. He told her about the credit card, the chaos left behind at the airport. A sign promised a gas station in two miles.

"Who was that woman? The one who gave me the shot?"

"I assumed she was with the ambulances. She acted like she was in charge. After she jabbed you, she left. She had to be a doctor, right? EMTs can't give shots, can they?"

Charlotte shrugged, rolled her neck, working out kinks. "She knew what was going on?"

"You mean in the big picture, or just at the airport?"

"At least the airport, but more. She took blood, you know."

"Isn't that normal?"

"I don't think so. She wanted to send me to the hospital."

"Just trying to bankrupt you with medical bills. Par for the course. Don't take it personally."

He pulled up to a pump and topped off the tank, while Charlotte found a restroom and cleaned herself up. When she came out, Seth was in the car with a bag of snacks and drinks.

"We lucked out hard here," he said. "The phones are down, but the manager has one of those ancient carbon sliding credit card things."

"And you had a card with raised lettering?"

"No. He wrote them out. I tipped him a hundred or we couldn't get gas."

"How lucky."

"Oh, yeah."

And then Charlotte fell to crying in a gush and threw herself across Seth's lap on the seat. She cried for a while there, face in his shirt, his hand caressing her hair.

"They're dead," she finally managed to say. "My parents. They killed themselves."

"How do you know?"

"I borrowed a phone on the bus. Their lawyer's been waiting for my call."

"I'm so sorry."

"They killed themselves for me," she said.

"Don't blame yourself for shit other people do."

"No," said Charlotte, straightening up. "It's what they did. They left a note. The medical bills were going to bankrupt them. My father would die from the disease, my mother from sadness and poverty, and they'd have nothing to leave me. They checked their insurance policy, saw the suicide clause, and two weeks ago both overdosed. Took a week for the neighbors to find them."

"Oh fuck..."

"'So you have everything we didn't have,' was what the note said. 'Pay it forward.'"

"What does that mean?"

"Kids. They've always pressured me to have kids. A guilt trip on the way out." She giggled at that, which turned to a stomach-shaking laugh and then into gasping, tears, and a scream that brought the man out to see what was happening.

Seth waved him away.

It took her only a moment to collect herself. She looked into Seth's face and felt embarrassed. She could see the added worry in his eyes, the impotent twitch of his chin as he searched for something to say.

"I'll be all right," she said. "It's going to take a while to process."

"We'll get you home," he said. "I want to get you home."

She might have resisted the first statement, but the second left no room for dissent. That's what he would do. That's what was happening.

Charlotte climbed into the front seat and slid the camera into the console, careful not to knock over the coffee Seth balanced in the cupholder.

"Didn't they have anything bigger?" she asked.

"Forty-four-ounce coffee. Newest thing. Why should cold drinks get all the diabetes?"

She chuckled. It felt good and she saw visible relief in Seth's face.

He drove the hot desert road, squinting at mirages a hundred yards ahead, while Charlotte studied an old paper map left in the glove box. Seth had asked her to find a route northward around population centers, off main freeways if she could. I-10 wasn't bad, but Seth worried what they'd find when they crossed into California. It was also basically the wrong way. They needed north more than west.

Charlotte turned them up Highway 95 just as traffic was becoming noticeable eastbound on the other side. They could hear gunshots through their open windows and thought a distant cloud might not be rain, but smoke.

The smaller roads were the way.

They drove in silence, Seth reaching once for the radio, but Charlotte putting her hand on his to halt it. The touch electrified him, gentle and pleading. He would rip the machine out of the dash for her, he thought, find the men who made it and murder them with machetes. The image flashed suddenly and shook him, partly because of its fervor, but also because of the violent turn.

Charlotte let the wind blow through the window, liked the feel of it in her hair. She let her mind wander with the wind, which wasn't hard. The sound was dampened.

"I was never good to them," she said after a long time.

Seth wanted to tell her not to beat herself up; the words had formed on his tongue, but he held back. This wasn't the time for that. She needed to talk.

"They were always old-fashioned," she went on dreamily, staring out the windshield at wastelands of tawny sand and thirst. "And they were. Single-minded. I don't think they enjoyed a single day in their lives. Every moment was work, every moment was running away."

"What from?"

"From India. From poverty. From demons they didn't talk about. They'd been there during some of the violence. They alluded to it, but never talked. I used to think they were cowards, but then I wondered if they'd had a hand in it."

"People want to survive. They do things to survive."

"I picture my dad killing and I can't bring myself to even picture how he did it. Gun? Rock? Machete?"

The mention of that implement made Seth uneasy.

"Then I thought about my mom killing someone and it was clear. Maybe because she was the authoritarian most of the time. I can see her cutting a throat, pushing a body into the Ganges River and wiping her hands on her sari before coming home to make naan."

"Bad ass."

"No. Not like that." She didn't explain and Seth let it go.

"They couldn't have but one child. Me. I was all they had. I wondered why they wouldn't adopt, but it was a genetic thing. Their issue. It was how they'd continue. It was their survival."

She paused and Seth filled the silence quietly with, "I can see that."

"And I let them down. I don't want children. Who in their right mind would bring a kid into this fucking hell?"

Charlotte didn't swear easily and the word had a bite. Seth nodded. "You're your own person, Charlotte. I'm sure what they really wanted was for you to be happy."

"Were you even listening?"

"I was, but their final message didn't say children. It said, 'Pay it forward.' That could mean to give a push to someone else when you can't go on."

"They meant kids."

"You don't have to read that in it."

"I do, Seth. It's what they meant. It's the weight they put on me. They'd be fine with me being a crack whore living in a box as long as I had a litter with me."

"That's a little much."

"Maybe. But the idea is there. My desires had to be put aside for the future generation. Just like theirs were. The only way I can pay them back for…for everything is to have children to carry on. My one responsibility in life, to my parents, to the clan, species, the biological imperative, is to procreate."

"Seems pretty basic – I mean, not like an obvious thing, more like an ignorant view, one that hasn't evolved into a standard of living and mind beyond the bare minimum."

She thought about that for a moment. "That fits. You can take the parents out of the slum, but you can't take the slum out of the parents."

"But you aren't from the slum."

A wind gust filled the cabin with sandy heat as a dust devil spun up to the right. Charlotte watched it dance to and fro, then leap the highway, skid and sputter. Then in a puff, it disintegrated and dropped its weight of sand rain-like to the ground.

"No," she said. "I'm not from the slum."

Chapter Thirty-Seven

The traffic was heavy but moved. At one point they pulled over to let a column of army vehicles pass. There were two dozen Humvees, trucks pulling tanks, covered trucks, all the strange desert-tan camouflage that reminded Seth of America's unpopular wars. Green camo could recall the Second World War, ignoring Korea and Vietnam in its 'good war' glow, but the desert pattern was all bad, all Middle East entanglements and body counts, all sour in his mind.

"Ever felt pride at seeing that?" Seth asked, watching a tank roll by, taking all of the two lanes on the back of a flatbed.

"No. Not like that. When they're in dress uniforms maybe. Blue and buttons. White gloves. Standing in the rain next to a flame, then maybe, but never like this. Never the equipment. Never the fatigues."

It took nearly an hour for the convoy to pass and then another half hour for Seth to fight his way back into traffic. It was now good and thick behind the column.

"Keep an eye open for General Hooker," he said.

"I get it," said Charlotte.

The military turned off in Las Vegas. Seth circled around the city as best he could. It looked fine, the city of sin he remembered. The lights were even on – flashy and glitzy in the early afternoon haze. But there was smoke in the air from the western fires and six black smudges in the city center. The radio was static or a recording declaring martial law in the city limits, promising to shoot looters on sight. Curfew was eight p.m.

In Beatty, neighbor to Death Valley, Seth was unable to find a gas station with any fuel that would take credit cards, even when he agreed to pay the ninety-eight dollars per gallon they were asking. Instead, he cut a length of garden hose from a rambler they found off main street watering the lawn in the middle of the day. Charlotte was aghast at his boldness. Walking up to the house, turning off the water and then cutting the hose twice for a neat five-foot length.

"Where'd you get the knife?"

"Gas station. Charged it. Same as the water. Drink this." He handed her the remnants of a gallon jug. They'd gone through two already. Seth kept the air off to save fuel and Charlotte liked the windows down. She dutifully finished the water while Seth pulled into a crowded church parking lot next to an early model Pontiac.

Like he did it every day, like it was his job, without fear or self-consciousness, bold as you please, he popped open the Pontiac's gas cap with the tip of his knife, plunged the hose down the hole, sucked it until gas spilled out over his shoes, and began filling empty water jugs.

Charlotte handed him a fourth water jug to wash his mouth out when he was done.

"Last one," she said.

He put the car into gear and found a park with running water and a flush toilet. Seth poured the stolen gas into the tank and Charlotte filled their last jug at the drinking fountain, the sun beating down on them like it was a heat lamp. Sweat clouding his eyes as he watched; she taking it in, genetically better for this than him. He could feel the sunburn on his arms already. Late July Death Valley sun had its way with his pale skin from three weeks in a dark cell. He welcomed the burn.

They drove until dark, invariably finding themselves on I-80 with thick traffic going both ways, exacerbated by numerous cars pulled off the road, stalled, broken, out of fuel or worse. Several had bodies in their cabs, bullet holes in their windows. Some people walked the shoulder, dragging pull-behind luggage like they were waiting for a cab.

In Winnemucca, Seth found a truck stop just far enough off the main road to be welcoming under the circumstances. It was full, but not packed, and when he pulled in next to a still-running tractor trailer with its orange running lights on and the sound of snoring coming from within, he felt soothed by the normalcy of it.

"Food?" said Charlotte.

"Hell yeah."

Seth collected his camera and paused before following Charlotte inside, catching the sunset in the haze, amber light, streaks of orange, a fading yellow orb turned red at the horizon, all tasting of soot, smelling like smoke, burning his eyes just to look at it. It was beautiful in its way.

Charlotte had intended to go inside, find a nice booth, down some water, order coffees and wait for Seth, but she hesitated at the door. She'd wait there, wanting the escort before she took her dark skin past the Confederate flags and gun rights signs on the door.

She glanced at the sunset that had distracted her companion and saw only burned sky. Nothing beautiful to film, but of course, they weren't making a beautiful film.

"You get it?" she asked.

"Suitable, don't you think?"

She slid her arm in his and together they went inside.

It was a convenience store connected to a café. On the store side, the shelves were bare. Not even candy or the ubiquitous beef jerky remained. It was clean, signs of someone picking up, but no one was there. The sound of radio static from the café made Charlotte jump.

"What?" said Seth.

"The sound."

"Is it back?"

"No, it's...it's the radio in there."

Seth wanted to ask her more about the sound, but it would wait.

Inside the café, the scene was surreal. Every chair was occupied, every face turned to a back counter where a blocky radio stood being tended by a fat man in a greasy baseball cap. He twisted the dials, changing the static's quality, but not its content.

A woman in a waitressing outfit, but not from this one, turned to see them come in. The movement drew the others, and in a slow synchronized pan, all were staring at Seth and Charlotte.

Seth brought his camera up to record it, careful to gather the crackling sound under the weighted silence with the little mic he had.

"We're just looking for something to eat," Charlotte said.

The pause stretched out.

"We can get you something," someone said from the back.

"What's with the camera?" asked a bearded man at a side table.

Seth noticed a shotgun by his chair. There were many guns now that he looked, revolvers in holsters like some western saloon, hunting rifles with scopes, pistols on tables, semi-automatic assault rifles like the kind they were still talking about banning, the favored weapon for mass shootings near you.

"You reporters?" A woman in jeans.

"Something like that."

Keeping his eyes on Charlotte, the man with the shotgun said, "Turn it off."

Seth lowered the camera.

"Have a seat anywhere." An older woman, gray hair pulled back in a bun, apron tight around her ample middle, carried water to them. "We still got power, and a generator besides. What'll ya have?"

They found a booth in back. "Anything," said Seth, sliding in.

"Grilled cheese?" said Charlotte.

"A woman after my own heart," said the waitress. "That we can do. A little short on the burgers and chili right now." She winked.

"A couple grilled cheese," said Seth. "Each."

"I'll get ya some soup too."

"Coffee?"

"Coming up." Her cheer sounded genuine, a strange and surprising flavor in this dour room.

The radio found a voice and the group turned back to it, slowly releasing the two from their binding gazes.

"The USGS has reported the possible detonation of several nuclear devices. Where and how big it is not clear, but three distinct events have been reported suggesting Asia and Europe. Listeners, this is it. I've been telling you about this day for years. This is it."

"Who are we listening to?" asked Seth to no one in particular.

"Patton James. 'News From a Secure Location.'"

Seth had heard of him. He was some kind of conspiracy firebrand, calmer than his predecessors and a little less fascist. He was in his seventies and swore by a regime of dubious dietary supplements he'd branded with his image. Some called him the voice of the 'moderate truth'. A soothing appellation in a troubled political climate that belied the wild conspiracy stories he sold via the internet and radio waves. And now shortwave, if Seth's recognition of the big device on the counter was accurate.

"I told you here first that the president had been assassinated. And I was right. Vice President Lensly spoke today from Air Force Two confirming it. Why not the White House? Or Washington? Could it be that I was right that there was nerve gas in the streets there? He didn't say. What he did say was nonsense, a call for calm that's about as effective as thoughts and prayers after a flood.

"What can I say? I hate being right. The best thing for all of us good folks to do," he said, "will be to hunker down, wait it out. Come out on the other side."

"The other side of what?" It was a man, middle-aged, graying at the temples. Armed but in a dress shirt and slacks. An office worker. "What the hell is going on?"

Static returned to the station and a short Black man in a red plaid shirt, bald, sweat down his back, went to work it.

When no one answered the clerk, Charlotte asked the question again. "We've been out of the loop. I'd like to know what they say is going on."

"You can't trust the media, missy," said a mustached man. A trucker perhaps. His eyes were red, his hands shook. Charlotte wondered if he were coming off of some drug, or maybe coming on.

"It ain't racial," said the man at the radio. "Many folks tried to paint it that way, but it's ripping our communities open as well as yours."

In another place, Charlotte might have called attention to the separation of communities, argued for unity, but it seemed out of place now, a Band-Aid placebo on a gunshot wound.

"Commies," said the waitress. "Started down in Mexico thereabouts."

"Brazil?" offered Charlotte.

"I heard that," said the clerk. "But that's down there. How does that translate to Russia nuking their own people? Nerve gas in Washington?"

"Is that confirmed?" asked Seth. "Patton James isn't exactly Reuters."

"It's confirmed as much as anything can be," said the man by the radio. "I heard it before. James is kinda late on it, actually."

"Jesus."

The grilled cheese sandwiches arrived. Soup and a pot of coffee. The lights flickered, went out and then came back on.

"That'd be the generator," said the waitress. "Looks like the lines are down again. But don't worry everyone. We're good here. We can wait it out."

"Wait what out?" said the clerk. "Really."

"Calm down," Charlotte heard herself say.

"It's a sound," said the man at the radio. He'd found a station, but the language was Asian. He glanced at Charlotte. "You understand what they're saying?"

"No." She felt insulted.

Seth put his hand on hers. "What about the sound?" he said.

"When I was in Palo Alto this morning, a station up north, a university station – off the air now – said they'd discovered strange doings with a low frequency. A sound below normal hearing of most folks, but in the range of younger ones."

"Yeah," said the dress-shirted man. "My students used something like that as a ringtone on their phones. When a call came in and I didn't hear it, they'd all laugh." So he was a teacher. "The sound affects children. Young people." He looked at Charlotte, who recoiled a little from his gaze. "The sound puts ideas in their heads."

Seth had noticed the look at Charlotte. A quick survey of the room confirmed that she was the youngest person there, with him at forty-six, probably coming in second.

"A weapon," said the trucker. "Oh my god, the commies got a super-weapon."

"More like the CIA," said another. "It's hitting everybody."

"Majestic 12," said someone. "Patton James said the UFOs would make a big move this year."

"Shut your ignorant mouth," said a woman with big hair and a bigger rifle. "That's not helping."

"Good as anything else," said the trucker. "Maybe it's like the COVID. Something got loose out of a lab."

"More ignorance," said the woman. "You people are what—"

"Hush," said the waitress, cutting her off. "All of you." She gestured around with a pot of coffee, taking in the room. "Ya'll looking the wrong way. It's just a passing thing. Whatever it is. Relax. Keep still. Have some pie. Don't work yourselves up. Too many guns here for that."

Charlotte bit into her sandwich, heard the crunch of toasted bread and tasted smooth cheddar within. She rolled her eyes in bliss. Seth was already on his second sandwich. He washed down a bite with his coffee.

"Maybe you should turn off the radio," he said after he swallowed. "Having speakers on maybe isn't a good idea if we really are dealing with a sound."

The man ignored him and hunted radio stations. Found a German-speaking one, skipped it. "It's coming from the ground," he said, without looking up. "That much is clear and confirmed." Everyone nodded in agreement. "The sound is coming from the ground."

Chapter Thirty-Eight

Whether the noise was responsible for the chaos, everyone had an opinion – coincidental, causal, a side effect – but the presence of some kind of vibration emanating from below was common knowledge and officially confirmed.

The man with the radio was Don. The waitress, Sue. The big-haired woman, Molly; the truck driver, Antony. The schoolteacher went by Weaver. Among the others was a Larry, the owner of the place, a Rita, a Beth, and a Bryan. Five others beyond that Charlotte had given up trying to remember. They didn't remember her name either, so, whatever. Sue and Larry were the only ones who had known each other prior to that day. Rita was traveling with Weaver – a hitchhiker. Molly had a husband somewhere who was expected back any minute from reconnoitering the town. He'd been gone three hours when Charlotte and Seth had rolled up, so closer to five hours now.

The radio had suggested people stay off the roads, stay home. Don't panic. A recording from the Civil Defense. Specifically, martial law was declared, looters beware, and the only vehicles allowed to move between dark and dusk were military. Seth and Charlotte were stuck.

"We ain't got no beds," said Sue, "but ya'll welcome to space on the floor. Ain't gonna get cold, that's for sure. Air conditioner don't run on the generator."

"It's safer if we're all together," said Weaver. He was inspecting his big black revolver for the third time that hour.

"What about the man outside?" asked Charlotte

"He's back?" Molly stood up to look.

"No. Someone's sleeping in a truck outside. We heard him snoring when we came in."

"He'll be fine," said Antony. "I'll get in my sleeper as well. Nighty-night, everyone."

"Is that safe?" asked Weaver.

"We're in the middle of nowhere," said the trucker, slinging his rifle over his shoulder. "Whatever is happening is happening far away. I'll just be outside."

He tipped his greasy ball cap to Sue and Larry and left through the front door into the thick darkness. The generator didn't work on the outside lights. The neon was dark. The pumps in shadow. Only the orange running lights on the sleeping camper and a distant stream of convoying lights – white spots one way, red the other – shone outside.

"We should lock it," said someone. Bryan, Charlotte thought. "The door. For protection."

"Why not?" said Sue.

"My husband," said Molly.

"He knows to knock."

Charlotte looked at Seth. He shrugged, an indifferent reaction to whatever question it was she was asking. She didn't know what it was, so couldn't fault his answer.

Sue had let them have their dinner for free; their credit card machine was out, and it was only the neighborly thing to do. "Now if you'd ordered the prime rib..."

"You'd have to shoot us?" It was a joke aimed at all the guns in the room.

"Wing you at least," she said with a wink.

Guns had always made Seth feel funny. He didn't like them as a rule. After Saõ Paulo, after seeing first-hand what one could do to a human being, he liked them less. Nevertheless, he wanted one. He was the only man without one. Charlotte, probably the only woman. Rita kept her hand near her purse. Sue mentioned she had something in the back, and Larry's shotgun was something out of a Western, double barrels and scratched all to hell. Molly had a little silver gun. He finally asked.

"What's with all the guns?"

"We were taking inventory before you came in," said Don. "What do you have?"

"My good looks and several cameras."

"You some kind of pacifist?" asked Larry.

"Some kind," he said.

"You're traveling across country without a gun?" said Molly.

"Looks like it."

"How did you plan to defend your wife?"

"She's not—"

Charlotte interrupted him. "We didn't know things were this bad. We've been out of the country."

"Oh."

Sue went and locked the door. Charlotte sipped her coffee.

"How're you feeling?" asked Seth.

"Tired."

"Do you still hear the sound?"

She shook her head. "Actually, I don't. I did at the airport. God, did I ever. It's been gone since."

"Since that shot the woman gave you?"

"Yeah. Since then. Interesting."

"That's good."

She forced a smile.

Seth put his hand on hers. "I don't know what to say and I want to say something."

"I'm good."

"No, you're not."

"How're you?"

"After months in a South American jail, I'm rolling."

"Was it bad for you?"

"Not so bad."

"It was," she said. "I can tell."

"I'm sure it was no worse than yours."

"I had clothes."

"Maybe a little worse."

The radio found music, something hard-edged and raucous. Blaring guitars finding distortion and coming back to screaming riffs. Larry and Sue were making the rounds with coffee pots. The kitchen was closed for hot food, but if anyone got hungry, they'd figure something out.

"They're so nice," said Charlotte.

"Gives me new hope for the human race."

"If only."

Seth watched her face, saw her track Sue and then Larry, then fade into unfocused. "How could they kill themselves?" she asked the air. "How could they lose hope so quickly?"

"That's not at all what happened," said Seth. "Hope is what your parents had. Hope is what they did."

"I don't want to hear it. Suicide is unforgivable. It's unnatural."

"They bolted."

"That's what I mean. They're cowards. Running away."

"No. Not like that. Not at all. I don't mean bolted like fled, I mean bolted like plants."

She shook her head, and looked at her fingers. "What?"

"I was growing cucumbers one summer," explained Seth. "Not all of them were doing well. Watering issue, soil. I never figured out why they were suffering. Some did better than others."

The lights flickered, dimmed. Conversation slowed.

"A strange thing though, the ones that were doing poorly, that didn't look like they'd make it at all, suddenly flowered. Still in the seedling cups, before I could put them in the ground, they flowered. One of them even began making cucumbers. They were bolting. That's what the book said. Bolting. It's when a plant facing extinction puts all its energy toward the next generation. No new leaves, no roots. All reproduction. It sacrifices its own life immediately and completely in the service of its seeds."

"Bolting?"

"Bolting," said Seth, softly. "It's not unnatural. It's born of stress, but it's not unnatural. Your parents weren't cowards."

"They died for a guilt trip then."

"No. They did what they thought was right. It wasn't about you. Well, maybe a little. But it was about them. What they thought they were about. They were done. Tired. Facing hell. That alone... And, before you get onto the guilt some more, I'd say they did what they did knowing your feelings about children. Knowing that you would never have any, but doing it just the same, for you. Their resources were better spent on you and your future, which no matter what, was brighter than theirs. That's it. That's why. They pushed what good they could offer into the future to you."

From outside, there came the sound of gunfire. Six or seven rounds. Loud. Clear. Don switched the radio off.

The sound came closer, different qualities, small gun, large gun. Nearer. Farther. Coming. They traveled on the rumble of motors.

One of the parked trucks outside burst into a pillar of gasoline-fueled flame and all the café was bathed in orange horror.

Then another truck, the one beside Seth's rented car, was engulfed in another plume of fire.

From the flames of the first one, a man stumbled out. It was Antony. His hair was on fire. His shirt was on fire. His shoes. He staggered and ran, dragging his rifle limply behind him, trailing sparks where the barrel skidded on concrete. He slowed. Stopped. Collapsed to his knees, and before he could fall forward, he jerked to his right, pushed over by a gunshot that pierced the roar of the conflagration. Before the echo had faded, Antony was but a smoldering mound in the darkness outside.

The café watched in shock, fear rising like a stink.

Glass burst beneath the sound of more shots. Shards of safety glass rained down in clattering cubes across the front; three round spidery holes popped through the door, chest high.

Charlotte ducked beneath the table. Seth grabbed his camera and starting filming.

He felt like an idiot for not capturing any of the café talk before, showing the faces of these people, thrown together, holed up under flickering fluorescents. He could have done it, they'd not have known. He hadn't even had a mic hot.

He panned across the room, taking in as many of the faces as he could, adjusting the mic to pick up sound, wondering then if he could adjust it to hear 'the sound'.

All clutched their guns and waited. Shifting behind chairs. Someone overturned a table. Seth caught only the movement, not the actor. Don took the radio off the counter and carried it into the back.

A hot wind carried the smell of burning plastic, rubber, and men into the café, and Charlotte became aware for the first time since the airport of the distant rising hum at the base of her skull.

"Seth, I can hear it again," she said.

"Fight it."

He didn't know what it was. She didn't know what it was. But it was. And it was a threat. It was premonition and motivation. Seth saw it in Charlotte's face, her tightening jaw and glazing eyes.

"Fight it."

And gunshots filled the air.

Seth turned his camera to the broken walls.

In the ghoulish green light of the flickering cheap fluorescents, a rush of bodies threw themselves forward. Even in the melee, the gunshots, the screaming that all arose at once like an ignited siren, Seth saw that they were children. Not young adults, not teenagers. Children. Five-, six-, seven-year-olds. Shooting heavy revolvers into the café with both hands. A dozen, two dozen.

The denizens of the café hesitated to return fire, even in the face of onslaught, and Seth, in panning quick to his left, saw the back of Molly's head explode.

The café fired.

All sound was noise, all sight smoke, and smell blood.

They were not unfamiliar sensations for Charlotte and Seth, but this was closer, this was on them. Here they would not escape the blood spatter.

After the rush of dead children came older ones. Here were the young people from Martha's Vineyard, armed and mad. Here were the followers of Sosa, though Charlotte guessed they didn't know who he was. Here the kindred of Bobby Weller, finding new parents to slay.

In a moment they were in and shooting continued.

Seth and Charlotte cowered beneath their table as bullet holes punctured the vinyl seats behind them. Seth filmed as he could, the light diffused in smoke, the sound uneven and so perfect for this chaos. His angle was necessarily low, making the attackers loom.

Charlotte searched Seth for help. He turned to face her. Was he measuring her? Trying to guess if she was with the children or them? His face calmed and centered her. She had come to trust his eyes, that chin. To like the stubble he wore now. He lowered the camera to more fully comprehend her.

"Keep filming," she said. "I'm fine. What else have we to do?"

And he understood.

The shooting stopped. Seth took in the dead bodies littered among chairs and tables. The patrons were all dead. They were there fighting and then they weren't. All in a rush, they were overwhelmed, silenced and now prone. Their bodies matched and doubled by those of the kids. A knot of teenagers went into the kitchen. Don made a startled cry and went still.

A young Black woman in a ragged yellow sundress, a breast showing through a tear, walked slowly toward their table. The crunch of glass under her feet was the only sound competing with their breaths and the burning of trucks in the parking lot.

Charlotte touched Seth's arm and he trained the camera on the approaching woman. She was close, and pulled back beneath the table as far as they were, the camera could only see her from the waist down. Scratched and bruised legs over stained white sandals. A pistol dangling from her right hand, in and out of frame as she swung it casually like it was a purse.

The woman stopped, leaned over and peered beneath the table.

She had short-cropped hair, deep brown eyes. Lip gloss. Maybe twenty years old. Maybe twenty-two. Maybe eighteen.

"Hi," she said.

Seth filmed her.

Charlotte stared.

"It's over," said the woman.

"What is?"

"Just this. For now. You can come out."

"But he's old," said Charlotte. "My friend here. He's old."

"What's that?" The woman looked confused.

And Charlotte listened for the distant chime. The ringing was small in her brain now, a distant soft chord, high and luring, but not overwhelming. Existent but unobtrusive.

"Nothing," said Charlotte. "Can we go?"

The young woman made a face. "I don't care," she said. Miffed, she turned, stepped over the waitress's torn and bullet-ridden body, skirted the corpses of three children, and put two more shots into the teacher's back before following the others into the kitchen.

Chapter Thirty-Nine

The light of the burning buildings was far behind them when they dared speak again.

"How's your head?" asked Seth.

"Better."

"Should I pull over? Let you sleep?"

"Let's just get home. Nobody's on this road."

The dark Nevada highway was as lonely as a grave and hot as a furnace. Between the isolation and the curfew, they'd seen only two other cars for the hour since they'd left Winnemucca. In the town, however, they'd seen military vehicles at the exits. Soldiers aimed their weapons as they passed, watched them, ready to shoot if they left their lane, sped up, slowed down, looked too hard – who knows what would have drawn their fire. Whatever it was, they did not do that, and though watched and fearful, Seth and Charlotte passed through the town with its fires and shootings, screams and smoke, and passed north toward home.

"I need an hour. Just an hour of sleep. Okay?" said Seth.

"You want me to drive?"

"No. Just give me an hour."

He drove several miles looking for a turnoff and finally found one far enough from the road that the darkness would hide them. He switched off the car.

"Get some sleep yourself," he said.

"Sure," said Charlotte.

Seth thought to take the back seat, or offer it to her, but chose instead to remain behind the wheel. He left the keys in the ignition and his seat belt on for the same reason: a quick getaway if need be.

He found darkness behind his eyelids and a serene emptiness where he could lay aside his worries for a moment, and in that moment, he slid into a deep, dreamless sleep.

Charlotte sat in the passenger seat and looked out on the stark desert scene. There was no moon, but after the remnants of the headlights left her eyes, the stars showed her the bleakness. The sands were light-colored and so took on a shine as if fed from below. Spots of dark, plants or shadowed rock, punctuated the wasteland like scars on a corpse. Such were her thoughts.

She closed her eyes but found the same themes there. She watched Seth as he slept, noted the breathing, intaking and outgoing of breath, reflexive and natural. She thought she could hear his heart beat in the stillness of the car, but it was her own. His face was quiet and unworried for a change. She'd tried many times to recall his face while locked in that cell in Brazil, and from her memory – always by placing him in a scene, usually the tennis pavilion for some reason – he looked decidedly different than he did now. Then again, different from Massachusetts, which was different than their arrival in Saõ Paulo. He looked so old now.

When she'd met him, really met him at the beginning of this nightmare descent, he still carried the jaunty rebel outcast persona his reputation reported. A damaged man from being too open, too willing to mix with the students, which he saw not as wards, but his peers. Then, burned by association to the decisions of those around him, he become a dangerous man, cracked, but grounded by virtue of being pounded into it. She wished now she'd known him before, known the woman who'd died in his house. She'd had her own bouts of depression but had never been suicidal. Maybe that made her unique, rare at least in the current world. It was easy to despair when looking ahead from here.

That had been her defense, she realized. She'd freed herself from the desire for children and thus freed herself from worry beyond the near. Driven to it by her parents' insistence, her rebellion against them was her insulation. The world burned. People suffered. All was fucked and would get worse, but she was okay now, and that was enough. Obligations beyond the near present were not her concern. She'd conducted herself with a solid progressive outlook, recycling, voting for the lesser of evils, but these things she did more for generational inclusion than actual concern. She'd removed her line from a far future. Maybe she was suicidal after all.

Back to the darkness. A bead of sweat trickled down the back of her neck, joined the pool dampening her shirt against the seat. The heat still here. Always here now. All her life she'd been aware of climate change, seen the effects, environmental and social. She'd shaken her head, given up straws and religiously brought her own grocery bags. And in the back of her activist mind, she had always thought that a degree in journalism would help the world. She could report and so enlighten, but always there was another side, shadowed and censorious, and in the darkness of this desert night, she saw her career differently but clearly. Without skin in the game, it was selfish, detached, and voyeuristic.

And then, in memory of sound, she saw the only thing that there was to do. The impulse of the younger generation feeling their futures burn, watching themselves starve so another billionaire can ride a spaceship. Feeling the batons of black-clad police drive the children into cages for breaking a chain-store window. These were steps of change but goddamn it – god dammit – they were not working. Too slow, too laden with compromise at a time when delay is death and disaster.

To her right on the horizon, flashes in the distance. Lights. Yellow-orange. Soundless struggle on a scale to challenge the dead desert night. Shadows of smoke, trailers of fire. The world more polluted, but in measure now. Now and no more?

And there it was, in the back of her mind, the sound. She recognized it there, not for its din, for it had shifted, but for its presence. She could remember when the sound was not there and recall what it had sounded like previously. Different now, she knew it was the same thing. From a chord to a chime to now a low hum. It was low for distance, a place in the background of her thinking, but also in register, like a deep bass. A hum you felt more than heard. She recalled standing by speakers at a concert once. Professional earplugs beneath headphones, the music muffled in her head, but feeling the bass inside her. Her hair would move, her fingers touching the invisible sound of the massive black wall. One sensory manifestation transformed to be understood by another. She could hear it, feel it, see it. If she'd have opened her mouth, she might have tasted it. She'd fled from it, feeling the overwhelming power, wondering if her organs were being damaged by the proximity.

A woman dead in a tub; amplified drum to her kidney; the energies of the universe upon witnesses.

She recalled her parents and felt a wave of guilt. They'd be pleased by that, she thought. They'd been scarred by their early lives. Some, more generous observers, might call it imprinting. Their struggles were survival, basic and immediate. Fight or flight. The world a serious place, always threatening. They were never unafraid. Every step they took was planning how to avoid the doom chasing them. She was their biggest step, but they could not put the fear they felt into her. Was that not the goal? That she should not have that? Had she not lived their dreams by not knowing their terror? Was she not everything they'd wished?

Strange that Seth had seen this before she had. She wanted to think, like Seth had inferred, that their final act was a celebration of their success, and that there was peace in them that she could live the life they couldn't.

Bullshit though. Total bullshit.

There had been no epiphanic understanding. No higher sense of her decisions to their intentions. It was a compromise at best. A resignation. A surrender. Having seen what they had seen, they'd at once put a huge value upon life, and also, at the same time, a low one. They'd measured their own, at the end, as base and hers higher. With their demise, she would have more. Whatever that was.

A fiery rocket trail arced over the mountain like an errant firework. Still no sound even after the white-hot flash of its landing threw the mountain into dark silhouette.

Was it not the way of things, though? Was it not the natural course to live and die, and your flesh would feed the next generation? She understood this clearly now. The hum ticked up a register, something brighter and clearer. Still distant, but warmer. Coming.

The next generation need not be her, need not even be human. The dead feed the worms who feed the birds who feed the men who feed the wolves. All of it the Earth.

She was dreaming now. Ideas cascaded into themselves, growing in scale, speed and sound to a river rapids soundtrack. The scale of it. The scale of it. Widening. Whole. The scale of it.

"What's that?"

Charlotte turned to see Seth rubbing his eyes.

"What?"

"What about the scale of it?" he said.

By the green light of the LED clock on the dashboard she saw that hours had passed. The night was dark again. No lights over the mountain to be discerned, the sound in her skull receded.

"The scale of this...thing."

"Yeah, I was thinking about that too." He stretched his arms above his head, hitting the ceiling, the car suddenly cramped.

"What do you think?" she asked.

"What do I think? I think I don't think about it."

"That's not helpful."

"It's all that I can do. Thinking big is a quick way to lose hope. Despair is recognizing scope, seeing how small you are."

"I thought tragedy was close up and comedy long shot?"

"Did I say that?"

"You and Chaplin."

"I can't fix long shots," he said. "Close-ups? Me? Maybe there's something I can do there. That I can work with."

"Next you're going to be singing 'Man in the Mirror'."

"Well, not that close. I can expand the frame a little. A two shot."

"It's good to be small though, isn't it? Absolved from responsibility."

"I know I'm arguing against my own position, but you made me remember that old phrase about no snowflake feels responsible for the avalanche."

"It fits with this shit."

"What about us?"

"What do you mean? Why did we get a front row seat to the end of the world?"

"Did we?" he said.

She opened a bottle of water and sipped, tasting the tepidness, swallowing but finding it unrefreshing.

Seth started the car, flipped on the headlights, and turned back onto the road.

"There was more in your question than apocalypse," she said. "About us."

Seth was glad it was dark. He felt his cheeks blush. "I don't believe in the apocalypse. People keep predicting it and have been wrong every time."

"They only have to be right once," she said, offering him the bottle.

He took it, sipped. Noticed how warm it was. He rolled down his window to let the air blow in. It came hot and dry, full of grit, smelling of smoke and despair.

"Do you believe in endings?" he said, aware he was avoiding her earlier question. "Is this that? Or just another cycle?"

"The end of a cycle is death to that cycle."

"Linear time, I hear, is a Western construct. Most other civilizations didn't have it. They saw rings."

"Perspective. If you're standing on the edge of a circle, it looks straight, the way standing on a big, round planet can make you think it's flat."

"My point," he said. "It's wrong."

Charlotte rolled down her own window, and leaned her head out. In the glow of bleeding headlights, he watched her hair whip her face in violent gusts. Eyes closed, facing forward, she let it waft over her. They were going eighty miles per hour.

She pulled back inside and rolled her window up.

"Should we do the air?" asked Seth.

"Let's save it for the daylight."

"Good idea."

Seth kept his window down and the wind, hot and unending, slayed the silence but made talking difficult. After a few miles, ten, twenty maybe, Charlotte said, "This could be a cycle. Just a long one. One we haven't been around long enough to recognize."

Seth rolled his window up and was surprised by the quiet of the car. Remembering that luxury cars were renowned for their quiet and isolation.

Charlotte said, "What if this is what the extinction event looks like? What are we on now? The sixth extinction?"

"Was that a book?"

"Yeah. It showed the big ones before."

"Asteroid and such?"

"Some worse than that."

"I don't think we'll go extinct."

"I do," she said.

"Now?"

"I'm thinking I'm safe in saying that eventually we will. The sun will burn out, right?"

"There you go," said Seth. "Looking at the big picture. Helping your mood?"

"You're back to cynical."

"Sorry."

"No, it's good," she said. "You've been treating me differently."

"How? When?"

She shrugged. "From deferent to protective to…what?"

"You tell me."

"You're ducking the question again." She slid her hand beside the seat and reclined it. Her eyes were still closed.

"I care about you," Seth said. "I feel protective of you. That's true. I feel guilty. I feel like all this is my fault."

"You brought on the extinction?" she asked. "You're more powerful than I imagined."

"I mean our part of it."

"Same response."

She was different. She had changed. How had it taken so long to notice? She was not panting and fearful. The horror of the child massacre from the truck stop had not affected her, let alone devastated her. There was hardness to her now. It frightened him.

"Maybe it was you," she said after a while.

"And I am sorry," he said. "If... If... I—"

"Your generation," she said. "Hasn't this become that? A generational war?"

He thought about that. He hadn't put it in those terms, but, as far as they knew, she was right.

"Jesus," he said. "It wasn't me. I'm on your side."

"Our side?"

"That's what I meant."

"I know. But you're still old."

"Wise," he said. "The revolution has nothing to hold against me. I'm an ally. A veteran in fact."

"You're old."

"Exactly."

Her breathing grew heavy and slow. Rhythmic. Sleep finally settling over her.

Seth turned on the air-conditioning just as the first blue line of dawn scraped the east.

They had gas enough until midday. Road signs promised there'd be places to refill. He'd find cars pulled over if he had to. They'd get home. He'd get her home. Seeing her vulnerable, battered, and now hard, his heart bled. Something in him stirred. A dedication he had not known before. He tried to compare it. Was it love? First love – the amber glow of the beginnings of an affair? No. It was more akin to the feeling he had when he'd first held his son Travis in the hospital. Like that, but more. It was... It was... It was purpose.

Chapter Forty

A couple hours after dawn, Charlotte still asleep, Seth pulled into a deserted rest stop. Parking next to a camper, he got out tentatively and called for anyone. No answer. He siphoned gasoline and refilled his tank. Afterward, taking the camera on a hunch, he went into the restroom to relieve himself. It was there he found the slaughtered family, throats cut, blood everywhere, flies thick as shadows.

He regarded their mutilated faces, their size, stature, coloring. All adults, father, mother, older sister and a grandfather. He tried to figure the scenario that put them all there in different twisted angles of death. None looked moved, but still their final crumpled shape where they died. All the crimson footprints on the white tile were small and childish. No match among the corpses for that frame. The room was in shade but brutal sunlight kept it all visible, the camera correcting the color. He became aware of a sound and jumped before realizing that it was just the screech of some desert cricket, a high-pitched whine that meant heat. He thought it was a cricket, but in truth he never actually found out what made that sound. It might have been the grass itself shrieking in pain at the three-digit temperature.

He went into the far stall, did his business and returned to the car, where Charlotte still slept. He filmed her serene face through the window, feeling the barrier of the glass as if it were steel.

As he turned the ignition of the car, he thought he heard a sound from within the camper. He didn't wait to find out what it was but pulled out quickly and returned to the dry artery of the burning highway.

Charlotte hardly stirred. Good. She needed rest.

Seth passed a few cars going the other way, but never found one in his own lane until he was well into Oregon. He'd found ninety miles per hour on the speedometer and slipped into cruise, the air-conditioning keeping the cab comfortable but never wholly overcoming the pounding heat.

He had time to think. Strange, he thought, how he'd had weeks in the cell in Saõ Paulo and hadn't used the time to really think this way. That was prison time, he decided. Thoughts were dangerous there, at least certain ones. Now, free, or as free as this was, he could assess things a little clearer, able to process more clearly what he had discovered.

He'd embraced the role of witness. Once Bobby Weller had opened his parents' skulls, he knew he was the eyes of the event. Others had seen it, it'd been broadcast live, but he and Charlotte, too, were there to understand it. The moments in the dressing room, the poolside, the boat, Kinsley become victim. It was all in a narrative. Surely it began before they were there, but it was shown to them in scenes of horror and meaning across the continents, to falling buildings and the rebels who killed scientists that dared to go against nature. Retribution, terrible and swift. Tens of thousands dead in Brazil. The scale ever increasing, intimate in close-ups, at airports and truck stops, but widening like spreading wildfire.

As if on cue, tawny smoke appeared on the horizon as they approached forest land. Beneath the churning clouds of soot was the only shade, and at speed he was quickly within it. He had to slow for how dense it was. Headlights on in the middle of the day, thirty miles per hour, twenty, ten at times to be safe. For hours they crept up mountain roads, cars on the shoulder, smoldering, adding perfumes of black burning rubber to the pine and grass cloud.

Then they broke through and the mountain was a charred smoldering wasteland. The blanket of smoke was gone, but like spirits haunting a cemetery, small white strands of it rose from puddles of dying debris, witnesses to the holocaust that had passed over this place only a day before.

Up the mountain they drove until they were again in living forest. Green pinnacles on mountaintops. The air finally cool. Down the other side to more charred land, where fire had raged the year before, or was

it the year before that? There were so many. The west was a tinderbox
and the fire season never ended.

"I didn't see a single fireman," said Charlotte.

Seth jumped to hear her speak.

"Calm down there, sport," she said.

"Sorry. I was woolgathering."

"Look there." She pointed. "Do you see it?"

Seth looked to his right at the barren moonscape of the fire's scars.
Black ground cover, charcoal thick as moss. Branchless trees standing
like shared needles, charred pointed spikes, waiting to spear some falling
thing like a tramp in the unending oubliette.

"I see nothing."

"There," she said. "The green. See the grass pushing up there? Green
as life in the gray shit around it?"

He hadn't, but then, looking for it, he saw the small, fragile tufts of
green pushing up. Maybe it was grass, maybe it was bushes. A resurrected
pine. "Yes," he said. "I see it."

"That's hopeful, don't you think?"

"Yeah."

"The ash will nourish the new growth. They say man has changed
the natural rhythms of the forests. Fires were common things before we
kept putting them out."

"Don't seem to have that problem anymore."

"No," was what she said. "But that's why the forests burn so badly
now. Or one of the reasons. We broke the cycle. We let the old trees
take all the light. The fire's putting things right."

Seth glanced at her as she stared forward to some middle distance
between here and there, sadness etched in her profile. He wanted to say
something, but didn't know what. She sounded like Sosa. Like Weller
at the pool, and in the heat of early August he shivered.

Another few miles and they crossed the fire break; a road hastily cut
through the forest by bulldozer to fight the inferno. On one side was
scorched wasteland, on the other green forest. Tall trees taking the light.

"We're almost home," Seth said after a long while.

Charlotte nodded.

"How're you feeling?"

"I'm okay. Hungry."

"We'll be home soon."

"You said that."

"It's true."

She rummaged in the back seat and found another bottle of tepid water. She was glad they were nearly home, but surprised at how much of the trip she'd missed. She couldn't remember the day at all. Not the dawn, not the afternoon, and now, late evening, them driving into the setting sun, it was as if she'd been teleported.

"I didn't dream," she said. "How long did I sleep? Ten hours? Fifteen? I remember nothing."

"Sounds great."

"Does it?" She considered it, pondering what oblivion was, comparing dreamless sleep to the perpetual one, wondering if they were the same. Had she been dead? What if she hadn't woken up? Wasn't that the dream, death? The pun made her smile. Seth raised a concerned eyebrow at her. She smiled in return.

"You're sweet," she said and saw him blush.

A painless death. What else was there to be hoped for? Her parents had achieved this greatest of all goals. They could be celebrated. No horror in their last moments, unlike so many other passings she'd witnessed. She was glad the building had sandwiched the way it had. Instant death to all. Unless some person was trapped in the rubble, then they could either be saved or die more horribly. A gamble. She remembered reading about people who'd starved to death in rubble waiting to be saved, the rescuers thinking no one could survive and slowing their efforts, thus ensuring the terrible outcome.

She said, "Some die badly. Some die well. But they all die. The real question is when, right?"

Seth regarded her, not certain if that was an actual question she'd asked, or if he'd just overheard seepage from her troubled mind. He left it in the air.

They entered the Bend city limits. There was life here, some semblance of normalcy. The lights were working. Traffic flowed. The smoke that lingered was not from here.

"How do you want to play this?" Seth asked.

"You're going to have to be more specific," she said. Yes, she had changed. She had grown harder. Seth felt a pang of recrimination for his part in killing something inside her.

"Shall I take you home? Should we separate now?"

"You don't actually think it's over, do you?" she said.

"No. So, I'll leave it to you. Do you want me gone?"

"You're saying that like you want to stay with me," she said.

"I do," he heard himself say.

She regarded him. "Okay," she heard herself answer, "but you need to shave the beard."

A flash like summer lightning against a creaking burning sky, pent-up stress and release. Seth broke into laughter.

Charlotte understood, but didn't join him. She felt the grin on her lips, felt it spread to her eyes, bleary and tired for all their sleep. "It'll do us both some good," she said.

"Wait," said Seth after he caught his breath, "just so we're clear and I'm not pushing. You're talking about sex, right? Sex with me? You'd like to sleep with me?"

"Yes, Seth Lian. I'd like to sleep with you. I wish I could tell you it's deeply personal, but I'm not sure it is. I need to feel alive and there's no one else in the world right now who I'm close enough with to even consider it. You'd be doing me a favor."

He laughed, heartily and loud, but then stopped himself. "I'm not laughing at you. I'm laughing at...at the... Hell, I don't know why I'm laughing."

"Are you happy?"

"Thinking of loving you? Yes, absolutely. But only if you—"

"Let's go to your place."

He made the turn toward the campus district. Here there were signs that things had deteriorated. There was a shell of a burned-out house – a duplex, he remembered. No one had picked up garbage in a while. Bags littered the sidewalk.

"Do you want to drive by the school?" Seth asked.

"No. I'd rather not see it."

"I'm sure it's fine."

"Then why go look?"

"Yeah. Okay."

She appeared as tired as he felt. The benefit of the few hours of sleep he'd managed had long dissipated. He yearned for his bed, to sleep in it. He smiled to think Charlotte would be there with him when he did. Depending upon his energy, he might even suggest that they just sleep when they got there, but banished that idea. For once, not having sex would be a selfish act.

There was a natural familiarity to his neighborhood but also something novel and dreadful. Many things looked as they had before, but nothing was the same. That tree was sinister, the air tainted by auburn haze. The garbage can knocked over as he'd never seen it before. It was the space, the time – the planet maybe. Changed, and not for the better. He could feel it. Whether it was a transcendent awareness coming from outside him and showing him truth, or an imminent one, created from his own fears and insecurities, shading it all in darkness, he could not tell. And, like the location of God which these two views often relate to, he decided it didn't matter. It was there.

"Whose car is that?" said Charlotte.

A red Ford Taurus was parked in his usual place. It took him a moment to remember who it belonged to. He had to delve into past lives to connect it. "It's Barney's," he said.

He pulled the rental in beside it, noting the gas gauge pegged at empty, and congratulated himself for getting home.

They got out, stretched, and looked around. Charlotte went to the trunk for her overnight bag, leaving the larger case where it was.

Seth scanned his neighborhood, noting the sooty air, seeing the setting sun orange between the houses. It was strangely quiet. No birds, no insects. No traffic or sound coming from nearby houses. The apartment above his, empty. The drapes drawn. No car.

He fished his camera out and panned the neighborhood in a slow establishing shot, coming to rest on the house, his apartment. It was in the viewfinder that he noticed the broken doorjamb leading inside.

Charlotte put her hand on Seth's shoulder, making him jump.

"We're still the witness," she said.

He turned the camera to her, shifted to catch her in the fading light of magic hour. She regarded him placidly. "It's what we got," he said.

"Do you really think there'll be anyone who'll care about what we saw when this is all over?"

"Someone was there to record Zeus's work, right? Else how would we know?"

"You don't think people will remember?"

Seth thought about that, admiring her eyes in the viewfinder, feeling shame and tenderness at her mussed hair and sooty neck. "The old will try to erase it."

"There won't be any old."

"The next old," said Seth. "It's the circle of life, Simba."

He waited for a reaction from her, a laugh or at least a smirk. A grimace, but instead she looked past Seth to the waning light and the orange glow reflected in her eyes.

A sound from within Seth's apartment drew their attention.

He turned the camera not too expertly and focused on the door.

Charlotte noticed the door then. "Someone's broken in. Did your friend do that?"

"I guess Barney didn't have a key."

"Why would he come here?"

"Let's find out."

Chapter Forty-One

Seth turned the viewfinder window up and checked the framing before walking forward.

"I'd say you were being overly dramatic," said Charlotte.

"But?"

"But that was before."

"This is just a suspense shot. It'll be dramatic with music."

"You're editing even now. Have a place for this shot already?"

"No, but I might. Or it'll be cut. Something's gotta be left on the cutting room floor. Not everything is useable."

He was trying to banter, but he knew it was defensive. Same for him filming. It was stupid to have his camera out recording the approach to his own house. Granted, the light was eerie and provocative, orange hazed in sunset, particles in the air thick enough to carry heat, catch shadows midair, streaks like a concert. Lines of light and darkness warm and fragrant. But this was a tourist shot if ever there was one. It was the artist in him, perhaps, that chose to make a dramatic gesture out of walking to his apartment, but like God and the neighborhood, there was something that scared him.

"Maybe you should stay outside," he said to Charlotte.

"Okay."

He was surprised by the answer, but before he could consider it, he smelled it. A sweet, cloying rot stench. Organic. The unique and pungent odor that comes from carcasses on the summer roadside; decay in heat.

He lowered the camera finally, put it on a low wall still running, a yard from the door, and stepped closer.

"Hello!" he called into the house.

No reply.

Charlotte saw him tense, saw him put the camera down, and felt sudden fear. She took a step forward and smelled it too. It reminded her of the garbage smells of Saõ Paulo, the rank rinds and rotting rats of the favela. Poverty. Desperation.

Seth went inside. Charlotte took two more steps, picked up the camera and filmed the gaping doorway.

The door swung open on old hinges, the latch free from the frame. Cracks ran up the side, splinters lay like needles in the threshold. Seth reached for the inside wall and turned on the light, ready to leap backward as he did.

The lights came on and his house came into view. Seth studied the furniture – the tables, the floors, the windows – looking for a difference from when he'd last seen it. It was cluttered, but it was always so. It showed still the remains of the party he'd thrown before he left for New England, so many days ago. One, two lifetimes past. He couldn't tell if anything had been shifted, but he didn't like it.

He glanced down and saw he'd balled his hand into a fist. His white knuckles stared up at him in unspent rage. He relaxed and noted the divots his nails had made in his palms.

"It's fine," he called back to Charlotte.

Charlotte took a step closer, shifted the angle and watched as the camera adjusted to the changed light.

"The smell?" she said. It was in her eyes now and they watered freely.

"Don't know yet."

"Then not fine," she said back.

"It's not coming from in here."

"Well, that's something."

In the kitchen, he found Barney's book bag lying on the table, a coffee mug beside it. There was mold in the mug, a gray-green film creeping up the sides. A half-filled coffee carafe sat in the maker, similarly adorned.

Someone had cleaned out his fridge. It was empty. The freezer still had things, microwavable meals, a piece of salmon he'd had in there for years. Ice.

"I think Barney came by to check the place," he called out to Charlotte. It was just the kind of thing his friend would do when Seth had failed to return from South America. The stack of sorted mail on the counter confirmed someone had been trying to be useful.

The bag and coffee cup worried him. Something had happened to Barney. Something within the last couple of days. The coffee in the mug hadn't all evaporated.

"Was he staying here?" said Charlotte from the doorway.

"Maybe. He left his stuff. Looks like he had to bug out of here quick."

"That's not good."

"We don't know what happened. Let's not jump to conclusions. I'm sure he's fine."

"That's a conclusion," she said.

"You know—" Seth's words were cut short as Charlotte stumbled sideways into the wall. The camera fell from her hands, bounced off her foot to skid into a pile of boots in the foyer. Seth was to her before it had stopped moving. He grabbed her, held her up, moved her toward the couch. "What is it?"

"You don't hear that?"

"Hear wha— No. No, I don't."

"But you did, right? You have?"

"I think so. At the beginning. Maybe something at the tennis center. Maybe a hint at the Vineyard, but nothing since."

"It's worse," she said. "Do you have anything?"

"I think so."

He carefully arranged her on the couch, shifting her so if she passed out, she'd topple onto pillows. She threw him a perturbed glance, but then the wave of sound, piercing and direct, found her brain and her eyes clenched.

Seth ran to his bedroom on the way to his medicine cabinet. Someone had made his bed. Someone had left a suitcase open on the floor with slacks and shirts. Someone had been reading a book in Greek and left it on the table, carefully bookmarked with a yellow Post-it note. Barney.

In the medicine cabinet Seth sorted through a half dozen orange pill bottles, reading labels, ignoring expiration dates until he found his emergency Lortabs. He carried them out to Charlotte and dropped three into her hand.

She handed one back and swallowed the two dry.

Seth went to the kitchen and returned with a glass of water.

"I forgot ice," he apologized.

"It's okay, Mom," she said.

Seth blushed.

She laughed.

"Those worked fast," said Seth.

"It comes in waves. I'm in a trough right now."

Seth sat next to her. He took her hand in his. She removed it and scooted around to lay her head on his lap. She closed her eyes and felt him smooth her hair. In some distant plane, drums and flutes and clattering spears sang a song of war. Distant now, sound overflowing a hill, the runoff finding her senses.

"Barney was sleeping here," Seth said after a minute.

"Wonder what happened."

Seth reached for the remote control and turned on the TV. It hummed and gave the message that the Wi-Fi was down. He skipped past it and found no regular channels. He ordered the machine to scan for signals.

Charlotte rolled over to look at the screen.

"That's not good."

"There's never anything on anyway."

The roll of numbers in the upper corner stopped, and the frame filled with images of rioting mobs shot from a balcony, maybe ten floors up. A phone camera no doubt. The city was unspecific but familiar, a western one. It could have been Portland, Houston, L.A., Washington, Madrid, or Hong Kong. A Coca-Cola sign. A Nike swoosh on a billboard. People rushing barricades. Gunshots and tear gas. Police on both sides of the melee. Seth kept the sound off, but a text crawl scrolled beneath the scene telling everyone to remain indoors, to not let anyone into their homes, not even children. "Not even children." It said that twice.

Another image, smoke thick over a burning city. Beirut? Sidney? Calgary? Dawn or twilight? A gigantic orange flash become a rising fireball, churning in upon itself, rising to the sky. The camera jarred by the late-coming shock wave. A black screen. Still the scrolling text. "Not even children. Not even children."

"Turn it off," said Charlotte.

Seth did.

She rolled over in his lap and looked up at him, seeing his bristly chin and trembling lips, then his worried eyes peering at her.

"It's hot," she said.

"I'll turn on the air."

As if on cue, the lights went out.

"Fuck," he said.

"Okay," said Charlotte.

The last of the daylight found its way through the broken front door. He allowed his eyes to adjust to the diffused amber glow. "Are you sure?"

"Yeah."

"I'm old enough to be—"

"Shut up," she said.

He shut up and she rolled off him, took him by the hand and led him toward where she thought the bedroom lay. She'd guessed right.

"Should I get a candle or something?" he said. "Would you like me to shower? Shave? I'm sure the hot water—"

His speech was cut off by her warm mouth spreading over his lips. Dim, dying, reflected light shone golden off her black hair. She smelled of sweat and sweet and the only person in the world he needed. His sex stirred. He heard himself moan. He felt her hands pull his shirt up and his found her blouse.

Feeding upon each other, clothes coming off in pieces and parts, they tumbled to the bed where skin bathed in skin.

Charlotte felt her breasts move against his hairy chest and she laughed for the fun of it. She hungrily kissed him, playing with his tongue, nipping his lips and feeling the heat of each advance spread through her like lightning. Her head swam as if drunk, full of dizziness and desire. The enduring soundtrack in her mind melding with her heartbeat and finding a rhyme as she pressed Seth to the bed and mounted him in a single glorious plunge.

She heard him moan again, heard her own breathing quicken. She rocked her hips to the driving beat, her breath keeping time. Sweat ran down her back and tickled her buttocks. She laughed again, and Seth moaned again. Her hands found his chest, felt the sweat there, the wet and the fur. Here was a man, she thought. Here was a man.

Seth's mind was a cascading barrage of heat and lust and disbelief. He'd done his share of drugs – more than his share – but never had he found a moment like this. He tried to retreat, to cling to some safe spot of detachment, if only to prolong the sex for her sake, but he could not find purchase. Once he noticed the fading light, once he felt the heat, but otherwise all was Charlotte, all was their sex, their union, their coupling. Inseparable.

Charlotte felt Seth buck beneath her, high and hard, and to it, she let go her orgasm in a wave of dazzling sensation that electrified her fingertips and shot her lungs into a scream.

Seth emptied himself inside her, her muscles constricting and guiding him – welcoming him in primordial dew. Forgiving him. In the din of his own swirling mind, her distant scream did not alarm him, but was right. And when his senses returned to him a moment, a minute, a lifetime later, she was panting atop him, bent over, her long black hair flowing over her face like water from a font. The sun long gone and even twilight fading.

It took Seth ten minutes to catch his breath. By the time he tried some pillow talk, the Lortabs had led Charlotte to sleep. He put his hand on her chest to feel her heart, leaned over her mouth to hear her breath. He stayed like that until full dark, careful to be sure that Charlotte would not die from his pills.

He finally lay beside her on his back, staring into the dark of his once-familiar ceiling. Heat poured in from the sunbaked world beyond. Too hot for covers. No power for air. He was glad Charlotte could sleep through this obscene night heat, breezeless and choked with the smell of forest ash and melting plastic.

He thought of the planet, what it would think, if it could think, of the current situation, and then what it would do, if it could do, about it. Such troublesome thoughts flavored his restless sleep until of a moment he was aware of new orange light seeping in from his eastern window.

He sat up and stole a loving glance at Charlotte only to find her staring back at him.

He jumped to see her alert and watching. "Jesus, you scared me," he said.

"I heard a noise," she said.

"*The* noise?"

Her eyes were glassy but awake. She nodded. "*A* noise."

Chapter Forty-Two

Charlotte had dreamt of Gaia, Cronus and Zeus, and the turning of the world. She'd dreamt of a fever, hot and healing – doubtless brought on by the miserable air in Seth's apartment. She'd dreamt of cleansing fire and the necessity of destruction. She dreamt of her parents, saw them alive and then dead, imagining their rotting bodies together, clasping each other's hands, stepping aside to clear the path for what they could only hope would be, never to be sure, only to try.

Seth slid into his jeans and stepped out of the bedroom. From a side table by the couch, he picked up a heavy cut-glass ashtray and dumped the debris onto the floor before lifting it above his head as a weapon.

Charlotte rolled out of bed, noticing her nakedness, but doing nothing about it. She took a tentative step just to the bedroom threshold. Seth turned and looked at her. He pointed to the front door and the back questioningly.

Charlotte pointed to the back.

Seth felt like an idiot with the ashtray. Not that it was a bad weapon, but he hadn't even searched his house before he'd gone to bed. There'd been extenuating circumstances, grand extenuating ones for sure, but still, now, he felt like a complete fool, sure that his own stupidity would rob him of the best thing he'd ever had in his life.

He opened the sliding door to the backyard. It wasn't locked.

There was the hot tub on the back porch, the tomb from before, the place where Gina had died, comfortable in soothing water. And he'd let her. God, why should he think of that now? God, why did he still have the damn thing?

The first rays of the morning sun burst over the fence and blinded him, so he had to look away. He could feel the rays of it on the back of his shading hand, upon his forehead. His neck. He thought of a Martian in a tripod walker, heat rays. Sunshine was now an alien weapon.

And the air was thick with smoke. Ash flakes floating like hovering leaves, telling him the fires were near. When California burned and the wind brought their soot to them up here, it was a particulate and faraway small. This was big and near. The air glowed in sickly tangerine brown. He squinted east and saw the painful sun as a tawny orb, round and distant. Poisonous and remote. Diminished by the choking air.

And that smell was back. The rot he'd encountered when they'd arrived. He scanned the narrow yard and followed the path around the house toward the front until he came upon his big blue plastic garbage can. It was twice as big as he'd ever needed, but his neighbors put out two of them every week. It was as big as an ice chest, bigger. Big as a refrigerator. Big as a coffin.

He coughed at the smell and turned away as he had before in the sunshine. A vampire afraid of light and also garlic, the sweet smell of organic decay.

He reached out, took hold of the trash lid, recalled the detritus he'd left there from the party so long ago, praying it was the same, and flipped it open.

Barney Faro, professor, his friend, stared up at him from inside the container, one eye dangling in its socket, the other cataract gray and cracked. His skull was cleaved open, a neat triangular divot just over the missing eye socket, exposing stinking black ooze beneath the bone, some of which had leaked out and hardened on his tousled hair. He was in a suit. His tie-pin sparkled in some reflected dying light.

"Dad?"

Seth jumped at the sound, dropping the lid and the ashtray in the same jolt. The lid plunked down with a plastic thud, but the ashtray crashed to the ground and shattered into a thousand jagged chunks of colored glass on the concrete.

"Travis?" said Seth. "Son? Is that you?"

"It's me, Dad."

"What are you doing here?"

Travis stepped around the corner of the house. "I came to see you. When all this shit hit the fan, I couldn't get ahold of you."

"Where're Ellen and Kyle?"

"Mom and Kyle are dead, Dad. I'm sorry to be the one to tell you. They didn't make it."

"Oh God," said Seth. "Oh... Oh shit. But you're safe? God, that's something."

"Yeah."

"Did you just get here? Lucky you. I wasn't even here yesterday."

"Been here awhile, Dad," said Travis, taking a step closer. "I've been waiting for you."

His son looked like him, same build, same stubble and mussed hair. He'd be thin all his life and never have to count a calorie. Handsome and driven. A good boy. He should be proud. He didn't know him, not like a father, not even as a friend, but still here was family. Here was his offspring. Here was his foray into the future. The captain of the genetic pool of all his fathers before him.

He felt a love for the boy, even as he saw him turn and raise the red fire ax above his head and step closer to cleave his skull in as he had his friend. There was a twinkle in his boy's eye, a purpose, a calling. A required thing he was all too willing to do.

But Seth would not let it happen.

He dove to the side, catching Travis's knee with a kick.

The ax plunged into the garbage can lid; broken glass into Seth's knee as he slid.

"Travis, you don't have to—"

The ax was free and falling on him again. Seth rolled into his son and the ax chipped the concrete behind him.

Seth spun and kicked at the backs of Travis's knees; Travis stumbled back, dragging the ax into Seth's shoulder. Seth felt a bone snap in his shoulder, and surprise turned to pain, turned to a scream.

Travis straightened up, a wide grin on his face. "Scream some more, old man!" he yelled and took aim at Seth's ankle, raising the ax.

Seth rolled and the ax again missed his flesh, chipped a divot in the concrete.

"Don't—" Seth pleaded. "Don't! You know I'd do anything for you," he said.

"Then die, motherfucker. Die die die die!"

Travis raised the ax and ran at his father. His face was wild. His lips were bleeding. Seth saw his teeth were chipped and wondered what he'd bitten to do that.

Seth grabbed the trash can and toppled it in front of Travis just as he reached him. The boy tumbled over and fell on top of Seth. The ax was out of his hand and Seth tried to wrap his arms around his boy, to stop him, to hold him, soothe him. Love him.

Travis kicked and hit and bit Seth's arm hard enough to draw blood, deep enough to take a piece of it.

He rolled back and Travis gave him a hard kick in the back.

Seth stumbled to his feet, feeling the glass embed itself into the calluses of his feet. He picked up the ax, choked-up on the handle, holding it in one hand, pointing it like a gun.

Travis lunged at him from the ground, arms outstretched, reaching for Seth's throat, but falling, then reaching for his chest, his head, his groin, his legs. His fingers splayed and grasping.

Seth stepped back and felt himself slipping. The ground was wet with his own blood, his feet lubricating his steps. He tried to balance, and took his eyes off his son to find a path. And that is when Travis leapt on him. Seth felt the blow up his arm that held the ax, a shock up his wrist to his shoulder to his heart.

The impact felled them both onto the bloody, glass-splintered cement. All was pain as Seth's broken shoulder broke the more and he screamed into the morning.

When his senses came back, a moment later, a minute, a lifetime, his disbelieving eyes showed him the ax embedded in Travis's face. From forehead to cheekbone, an inch inside the brain, the ax hung from his son's once-beautiful face, the handle some elephantine decoration, a party favor. A gag.

And he imagined — or did he hear — that distant drumming in his ears. It rose from below to above and echoed the crack of his breaking heart till Seth screamed to drive out the din.

Charlotte had seen the fight. She had been there when Travis rounded the corner. She had seen him before Seth had, had noticed the ax, had discerned the contents of the trash can. But she had done nothing. Instead, she had filmed the encounter. When the wave found her brain, and filled her thoughts with blood and noise, drums and shrieks, musical mayhem — a fever pitch, hot, deliberate, desperate, and maternal — she'd lowered the camera and filmed only her feet until it passed enough for her to aim it true again.

She caught the best of it though, she thought, the end of it. The coup de grâce, the tumble, and Seth's terrible shriek. High drama. Powerful. Poignant.

"We are witness," she said when the echo of Seth's scream had subsided into his panicked panting.

He turned to look at her.

"Charlotte..." he said, then choked and screamed again.

She went to him and led him into the house, the camera still rolling, but dangling from her wrist. The sound catching the pants, the shrieks, the cracks of glass under their feet. She laid it on the counter by the sink, aiming it as best she could at Seth, his bloody clothes, and dangling arm.

"Charlotte..." he said. "My god, what—"

"Shhhhh," she said and kissed him.

He noticed then that she was naked.

"Did you step on glass too?" he asked.

"Just a little."

She poured cold water over his foot, and he saw the blood pool on the floor in pink puddles. She plucked out a piece of glass, then another, then poured more water.

The pain was so bad he could see it, and he pushed Barney's bag off the table with the coffee mug that shattered like the ashtray.

"Now, don't do that," said Charlotte. "But since you've made space, why don't you lie down there."

Seth's mind was red with pain and black with despair. He did as he was bade and lay down upon the cheap kitchen table. He closed his eyes and dreamed of his Lortabs. He felt Charlotte attend his knees, felt the water run off his legs. Tears formed in his eyes. "Travis..." he muttered.

"Something's gotta be left on the cutting room floor," said Charlotte.

The words were familiar, the voice known to him, the meaning of them altogether strange and distant, wrong and portentous.

Charlotte stepped to the sink and rinsed a towel and examined the hanging pans, the magnetic cutlery strip over the counter. Normal and domestic, but eerily so. The light filled the kitchen in orange haze. With the door open, the air inside was the same as out, hot and thick. She felt her mind wobble, noticed her knees knock, felt as if she were riding some roller coaster. A rise after a fall, returning to a height. Her hands gripped around it. The drums echoed in her head, each beat feeding upon the last, growing denser, louder. The song, motherly and plaintive, lovely, forlorn.

Ideas. Plans. Decisions. Actions formed.

She bent in close, tracing a line from Seth's brow, down his jaw, to his neck.

A moment of pressure and then a sound like splitting leather. Sweat now sticky, now hot and flowing. Rhythmic. Smelling of warm copper.

"Charlotte," he said, though his voice was gurgly and wrong. "What have you done?"

She looked at him lovingly, wonderingly. Compassionately. "Nothing personal," she said.

He sat up and touched his neck. He felt the heat, the wet, the sticky. His fingers were red in blood.

"I love you," he said.

"I love you too," she answered.

And the music rose up and he smiled. "I can hear it."

"Yes," she said. A tear rolled down her cheek. The knife fell from her hand to the floor.

"Help me to the tub," he said. "Quickly." He was growing dizzy.

Charlotte led him outside and kicked the cover off the hot tub. A good amount of water had evaporated even for its being covered, but there was enough there for Seth to slide into up to his chest if he lay low.

"I hope we have a girl," he said to her. "I hope she looks like you."

Charlotte kissed him on his mouth, felt his cold lips, tender and giving even now. He touched her tummy and smiled at her with his fading eyes.

She did not know how she knew, but she knew he was right. She was pregnant and it would be a daughter. She knew this as certainly as she knew that the old had to be removed for the young to have any chance at all. It wasn't personal. It was required. It was the last chance for there to be any chance. Perhaps a long shot even now, but the time for half measures was long gone.

Seth slid lower into the water, curling his legs up underneath him to where only his head rose above the water. The hot tub swam in a crimson swirl.

Charlotte returned with the camera and aimed it at Seth.

He reached for it, and she passed it to him.

"You're the talent," he tried to say, though no words came out. "Easy to look at."

He couldn't focus on the screen. Didn't make the shot. The cool water was everything now. The hot day finally relaxing. He dropped the camera in the tub.

Charlotte regarded him there for a while, listening to the chimes and rising chords, lost in the sound of it, fearing the horror when it would go and leave her with what was left.

She studied her lover's face, ashen now, lifeless. It looked old. Ancient-old. A terrible face now. A face that had gone on too long. And in its hardening features, to the rhyme of that uncanny song, she saw the faces of a hundred thousand devouring fathers, each generation feasting to the famine of the next, until Gaia herself called for aid.

"Cronus ate his own children," Charlotte said to Seth. "Remember?"

His reverent response was adequate and right.

She touched her belly and tried on a fearful but uncertain smile before fishing the camera out of the pool and turning it off.

Acknowledgements

I'd like to thank Flame Tree Press for their continued faith and support. The wonderful Nick Wells first and foremost, of course, but also, every editor, typesetter, proofreader, intern – all! You are a blazing lighthouse in the storm of publishing. I'm genuinely honored to be a part of it.

Special mention and eternal gratitude to my editor, Don D'Auria, who is the gentle guiding hand beneath the page. Knowing Don is there is worth a thousand words a day and a good night's sleep every night.

Finally, a note. This book is a work of fiction, a snapshot of a dark vision of madness, spawned in the COVID era, tortured by politics, nurtured by fear. It is a cautionary tale, not a manual.

About the Author

Johnny Worthen is an award-winning, multi-genre, tie-dye-wearing author, voyager, and damn fine human being! Trained in literary criticism and cultural studies, he earned his Bachelors and Masters degrees from the University of Utah. Beyond English on a good day, he speaks Danish and reads Latin. He is a Utah Writer of the Year.

Johnny writes up-market stories from the inside out, beginning with theme and pursuing an idea through whatever genre will best serve it. So far he has published fiction novels as mystery, young adult, comedy, urban fantasy, horror and science fiction, both traditionally and indie.

A frequent presenter and panelist at writing conferences and fan conventions, he is active in local communities of artists and writers. A long-time volunteer for the League of Utah Writers, the state's oldest and largest writing organization, he has served several high positions of leadership, including President from 2018–20.

When not writing his own stuff, Johnny edits professionally for a small dark fiction press in Los Angeles and teaches Creative Writing at the University of Utah as an Associate Instructor. He lives in Sandy, Utah, with his wife, sons and cats. There's also a lawn.

His previous books with Flame Tree include the science-fiction *Coronam* series: *Of Kings, Queens and Colonies, Of Civilized, Saved and Savages* and *Of Heroes, Homes and Honey.*

FLAME TREE PRESS
FICTION WITHOUT FRONTIERS
Award-Winning Authors & Original Voices

Flame Tree Press is the trade fiction imprint of Flame Tree Publishing, focusing on excellent writing in horror and the supernatural, crime and mystery, science fiction and fantasy. Our aim is to explore beyond the boundaries of the everyday, with tales from both award-winning authors and original voices.

•

Other titles by Johnny Worthen:
Of Kings, Queens and Colonies: Coronam Book I
Of Civilized, Saved and Savages: Coronam Book II
Of Heroes, Homes and Honey: Coronam Book III

You may also enjoy:
Shadow Flicker by Gregory Bastianelli
October by Gregory Bastianelli
Second Lives by P.D. Cacek
Fellstones by Ramsey Campbell
The Lonely Lands by Ramsey Campbell
Somebody's Voice by Ramsey Campbell
The Queen of the Cicadas by V. Castro
Hellrider by JG Faherty
Dead Ends by Marc E. Fitch
The Toy Thief by D.W. Gillespie
One By One by D.W. Gillespie
Black Wings by Megan Hart
Stoker's Wilde by Steven Hopstaken & Melissa Prusi
The Portal by Russell James
The Dark Game by Jonathan Janz
Will Haunt You by Brian Kirk
Hearthstone Cottage by Frazer Lee
Those Who Came Before by J.H. Moncrieff
Tomb of Gods by Brian Moreland
That Which Stands Outside by Mark Morris
When the Night Falls by Glenn Rolfe
Lord of the Feast by Tim Waggoner

•

Join our mailing list for free short stories, new release details, news about our authors and special promotions:

flametreepress.com